The explosion shook the whole small adobe building. I heard the crash of broken glass as the big French doors at the rear of the house were blown into the bedroom.

I was on my feet, snatching the hidden Smith & Wesson revolver from under my shirt and starting for the side door. Then I came back to the gun rack and yanked the big bowie fighting knife out of its sheath.

I moved over to the path at the side of the house—and a heavy body dropped off the roof and landed behind me. Out of the corner of my right eye, I was aware of something black whipping toward my face. I thrust the big bowie upward to ward it off, but it wrapped itself snakelike around both the knife and my neck and tightened instantly; there was a moment when I thought I was going to be forced to cut my throat with my own blade.

THE THREATENERS

DONALD HAMILTON

FAWCETT GOLD MEDAL • NEW YORK

A Fawcett Gold Medal Book
Published by Ballantine Books
Copyright © 1992 by Donald Hamilton

All rights reserved under International and Pan-American Copyright Conventions. Published in the United States by Ballantine Books, a division of Random House, Inc., New York, and simultaneously in Canada by Random House of Canada Limited, Toronto.

Library of Congress Catalog Card Number: 92-90159

ISBN 0-449-14681-2

Manufactured in the United States of America

First Edition: September 1992

In Memory of Kathleen Hamilton 1915–1989

Chapter 1

SPOOKY was behind me again as I headed for the rifle range, which is about five miles southwest of the city of Santa Fe. It's a fairly complete gun-club operation and also includes facilities for pistol shooting, but at the moment I was concerned only with long guns, and only in .22 caliber. It was kind of a return to the womb. Like most ranch kids, I'd been given, as my first gun, a single-shot .22 just like the Anschutz now resting behind my seat in its fancy foam-lined case. Well, maybe not *just* like it. Back then, the little old Iver Johnson birthday rifle had cost my dad seventeen bucks secondhand at the local general store; the Anschutz, ordered new from an importer in the east, had recently set me back well over seven hundred. It was a special rifle made for a special kind of shooting.

The Mexicans started it, I believe, and called it *Siluetas Metálicas*. They set up silhouette targets cut from heavy sheet steel, *gallinas, javelinas, guajalotes,* and *borregos*, at distances ranging from two hundred to five hundred meters. The original idea was that, standing on your hind legs like a man instead of lying on your belly like a worm—most serious target shooting is done from the prone position because it's the steadiest—you'd try to knock over these heavy metal chickens, pigs, turkeys, and sheep with one shot each, using your ordinary hunting rifle. It was a challenging sport, it caught on fast, and pretty soon it spawned some fairly specialized equipment and several variations, one being a small bore version using .22-caliber rifles at shorter ranges with smaller targets.

1

I love the big guns, but in this line of business—never mind what business—I have to fire a lot of heavy stuff for practice. I don't go out of my way to tenderize my shoulder and rattle my eardrums for pleasure. But I still enjoy all kinds of shooting, and I'd read about this small bore silhouette stuff, so when a man I met at the range while I was checking out a new .38 revolver mentioned that there was to be a match there the following Sunday, I borrowed a secondhand .22 from a friendly dealer, had him dress it up with a secondhand telescopic sight, spent a couple of hours on the range on Saturday calibrating the half-baked outfit after a fashion, and drove back out bravely on Sunday to see what it was all about.

With that inadequate gun and no experience, it was a slaughter as far as I was concerned. I only hit—hush, don't tell anybody—five of the little steel animals out of the possible forty; but I had a lot of fun.

Now, with the proper gear, and another match under my belt, I was hoping to graduate from Class B, the cellar division, into Class A. Two scores over fourteen were required, and I'd recorded a sixteen last time out, so I only had one more to go. Maybe this seems like a small ambition for a man who's spent most of his life using firearms for real—at least, being such a hero marksman, I should already, on my third competitive outing, be knocking off twenty-fives and thirties with my eyes shut and shooting for Triple A or even Master, right?

Well, few new sports are that easy to conquer, and that goes for new target rifles, too. My Anschutz had a special trigger mechanism with a tricky two-stage pull much lighter than I was accustomed to. Furthermore, my skull had acquired a bad bullet crease on a recent mission, and I'd also taken a slug lower down. The physical machinery had recovered pretty well, and I'd spent some time at our training and rehabilitation center in Arizona, known as the Ranch, being healthified until I could hardly stand myself; but while I'd managed to fudge enough qualifying targets with rifle and pistol to get myself sprung out of the hands of the doctors

2

and trainers, I knew that the mental apparatus was still a bit shaky and my concentration wasn't all it should be. The discipline of shooting offhand (our jargon for standing) at unreasonably small targets at unreasonably long distances, with a gun that produced hardly any noise or recoil to lacerate my nerves or aggravate my healing injuries—pure, basic marksmanship—was exactly what I needed.

Except for Spooky. Spooky I didn't need at all. Actually, I'd spotted four Spookies over a period of weeks. The one escorting me around today was Spooky Three—I'd numbered them in the order I discovered them—the only female member of the crew, a sturdy, dark-haired dame in her mid-twenties, wearing a teenager costume of torn T-shirt and faded skintight jeans ragged at the knees, and driving a battered tan Volvo wagon that must have been brought over from Scandinavia by Leif Eriksson about the year 1000 for his tour of Vinland the Good. That was her image today. Last week she'd been a neatly dressed blond matron in a beige pantsuit and high heels, driving a shiny blue BMW.

The rifle range is, of course, located well out in the boonies so that if a ricochet or wild bullet should sneak over one of the bulldozed dirt backstops, which doesn't happen often, it won't find anybody to hurt. It's the usual arid, rolling New Mexico landscape: stony yellow-brown earth scantily covered with tough yellow-green grass and weeds, and an occasional cactus, and dotted with widely spaced, dark green piñons and junipers not much higher than a man. Bulging up against the horizon to the north are the Sangre de Cristo peaks; to the east are the more distant Jemez Mountains; and on a good day—and we have lots of them out there—you can see Los Alamos. If you want to see Los Alamos.

Ms. Spooky was still astern when I left the pavement and headed out the gravel county road. The weather was clear and dry, and I could see the dust kicked up by the ancient Volvo a discreet distance behind me. This early on a Sunday morning there wasn't much traffic to confuse the issue. My sturdy lady was still hanging on back there when I negotiated the steep dip where the road ran through the arroyo near the

3

county dump; but soon after that there was no more dust behind me, and I knew that she'd taken the turnoff to the dump. Well, these double-talk days I believe I'm supposed to call it a landfill or maybe a sanitary refuse disposal area, but I'm old-fashioned and it's still a dump to me.

If she followed their established routine—I'd been coming out here several times during the week to practice on the deserted, or almost deserted, range, and after a while they'd settled on this observation scheme—she'd park there, probably leaving the wagon open in the rear as if she'd just finished unloading the family garbage. She'd hike a hundred yards to a small hill that let her look down on the distant club grounds beyond. From there, she could keep an eye on my activities with binoculars and see me preparing to leave in time to get back to her car and pick me up again on my way home.

There were already eight or ten cars, vans, and pickup trucks in the gun club's parking area when I drove up. Stopping at the end of the row, I turned the pup loose to run while I opened the rear of the Subaru I was driving that autumn to get my gear out. I'd owned a Mazda RX-7 for several years. It had been fast, reliable, and pleasantly flashy, and it had got the sports-car kinks out of my system, but the low-slung little two-seater had never been an ideal vehicle for a man who went in for hunting and fishing. After I acquired a young Labrador retriever and he filled out to a solid ninety pounds, the situation had become critical. When a gent with a Mazda deficiency offered me a respectable sum for my pretty car one day when I was having it serviced at the local dealership, I took his money and borrowed a company vehicle I'd used on a recent assignment to keep me rolling while I was making up my mind what personal transportation to buy next.

I got the rifle and associated gear from the rear of the station wagon. After lugging the stuff to one of the tables under the long canopy behind the firing line, I went over to be signed in by a guy named Jack, who told me I was shooting with a guy named Mark, second relay, meaning that at each distance Mark would shoot his two five-shot strings first while I scored him, after which he'd score me while I shot mine. Then we, and all the other pairs of shooters on the line, would move over one set of targets and repeat the process.

Today Mark and I were scheduled to start with the pigs—excuse me, *javelinas*—at sixty meters, after which we'd do the turkeys at seventy-seven, the rams at a hundred, and then crank our sights back down to handle the chickens at forty. To give you an idea of the accuracy required: the rams, also called sheep, are about six inches long, and the other targets are scaled down in proportion to the shorter ranges at which they're shot at so they all look about the same size from the firing line. Think of trying to hit, from a wobbly standing position, a six-inch toy woolly-woolly at the far end of a football field.

Looking around for Mark, I was careful not to glance at the distant, low hill from which Spooky was presumably watching; if she was dumb enough to think herself undetected, I didn't want to disillusion her. Mark was busy undermining the loyalty of my one-man dog; they'd got acquainted during various practice sessions when we'd happened to pick the same time of day to use our range keys. As a matter of fact, he was the man I'd encountered out here earlier in the summer, who'd got me into all this by telling me about the following Sunday's match. He was scratching Happy's ears expertly and laughing at the big yellow dog's blissful reaction.

"That is truly one friendly Labrador," he said, straightening up and giving the pup a final pat. "Well, they all are. It looks like we have a good day for it. No wind to amount to anything. How has the gun been shooting?"

A gun club like ours is an odd place: you know a lot of first names and the faces that go with them, you talk guns and hunting with the guys, but you seldom know their last names or what they do. They just kind of spring out of the woodwork once a month on match Sundays. Occasionally you say hi to one of them and chat a bit, if you happen to meet him practicing on the range between matches, or maybe you bump into one in a local sporting-goods store, but there's no real social contact. Whether it's the same around golf courses and tennis clubs I have no idea, since, having found a sport I like better, I don't mess with those bat-and-ball games.

Mark was a bit of an exception to the general run of gun-club relationships, as far as I was concerned. He was a solidly built gent in his forties with thick, straight, black hair combed neatly back from his forehead. Say five nine or ten, say a hundred and seventy or eighty. He had a round face, bright brown eyes, a short snub nose, and smooth olive skin. I knew that he shot in Class AAA, and that his last name was Steiner, which had surprised me a bit when I first heard it since it had sounded like a Jewish name to me and I'd have guessed at Latin heredity, not that it mattered. I knew that he had a thin blond wife who looked considerably younger, and two little girls; and that he lived in a development at the south edge of town. I also knew that he was a helpful guy and clever with tools.

I knew all this because when I first got the Anschutz I'd been having trouble getting the big Bushnell telescopic sight properly lined up and he'd invited me to his house and solved the problem in a little workshop he had in his garage—a couple of shims cut from a Coca-Cola can had done the trick, in case you're interested. I still didn't know what he did for a living, and I hoped he didn't know what I did. It's information that's not supposed to be available to the general public. As a matter of fact it's not supposed to be available to anybody except on a strict, official, need-to-know basis.

"Nothing wrong with the gun," I said. "Now it's just the guy behind it who needs fixing. I've got our scorecards here; you're shooting first." The pup at my feet looked around sharply as a .22 cracked at the firing line; the targets are set out early to allow us to warm up our guns with a little pre-match practice. Gunfire means birds to a retriever; and birds are his business in life. I said, "I'd better put him in the car or he'll be out there looking for some crippled tin chickens to retrieve."

6

A rifle match, to an observer, must be about as exciting as watching the snow melt in the spring, although silhouette shooting is a little better in this respect than drilling holes in paper targets: at least you get to see the distant little black metal figures leap into the air at the impact of the bullets, or go spinning off to one side or the other or, heartbreaking for the shooter, turn a little at a glancing hit but remain standing firmly on the base for a big fat zero on the scorecard. Or stay totally unmoved by a miss. But there's nothing boring about it for the shooter, who, once the match has started, has his past misses to mourn and future hits to hope for.

The one thing you must not do, if you get off to a good start, is start calculating what a wonderful score you'll make if you can just keep it up. So I did it. I cleaned off the first five pigs without a miss. Then I left one standing out of the second five; but that was still better than I'd ever done in competition, and I began to imagine myself finishing right up there with the local experts, or maybe even beating them. So of course I tightened up like any stupid novice—you wouldn't know I'd been shooting all my life—and blew it on the turkeys, missing all but two. Well, never mind the play-by-play. I wound up with a score of eighteen, sending me up one class, which after all was what I'd hoped for; but I couldn't help wondering how much better I'd have shot if I hadn't been constantly aware of the binoculars watching from the distant hilltop, and asking myself who the hell were these creeps anyway, and what the hell did they want? I was getting a little tired of constantly wearing an extra shadow.

But Mac's original instructions had been for me to play it cool and continue to pretend the fearsome foursome didn't exist while he had the situation investigated.

"Only four, Eric?" he'd said when I first called Washington to report that I seemed to have acquired a guard of honor. My real name is Matthew Helm, but except under special circumstances, we use the code names for official communication.

I said, "Four are all I've spotted so far; three men and a woman. Of course, they could be deliberately showing themselves to hold my attention while a backup crew plays it cagey and keeps out of sight, but I don't think they're being that clever. My instinct tells me that they don't feel any need to get fancy because they think they're still invisible as far as I'm concerned.''

''Clearly they haven't determined your true occupation.''

''How do you figure that, sir?''

''If they knew you were a professional, they'd know it would take more than four watchers to keep you covered around the clock without alerting you. Apparently they're under the impression that you're just an innocent, free-lance photojournalist who has enough of a private income that he doesn't have to work very hard; that's the cover you've always used around Santa Fe, isn't it?''

I said, ''It wasn't a cover when I started, you'll recall, back in the good old days when I'd escaped from your clutches, before my wife left me and you lured me back into the Washington fold—well, sheepfold is hardly the right descriptive phrase, is it? Call it a wolf den.'' I grimaced at the phone, although my expression would hardly reach him two thousand miles to the east of where I stood. ''You may be right, sir. I still keep a couple of cameras around and snap them occasionally for show. Anyway, these people don't seem to know I've spotted them, and they certainly aren't taking any serious precautions; I could have had each of them half a dozen times. I'd say you're right, and they don't know what I really do for a living, or what a truly nasty person I am.''

''Well, we do try to keep it a secret,'' Mac said dryly. ''Now tell me what you've done to deserve all this attention.''

''I haven't the slightest idea, sir.''

''You have a lady living with you at the moment, I believe; a divorced lady. Ex-husbands have been known to do some strange things—''

''Unlikely in this case. The guy is a young doctor and I shouldn't think he'd have enough money yet, judging by what Jo told me about him, to mount this kind of an operation even if he's mad with jealousy, which seems unlikely since he remarried a few months ago. Besides, Jo has gone back to Tucson."

"Permanently?"

I said, "If you practice with a golf ball on the office rug, or whack a tennis ball against the backyard fence by the hour, you're merely an enthusiastic sportsman. The gal may think you're kind of childish; but boys, even grown-up boys, must be allowed to play their silly games, right? But if you buy a new gun, even just a lousy little .22, and spend a few afternoons a week at the rifle range learning how to put a bullet in the right place . . . After the way we met down in Mexico under fairly violent circumstances, Jo was already uncertain about me. Seeing me spending considerable amounts of time and money on my shooting made up her mind the wrong way; I guess to her it seemed like watching Jack the Ripper sharpening his knife. Maybe I should have taken up golf."

"My condolences," Mac said. He's not the most sympathetic man in the world; and he's always uneasy about our amorous entanglements, although as far as I know he's still got his own lady, a high-powered businesswoman he sees at odd intervals. "Tell me about this recreational shooting you've been doing. Whatever it is, I find it commendable, since I'm told that your latest scores at the Ranch, while acceptable, weren't up to your usual standards. And we have found that just about any shooting practice carries over to all shooting."

"Yes, sir." I explained the basics of the small-bore silhouette game. He seemed to find it amusing that one of his sinister senior operatives was spending his convalescent leave knocking over little metal animals and birds with a .22, like a kid in a shooting gallery. I finished with: "Hell, I can't figure out what these weirdos are up to, following me around."

"Of course, over the years you have made a few enemies in the line of duty, but as a prelude to revenge this does seem a little overelaborate." Mac was silent briefly. Standing by the filling-station pay phone while the attendant pumped gas into the Subaru—since I was being watched, it was highly possible that my home phone was tapped—I visualized him in his office in front of the bright window he likes to make us face, a lean, gray-haired man with black eyebrows, wearing a gray business suit, always. He went on: "In the absence of clear private motives, we'd better investigate the possibility that you've become involved in a government operation of some kind. The questions are, what kind, and what government? Can you think of anything you've been doing that would bring you to official attention?"

"No, sir."

"Well, I'll check here in Washington and try to find out if some other agency is operating in your area. Or if there's a possible foreign interest. That close to Los Alamos it's not inconceivable; they still do strange work up on that mountainside, don't they?"

"We call it the Hill, sir, and they like people to think they're harmless nowadays." I laughed. "Last summer around the Fourth of July I drove up that way to visit some friends; it's only forty miles. Coming into town I passed a big sign at the city limits: FIREWORKS PROHIBITED. The home of the atom bomb, for Christ's sake, and they won't let the kids shoot off a few whiz-bangs on Independence Day!" Apparently he didn't find it amusing; I heard no laughter on the line. Well, his sense of humor isn't very highly developed. Or maybe it wasn't really funny. I went on: "So what do I do about this flea circus, sir?"

"Nothing, until I've made an investigation here. You'd better give me the descriptions; but unless they take positive action against you, continue to ignore them."

Well, as I said earlier, those had been his original instructions.

Chapter 2

THEY gave me a little blue ribbon for my farewell performance in Class B. I'd beaten three other novices who'd made scores of ten, eleven, and thirteen; there was also a first-timer who'd managed a seven, better than I'd done on my initial venture into silhouette competition. Mark had cleaned up in AAA and was top gun for the day with a fairly spectacular score of 32x40.

At his suggestion, before taking off for our respective homes, we relaxed with a couple of beers from the cooler in his van. It's not my favorite tipple, but beer lovers are almost as bad as teetotalers for condemning you as a hopeless alcoholic if you indicate your preference for something harder. Anyway, after standing in the bright New Mexico sun for a couple of hours, I didn't find the idea of beer completely revolting.

"Hey, you got that new Anschutz hitting pretty good," Mark said.

I grinned. "Your antique wasn't doing too damn badly."

What he was using was a home-built rig based on an old Winchester Model 52, no longer in production, but one of the best small bore target rifles ever made. (In target-shooting jargon, "small bore" stands for a .22; all other common calibers are "big bore.") He'd cut down the barrel—within wide limits, a short gun barrel is just as accurate as a long one; and it isn't knocked about so badly by the wind on a gusty day, important when you're shooting offhand. He'd improved the trigger pull, mounted an enormous Leupold target scope, and set the whole thing into a sad-looking lam-

11

inated stock on which he kept whittling and sanding to make it fit him better when he wasn't adding to it elsewhere with tape and moleskin. When he got it just right, he said, he'd use it as a pattern for a really good-looking stock. As far as I could make out, he'd been getting it just right for at least two years now, the length of time he'd lived here in Santa Fe. Right or wrong, the old patchwork rifle consistently outshot a lot of new and expensive equipment, including my Anschutz.

"Well, that is enough of this childish play," Mark said, draining his Budweiser. "Now I must go home and take care of serious matters, like raking the dead leaves from the yard, or my wife will divorce me. Too much shooting, she says, and not enough work around the house."

"I know how it is," I said, thinking of Jo Beckman, who'd been very nice to have around, and wasn't around any longer. "Well, thanks for the beer."

I whistled for the dog and had a moment of uneasiness when he didn't appear at once, although instant obedience is not his thing; we run a partnership of sorts, not a master-slave operation. But with Spooky constantly on the horizon I couldn't help figuring my vulnerabilities. Jo was no longer around to be threatened; that left only Happy. And me, but I've lived in a state of threat most of my adult life and so far I've managed to cope with it, one way or another.

Then the pup came bounding over the hill and plunked himself at my feet to catch the junior-grade Milkbone biscuit I tossed him to console him for having to leave his business in deference to mine. Mark's van was just pulling away. I frowned, watching it go. He seemed a nice enough guy, easy to get along with and comfortable to shoot with—you never had to worry that he'd let his gun muzzle wander carelessly in your direction—and he was certainly a fine marksman, but there was something lacking. Then I realized what it was: triumph. Hell, the man had won the damn match, hadn't he? He'd beat out a dozen good local shots, and several more not-so-good ones like me, with a score that would have been nothing to be ashamed of in national competition; you'd have thought he'd be walking on air. Of course a little modesty is expected; but so is a certain happy glow, which had been conspicuously missing.

Well, I wasn't glowing much myself, even though I'd won my stumblebum class decisively and shot my best score to date in this type of competition. I was gaining on it, which was nice; but it was, after all, just a game. When you've been shot at for real and have shot back and survived, you may find target games enjoyable but you're not going to be too depressed when you lose or too elated when you win. The stakes aren't that high; your life isn't on the line.

It was a disturbing thought: maybe Mark Steiner wasn't conspicuously, deliriously happy about his win today because he had, in the past, competed with firearms in other ways and in other places where the stakes had been higher. I stood there for a moment reviewing the past summer in my mind: Could the guy be something other than the simple citizen he seemed? Could he have been planted on me? The fact that we'd been assigned to shoot together today was probably of no significance, the luck of the draw, but we'd met with some frequency on the range on weekdays, apparently by accident; but was it? Well, I could think of other club members I'd encountered out here, sighting in their guns and practicing their shooting, almost as often. But he'd been very friendly and helpful and had invited me to his house and introduced me to his family. It made me feel disloyal to the guy, although we weren't by any means bosom pals, but I found myself wondering uneasily if he could be another Spooky, Number Five, gradually moving in on me, fixing my rifle, plying me with beer, while his four associates kept watch on me from a distance. . . . Or maybe he was just a stolid gent who didn't ever show much emotion and I was getting paranoid after weeks of being watched.

It was still a clear, sunny, fall day, but up the Rio Grande valley white clouds were starting to form; eventually they'd pile up high and turn black, probably, and give us our usual afternoon thunderstorm. Spooky Three picked me up on the way home. Now that I'd finished shooting and the pressure was off, I felt kind of benevolent toward her; after all, I'd more or less saved her life, at least for the moment. Well, hers or one of her friends'.

"I've still found no government organization that will admit to employing anybody fitting the descriptions you gave me," Mac had told me when I checked back yesterday for the third or fourth time. "Or to conducting any operations in the Santa Fe–Los Alamos area. Of course, they do not have to be telling the truth; they seldom are."

"Some years ago we had another situation like this down in Mexico, if you'll recall, sir," I said. "I did my damnedest to find out if a certain dame I kept bumping into belonged to us, but nobody'd claim her, so I figured she had to be on the other side and wound up shooting her when she started waving a gun around. It turned out that she was working for a certain Washington would-be big shot who was concealing her identity for some dumb security reason; as punishment for her death, he wanted me skinned alive and roasted over a slow fire."

"Yes, I remember," Mac said. "I have been careful to point out during my inquiries that if nobody admits responsibility for these people, we'll feel free to deal with them as we please; and we will entertain no complaints afterward. . . . Oh, Eric."

"Yes, sir."

"Does 'Lapis' mean anything to you?"

He pronounced it as a Latin word: "Lahpis." I'd more often heard it pronounced "Laypis," and it took me a moment to make the connection. Well, Lahpis or Laypis, at least he seemed to have a lead after all; he just had to be coy about it.

I said, "Well, lapis lazuli is a semiprecious stone, kind of blue, if I remember right. I believe they used to find some in Colorado. I have a vague memory that the ancients used to grind it up to make ultramarine pigment."

"Very good, Eric." He sounded like a teacher commending a backward student. "Actually, the main sources of lapis lazuli are Afghanistan and Chile. However, I doubt that the man who used the word was referring to gemstones.''

Clearly, he wanted me to kick it around a bit. "A man, a woman, or perhaps a town?" I suggested. "I've never heard of a Lapis, Colorado—I don't think that, unlike turquoise, the rock in question was ever found in New Mexico in significant quantities—but a lot of old southwestern mining camps with odd names have vanished from the map. I'll check it out with one of the local historical geniuses if you like, sir.''

"I'm afraid it would be a waste of time. I doubt that we're dealing with a treasure hunt involving a lost mine. The word may be a coded reference to a man or a woman, as you suggest, maybe even one of the men, or the woman, currently watching you, but more likely it refers to an undercover organization, or a secret project, probably the latter.''

"Operation Lapis?"

"Perhaps.'' He hesitated and went on: "I recently encountered an immaculate young fashion plate of an executive assistant who was apparently quite a partygoer in his free time. At least he was suffering from a bad hangover that day. It made him less circumspect than he might normally have been. I chatted with him as he guided me to the sanctum of his superior—some of those Washington office buildings are as confusing as the Pentagon—and he had an interesting reaction when I mentioned casually that I'd been checking on current government activity in the southwest, so far without result. First he said he wasn't aware of any, then he apologized for yawning by saying that it had been a long night and the liquor had flowed a bit too freely but the lady had been pleasantly cooperative, and finally he yawned again and said, 'Well, there's Lapis, of course,' as if it were something known to everybody. Then, realizing that it hadn't been known to me, he seemed aghast at his breach of security and delivered me to the proper office without speaking again.''

"I'll keep my ears open," I said.

"Eric.''

"Yes, sir.''

15

"It occurs to me that there is one way of determining who is responsible for these people who have you under surveillance. I have been thinking of that incident in Mexico you mentioned. It suggests a possible approach, doesn't it?"

I'd hate to say how many years I've worked for him, but sometimes he still manages to startle me a little.

I said, "You mean, I knock off one of them here and you see who in Washington gets mad at the loss of a precious agent and comes roaring at you to demand my head?"

"Precisely. You don't approve?"

He was getting bloodthirsty in his old age. Well, his humanitarian impulses had never been overwhelming. What disturbed me wasn't the fact that he was suggesting a touch, as we call it—use "hit" if you prefer—on someone who might be a colleague of sorts in the murky world of U.S. undercover operations. We are no longer a little band of brothers and sisters, if we ever were. Today's government is full of wild men and women ruthlessly saving the nation their own way, rabid spy catchers and fanatic drug hunters and hungry empire builders, who'll kill you as soon as look at you, even if your office is right down the hall, if they get the notion you're an obstacle to their ambitious campaigns. I owed the new groove in my skull and the fresh bullet and operation scars on my left midsection to just such a U.S. zealot with a shining cause. So I don't pay much attention nowadays to birth certificates, passports, or even badges or IDs. It's a jungle out there, man, if you'll excuse the phrase; and you're just as dead if you're shot by a true-blue Yankee as by a dirty red commie. What counts is the gun. If it's pointing my way, I'll do my damnedest to blow away the guy behind it at the earliest opportunity, and if he happens to be a great American patriot named George Washington, it's just too damn bad; he should have aimed his lousy musket in some other direction.

16

However, the survival instinct can be followed too far. While I'm no great humanitarian, either, the idea of casually eliminating people who'd merely annoyed me a bit by walking in my footsteps, didn't appeal to me, if only because it would create more problems than it solved. I reflected that it was an odd reversal of our customary roles, for me to be the advocate of restraint and caution. I had to tread cautiously or Mac might think my recent wounds had left me in a state of mushy sentimentality, and order me back to the Ranch for toughening.

I said mildly, "It just seems a little premature, sir. Let's wait a little longer; maybe they'll reveal what they're up to. Anyway, we don't know that they're taking orders from Washington rather than Moscow. Or Peking, whatever they call it nowadays. Or Havana, or Baghdad, or Qaddafiville, whatever the name of *that* dump is, and however the paranoid bastard spells his name."

Mac said, "That is just the point. If the surveillance orders originate here in Washington, with one of his operatives dead, the person responsible will be forced to identify himself and open communications with me quickly, before I order you to wipe out the rest and send you whatever help you need to accomplish the task. I think it is fairly well known that I do not take kindly to having my people harassed, on or off duty. If we get no official complaints here, we've more or less eliminated Washington as a source of your problem, a considerable step forward. I'm sure you can arrange it so the local authorities will accept it as self-defense, with a small hint from me. Unless, of course, you prefer to make it an accident."

I had it now. His professional feelings were hurt. He'd learned that somebody in Washington had a big operation going out here. Operation Lapis, for God's sake! He knew that one of his people was under heavy surveillance, very possibly in this connection, yet nobody'd had the courtesy to tell him what it was all about even when he'd gone out of his way to ask. Okay. They'd had their warning. He'd stated clearly and repeatedly that if the operatives haunting one of

17

his men remained unidentified and unexplained he'd take steps to have them dealt with. Having got no answers with polite questions, he intended to see what he could blast loose with a gun. My gun.

I said, "I have a hunch we're barking up the wrong tree, sir." Well, he was doing the barking, but it wouldn't have been diplomatic to say so.

"What do you mean?"

"There's something amateurish about this surveillance that makes me wonder if it isn't an independent project with no connection to Washington or any other national capital. I'd appreciate it if you'd give me a little more time, sir. I've just been riding along pretending to be blind and deaf; now let me see if I can't figure out a way of prying loose some information without cluttering up the place with dead bodies."

There was a pause; then his voice came through the phone, with a hint of impatience: "Oh, very well. But be careful. According to the reports I've received, you're not in good enough condition yet, physically or mentally, to cope with any truly demanding situations. That was quite a blow you took on the head, not to mention the other injuries."

Which was his way of telling me that he was only yielding to my request as a concession to my temporary disabilities.

For a long time after my marriage broke up for pretty much the same reasons that had caused Jo to leave me, I'd told myself firmly that my home was now Washington, D.C., handy to our base of operations, where I had a nice little bachelor apartment; and that Santa Fe was an okay town to visit occasionally for old time's sake but I wouldn't want to live there. The trouble was that the crowded east gave me claustrophobia and I found myself coming back out to New Mexico more and more often for a breath of more or less unpolluted air. Finally, after years of imposing on friends or camping out in hotel and motel rooms, and each time kidding myself that this was positively my last nostalgic visit to my

18

old hometown, I broke down and bought a small house on the east side of Santa Fe, up toward the mountains.

For a man in my line of work to support two establishments when he spent much of his time in the field, or at the Ranch being patched up between missions, wasn't very economical, but the danger pay does tend to pile up in the bank, and I needed a place for the dog. My new domicile is an old adobe on a tight little lot surrounded by a six-foot board fence. Esthetically, I'd have preferred a traditional mudbrick wall—Santa Fe is a city of walls—but nobody asked me, and the high fence still makes it a safe haven for Happy. Fortunately he's not a chewer. A big rolling gate lets me bring my car into the diminutive yard, necessary because the narrow street outside is a fairly busy one and drivers, particularly late at night when they've had a few beers, have been known to take the bend below the house too fast and clobber a car parked out front. As a matter of fact, I'd been told that they even take out the fence every few years, and that this was the reason I'd got the place at a fairly reasonable price—the previous owner had found the midnight crashes traumatic—but folks in my line of work had better be hardened to midnight crashes and so far there haven't been any.

As I came around the last curve and saw my place up ahead on the right, I swore to myself; you can plaster a fence with no-parking signs until no wood shows and still people will put their lousy cars right in front of it and go off and leave them. This was a fancy Mercedes, and it wasn't just taking up part of my very limited parking space, it was right in front of the gate in spite of my pitiful signs begging folks please, please not to block the driveway. Pulling up behind the chocolate-brown sedan, I saw that there was, after all, someone in the driver's seat. I got out and started forward to request that they haul ass pronto. Then a woman got out and turned to face me.

It took me a moment to recognize her. She hadn't changed all that much, but it had been five years. Then I exchanged my scowl for a welcoming grin and hurried forward.

"Madeleine! Damn, it's been a long time! It's good to see you!"

There was no answering smile on her face. "What are you trying to do to me, Matt?" she asked as I came up. "What in God's name are you trying to do to me?"

Chapter 3

LOOKING at her, I remembered certain things, of course, the kind of things you remember about a woman to whom you've made love, particularly a woman to whom you've made love in times of peril. We'd shared some violent adventures and some tender moments; but while I'd found myself deeply involved at the time, she'd never let herself be drawn into a full commitment.

A bright and ambitious young woman from good family with a shining law career before her, not to mention a happy marriage, Madeleine Rustin Ellershaw had suffered intolerable disgrace and lengthy imprisonment for a crime involving national security of which she had not been guilty. Freed at last, and eventually exonerated, but with her career and life in ruins—her husband, a scientist employed at one of the secret government installations near Los Alamos had been murdered at the time of her troubles—she'd been determined to achieve the kind of complete social rehabilitation no gun-toting secret-agent type could give her, even if he'd been instrumental in proving her innocent.

I'd thought she'd attained her goal with her second marriage, to a very respectable young lawyer named Walter Maxon. I'd made a point of keeping away from them—no marriage needs old lovers hanging around the bride—but after a couple of years I'd read about the divorce in the newspapers and heard that she'd left town. I'd been sorry, the way you are when things don't work out for people you like, but not sorry enough to look her up wherever she'd moved to. I mean, that hand had been played.

The autumn sun was bright and hot and I remembered that I'd left Happy in the closed station wagon with the engine, and therefore the air conditioner, turned off.

I said, "Just a minute. Let me get the dog."

"Matt—"

"Hold everything, this is no place to talk. Lock up your car and get out of the street, they take this corner like it was Indianapolis on Memorial Day."

I snapped the leash on Happy, grabbed the gun case, waited for an old pickup truck to roar past, and joined her at the entrance to my miniature estate. She was looking at the yellow sign indicating that the premises were protected by the Guardian Security System, known as GSS. I dealt with the padlock. Although the hasp is on the inside, a hand-sized hole lets you work the lock from outside. I rolled back the heavy gate far enough to admit us and rolled it closed again.

"Give me time to turn off the alarm," I said, leading the way to the front door, which is actually at the side of the house. "Once the door is open, I've got about sixty seconds to push the right buttons or all hell breaks loose. . . . Here, hold the dog."

I must admit that the crazy burglar alarm has me bugged; I'm always terrified that I'm going to forget the code and run out of time trying to remember it, or punch it wrong even if I do remember it. I don't know why I make such a big deal of it; it's not as if the system was wired to a lethal load of plastique or TNT. If I don't turn it off within the allotted sixty seconds, all that'll happen is that the noisemakers will scream and disturb the neighbors a bit, and the private security outfit monitoring the system will phone to find out if I goofed or if they should really call the cops. However, I made it to the control box in time and punched the right number on the keypad, and the little red light went out.

"Okay, all clear."

After letting Madeleine enter, I took the leash off Happy and put him out into the yard, hearing Madeleine laugh as I closed the door behind him.

"He's kind of sweet, like a big friendly teddy bear, not at

all the kind of dog I'd expect you to have," she said as I turned back to face her.

"You think I'm more the snarling pit-bull type?"

"Or killer Doberman." Her voice was expressionless, but there was a hint of mischief in her eyes.

I grinned. "I don't need a dog to defend me; I can defend myself. But I'm very lousy at fetching ducks out of deep water in freezing weather, which is Happy's specialty. Well, what do you think of my cozy domicile? Living-dining room before you. Bedroom to the left. Kitchen and bath to the right . . . Did I say something interesting?"

"I've been waiting out there for quite a while," she said.

"Sure," I said. "Into the kitchen and hard left. Guest towels on the top shelf. In the meantime, I'd say the sun is practically over the yardarm, wouldn't you, ma'am? As I recall, the drink is Scotch."

"Your recollection is accurate, sir."

I watched her move away from me, a slender woman in her thirties, looking very competent in a severely tailored business suit, black with a fine white stripe. Nylons black, very sheer. Pumps black, with high, slim heels. Height medium. Hair brown, not too long, carefully arranged about her head. A lady who, five years ago, had made a spectacular comeback from almost total disaster with, although I wouldn't have dreamed of reminding her, some help from me.

She'd been in bad shape, defeated and hopeless, when I'd picked her up at the prison on the day of her release, with orders to keep her alive, never mind why. There had been others around who'd had instructions that conflicted with mine. Playing bodyguard, I'd wound up having to throw myself heroically between her and a distant rifle, taking a bullet in the shoulder. After getting patched up locally, I'd had her drive me to the Ranch in Arizona for more permanent repairs. The reconstruction had taken some time, and I'd arranged for her to be put through the less classified parts of our basic training course so she could help defend herself while I was semidisabled. The experience had taught her a number of things most women don't know, and our demanding exercise program had turned her from a soft, helpless victim into a lean female predator who'd repaid me for saving her life once by saving mine twice. I was glad to see that she'd kept the taut figure she'd attained back then. I wondered how much else of the Ranch course she retained. No one unaware of her history would associate knives and guns and unarmed combat with the handsome businesswoman in the pinstripe suit and severe silk blouse who emerged from the kitchen.

She took the glass I offered her and sipped from it while looking around the room. It was typical Santa Fe, with heavy mud-brick walls plastered smooth and painted white, a rounded kiva fireplace in the corner, and a rather low ceiling with the round exposed roof beams, natural timbers, that we call *vigas*. The wooden dining table and four chairs at one end of the room, and the cocktail table and the two big wooden armchairs facing the fireplace at the other, were all of local manufacture, heavy and dark and picturesque and ethnic as hell, but, I'll admit, not remarkably comfortable.

Madeleine said, "I always thought people who went in for burglar alarms must be slightly paranoid."

"It was already installed when I bought the house," I said. "The lady who lived here used it as a summer home; she spent the winters in Scottsdale, Arizona. The place was ripped off twice in her absence, so she put in the alarm system; but nothing could keep the crazy drivers from knocking down her front fence occasionally, and she was getting pretty old, so she decided to live in Scottsdale full-time and sold me the property complete with furniture, kitchen appliances, and security system. Considering my line of work, I feel I'd be tempting fate if I didn't use it; and it does make me worry a bit less when I'm away on business. These days, around here, most people feel obliged to hire house sitters for protection while they're gone." I grimaced. "I can remember a time in this town, not too many years ago, when we didn't even lock our doors."

I took the Anschutz out of its case and slipped it into its

place on the five-gun rack on the wall beside the fireplace, below the two shotguns that are designed to cope with big birds and little ones, and the two hunting rifles intended for use against larger animals and smaller ones. The firearms designed to cope with people of all sizes I do not keep on display; but there was a large knife in an elaborately carved leather sheath lying on the shelf below the guns. It was a giant Bowie of presentation quality, with elaborate grips and engraved blade.. At fourteen inches it was really too big to be a practical fighting knife unless you had Tarzan dreams and a tiger in mind. It had been a tongue-in-cheek Christmas present from Jo, my late lady love. I locked up the gun rack and gestured toward one of the chairs by the fireplace, picked up my drink, and settled into the other.

Madeleine sipped her drink, watching me. ''Matt?''

''Yes, Madeleine?''

''Why are you having me followed?''

We'd taken the long way around, but we'd finally got to it. I regarded her for a moment, thoughtfully.

''How many people do you think I have following you?'' I asked.

She glanced at me sharply, but answered the question: ''I made it four at the last count, but there could be more.'' Then she said, angrily, ''Damn it, I thought it was all over, five years ago when my conviction was reversed and my record was cleared and full citizenship was restored to me. . . . It didn't make up for my lost career, or the years of my life wasted in that ghastly federal penitentiary, but goddamn it, at least it was *over*, or I thought it was. And then, just recently, I started seeing little men trailing me like before, when they were trying to pin all the treason in the world on me, Jesus! It was like a crazy time warp taking me back to that terrible year before the trial. . . . What are you trying to do to me, Matt?''

''When did you first spot these people watching you?''

She glanced at me irritably, but again answered the question: ''It must have been three or four weeks ago. And I shouldn't say 'men'; there seem to be two of each sexual persuasion—well, of the two standard sexual persuasions. An equal opportunity employer, hah! They could have been following me quite a bit longer. Denver is a big city; and it took me a while to realize that I kept seeing the same cars too often, and the same faces. I guess, after five years, I'd started to forget some of the lessons they taught me at that gruesome spy school of yours.''

''What makes you think these people are taking orders from me?''

Madeleine didn't seem to hear the question; she drew a long breath and went on harshly: ''Don't you have any imagination at all, can't you understand how being followed like that makes me feel? But to hell with my feelings, don't you realize that even if my record has been cleansed, purged, completely purified, I can't *afford* to be under surveillance? This new law firm has been very good to me, but if it got around that I was being tailed, as we ex-cons say . . . It would destroy everything I've built since I moved to Denver. No respectable firm can afford to employ a woman, innocent or guilty, who has teams of government agents following her around.''

''What makes you think they're government agents, Madeleine?''

When she didn't answer at once, I reached over to take her black purse out of her hands. I'd already noted that she handled it as if it was heavier than it should be. I looked inside and saw one of the smaller Colt revolvers, .38 caliber, with a four-inch barrel. I closed the purse and gave it back to her.

She spoke defiantly: ''It's perfectly legal. All my civil rights were restored, remember, including the right to buy a gun.''

Actually, while owning the pistol was legal enough out here in the west, where no pickup truck is properly equipped without a couple of firearms across the back window, carrying it concealed like that probably wasn't; but it was no time for technicalities.

I repeated my question: ''What makes you think they're

26

government agents, Madeleine? And how do you know I sent them?''

"They've got to be government agents if you're involved, don't they?'' She smiled grimly. "One of them told me, Matt. Oh, not willingly, but eventually she spoke up like a good little girl and told me everything.''

I studied her face carefully and saw the burning anger she was trying to keep in check. "I see. You're getting tough in your old age.''

She said harshly, "Remember, when we were traveling across the country together, after you picked me up at Fort Ames, that man you wanted to answer your questions who wouldn't? Well, at first he wouldn't. He must still be carrying the scar you gave him, unless he's had a plastic job done. I catch on quickly, Matt; it only takes me five years or so to take a hint. So I cut the pretty one out of the herd and pistol-whipped her a little, following in the footsteps of the master.''

She was waiting for something, perhaps shocked disapproval. I said, "I had a hunch it was going to turn out to be all my fault.''

"Well, whose else? You shouldn't have set me such a brutal example, back when I was weak and impressionable. And you shouldn't have put me through that lethal course and then sent a bunch of wet-nosed kids after me. It didn't take much to make the little bitch talk, just one good taste of the gun sight. I left her blubbering about her lousy face. To hell with her face, it's my lousy life she and her friends are wrecking, damn it. What little of it I managed to save out of that other wreck!'' She drew a long, shuddering breath. "Give me another drink, damn you!''

I took her glass away, refilled it, and returned it to her. She drank and sat for a moment staring into the glass.

"If you think I'm sorry for spoiling the stupid brat's looks, think again! I'd happily mangle the whole lot of them. I didn't fight back last time. I let them humiliate me and walk all over me and give me a farcical trial and call me a traitor to my country and lock me away; but this time it's going to be different. Last time I was a starry-eyed young lawyer and I was naive enough to trust the law to protect me, ha! Well, I'm still a lawyer, because it's the only way I know how to make a decent living, but I'm not starry-eyed and naive any longer. This time I know where the real protection is, right here!" She slapped the purse in her lap and lifted her head to look at me. "You see? You see what you've done? I was almost civilized again, almost human. I'd almost forgotten the gutless, prideless slob who crawled out of prison and the savage fighting beast you and your trainers and weapons instructors made of her. I'd almost forgotten about killing two men to save your life. But it's coming back to me, darling! Nobody'll ever put me behind bars again. They may kill me, but I promise you I won't die alone, and if the bastards I take with me are wearing police badges or government IDs, so much the better. They still owe me for the years they cost me—'Oops, just a slight mistake, ma'am, but it wasn't really our fault, ma'am, we hear so many perpetrators claim they've been framed, sorry about that, ma'am.' Well, this time, damn it, I'll make them regret their little mistakes in spades, and that goes for you, too, Matt, if you're trying to use me for something tricky!"

"Sounds like a threat," I said mildly.

She glared at me. "Are you laughing at me? Oh, I know you're tough and trained and experienced, and undoubtedly armed to the teeth, and all I have to work with is one crummy little pistol and a quickie course in mayhem that's five years old, but don't fool yourself that I'm going to be such an easy patsy a second time—"

"Nobody's laughing," I said. "Come on, let me show you something."

"Matt, damn you—"

"Come on!" I rose and took her reluctant hand to help her out of her chair. "We'll go out the back way through the bedroom."

She started to protest further, but checked herself and allowed herself to be guided out of the living room and past the big double bed to the French doors opening onto the patio

28

at the rear of the house. Happy, who spends most of his time in the front yard—perhaps he enjoys listening to the cars going by in the street outside—came charging around the corner to greet us as if he hadn't seen us for a week.

I coped with his enthusiasm and said, "This way."

The lot is a narrow one, leaving only room for a flagstone walk along the side of the house and a flower bed—well, decorative shrubs and small rosebushes—along the fence. Madeleine followed me with due regard for her nylons.

"It must be pretty when they're in bloom," she said. "I didn't know you were a gardener."

"I inherited the stuff. It seemed a pity to let it all die, the old lady had spent a lot of time and love on it, so I have a man come in once a week. . . . Okay. Do you see that knothole in the fence over there near the gate? Take a peek through it and I'll tell you what you see."

"Isn't this kind of silly?" Madeleine asked, making her way to the indicated spot. "Why don't you just tell me—" But she rose on tiptoe to look through the hole.

I spoke in tour-guide fashion: "You are now looking up a typical old Santa Fe thoroughfare, ma'am, with houses and property walls right on the street, not much in the way of sidewalks, no front lawns, a few parked cars. Well, I don't have to tell you about Santa Fe; you've lived here. There's a gray Honda parked next door on this side, you can just see the rear of it, and a blue Audi across the way. At least they were there just now when we came inside. And somewhere well up the street, with some other heaps, probably on the other side facing this way with a good view of my gate, is an old tan Volvo station wagon. There's a dark-haired woman sitting behind the wheel. Am I right?"

Madeleine hesitated. "Oh, up there. Yes, you're right, although I can't be sure it's a woman, but what makes her so special—"

"They're very systematic," I said. "Six-hour shifts; this gal still has a few minutes to go. At noon sharp she'll be relieved by a skinny young fellow with ragged jeans and a lot of dark beard, driving a white Chevy van. He was the first one I spotted, so I call him Spooky One; the lady is Spooky Three. At six in the evening, One will be replaced by Four, a sharp-looking Latin gent in a suit—with or without a tie depending on the mood of the moment—who'll take up the watch in a sporty little red Pontiac of some kind. At midnight, a tall blond character in boots, jeans, and a cowboy hat, driving a husky blue Ford pickup with four-wheel drive, one of those jacked-up monsters with a row of lights over the cab, will take over. Spooky Two. At least that describes the costumes and rolling stock as of yesterday; they switch things around occasionally to confuse. . . . Now what's happening?''

She'd suddenly become very intent on the knothole. ''The station wagon is driving away, but there isn't any—oh, yes, here comes the van. He's parking a little closer. Like you said, a real Castro beard.'' She drew a long breath and turned to face me. ''What are you trying to tell me, Matt?''

''Join the club, baby. We're all wearing extra shadows these days, it's the latest fashion.''

She said sharply, ''You mean, you want me to believe you're being watched, too? What makes you think I'll fall for a crazy story like that? The way you know their schedule to the minute, they're probably your bodyguards, assigned to protect you from people you've driven crazy, like me. . . . Oh, damn!''

Intent on our conversation, she'd snagged a stocking, cutting too close to the corner of the flower bed.

I said, ''Why don't you drop the act, Madeleine?''

She looked at me for a moment; then she bent over and touched a dampened forefinger to her damaged hose. I've never figured out why they do that; do they expect saliva to heal the broken nylon threads magically? She straightened up slowly to face me.

When she didn't speak at once, I went on: ''It's the standard toughie-lawyer routine, isn't it? Intimidate the witness by treating him as guilty and coming at him hard and watching his reactions, hoping he'll give himself away, one way or the other. But this is Matt, sweetheart. You don't have to run a bluff on me or put on an act for me. I'm on your side."

Her voice was harsh: "I had some people on my side once, long ago at the time of my trial; a lot of nice, friendly, helpful people. I have them to thank for my conviction. It made me, let's say, a bit mistrustful of folks claiming to be on my side." She drew a long breath. "That girl said she was there—they were all there—on account of you."

It was an odd way of putting it, but this wasn't the time to analyze it. I grinned. "That just means you didn't hit her hard enough, or often enough, sweetheart. It would be interesting to know what other stories she'd have come up with." I regarded her for a moment, rather grimly. "No matter what anybody said, you don't really believe I'd send a bunch of creeps to harass you without a word of warning, do you, Madeleine?"

There was a little silence as we faced each other. I'd forgotten—I'd made myself forget—what a lovely thing she was, if you like your lovely things brave and brainy. At last her glance dropped away from mine. She licked her lips before speaking.

"I had to be sure." Her voice was soft. "The man I knew five years ago was on my side, but you could have changed."

"I'm hurt. Whatever happened to faith and trust? Come on, let's get back inside. . . . No, not you, you big mutt; you stay out here and pretend you're a savage watchdog."

I closed the French doors behind us. Madeleine was busily brushing herself off as if she'd covered several miles of trackless wilderness instead of about twenty yards of fenced yard. She looked down at herself ruefully.

"Damn, it doesn't matter how nicely you're dressed, just one little run in your nylons makes you look as if you'd been sleeping in your clothes."

That was an exaggeration, but the slight damage was a breach in the businesswoman armor, an intriguing hint that severe and untouchable as she looked, she wasn't completely invulnerable.

She went on without looking up: "You never came, Matt."

31

She licked her lips. "I thought maybe, when you heard about the divorce . . ."

I cleared my throat. "You picked the other guy, remember? Am I supposed to spend my life chasing after dames who don't know their own minds? If you wanted me, all you had to do was grab a phone. You knew that."

"Yes, I knew. I guess I was . . . just too proud to admit I'd made a terrible mistake." She looked up at last. "He was a mouse, darling! A sweet mouse, but still a mouse."

"Hell, you knew that when you married him."

"I thought you'd come. I told myself, when you learned of the divorce you'd surely come. And then . . . and then I realized at last that I was kidding myself and I'd have to be the one, but I kept waiting. . . . I guess I was waiting for a good excuse. Well, I got it. These Spookies, as you call them. So I came down here and put on my silly act because I'm a proud bitch who has a hell of a time admitting she was wrong. Matt, I—" Then she stopped, and drew a long breath, and asked with sudden anger, "Are you just going to stand there? Well, if you're too stiff-necked to come six feet to me, after I've driven four hundred miles to you, I suppose I can manage to make it the rest of the way!"

She did.

Chapter 4

AT the last moment before the reaction went critical I closed the drapes and blinds at her request. No neighbors can look into my little rear patio or the bedroom window at the side of the house without doing some tough fence climbing, but I guess she was feeling shy in that respect, although in no other. Later, after a long time had passed—after our breathing had returned almost to normal—she stirred in my arms as we lay on the big bed in the vague, soft daylight that sneaked into the room in spite of the obstacles I'd put in its way. I heard her laugh softly.

"Oh, God," she whispered. "I'm so tired of being respectable, darling! I'm so tired of being the smart and well-groomed professional woman!" She laughed again. "Well, we've pretty well taken care of that, haven't we? See the high-class lady lawyer lying on the untidy bed all naked and tangle-haired and sweaty with her high-class lady-lawyer costume scattered over the floor getting all wrinkled and dusty. God, it's like getting out of a goddamn straitjacket!" After a little pause she went on: "Walter would have hung it all up neatly for me, you know, before he allowed himself to join me. He was a very neat boy."

I said, "That's why you married him, wasn't it, for his neatness and respectability?"

She nodded. "But it wasn't one of my very best ideas. After spending years being pushed around in prison and then coming home to receive the ex-con treatment—you remember—I wasn't thinking very straight, I guess. I just wanted to show all those smug, self-righteous bastards. . . . But I

33

shouldn't talk mean about Walter. I gave him such a hell of a time toward the end, poor guy, and he never did figure out why. He thought it was because I was in love with you."

"Gosh, aren't you?"

Her face was suddenly unsmiling in the dusk. "Don't be silly, Matt. I have to hate you, don't you know that?"

"You have a funny way of showing it."

She licked her lips. "Why shouldn't I hate you? You practically brought me back from the dead, and I don't just mean the way you stopped a bullet to protect me. I owe you a ridiculous debt of gratitude, and the fact that at the end I managed to save your life a little doesn't go very far toward canceling the awful obligation. . . . Don't all debtors detest their creditors? And you, you bastard, you saw me the way I was when I got out of prison, a flabby, broken-down, self-pitying . . . How can I help hating a man who remembers me like that? How can I help hating the man who practically rebuilt me from scratch? I bet that monster he created hated Dr. Frankenstein's guts for doing such a clumsy job. Well, I'm your very own do-it-yourself female monster, darling; and you'd better figure out what to do with me, now that you've got me all constructed, because you seem to have built me so I don't function too well by myself."

I looked at her for a moment without speaking; then I sat up and reached over the side of the bed for a couple of garments, passing her a creamy slip with lace top and bottom and satin in between, and hauling on my own well-worn white cotton-and-polyester shorts, JC Penney's best.

She looked at the lingerie in her hands and smiled faintly. "You got something against nude women, buster?"

"That's asking for a dirty crack, but I'll restrain myself. Put it on, if you want to have zee great Herr Doktor Matthias Helmstein his mind on your problems keep. Another drink?"

"If you're planning to feed me some lunch pretty soon to soak it up."

"That can be arranged."

When I returned with two glasses, she'd smoothed out the bedspread we'd rumpled and piled up the pillows we'd tossed

34

aside. She looked like a little girl sitting there demurely against them, bare-legged and bare-shouldered in her pretty slip. I noted, however, that the little girl had been adult enough to run a quick comb through her tousled hair and make hasty repairs to her damaged lipstick. I noted also that she hadn't bothered to pick up her suit or blouse or stockings, leaving them on the floor with her high-heel shoes like the fragmented, discarded shell of a past stage of her development. I wasn't about to disturb any significant symbols of liberation she wanted to leave lying around, so I stepped over the crumpled clothes and, after giving her both glasses to hold, settled myself beside her and retrieved one.

"Ve vill now zee analysis commence," I said, after taking a healthy sip. "What's bugging you besides a bunch of snoops in your hair, babe?"

She said, "I'm not making it, Matt."

I regarded her for a moment. Fear stirred within me as I remembered another woman I'd met in times of desperate trouble who, unable to find her way back to a satisfactory way of living afterward, had wound up killing herself.

I said, "You indicated you were doing pretty well with that law firm up in Denver."

"Yes, and I was doing pretty well as Mrs. Walter Maxon, too, for the first year or so; at least Mr. Maxon seemed to think so. For God's sake, darling, I'm not bad-looking and I'm not dumb. I know the moves and I can fake them pretty well even when I don't, well, feel them. I can put on a swell loving-wife performance for a husband and I can manage a very convincing bright-but-modest-associate routine for the partners. All it takes is a little hypocrisy and a little acting ability. And all the time I'm bored out of my skull. My God, two years with that sweet little boy in that sweet little house— well, it wasn't so damn little—with the biggest excitement of my day being whether or not I got his eggs soft-boiled just right in the morning. Even then there was no danger of his beating me if I goofed, dammit, or even complaining; he'd just look a little sad. Well, I made a showplace of his lousy shack in return for his giving me his veddy, veddy respectable name, and I entertained his business contacts beautifully, if I do say so myself, and I was very sneaky and clever about helping him with his work without ever letting him know that as a lawyer, he made me want to scream. Not that he didn't know his law, he was a walking law library, but he had about as much gumption as a three-toed sloth, no enterprise, no inspiration, just meticulous hard work, which is okay in its place, but occasionally you've got to come up with something a little more dramatic, and there was no drama in him. Not in the courtroom and not . . . not in bed."

After just making love to the lady, I didn't feel right about discussing the sexual prowess of her former husband or listening to her discuss it.

I said, "Well, come to that, I've never considered myself a particularly dramatic lover."

She said judiciously, "Maybe you're not quite Casanova reincarnated, but at least you act as if there was another human being in the bed with you, willing and reasonably durable, not a porcelain doll too precious and fragile to . . . No, damn it, that's dirty. I mustn't talk about him like that. He was just as sweet as he could be and he loved me; loved me enough that, when I had to leave, he let me go without making me feel too awful about it. Just as you did when I decided to marry him. I've always respected you for that."

In spite of my modest disclaimer, I wasn't quite sure I liked not being Casanova reincarnated. I said, "Golly gee, ma'am, it makes me feel warm all over, being respected like that."

"You bastard," she said. "You know what I mean. You're not—and neither is Walter—the kind of selfish and possessive lover who grabs a gun when he finds the gal with another man and blows away the two of them. That kind of hysterical freak doesn't really love anybody but himself. He's just telling the world how badly his poor little feelings have been hurt. If you love somebody, you want them happy, preferably with you but if not with somebody else, don't you? If you *really* love them, you certainly don't want them dead!"

36

I said, "It's very pleasant to lounge on a bed alongside a pretty girl in her underwear, drinking whiskey and talking about love, but I'm afraid it isn't getting us very far. . . ."

I stopped, hearing a sound outside. Happy was barking in an odd way. Labradors don't bark much as a rule and he's pretty quiet even for a Lab, although like most dogs he will serenade the postman and the UPS man—I sometimes wonder what those guys do to attract so much loud canine attention. But this was a sharper and more excited bark than the deep routine woofing designed to warn me that the defensive perimeter was again under attack by dangerous delivery personnel. . . . Then there was the crack of a shot, and silence. I felt a sudden panic.

"Oh, Jesus, if some trigger-happy bastard has shot my dog . . . !"

I rolled off the bed, kicked my feet into my shoes, and ran into the living room. It took me a moment to unlock the rack and get down one of the shotguns. There are two theories about the home storage of firearms. One says you never load a gun in the house, the other says an unloaded gun is a useless piece of iron and you're supposed to treat every gun as if it were loaded, anyway, so it might as well be. With no kids around, I go for Theory Two to the extent that while the chamber was empty, the weapon in my hands, an old Remington 1100 auto, had four buckshot shells in the magazine. Heading for the door, I yanked back the charging handle and let the bolt slam forward, readying the gun for firing.

Normally, I might have taken a few precautions like, say, going out the bedroom door as before so I wouldn't be stepping right into the line of fire; but the ugly silence, after the odd-sounding barking and the single shot, did things to my judgment. I had an ex-wife and some offspring in the east somewhere, but the big yellow retriever in the yard was my only immediate family, and maybe you wouldn't die for your dog but I'm not so sure about me. I'd certainly kill for him. As far as I'm concerned, any two-legged creature that would harm a dog isn't really human, so where's the problem?

I yanked the door open and made a dive for the bushes on

37

the far side of the path, wishing the old lady from whom I'd bought the house had gone in for anything but roses. Nobody shot at me. I came up scratched, with the gun shouldered ready to fire, safety off. Then I drew a long breath of relief. Happy was standing over something by the front gate, his thick yellow tail slashing from side to side. Wherever the single bullet had gone, at least he was still alive and on his feet.

I extricated myself from the thorny cover into which I'd plunged and moved forward cautiously. My initial impression was that my gentle hunting dog had brought down the intruder and was now busily tearing him limb from limb; which was strange behavior for a soft-mouthed retriever who never left a tooth mark on a bird. Then I saw that the invader was a woman; and that Happy was merely licking her face in his friendly fashion. She didn't seem to appreciate his attentions. Hearing me approach, she pushed herself up, her face white, her eyes wide with fear.

"Take him away!" she gasped. "Oh, please take him away!"

I saw her pistol come up, a small automatic. I didn't know if she was even aware, in her panic, that she was still holding it; but it was swinging my way, and a gun is a gun, and dying accidentally isn't a great improvement over dying intentionally. I kicked at the weapon and swung the butt of my shotgun hard, keeping the muzzle high so that if there was a discharge, it wouldn't blow my head off. The shotgun didn't fire, but the wooden stock made a solid thunking sound as it hit the woman's skull just above the ear.

Chapter 5

I picked up the pistol where I'd kicked it. Checking it, I saw that its seven-shot magazine lacked two cartridges: the one that had been fired and the one that was in the chamber ready to fire. It was a small .380 Spanish automatic called Llama—well, semiautomatic, if you want to get technical. I was reminded of somebody's long-ago jingle to the effect that a one-l lama is a priest, but a two-l llama is a beast. Edgar Guest? Ogden Nash? This little beast seemed like a reasonably well made gun. I replaced the magazine, set the safety catch, and having attended to all stray firearms, always the well-trained agent's first concern after a crisis, laid it aside with my shotgun on the rough wooden box built against the front fence that concealed my garbage cans.

I turned anxiously to examine Happy. He'd been hovering nearby, looking hopeful. He was clearly of the opinion that with two firearms in sight and one shot fired there should be something for a good retriever to retrieve, damn it, just tell him where. I called him to me and inspected him carefully for blood, poked him for indications of pain, and drew a long breath of relief when I found neither; apparently the bullet had gone elsewhere.

"Will you stop playing with your damn dog; this woman is badly hurt."

I gave Happy a pat and released him, looking around. Madeleine was kneeling beside the unconscious figure by the gate. She was wearing an old plaid robe of mine and her high heels.

I said, "You're making me feel bad. I was trying to brain her. You mean I failed?"

"Don't be so tough. And you didn't have to hit her all that hard!"

I looked at her in amazement. "The dame was waving a gun, baby! If she's breathing at all, she's way ahead of the game; she should be dead."

Madeleine started to speak hotly; then she threw back her head and laughed instead. "Sorry, Matt, I've just been living too long with respectable people in that beautiful dreamland they inhabit where violence is unspeakable and death is unthinkable and if you have a problem you just call a policeman and he'll come right over and fix it for you. Wish-fulfillment country. Thanks for kicking me back into the crude real world again; it's like coming home." She looked down at the woman on the ground. "So what do we do with this, cut its throat?"

Something was nudging my thigh. I said, "Happy, stop it, I can't play with you now."

"He wants to give you something," Madeleine said. "It looks like a purse."

Getting no cooperation from me, he'd found a retrieving object on his own; and he was holding it in his mouth, sitting properly to deliver it with his tail working happily. I told him what a great dog he was and took the rather shabby brown leather bag. It was of good quality, I noted, just well-worn; perhaps a favorite best purse relegated, after many years of faithful dress-up service, to informal occasions when the owner was wearing jeans and shooting people. Happy had left a little saliva on it, but no tooth marks. Like I said, softmouthed. I wiped it off and opened it. A small wallet inside, also pretty good leather, yielded up several credit cards and a driver's license in the name of Ruth Stephanie Steiner, 22 Butterwood Road, Santa Fe, New Mexico 87501.

For a moment the name meant nothing to me; then I put the stuff into the hands of Madeleine, who'd come over to look, and knelt beside the unconscious woman, turning her over carefully so I could see her face. I hadn't really got a good look at her during the action. Pale and dirt-streaked, her features didn't look very familiar; the girl I was thinking of had been very different in appearance, a grave young woman with big blue eyes hiding behind big horn-rimmed glasses, and a ragged mop of short blond hair. I spoke a rude word as I got to my feet, realizing belatedly that I was wearing only shoes and underwear shorts, and a number of rose-bush scratches. I listened for a moment, but the lone shot seemed to have aroused no neighborhood interest. I noted that the woman hadn't got the gate completely closed after slipping into the yard. I closed and padlocked it, reminding myself not to leave it unlocked again, since there seemed to be no telling what might come through it.

"Keep an eye on the dame, I've got to get to the phone," I said.

"You know who she is." It was a statement, not a question.

"Yes," I said. "I'll tell you later. Hold the fort."

Although I'd called the number a couple of times in the past few months, I didn't have it in my head or written down; I had to dig it out of the book. A young-girl voice answered on the fourth ring. I asked the kid to call her daddy.

"Popsy, it's for you," I heard her shout.

Footsteps approached the phone. I heard a male voice say distantly, "Your mama does not like you to call me Popsy, Andrea. Show a little respect, huh, small one?"

"Yes, Papa."

Then the voice was speaking directly into the phone: "Steiner here."

I said, "Mark, this is Matt. I've got something of yours. A Llama pistol, the small-frame model, caliber three-eighty, one shot fired. It didn't go off of its own accord. I think she was shooting at Happy but she missed."

"Oh shit!" There was a pause; then Mark spoke carefully: "Ruth has been terrified of dogs ever since the time they tried to run her down with hounds when she escaped from . . . Never mind. I was not even aware that she had gone out; I thought she was taking a nap. Is she okay?"

"No, I had to thump her pretty hard, disarming her. Do you want me to call nine-one-one for an ambulance?"

"Damn it, amigo, you did not have to . . . !"

I said irritably, "Amigo, it's only my gentle nature that kept me from putting a load of number-four buck into the trigger-happy broad. Now, having softheartedly spared her life, I'm giving you and her another break, calling you instead of the cops. Be grateful. What about that ambulance?"

After a moment he asked, "What is the police situation?"

"I haven't called them, and I don't think anybody's reported the shot. That nine-millimeter Kurz isn't a very loud cartridge, and the Hispanic kids in the neighborhood don't wait for the Fourth of July to set off firecrackers; there's always something popping around here."

At the other end of the line, Mark Steiner cleared his throat. "Please call nobody, I will take care of it. What is the address?" I remembered that I'd been to his house, but he'd never been to mine. When I'd told him how to get there, Mark said, "Wait for me; I will be right over. . . . Matt."

"Yes."

"I will contact some people I know. I must come clear across town; they may arrive before I do. Let them in. They will take care of her."

I said, "There have been some funny things going on around here lately. You'd better give them a word so I'll know they belong to you."

"Do we need this TV melodrama?"

I said, "As far as I'm concerned we've already got it. A strange dame trying to shoot my dog and me for motives unknown seems melodramatic as hell to me."

"Very well. The password is . . . How about Lapis?"

He pronounced it Lahpis, as Mac had done. I kept my voice even, I hoped, and said, "Like in Lazuli? Good enough."

"I will be on my way as soon as I make the one telephone call. . . . Oh, and thanks."

"I'll tell you later if you're welcome."

I hung up, selected the male garments from the jumble of

clothes on the floor—witnesses to the sudden passion that now seemed to belong to the distant past—and pulled them on, trying not to think about the word Mark Steiner had given me because I had absolutely no relevant data to plug into the mental computer. Except that a hung-over young bureaucratic type, talking to Mac, had once let slip the same word in connection with secret government operations in the southwest. Lapis. Latin for "rock," or "stone." To hell with it.

I called Washington hurriedly and left word that interesting things were happening here and I'd report in detail within the hour; if I didn't, an investigation would be in order. After getting the shell out of the chamber and back into the magazine, I hung the shotgun back on the living-room rack, equipped myself with other arms more suitable for the occasion including the Llama, grabbed a spare blanket from the closet, and went back out into the yard. Madeleine was sitting on the edge of the garbage box. She was scratching Happy's ears with one hand and holding her Colt revolver in the other.

"How's she doing?" I asked.

Madeleine shrugged. "Still breathing. Should we carry her inside?"

"I think you're not supposed to move them unnecessarily. It isn't raining and it isn't cold. Somebody's coming for her." I hesitated. "You wanted to know who she is. She's the wife of a guy named Mark Steiner. I shoot targets with him occasionally. Don't ask me what she's doing here because I don't know." I gestured toward the borrowed robe. "You'd better get some clothes on before we have company."

"Well, I'm not getting back into my lawyer suit; I just put that on to impress you. Get my suitcase out of the Mercedes, will you? The keys are in my purse, somewhere in that love nest of yours. . . ."

"You might have told me you wanted stuff from your car before I locked the gate."

But it was a comfortable kind of bickering, and I realized that I liked having her around—and at least this one wasn't

43

likely to be turned off by my violent profession at this late date; she'd known me too long. While she was dressing in the house I covered Ruth Steiner with the blanket and, kneeling beside her, pulled back her eyelids the way I'd seen it done. Her pupils were the same size, which could indicate that her cranium wasn't too badly damaged. Her left ear was split near the top, swollen and bloody, and the growing lump on the side of her head was already spectacular. Still kneeling beside her, I knew, by the change in her breathing, when she started to become aware of her surroundings.

I said, "It's all right, Mrs. Steiner. Mark's coming."

She turned her head painfully to look at me. "What happened . . . ? Oh, take him away!" She was staring past me fearfully.

I said, "He's a very gentle dog and he's never bitten anybody in his life, but if he bothers you, I'll put him inside. . . . Come on, Happy."

I rose and went over to open the front door and let him in; when I returned, Ruth Steiner was sitting up, pressing both hands to the left side of her head.

"Gentle!" She was rocking back and forth with the pain, and her voice was angry. "Gentle? You should have seen him; he leaped right for my throat; if I hadn't shoved my purse between his jaws, I'd be dead now!"

I laughed. "Lady, you had a pistol in one hand and an interesting object in the other, didn't you? Happy thought you were going to fire the gun and toss something for him to fetch, just as I do when I'm training him. I use a blank pistol and a training dummy, but you can't expect him to tell the difference. Well, you fired the gun, but you were a little slow with the throw, so he got impatient and jumped for what you were teasing him with, he thought. He had no interest in your throat; all he wanted was your purse." I looked down at her grimly. "And just for future reference, Mrs. Steiner, if you ever take another shot at my dog, hit or miss, I'll use the other end of my shotgun on you."

"Well, that figures!" she said sharply. "I can well believe you'd consider a dog more valuable than a human being,

44

considering how you and your friends behave toward human beings!"

I looked at her for a moment. "What friends?"

"You know what friends! There's one sitting up the street from our house right now, if he hasn't followed me here. Oh, damn you, damn you, damn all of you, why can't you leave us alone? Hounding us, hounding us, finally making us live in this ghastly desert where the wind never stops blowing and there's always dust in your teeth. . . . Well, maybe we can go back to civilization now that you've found us again! Obviously we're no safer from you hiding under a phony name in our miserable little development shack in this primitive mud-brick town."

I said, "You've lost me, Mrs. Steiner. I don't know where you came from or why you had to leave there; and if any friends of mine are parked near your place here in Santa Fe, they haven't told me about it."

She laughed angrily and winced at the pain in her head. "That's what you *would* say, isn't it? But did you really think Mark was fooled when you went out of your way to strike up an acquaintance with him at the gun club last summer and then acted so very helpless with that new rifle that he was obliged to invite you home and fix it for you? You're not much of an actor, you know; and when Mark realized he was being followed again, it became obvious that you had to be part of the conspiracy, the inside man, I suppose you'd call yourself. . . . What are you laughing at?"

"Never mind," I said.

I'd laughed, of course, because Mark Steiner's suspicions of me echoed so faithfully mine of him. And then, of course, there was Madeleine and her suspicions. If the Spookies, whoever they might be, had been trying to turn us all against each other, they'd succeeded brilliantly. Hearing a car pull up outside, I took out the little Llama pistol, it being SOP that you never shoot anybody with your own gun if somebody else's is available and will do the job. I had no doubt the Llama would do the job. Whatever Mark Steiner might be, he wouldn't have a gun around the house that wasn't

45

sighted in properly. Somebody tried the gate and then pounded on it. I walked over there and paused before reaching for the padlock key.

"Give me a word," I said.

An impatient male voice said, "Lapis, damn you. Now open up."

I was interested to note that this one called it Laypis.

Chapter 6

THE first man who entered my little front yard was tallish and blondish, wearing expensive prefaded jeans, a short, prefaded, denim jacket, and a dark blue turtleneck, all very casual, but I got the impression it was merely a costume he put on for slumming out here in the crude southwest; he was an eastern three-piece-suit man at heart. It showed in the neatly pressed jeans—no true westerner ever put iron to denim—and in the white, capped, well-brushed teeth, the crisp, closely trimmed, slightly wavy, light hair, and the shining, newly shaved face.

On the other hand, he had said Laypis, which placed his origins somewhere west of lah-di-dah Boston. A man of contradictions, obviously. He smelled pretty. If I were to shoot him, at any reasonable range, it would be an easy retrieve for Happy, I reflected, since if I could detect the after-shave lotion and cologne at ten feet, my dog, with his far superior olfactory apparatus, should have no trouble tracking it out to at least a hundred yards even if I dropped the guy in heavy cover.

Our visitor was wearing a gun high on his right hip under the unzipped zipper jacket: a flat automatic, probably chambered for the 9mm Parabellum cartridge that seems to be replacing the good old .38 Special in the affections of the bureaucracy.

"Where is she?" he snapped.

"Right over there, " I said, inclining my head toward the woman sitting on the ground, watching.

The newcomer looked that way and back to me with suspicion in his baby-blue eyes. He was quite a handsome fellow; the clean-cut, freckled, all-American-college-boy type that some government departments seem to cherish. Somehow, I'd been quite sure from the instant I first sighted him that like me, he got his orders from Washington. As they say, it takes one to know one.

"Steiner says your name is Helm?" He made it a question.

"That's right. Who are you?"

He flipped a fancy ID folder at me, too fast for me to read what was engraved on the gold shield inside.

"U.S. government," he said. "We were informed that it was an emergency; that the woman was badly hurt, unconscious, an ambulance case. She doesn't look like an emergency to me. If this is some kind of a trick . . . Check her out, Mike."

The second man in was shorter and darker than the first, and his black hair was somewhat longer. He wore a light sport coat instead of a windbreaker, but a slight hip bulge indicated that the gun was in the same place and probably of the same configuration and caliber. They do like to standardize. He walked over and squatted on his heels beside Steiner's wife. It's a position that doesn't come naturally to many Anglos, although I've known some cowboys who could make it look comfortable—when I try it, I don't last very long—but people of Spanish descent seem to be able to sit that way by the hour. He examined her bruised head gently.

His partner spoke to me: "I'll take the gun."

I looked at the well-manicured hand he held out for it. There was really no reason why I shouldn't give him Ruth Steiner's gun. But then again, there was really no good reason why I should. I get very tired of these officious jerks with badges who march onto the premises and lay claim to every firearm in sight. The weapon goes for around three hundred bucks, retail. He was probably under the mistaken impression that it was my property; but in any case he knew damned well it wasn't his. I should make him, or the U.S. government, three hundred bucks richer without even a please?

I said, "That's a pretty reckless statement, isn't it? The piece is in my hand and yours is in your holster. How are you planning to work this confiscation?" He stared at me, shocked. Representing the U.S. government as he did, he hadn't expected a refusal. I went on: "You came for a dame, mister; just take her and blow."

"Listen, you . . . !" Then he stopped, looking past me.

Madeleine's voice spoke behind me: "Visitors, Matt?"

I answered without turning my head: "The *federales*, ma'am. They've supposedly come for Mrs. Steiner, but this one seems eager to cart away everything that isn't tied down. He's starting with the firearms, but he'll undoubtedly go for the patio furniture next, after which it's good-bye to the stove, sink, refrigerator, and TV. We call him *El Hombre sin Nombre*, since he's very shy about revealing his name, assuming that he has one. That one over there is less anonymous; he's called Mike. See if he needs help with Mrs. Steiner, will you, please?"

The man in front of me didn't like it. In fact he was pale enough with anger that the boyish freckles stood out very clearly. However, he couldn't think of a move to make that might not earn him a bullet. He tried to convince himself that I couldn't possibly shoot a fine government employee like him, and failed.

Madeleine came into my field of vision, dressed in jeans and a man's shirt, white, with the tails hanging out. I won't say she looked as good in those sloppy garments as she had in her smart legal costume—I like dressed-up ladies—but for a denim girl she didn't do at all badly. On her feet, Reeboks or Adidas or whatever; I can't keep track of them all. Life was simpler back in the Keds era. She was carrying, incongruously, the smart black purse that went with her business clothes. As I say, dressed up or dressed down, she was still very pleasant to look at. The man called Mike regarded her with frank Latin admiration.

After a moment he cleared his throat and said, "If you can give me a hand, we'll get her to the car, Miss. . . ."

Madeleine took her hand out of her purse, which didn't

leave the purse empty. What had started as a peaceful Sunday, with just a few target .22s popping for fun, seemed to be getting pretty heavy with serious firearms.

"Rustin," Madeleine said. "Madeleine Rustin. Are you a doctor?"

"Miguel Ortiz at your service, Miss Rustin. No, I'm not a doctor; but they've got me kind of specializing in making temporary repairs until the real doctors can take over."

"How is she?"

"It looks messy, but there's not enough external bleeding to worry about; they can patch up that ear later. I'd say what she needs is a bed, some X rays to determine if there's a skull fracture, and in any case plenty of rest until it's certain there's no serious concussion or internal seepage. Let's get her on her feet. . . ."

As the three of them moved awkwardly toward the gate I said to the man before me: "Well, what's it to be, Mr. Government Man?"

His glance wavered briefly; he steadied it and said contemptuously, "You're bluffing, Helm, but I haven't got time to play macho games with you. You may keep your weapon if it means that much to you." He fixed me with a hard and intimidating stare that he'd undoubtedly practiced in the mirror. "But you will forget all this. You will also forget the code word we used, which should never have been given you. Is that understood?"

I regarded him for a moment. He was slightly incredible, but they all are. "It's understood and rejected," I said. "Pull in your horns, buster. You come onto my property and announce that you're going to take this and I'm going to forget that, just because you're carrying an ID you won't even give me a good look at, that you probably found in a box of cornflakes. Well, you'll take nothing except what you came for and I'll forget nothing except what it pleases me to forget. Good-bye now."

He tried the stare again and, when I displayed no signs of terror, opened his mouth to speak, changed his mind, turned on his heel, and marched out, making no apology for bumping against Madeleine as she returned from the street alone. She glanced after him, shrugged, and watched me roll the gate closed and snap the padlock.

"What was all that about?"

"All what?"

"You acted as if you wanted a gunfight or something."

I grinned. "The man who takes care of the yard, Juan, says we should get some manure for the compost heap to make it work right with all the leaves he's raking this fall; apparently there's some kind of chemical reaction in there that requires excremental stimulation. It occurred to me that Mr. No Name would do fine, full of shit as he is. But I guess we'll just have to buy it, although I'm always reluctant to pay good money for it when there's so much of it around, and more generated every minute." I realized that I was talking too much. I hadn't really thought the guy would go for it, but it's always a strain. I took Madeleine's arm. "Come on, I promised to feed you. I'll let you pick the can. I'll open it and warm it. How's that for a deal?"

She grimaced. "Damn, what happened to all the glamorous secret agents who dish up gourmet meals at the drop of a bullet-proof vest?"

"You came to the wrong place for glamour, babe; around here all you get is Dinty Moore's beef stew."

Actually, she settled for a plate of corned beef hash with a poached egg on top—Prairie Farms AA Extra Large, if it matters. Since they're just about the only things I cook, aside from an occasional steak and a few potatoes, I'm particular about eggs. After cleaning up the kitchen, we took our coffee into the living room. Earlier, I'd touched a match to the firewood I keep laid and ready during the colder seasons of the year. Madeleine, in one of the massive wooden chairs before the flames, let her jean-clad legs sprawl apart in an unladylike manner.

"Just what were you trying to accomplish, Matt, being so tough with that government character?" she asked lazily at last. "Not that he didn't ask for it, but you were really pushing."

I shrugged. "I'm hoping his feelings are hurt enough that he'll phone Big Papa in Washington to report that a nasty man was very rude to him."

"If he does call Washington, what will that accomplish?"

"Then his chief will, we hope, check out a certain individual named Helm and, if he looks hard enough in the right places—it can be done, if you're persistent and have good government connections—find out that I also work for the government. If the pushy character who just departed is professionally interested in the Steiners, he should have had me traced when I first got friendly with Mark last summer. Maybe that's what made him so hostile; he realized that his sloppy operational habits were going to be exposed. Anyway, having identified me, his chief will lodge a protest with my chief in the name of interdepartmental cooperation. That way we'll know what bureau or department we've come up against without going to the trouble of tracking down the only name we've got, Miguel Ortiz, which could be a lost cause. Hell, you're a New Mexico girl, you know that in Spanish-speaking circles, there are almost as many Ortizes as there are Martinezes and Montoyas; and Miguel isn't exactly uncommon, either. And neither name necessarily belongs to the man who was here."

"Kind of like looking for a phony John Smith, you mean?" When I nodded, she said, "But even if you do find out who nice little Mike and his tall, obnoxious colleague are working for, that still won't tell us about the others, the ones who have both of us under surveillance and apparently the Steiners as well—"

She was interrupted by a shrill, screeching sound; nobody will sell you an honest bell anymore. All they have to offer is these electronic screamers.

I said, "That should be Mark Steiner now. Maybe he knows something about the Spookies we don't."

The harsh screech that tells me somebody's at the gate wanting in sounded again, impatiently. I tucked the little Spanish pistol into my waistband and went out there. It took me a moment to find the right key on the ring.

"Come on, let me in, Matt. If you want the password, it's Lapis. I caught hell for using that!"

It was definitely Mark Steiner's voice. I removed the padlock and stepped aside, letting him slide the gate back. He came inside and looked around for me, and smiled thinly when he saw me back against the fence with the little automatic ready in my hand. He was dressed as he had been at the rifle range, in well-worn khakis, and he had the same khaki cap, with a moderately long bill, on his head.

"I recognize the pistol," he said.

"I saved it for you," I said. "One of those government freaks you sent wanted to liberate it. If I know my G-men, you'd never have seen it again. Here."

He took it and checked the chamber and safety the way any knowledgeable person does when handed a firearm. He stood looking down at the gun for a moment.

"I always wondered why anybody would name a pistol after a South American beast of burden," he said. "I didn't know she'd taken it, but it's the one she really learned to shoot with, after we'd done a little preliminary work with a twenty-two, so I guess she felt most comfortable with it." He looked up sharply. "You haven't asked how she is."

I spoke deliberately: "The health of folks who barge onto the premises with loaded firearms and homicidal intentions concerns me very little."

His lips tightened. "She was upset. She wasn't . . . responsible."

I didn't have to listen to that crap. I said, "Neither, I'm told, was the gent who shot President Reagan. But I've never understood why being an irresponsible loony should give an individual free shooting privileges not accorded to responsible, sane folks."

"Damn it, she's not insane!"

"A gal who blows her stack and runs off to kill somebody without even making sure she's got the right guy and then practically goes into convulsions when a friendly pup licks her face isn't exactly a well-balanced personality in my book." I looked at him hard. "And I'm damn well *not* going

53

to apologize for giving her the gun-butt treatment, which is what you're plugging for, isn't it? I almost lost my dog to your well-balanced wife, and there was even a moment when I thought I might lose me. And I haven't heard any apologies from you for turning a crazy lady with a gun loose on me."

"I didn't—"

"The hell you didn't. She didn't cook up the notion that I was one of the people who were hassling you, maybe even the main man, all by herself. . . . Yes, she talked a little before your federal friends arrived. From what she said, I know you must have told her all about me: that overfriendly Helm character with the affectionate pup you kept bumping into just a little too often at the rifle range. Well, I've kind of wondered about you, too, for exactly the same reasons. I guess it doesn't pay to be friendly these days. However, I didn't share my suspicions with a gal I'd taught to shoot whom I knew to be slightly off her rocker, and I didn't leave a loaded gun where she could get her hands on it. So let's just call it even, apology-wise, shall we?"

We faced each other for a long moment; then he looked down at the pistol in his hand. He smiled thinly. "You're a damn fool to talk to me like that after handing me a gun, Matt."

I shook my head. "I wouldn't have talked to you like that if you hadn't been holding a gun. You'd have slugged me. But we learn not to yield to our violent impulses when there are firearms involved, right?" I grinned. "And you're covered from the corner of the house. . . . Miss Rustin, allow me to introduce Mr. Steiner, and vice versa."

He glanced that way and laughed shortly as Madeleine stepped into sight, holding her small revolver. Steiner checked the Llama pistol once more, opened a couple of the lower buttons of his khaki shirt, slipped the gun inside, and buttoned himself up again, moving forward to make the lady's acquaintance.

Madeleine offered her hand, frowning a bit as she looked at him. "It's a dumb thing to say, but haven't we met somewhere?"

Mark bowed over her hand. "If I wasn't happily married, Miss Rustin, I would certainly invent a very fine previous acquaintance between us, but I am afraid it is not the case."

"I was sure . . . Well, never mind. How is your wife?"

I turned away to lock the gate. When I returned, Mark was saying: ". . . a mild concussion but no fracture. They're keeping her in the special rest home for a few days. Thank God the girls are old enough to stay by themselves for reasonable periods of time."

"Your children?"

"Andrea, thirteen, and Beatrice, eleven." Mark glanced at me. "Andy said you sounded like a nice man over the phone."

"You'd better teach the kid better judgment," I said. "Come on, let's go inside."

I waved him ahead. As we made our way along the side of the house to the door I glanced at Madeleine. It was the second time she'd been right behind me with her little gun when things could have got sticky.

"Thanks for the backup, babe," I said.

"Any time, buster," she said. "Any time."

I remembered that we'd worked very well together five years ago. I remembered other things from five years ago, but it wasn't the right time to compare nostalgias. After a moment she went on to follow Mark into the house. Happy greeted his friend exuberantly as we entered and got his ears scratched briefly before I put him out into the yard.

I asked, "Have you had any lunch, Mark?"

"No, I was just fixing something for the girls and me when you called. Ruth had gone to lie down with a headache. At least I thought that's where she was."

Madeleine said, "I'll get him something. . . . What do you want with it, Mr. Steiner? There's coffee, and I think I saw some beer in the refrigerator."

"Beer, please." When she'd disappeared into the kitchen, Mark looked at me. "Nice lady. But she holds a gun as if she'd seen one before."

"Never mind her," I said. "Let's talk about you."

He shook his head. "There's nothing I can tell you."

"Bullshit," I said. "What you mean is, you could tell me a lot but you're not allowed to."

"If you want to put it that way."

He looked around as Madeleine returned to put a plate and a bottle on the table. Carta Blanca, if it matters.

"Do you want a glass?" she asked.

"No that's fine, thanks, Miss Rustin."

"Let's make it Madeleine and Mark. What about you, Matt? More coffee?"

I said that would be great, and I told Mark to sit down and joined him at the table. It gave me an odd feeling to play host with a pretty lady playing hostess; I realized that it reminded me of my long-ago marriage. I wondered how Beth was getting along these days. The breakup hadn't been my idea. I'd just been young enough to fall in love, and foolish enough to think I could dismiss the past and settle down to a nonviolent life with a nonviolent wife. I seemed to have spent my life with disapproving ladies. Maybe what I needed was one who'd played my game and knew the score. . . .

"There you are," Madeleine said, placing a steaming cup in front of me and sitting down beside me with another.

"Real service," I said. I looked at Mark Steiner. "If you can't tell me anything, why are you here?"

He swallowed a mouthful of hash and washed it down with Carta Blanca. "Officially, I am here to impress on you the fact that you are not going to be told anything and that you are not going to snoop around trying to find it out."

"And unofficially?"

He grinned. "I am here to punch you in the nose for slugging my wife."

"Just how do your friends plan to stop me from snooping if I feel like snooping?"

He said, "They have discovered, much to everyone's surprise, that you also work for Uncle Sam in some mysterious

56

capacity, and they are having their top man in Washington demand that your top man in Washington order you to keep your long nose out of their business." He laughed. "I don't think Mr. Dennis Morton likes you very much. What did you do to make him so angry?"

Madeleine said, "Need you ask? He made you angry, too, didn't he? Earlier, he made me angry. He makes everybody angry. It's the secret of his success."

I said, "Dennis Morton? Is that his real name or did he make it up for the occasion?" When Mark didn't answer, I said, "Demand? That should lead to fun and games. My chief just loves other departments demanding that he run his agency to accommodate them; it gets his adrenaline flowing very nicely, thank you."

Steiner smiled thinly. "It seems that all governments operate in the same ridiculous fashion, each branch fighting with every other."

I studied him for a moment. "Under circumstances of such fearful security, I don't suppose you're going to tell me what the hell Lapis is all about; why my chief, who's pretty good at digging things out, could get only a hint of it in Washington, and why Morton blew his stack when you picked it for a password."

He started to say no, he wasn't going to tell me. His intended refusal was quite obvious. Then he checked himself and looked at me more sharply, frowning.

He spoke carefully: "The hair covers it now, but early in the summer . . . I would say you received a bullet crease along the head not too long ago. Although you are tall enough, I do not think you got that scar from cracking your head on a low doorway," he said. "And from the cautious way you moved when we first met, I would not be surprised if you'd had another projectile taken out of you. Just what is it you do for the U.S. government, amigo, that gets you shot up like that?"

I looked at him for a moment. I suppose I should have told him he had a hell of a nerve expecting me to answer his questions when he wouldn't answer mine, but that kind of verbal sparring would only waste time. He was leading up to something and I needed to know what it was.

"We call it counterassassination," I said. "In other words, if a certain department of the government—say Dennis Morton's gang—starts losing people to somebody or somebodies too tough for them to deal with, they call in the specialists. Us."

He studied me for a long moment. "So you have killed people?"

I nodded and remembered my thoughts at the rifle range. "Haven't you?"

He shook his head quickly. "Shooting is a sport with me. I love firearms, yes, but I have never pointed one at a human being."

"Lucky you," I said.

"You do not believe me?"

"You were a little too casual about winning this morning for a gent who's never fired a gun in anger."

He smiled thinly. "Matt, before I had to flee my country, I was national champion with the large-caliber rifle and the big silhouettes. That is real shooting, out to five hundred meters, where only a small wind will carry the bullet far off target. Should I clap my hands and jump with joy because I win a small-caliber match at no more than a hundred meters, against a few Sunday shooters who, if you will excuse me, are not really very good?"

It was a fair enough answer. I said, "So you aren't an American citizen?"

"You flatter me. Is my English so beautiful, then? I have still some years before I can become a citizen here."

I said, "Hell, you communicate real good, and Spanish accents are a dime a dozen here in this great southwest of ours. I never thought about it one way or the other."

"You mean, to you I was just another goddamn greaser, hey?" He grinned and stopped grinning. "You ask what is Lapis."

58

"Yes."

He poked himself in the chest with his thumb. "Me," he said. "I am Lapis."

Chapter 7

ONE of those damn cedar logs exploded loudly and we all jumped. I got up, kicked back into the fireplace some coals that had been expelled, and returned to my chair, trying to make sense of what I'd heard.

I remembered discussing with Mac the question of whether Lapis was a person, an organization, or an operation. It seemed that I'd found the answer: Lapis was an operation organized to protect a person, a foreign national, male, who'd married an American girl—there was nothing Latin about Ruth Steiner, either in appearance or accent—and lived elsewhere in wedded bliss for a while, but had been forced, with his family, to flee that happy home and hide out here in New Mexico where his wife hated everything. The big question was: what made Mark Steiner important enough that the U.S. government, at least Dennis Morton's minor branch of it, would take the trouble of establishing a new identity for him out here—I assumed he'd changed name as well as residence—and watching over him?

I saw that Madeleine was studying Mark thoughtfully. Suddenly she snapped her fingers.

"Lapis! That's it! Lapis means 'stone' in Latin, doesn't it?"

I said, "Great. There's nothing like a classical education, I always say."

"And stone is 'stein' in German. Mark Stein. Mark Steiner." She went on without waiting for my comment: "And stone is also *piedra* in Spanish. Don't you get it?"

"Not yet," I said. "Keep trying."

60

I saw that Mark was listening with a total lack of expression.

"*Piedra*, for God's sake!" Madeleine said impatiently. "Doesn't that mean anything to you? Marcus Piedra. It was in all the papers and all over TV a couple of years ago."

I said, "It doesn't mean a thing to me. Who's Marcus Piedra?"

"*That's* why his face looked so familiar! It was on the dustcover of his book, *The Evil Empire*. Somebody down in South America didn't like what he'd written and put a price on his head, a million dollars. As far as I know, the reward has never been withdrawn."

I glanced at Mark. It hadn't occurred to me that he might be a writer, but I guess they come in all shapes and sizes. Hell, I'd beat on a typewriter a bit myself, once, in between bouts with a camera.

"I always wanted to make a quick million," I said. "But I thought the name was Rushdie and the book was called *The Satanic Verses* and the price offered by a certain bearded Iranian gent, since defunct, was five million. Sounds like our friend here is dealing with a bunch of Latin cheapskates. What kind of a takeout man can you get for a mere one mil?"

"The Latins obviously got the idea from the Rushdie case," Madeleine said.

"Not necessarily." Mark spoke at last. "Bounties and bounty hunters go far back in history. Many an ancient king offered a reward for the head of someone who had annoyed him. And Gregorio Vasquez has as much power as many ancient kings, or even our more modern ayatollah, the only difference being that Khomeini dealt in Mohammed, and Vasquez deals in cocaine. The point seems to be that it is not safe for irreverent writers to criticize either religion—and if you do not believe that cocaine is a religion, you should interview some true believers, as I have done."

"Cocaine?" I sighed. "Oh, God, here we go again! You mean that government character I almost shot is just another dope hound?"

"Morton's organization is concerned with illicit substances, yes. Actually, it is a task force that was originally constituted to deal with the South American threat, but has widened its target area in response to recent developments.''

"That figures," I said. "A bureaucrat like Morton is always going to find an excuse to widen his target area." I drew a long breath. "Maybe I have the wrong attitude, but I can't help remembering that the world has a few other things besides dope to worry about. It scares me, the way we're all getting obsessed with a bit of feel-good powder to the exclusion of everything else."

Madeleine was frowning. "But don't you agree that the trade must be stopped?"

I laughed at that. "Stopped? Who the hell is stopping anything? My God, I'm not in favor of the stuff! If they were stopping it, I'd have nothing to say, I'd be all for them." I drew a long breath. "But the whole business reminds me of a guy I went hunting with once. The flies were pretty bad around camp, the way they get in those mountains in the fall, and some of them even bit a little—deerflies or something—but what the hell, if you spend any time outdoors at all, you learn to put up with a few bugs. What drove me nuts wasn't the flies, it was that jerk fighting a hysterical pitched battle with every fly that came near him. My God, I couldn't drink or eat or sleep in peace for him chasing winged insects frantically around the lousy camp. Just like the way, these days, I can't seem to do a simple job in the line of duty without running into a bunch of single-minded fanatics who don't give a damn how important *my* mission is. If I'm not helping *them* eradicate the traffic in chemical evil, I'm just something in the road and they'll drive right over me. Or try." I made a wry face. "Granted it's a menace, but like I said it's not the only menace we have to deal with these days. We do have a few other minor problems, like AIDS and nukes and starvation and oil and war and terrorism. I could bear having these crusaders in my hair if they were accomplishing something. But they aren't stopping it, any more than that frantic hunting partner of mine was stopping the buzzing insects. I think he managed to get one horsefly or deerfly or whatever they were in one whole evening of waving his arms like a windmill. That seems to be about par for the course, with flies or drugs."

Madeleine said, "That's a pretty negative attitude, Matt. Do you have a better answer to the problem?"

"Sure," I said. "It's simple. Create a world in which living will be such a pleasure that nobody'll need to resort to chemical joy. Nothing to it. The market for drugs will collapse and we'll all be happy. Next question?"

She made a face at me. Mark Steiner cleared his throat. "I gather you have not read my book, Matt."

I shook my head. "I'm afraid I hadn't even heard of it until just now. I must have been incommunicado on a mission somewhere when your big fuss took place. Sorry about that." I looked at him for a moment. "Are you hiding out here in Santa Fe to do another book, a sequel to *The Evil Empire*, perhaps? What's this one called, *The King of Coke*?"

As long as he'd been Mark Steiner, his accent had been minimal and his attitudes had been Yankee and it had been possible to kid him safely. But now he'd dropped his *Americano* act for the moment, and the real Marcus Piedra seemed to be a stuffier Latin type, with more strongly accented English, who liked to be taken seriously.

He spoke stiffly: "I am working on a sequel, yes. My first book was an intensive study-in-depth of the relevant countries of South America with emphasis on the political, economic, and social effects of the trade in drugs, particularly cocaine." There's nothing quite as pompous as an author explaining his own book to a heathen who hasn't read it. He went on: "I reported on the illicit organizations involved, like the Medellín cartel in Colombia, and I suggested that rather than being independent kingdoms of crime, they had recently become only parts of a greater illicit empire that included the whole continent of South America, plus Central America, ruled by an upstart former lieutenant of the Ochoas—"

I interrupted. "What's an Ochoa?"

Mark looked impatient at my ignorance. "That is the

Medellín family that, with certain associates, manages the big Colombian drug cartel that gets all the publicity. However, a few years ago some of those associates, led by an older gentleman named Gregorio Vasquez Stussman, a man who had for many years been satisfied to serve the cartel in a subordinate capacity, formed a new organization. No one expected it to survive against its entrenched opposition, and as a matter of fact little was heard of it for a while, but gradually it began to emerge as a giant criminal conglomerate that has quietly managed to gain effective control of all the South American drug operations, including the Medellín group.'' He gave a grim little laugh. '' 'Quietly' may not be the proper word. There was considerable violence, but there is so much violence connected with drugs anyway that a little more went almost unnoticed except, of course, by the people directly concerned, who were suitably impressed. A measure of the effectiveness of Vasquez's tactics, and the ruthlessness of his companions, is that by murder, kidnapping, torture, and intimidation on the one hand, and liberal financial inducements on the other, he has managed to gain power over some very tough and wealthy and important people on both sides of the law—people one would have said would be quite immune to threats or bribery.'' He looked up. ''May I have another beer?''

I waited until Madeleine had brought it; then I asked, ''At what point did Mr. Vasquez Stussman become interested in you?''

''When my first book came out, of course.'' Mark took a swig of Carta Blanca from the bottle and wiped his mouth with the back of his hand. ''As a matter of fact, his violent reaction to *Empire* was what led me to consider a sequel. It seemed like overreaction. To be sure, he had reasons not to be happy with me, I had given his drug super-cartel unfavorable publicity and revealed some unpleasant truths about him, but it was done. The book was in print; it would not be withdrawn no matter what happened to me. To have me killed for writing *Empire* would be mere childish retaliation, and he is not a childish man. Clearly he was offering a million dollars for my death, not because he was so very angry at what I had written, but because he was afraid of what I intended to write next. Which told me that there was something to be written next. I looked for it and found it."

He drank some more beer, and glanced toward the fire as the cedar snapped again. I got up and kicked a couple of coals off the floor and put the screen in front of the fireplace, although I always feel that a fire burning behind a screen is half-wasted.

Madeleine said impatiently, "Well? Don't keep us in suspense!"

Mark said, "As a matter of fact, that title you suggested, Matt, is inaccurate, and so were the geographical limits suggested in *Empire*. Vasquez's combine is no longer dealing merely with cocaine. He's not satisfied with being the king of coke, he's reaching for control of cannabis in all forms from marijuana to hashish to ganja, and of all significant opium-morphine-heroin operations, not only in South America—where the opium poppy doesn't do very well, although it's being tried—but elsewhere in the world, like the Golden Triangle and the Golden Crescent." He glanced at me, saw me looking blank, and explained: "The Golden Triangle is the Southeast Asian poppy-growing countries of Burma, Laos, and Thailand. When their production started to lag in the late 1970s, the slack was taken up by the Southwest Asian countries of Pakistan, Afghanistan, and Iran; the so-called Golden Crescent. This is what Vasquez did not want me to put into a book: the fact that he is well on the way to having a worldwide monopoly of the more popular mind-altering drugs. He also feared that I would reveal his motive in creating this monopoly."

Madeleine stirred. "Is there a mystery? Everybody wants to be rich."

Mark shook his head. "The Medellín people take care of their own and they have fantastic amounts of money to spread around. Vasquez had become wealthy enough, working for them in an administrative capacity. No, it was not the money. However, his son, Jorge, a pilot for a small Colombian airline owned by them, also flew occasional smuggling runs for them—moonlighting, I suppose you would call it. One of Papa Vasquez's duties had been to set up a smuggling route through the Bahamas with a transshipment point on one of the smaller islands, Roman Cay, that boasted an airstrip of sorts. He had made financial arrangements with the proper Bahamian authorities—one might call them improper Bahamian authorities—to ensure that the operation on the island would be ignored; and he had organized a small fleet of speedboats to carry the shipments across the Florida straits to a 'safe' marina in the Florida Keys. One day son Jorge was called upon to take over a run from a pilot who was indisposed. Flying into Roman Cay with a sizable shipment of cocaine, he ran into an unexpected welcoming committee. Secretly, the U.S. had put pressure on the government in Nassau, and the Bahamian police, accompanied by some American agents of the DEA, were waiting to arrest him. However, as Jorge was coming in to land, somebody fired a burst from an automatic weapon. It hit nothing; it is believed that one of the Bahamian officers who'd been paid by Gregorio was trying to warn Jorge off; but the effort backfired badly. The armed and trigger-happy officials on the ground all opened up at the first sound of gunfire. Riddled, the plane crashed and burned, incinerating Señor Vasquez, Junior. This did not meet with the approval of Señor Vasquez, Senior; and of course he blamed the U.S. of A.''

I said, ''Why not? Everyone else does.''

''Actually,'' Mark said, ''the DEA agents present claimed that they had not fired a shot, but this was ignored. In Vasquez's view, that great, overbearing bully, Uncle Sam, had coerced the officials of a small independent neighboring nation into betraying their contractual obligations to him, and their honor as gentlemen, and murdering a fine young man whose only crime, if it could even be called a crime, was transporting some merchandise to American citizens who, whatever their government's irrational attitude might be, were eager to have it and willing to pay well for it.''

Madeleine said, "I'd think Mr. Vasquez would be mad at either the Bahamians who did the shooting or the cartel that sent his son into a trap."

Mark shook his head. "The Bahamians he considers beneath contempt, mere tools in the bloody hands of the wicked USA. As I've already indicated, he did turn against the Medellín people; but like the late ayatollah, he reserves his big hate for the Great Satan, as Khomeini liked to call you. And he's going to fix you, amigos. He is going to get a stranglehold on all the major sources of drugs in the world. And then he is going to destroy the U.S. by flooding the country with drugs at bargain prices that no one can resist."

There was a short silence. I grimaced. "Well, like his bounty routine, it's not exactly a new idea. I seem to remember that the British used opium in just about the same way, in China a century or two ago. So Vasquez is going to turn us into a nation of helpless hopheads? Cute." I frowned. "Can he do it? I mean, does he have the power to control all the members of his far-flung conspiracy well enough to make them forgo the fantastic profits to which they are accustomed and market their products at more reasonable, and popular, prices?"

Mark shrugged. "*Quien sabe?* Who knows? I address that question in my book, but I'm afraid my answer is inconclusive. I do believe he *thinks* he can do it, and he is not a man given to deluding himself. But there is another, equally important question to which you *Americanos* can probably give a better answer than a transplanted Peruvian."

"And that question is?" I asked.

"Given the opportunity, will the American people destroy themselves in this way?"

He glanced at Madeleine, who said, "If truly cheap drugs became readily available, there would certainly be a lot of people flying high at first. In the long run . . ." She shook her head dubiously. "I really don't know."

I said, "Hell, there's a liquor store on every street corner now, and we aren't all running around drunk; and it isn't the price of Scotch, or beer, that's keeping most of us sober most of the time. I think Mr. Vasquez is kidding himself, with the help of a whole lot of guys and gals like Dennis Morton, whose livelihood depends on making us, and maybe themselves, believe that drugs can sink the good ship America and only they can save Old Glory from drowning in a sea of coke and hash. Well, I've spent a good deal of my life working for this country in various risky and unpleasant ways and my impression is that it's a fairly tough country inhabited by fairly tough people who may have some bad habits but aren't about to commit national suicide on some bargain-basement happy dust. Wow, listen to me, you'd think this was the Fourth of July or something! So Vasquez put a price on your head after your first book came out.''

Mark laughed shortly. "In a way, he did me a favor. Who was going to read a dull nonfiction work about distant South American problems? My American publishers printed a few thousand copies and thought they'd probably be stuck with many of those; but the press got wind of the reward and, as with Rushdie, turned my book into a big best-seller. The publicity brought me to the attention of Dennis Morton's superiors, who hadn't bothered to read *Empire* when it first came out. They decided that I was someone to be protected since I seemed to have considerable amounts of potentially useful information beyond what I'd already revealed— protected at least until I could be wrung dry. Now they keep telling me that it is my patriotic duty to jettison, or at least postpone, my new book and turn all my data over to them for appropriate action. Patriotic? To what country? I am a Peruvian citizen, amigo, and no official of *my* country has requested enlightenment. In fact, we left Lima very hastily after being warned that I was to be arrested and silenced, presumably at the request of some very influential and wealthy Peruvian gentlemen. I have no proof, but I am certain that Vasquez, the source of their drug-based wealth, put them up to it. So I told your Yankee officials: make me an *American* citizen and then we can discuss my patriotic *American* duty. But that branch of your government is apparently not willing to cooperate, at least not rapidly. In the meantime, I told them, the information is probably still available where I found it. If you want it, I said, why do you not simply obtain it from the source, as I did?" He gave me a wry look. "Why is it that these law enforcement agencies always expect us journalists to do their work for them and then turn it over to them gratis?"

I laughed at that. It was the ancient complaint of the working press. "So they're giving you a hard time, but at least they're keeping you alive after a fashion, right?"

"Yes, and while they could not keep Ruth from being abducted, they did find her and set her free, although it was a close thing and the hounds brought down and killed the man who had gone in to liberate her."

I said, "I suppose the idea of the kidnapping was to trade her for your notes and tapes and whatever."

"Yes."

His voice was curt; he didn't want to be asked if, had the lady not been liberated, he would have made the trade. It's not a choice we ever have to make, thank God. The standing orders are rigid: no matter who dies, we don't deal, ever.

Madeleine said, "And then you were moved out here, to keep you safe."

Mark said grimly, "Yes. Safe until they found us again."

"If you don't mind my asking," she said, "I get the impression you haven't been married very long, but you said your daughters were eleven and thirteen. . . ."

"Ruth is the mother of the girls, but I am not the father. Her husband was in the U.S. Foreign Service, stationed in Peru. He died in a car-bombing incident about four years ago. I had met him and become friends with the whole family while covering various diplomatic functions in my capacity as a journalist. After Richard Harrington's death . . ." Mark shrugged. "Please do not think there was anything between Ruth and me before that; but afterward . . . Anyway, we were married. I consider her children as my own; and I flatter myself that they accept me as an adequate substitute papa. Please do not judge Ruth by the little you have seen of her. She has never really recovered from the trauma of the kid-

69

napping; she has lived with fear ever since. Fear not so much for herself as for her children.''

Madeleine had another question: "Who are Vasquez's companions?" When he looked at her sharply, she said, "You talked about Vasquez's ruthless companions. Companions? It seems a funny choice of words. Do you mean his business associates?"

Mark laughed shortly. "Not exactly. They are his acolytes rather than his associates. They call themselves *Los Compañeros de la Hoja*."

He pronounced it "Oh-Ha," and it was a new word to me; my Spanish vocabulary is fairly limited. "What's an *hoja*?" I asked.

"*Hoja* means 'leaf.' The Companions of the Leaf. Of the coca leaf." Mark grimaced. "I told you it was a religion. Gregorio Vasquez is the high priest. For business and personal reasons he has become involved with other drugs, but cocaine is more than mere merchandise to him. And the people shadowing me, I think they are all Companions of the Leaf, prepared to do the old man's bidding when he sends them the word, after purifying themselves by certain dark rituals involving the sacred drug."

I said, "They're also watching Madeleine and me, you know, and have been for some weeks."

He frowned. "That is strange. Are you certain?"

"I can show you one sitting just up the street from here." After a moment I went on: "Let's work it out. You disappear from your old haunts after the kidnapping. They track you out here somehow. Their instructions state, presumably, that you can't be killed until it's certain that your research materials can be confiscated or destroyed at the same time. It's also customary, before drastic action is taken, to learn something about the habits and acquaintances of the victim, to see if they could cause any problems. I don't know how many friends you and your wife have made in Santa Fe—"

"Not so very many," Mark said.

"But among them," I said, "is a certain character who seems to be very familiar with firearms, a tall, skinny galoot

70

who's always out shooting with one gun or another. Well, if you're planning a takeout operation, you want to know exactly what you're up against. You don't want an ugly gunslinger, six four, opening up from the bushes with an Uzi or M16 as you move into the target area for the kill.''

Mark looked surprised. "You mean they think I've hired or drafted you to . . .''

"Or they believe that I'm associated with Dennis Morton's outfit in some way, God forbid, and that you were sent out here where I live to be under my wing, but we were supposed to be sneaky about making contact so they wouldn't suspect me. But they were too smart for us; they spotted me immediately, or so they figure.'' I laughed. "Hell, you wondered about me. I wondered about you. These people wouldn't even wonder. They live by the conspiracy theory of human relations. If two people meet fairly frequently, it can't just be that they both like to shoot and are members of the same gun club; there's got to be a plot brewing. In this case, obviously a plot for me to protect you against them.''

Madeleine said, "That explains why they're watching you, Matt, but where do I come in?''

I said, "When they checked up on me, they probably didn't have the clout to learn my Washington connections; however, the local history wouldn't be hard to come by. They'd only have to go back through the newspaper files a few years to discover that I'd been involved in quite a hassle right here in Santa Fe—accompanied by whom? A tough dame just released from prison who'd saved my life twice during the proceedings and killed two men doing it.'' I glanced at Mark. "Never mind the details right now. But anybody doing a thorough job of planning a hit on you, and thinking I was acting as your bodyguard, would want to know where my dangerous female associate was now and whether or not she might turn up unexpectedly.'' I turned to Madeleine. "So they traced you to Denver and found, surprise, surprise, a high-priced lady lawyer in a smart business suit. But when they became annoyingly persistent in their surveillance, said high-priced lady lawyer produced a gun and behaved in a

71

very unladylike manner, undoubtedly confirming their worst suspicions.''

"It's crazy!" she protested. "You mean these Companions think I'm a gun moll or something?''

I grinned. "Well, aren't you? I remember, at the Ranch, doing my damnedest to have you turned into one. I wouldn't be alive now if I hadn't.''

After a moment she laughed. "Poor Mark doesn't know what the hell we're talking about. You'll have to give him the details of my gaudy past some day.'' Then her expression changed. "The Old Man of the Mountain!'' she exclaimed.

"What?'' I asked.

"He lived up in the rocks of . . . well, I can't remember where, but it was somewhere in the Middle East. He had a kind of religion, I believe, a murderous kind of religion, and a bunch of fanatic followers. He fed them hashish and sent them out to kill. Hashishin, assassin. That's where the word comes from.''

Mark said, "It is not unique. There are other religious cults involving mind-altering drugs, for instance the peyote cult among the Indians in this country. However, I have never heard of peyote being used for any but peaceful purposes.''

I said, "The Old Man of the Mountain, eh? Maybe we should call our South American friend the Ancient of the Andes. I gather he isn't a kid.''

Mark laughed shortly. "You are guessing well. He is actually referred to nowadays, very respectfully, as *El Viejo*, the Old One. He will have seventy years next month. It will be a cause for celebration among the *Compañeros*. If he achieves that age.''

I looked sharply at the stocky man occupying the chair beside mine. "Have you any reason to think he won't, aside from the fact that he's already no chicken?''

Mark hesitated. "One gets tired of being pursued,'' he said slowly. "Amigo, if someone offered a million-dollar reward for your death, what would you do?''

I said, "That's easy. I'd get one of my rich friends to offer a two-million-dollar reward for his death. Assuming I had some friends that rich, which I don't.''

''So what *would* you do?''

I shrugged. ''Hell, I'd sight in my old .300 Magnum and go after the son of a bitch.''

Mark smiled thinly. ''That is a fine, uncivilized answer. I wish I—'' He stopped, and his smile vanished. He licked his lips. ''But if you had never in your life shot at anything but paper or metal targets . . . I gather that you have some experience, Matt. Will you show me how? I am very sick of living like a hunted animal and watching my wife breaking under the strain. Will you help me find this man so I can kill him, this Gregorio Vasquez, *El Viejo*?''

Chapter 8

I became aware that Happy was barking outside, giving me an excuse to stall a little before responding to the outlandish proposition that had been put to me. I don't mean that I'd never before been asked to participate in a wet operation, as the Washington spooks so colorfully call it, but it was the first time I'd been asked to hold the coat of an amateur while he did the actual shooting. At least I gathered that was what Mark had in mind, and I didn't know quite how to answer without hurting his feelings or giving him the impression that I disapproved of his project morally, which I didn't—anyone who sends out the wolves can't complain if he finds a few toothy predators on his own doorstep. Outside, Happy was still sounding off. I went to the side door and stuck my head out and saw, over the fence, the brown top of a UPS truck parked in front of the next house up the street.

"Happy, shut up!" I said, and he came to me, wagging his tail, proud of protecting the premises so efficiently. I scratched his ears. "Take it easy, you big loudmouth, you'll disturb the neighbors," I said.

I went back inside. He went back to yapping happily at the UPS truck. Discipline. Actually, my neighbors had fairly loud dogs of their own, which were also tuning up, and nobody locally paid much attention to an occasional canine serenade. I was glad to be living in one of the older parts of Santa Fe, where barking dogs were still an accepted part of the environment, even though the mournful coyotes we used to hear when this was the edge of town were long gone. To hell with modern communities that serve up nothing but car horns and rock and roll and motorcycle exhausts.

When I returned to the table, Madeleine was saying angrily to Mark: ". . . hell of a thing to ask him! Even if it were the way to do it, which it isn't, it's your fight. It isn't his fight!"

Ever since our brief moment of passion, I'd detected a certain possessiveness in her attitude as she served lunch to our guest and, now, tried to protect me against his unreasonable demands. I found that I didn't mind it in the least.

"If that is not the way to do it, what is?" Mark demanded. "If you were sitting here with a price on your head, what would you do?"

"There are civilized ways of handling—"

"What civilized ways? I have already done the civilized things. I have fled my country with my family to avoid violence. I have trusted your government's protection and had my wife kidnapped. I have fled again and hidden under a false name, and they have followed and found me. Should I now give up and wait for the knife or the bullet? Is there a law saying that this man can strike at me, but I may not strike at him?"

"I don't know about laws and rights; I just know you'll never make it. You'll just get both of you shot. This man will have all the protection money can buy!"

"All the money in the world will not protect him out to a thousand meters or even five hundred, unless he is willing to live in a bunker like Hitler. I am a good marksman, a very good marksman. I am not asking anyone to kill for me; I will do the killing. With great pleasure. However, I will need a guide."

"A guide? I don't understand."

"Hunters hire guides, do they not? Never having hunted animals, I would hire a guide if I were after moose or elk or deer for the first time; a guide who was familiar with the habits of the quarry, one who could bring me into position for a shot. It occurred to me, just from what I have already learned about him, that our amigo here would make a very good guide for anyone who was hunting a man; I simply do not know what I can offer him in return."

When he looked my way, I shook my head. "Sorry. I'd like to help out, but I'm hardly in a position . . . Christ, what's the matter with those damn dogs? I wish that UPS guy would get the hell out of here."

Happy had switched his serenade to the backyard now; apparently the truck had moved on to make a delivery to my neighbors on the other side. Their little terrier-type mutt was singing tenor to Happy's deep Labrador bass. It was getting just a little too noisy, even for our neighborhood, and I started to rise, but Madeleine was on her feet before me.

"I'll go bring him in the house; it'll give me a chance to get acquainted with him. You finish your coffee."

There seemed to be a kind of understanding between us, even though nothing had been said. Well, I had no objections. In fact, it gave me a kind of warm and comfortable feeling that I hadn't known in all the years of transient ladies, no matter how nice.

When she had left the room, I said to Mark: "As for this proposal of yours, I sympathize with your motives, and as I told you, if I were in your shoes, I'd take my gun and go hunting; but there's only one man who can give me killing orders and I doubt very much that I can persuade him that this is a mission suitable for our organization. . . ."

The explosion shook the whole small adobe building. I heard the crash of broken glass as the big French doors at the rear of the house were blown into the bedroom. Shocked, I was aware of a sense of outrage and anger at my own stupidity: anybody can buy a van and paint it brown. *It's Sunday, you moron; since when does UPS deliver on Sunday?*

I was on my feet, snatching the hidden Smith & Wesson revolver from under my shirt and starting for the side door, strangling the suicidal impulse to dash straight to the scene of the explosion and learn the worst. Then I came back to the gun rack and yanked the big bowie fighting knife out of its sheath. In tight places like my limited property an edged weapon can be worth a dozen firearms; besides, the atavistic instinct that I've learned never to ignore told me it was now knife country out there.

I snapped instructions to Mark, who had his gun out: "Stay right here. This is my kind of game, not yours; let me handle it. Besides, I'm a real trigger-happy character and I don't want to have to worry about shooting you by mistake. Your job is to use the Llama on anything that comes in here that isn't Madeleine, Happy, or me. Don't think about it, just purely shoot the living hell out of it, okay?"

"Okay."

Moving to the door, I was bleakly aware that the chances of his having to worry about Madeleine or Happy, after that backyard blast, weren't very great—the delivery made by the phony UPS truck had sounded like a grenade—but they were not my immediate concern. Survival was. The gun in my left hand and the big knife in my right made opening the door something of a problem, but I solved it, wondering how many boom-booms awaited me outside—well, in the narrow space between the fence and the house it would only take one. With the door open, I could hear the whimpering of a dog in pain. Earlier, I'd rushed heedlessly to Happy's rescue and got away with it, but the little voice inside was telling me that death was now waiting for me to answer the cry of my hurt dog.

I took a moment, standing back a bit from the open doorway, to scan the neighboring roofs for a sniper; then I made my death-defying dive into the rosebushes for the second time that day. This time, at least, I had pants on. Nobody shot at me or threw anything at me. Crouching there, I could see, past the rear corner of the house, the dust of the explosion still settling in the patio. I rose cautiously and moved over to the path at the side of the house—and a heavy body dropped off the roof and landed on the flagstones behind me.

Out of the corner of my right eye, I was aware of something black whipping toward my face. I thrust the big bowie upward to ward it off, but it wrapped itself snakelike around both the knife and my neck and tightened instantly; there was a moment when I thought I was going to be forced to cut my throat with my own blade. I was holding it edge outward, but the back of a bowie is also sharpened for several inches back from the point. With a major effort I sliced downward and outward, grateful that the strangler wasn't a wire man. The noose parted.

I didn't wait to give a sigh of relief. I simply spun to my right, swinging the heavy blade like a scythe, backhand. As I turned, the strangler came into my view, a black-clad figure, trying to duck; but I allowed for that and chopped him across the side of the neck, leaning into the blow. I must say I found the impact highly satisfactory, feeling the keen edge drive through flesh and bone. *Bomb my home, will you, you son of a bitch?*

It wasn't quite a beheading, but it was close enough, and I stepped back to avoid the spurting blood as the man fell, still clutching a remnant of black cloth. The clumsy old Thuggee scarf, for God's sake, in this age of efficient wire and nylon nooses! How obsolete could you get?

A sharp pistol report from the back patio reminded me that I'd better postpone my study of ancient weapons of assassination. But the scarf had added to my sense of unreality. The idea of modern grenades blasting my patio and old-fashioned stranglers dropping from my roof was hard to accept. I cast a wary eye upward as I made my way toward the rear of the property, but there were no more acrobatic surprises; then I made a rolling dive past the corner of the house and came up to take in the nightmare scene: the shattered outdoors furniture and torn plantings, the wounded dog who saw me and tried to drag himself toward me, the dead or unconscious woman lying in a pool of blood—and the dead man in khakis with his once-fired gun still clutched in his hand. Well, twice-fired if you count the shot let off by his wife, earlier.

Mark had to be dead; his head was cocked at a crazy angle to his body. Later, I might miss the guy; at the moment it was merely another loss on top of the losses I hadn't begun to assimilate, and I just thought grimly, *Stupid bastard asks for help and then won't stay where he's told!* So much for Mr. Marcus Steiner, whatever his real patronymic might have been in German, Latin, Spanish, or English. He'd got brave instead of obeying orders, and somebody was richer by a million bucks.

Not that I called time out to think all this, it simply went through my head as I took stock of the live ones—first the girl in jeans and a dark jersey reaching into a big woven shoulder bag. Over the fence behind her, parked in the neighbors' driveway, I could see the roof of a brown truck, the one I'd so carelessly assumed to be UPS. Well, the neighborhood dogs had also been fooled, and whoever said I was smarter than a dog? In addition to the girl, there was a black-clad man in the patio, just rising from Mark's body with another scarf in his hand. He leaped toward the fence, which made him no immediate threat.

I gave my attention, instead, to the girl, who was smallish, with long black hair and mad brown eyes. A big white dressing, not quite clean, was taped to one side of her face. Except for the crazy eyes, which had not been mentioned, she fit a description I'd heard: she was undoubtedly the girl Madeleine had caught in a Denver alley and pistol-whipped. Her hand came out of the bag with a grenade. Her other hand fumbled for the pin. The fact that we'd both die in the explosion, in this confined space—she must have tossed the first one from behind the shelter of the fence—obviously didn't concern her a bit. I didn't trust my left-handed pistol marksmanship for the job. The heavy fighting knife, thrown hard, drove through her like a spear and nailed her to the fence. She dropped the grenade. It rolled toward me. I fielded it and checked it; the pin was still in place. I won't say it wasn't a relief. The second strangler had vanished. I heard the phony UPS truck pull away with a roar.

Like a butterfly on a pin, the girl was still hanging there, both hands clutching the hilt of the enormous bowie that transfixed her. To hell with her. Mark was dead. Madeleine was either unconscious or dead; at least she wasn't hurting at the moment. I went to my dog, who was.

Happy was still trying to get to me, but his rear legs weren't working. He was badly cut up and his thick yellow coat was bloody. His soft brown eyes were asking me why anybody would do this to a good hunting dog who'd never hurt anybody, not even a duck. He'd stopped whimpering; he was licking my hand instead. His back was obviously broken. I started to reach for the .38 I'd put away, but I found I couldn't do it that loud and brutal way. I patted his head and went into my shattered house and managed to find the little kit we carry on duty. I loaded the spring-operated hypo with the red capsule that kills men instantly, hoping it would work as well on a dog. I went back and let him lick my hand some more and scratched his ears gently and talked to him a little. Never mind what I said; that's between the two of us. The red capsule worked just fine.

Then it was very quiet in the blasted patio. When the rough tongue had stopped licking my hand, I rose and made certain that Madeleine wasn't breathing. It should have meant something to me, it should have meant a great deal, but it didn't. In this business you lose people; it goes with the territory. This wasn't the first loss I'd ever sustained; and I knew there was only one way to deal with it: don't. Pull down the riot shutters and seal it off. Don't think about what could have been. Don't think about the fact that if you hadn't been too stubborn or proud or stupid to go to her when you learned she was free, the two of you might have had at least a couple of good years together, and maybe . . .

The girl with the knife through her suddenly tumbled to the ground, but the blade had merely pulled out of the wood of the fence; she was dead, too. Everybody was dead but me. Maybes were a waste of time, I told myself firmly. Sirens were beginning to scream in the distance. Suddenly, guiltily, I remembered something: they wouldn't have come for Mark at last if they hadn't worked out a plan for dealing with his notes and tapes. I hurried into the house and found that the phone still worked. I called the same number I'd called earlier in the day and drew a long breath when the same young-girl voice answered.

"Andrea? Do you recognize my voice? I talked to you earlier."

"Yes, I recognize you. You're Mr. Helm, aren't you?"

"That's right. Your daddy has a message for you. Take your little sister and get out of the house and run away. A couple of blocks away, at least. If you have a place you like to hide away from home, go there."

"I don't know what you mean, Mr. Helm. Why would we have a place to hide?"

In my day every kid had a favorite cave or bush or tree or old shack in the neighborhood that was his own place that nobody knew, but I suppose they don't wander so freely around the countryside, or cityside, these civilized days.

"Never mind," I said. "Just get out of there. Some bad people are coming, Andrea. Take your sister and get out. Pretty soon you'll hear sirens and see police cars. Then you can go up to a policeman and tell him who you are. Okay?"

"I don't understand. . . . Oh, okay, if that's what Popsy wants."

"That's what he wants."

I stood there for a moment, not wanting to go out back again. I'm pretty hardened to dead people, even dead people I've loved, but dead dogs kind of get to me. I waited for anger, but it didn't come. What was there to be angry about? The girl who'd thrown the grenade was dead; there was no point in getting mad at her. The man who'd killed Mark Steiner had got away, but Mark hadn't been a good enough friend that I felt obliged to work up a rage at his murderer. There was, of course, work to be done, but cursing and beating the wall with my fists wouldn't get it done any faster or better, so I stood in my living room smelling dust and explosives, realizing that I was in the wrong place. *What am I doing here?* I asked myself. *What the hell am I doing here?*

What was I doing there, a guy like me, in my line of work; what was I doing with a rose garden, and a pretty little house with a burglar alarm, for God's sake, and Sunday-morning target games with a .22, and a dog who loved everybody but the UPS man . . . ? Who the hell did I think I was, Joe Average Citizen?

I realized that I'd been sneaking up on it again, the normal life that I'd tried once before, years ago, until it blew up in my face. Nobody I loved had been badly hurt that time; my wife had simply done the smart thing and left me, taking the kids with her. She'd realized then, as I had, that I was simply the wrong man trying to live the wrong life.

But I seemed to have forgotten the lesson I'd learned back then, so many years ago. I'd made myself a pleasant and peaceful little nest here; I'd even begun to give serious consideration to sharing it with a certain woman, a woman I'd asked once before. Now she was lying out in the patio, shrapnel-torn and dead, and my dog was dead with a broken back, and my cozy refuge had been blown wide open. It was very unfair to Madeleine and Happy, but it served me right for trying to be something I wasn't and could never become.

The sirens were closing in. I went out to open the gate for the police.

Chapter 9

WE hung out over Dallas, Texas, for a while, or maybe it was Fort Worth, or maybe both, waiting for a thunderstorm to pass so we could land at the airport they share, called DFW. Meanwhile I tried to digest my American Airlines lunch, with some difficulty—those rocket-propelled flying coffins are bad enough when they're traveling in straight lines in clear weather; when they start wandering in circles through a sky full of dirty absorbent cotton, they don't do my gastric processes a bit of good. Besides, the lunch had consisted mainly of a salad of some kind of cold pasta that looked like curly white maggots. There had also been a chunk of wooden brownie for dessert, mahogany by the color. Fortunately, I'd managed to promote, for three bucks, a miniature of J&B to help it all down.

Landing on a wet runway, with the storm still black in the distance, we taxied halfway across Texas to the gate, and then hiked, it seemed, the rest of the way over into Louisiana to pick up our connecting AA flight to Miami. I'd assumed that continuing on the same airline would make the plane-change easy; there was also a time when I believed in Santa Claus. Airborne again, we were treated to a snack consisting of a tough little breadroll surrounding some sliced ham. I helped it down with another three-buck dose of J&B.

Having done some flying over water, presumably the Gulf of Mexico, we found land again and started losing altitude over jungly-looking terrain that I guessed to be the Everglades. We swung out over more water, presumably the Florida straits, curved back over the land, settled down onto another runway—dry this time—and taxied another fifty miles, more or less, to find a gate. Those jets seem to cover almost as much distance on the ground these days as they do in the air. Not to mention the mileage the passengers have to rack up on foot inside the interminable terminals.

Reaching the baggage-claim area in Miami involved a typical airport exercise in pedestrian endurance, aggravated by the fact that we were both lugging the sizable carry-on bags that had been issued to us, baby blue with black lettering: WESTON WORLD TOURS. They were fairly heavily loaded, mine mostly with tourist camouflage in the form of camera gear and film. I had no idea what was in my companion's. She'd refused to let me help her with her burden, telling me to restrain my condescending male chivalry; she was quite capable of managing her own belongings, thank you.

The wait at the carousels was, as usual, considerable. When our patience was rewarded at last with two suitcases that matched the claim checks, I hired a gent with a uniform cap and a trolley, at an exorbitant price, to trundle our luggage to the centrally located airport hotel called MIA, not to sleep—the longest leg of the journey was still ahead of us—but just to kill time until we had to report for jet duty again, and to further indulge my alcoholic proclivities, in the rooftop restaurant and lounge that had been recommended to me by someone, I forget who. It seemed quite pleasant, but then, after a day in the air almost any place firmly attached to the earth would have.

"Do you really think you should?"

The woman on the far side of the cocktail table was watching me tackle my latest Scotch. I spread some cheese on a cracker and offered it to her.

"Have some Brie," I said. "Keep your strength up. We're supposed to take off again at nine P.M., but it'll probably be close to midnight before they get around to feeding us dinner."

Ruth Steiner accepted my offering, but said stiffly, "Thank you, Mr. Helm, but I'm quite familiar with the schedule. I've

84

made this flight before, many times. My first husband was stationed in Rio for several years. He was in the Foreign Service. But you know that."

"Yes, Mark told me." I picked up my glass again and got the same pained expression as before. I said patiently, "Look, ma'am, what's your problem? It's not as if I'll have to drive this DC-10 or whatever the hell it is we'll be inhabiting next. Varig's got a nice sober young chap in a natty uniform to operate it for us, I'm sure. If I want to go along for the ride slightly anesthetized, why not? As far as I'm concerned, it's the only way to travel by air."

Looking across the table, I decided that skinny, big-eyed blondes with ragged hairdos and big spectacles were not my favorite people. I gathered, from her expression, that she didn't think much of me, either. If there had ever been a chance of our becoming soul mates, it had vanished when I whacked her with a shotgun butt. There was still a small scab at the top of her left ear. I could see no other evidence of the blow she'd taken, although there could be some fading cranial bruises covered by her hair. It was one way of getting acquainted with a lady, but it hardly made for a warm relationship.

"Well, you'll just have to get along with her anyway, Eric," Mac had said when I mentioned the problem.

He'd summoned me to Washington after using his clout to get things settled in Santa Fe. They'd taken quite a bit of settling. The fact that the man I'd almost decapitated with my king-size presentation bowie had been trying to crack my neck with a Thuggee scarf, and that the girl I'd skewered with the same giant blade—that Jo had given me as a joke and a wall decoration, never expecting a knife that size to be used in anger—had been about to blow herself and me to hell with a fragmentation grenade, had helped with the police, of course, but it had still been a considerable circus. The murder of a fairly well known author with a price on his head placed there by a kingpin of the drug trade would have been big news even without the gaudy trimmings.

"How far along with her do I have to get?" I'd asked.

Mac frowned. The bright window behind him that he likes to make us stare into made his expression a bit hard to read, but I'd had lots of practice; we'd faced each other across that desk more times than I cared to remember. His hair was no grayer than it had ever been, and his eyebrows were no less black. I couldn't see that he'd aged significantly in the years that had passed since we'd first worked together. There were playful rumors around the place to the effect that he'd sold his soul in return for eternal life, but I didn't believe a word of it. What soul?

He spoke carefully: "It seems that the lady knows where some needed information is located. It also seems that the South American contacts that will enable us to obtain that information cannot be made without her."

I said, "Do I gather that contrary to what appeared on the evening news, Mark Steiner's new book and all related materials did not perish when his house went up like a torch?"

Mac looked surprised. "Didn't Mrs. Steiner tell you?"

I said, "After things quieted down a bit she called me on the phone and asked me how to get in touch with you—well, with the head of my agency. I gathered she was disenchanted with Dennis Morton and his bunch of undercover clowns. I didn't try to find out what was on her mind. She still had a headache I'd given her, and her husband had died in my house. I figured I probably wasn't one of her favorite people and I'd just antagonize her by asking questions; I'd better leave her to you."

Mac nodded. "You're aware that the man you knew as Mark Steiner, who wrote under the pseudonym of Marcus Piedra, was actually Raoul Marcus Carrera Mascarena, scion of a fairly prominent Peruvian family. After all the political upheavals in the area they are not as outrageously wealthy as they used to be, but they could still afford a good U.S. education for young Marcus. It didn't please them, however, when he left Harvard to study journalism in Columbia, Missouri; they wanted a Harvard MBA in the family to manage their remaining interests profitably. And they certainly did not applaud when he began investigating the various South

86

American drug combines for different publications, and publishing his findings. I do not believe his family was actually involved with drugs, but in those countries there's an elite that continues to exist by accommodating itself to power according to certain rules, the main one being: one survives. One does not antagonize the dictator, or the junta, or the generals, or the drug lords. One does not necessarily make friends with them or entertain them socially, one may disapprove of them, one may even sneer at them in private as crude peasants, but one does not go out of the way to attack them publicly as Marcus did.''

It seemed strange that now that he was dead, I was getting to know more about the man I'd called Mark Steiner than I'd ever known while he was alive. I'd been aware of his Latin origins, of course, but his English had been good, and as I'd told him, it isn't something you pay much attention to in New Mexico, where half the people you meet have the same accent and ancestry. I'd wondered what he did for a living, but I'd never got around to asking, perhaps because I hadn't wanted him to ask me the same question. It had surprised me to learn that he was a writer; it had surprised me even more to discover that he was kind of a celebrity.

I said, "I don't suppose his family was any more enthusiastic about his marriage than about his career; they'd undoubtedly have preferred to welcome a high-class Peruvian girl into the fold. However, families tend to be kind of clannish down there, and you can't kill one of them, even an unpopular one, without taking a big chance of starting a blood feud.''

Mac said, "Mrs. Steiner made the same point, indirectly. She seems to feel that she may be able to get some useful assistance from her relatives by marriage and their contacts in other South American countries, now that her husband has been murdered, even though they disapproved of the marriage while he was alive.''

"Useful assistance in doing what?" I asked.

He said, obliquely, "Like many modern households, the Steiner ménage included a personal computer. I gather it was used entirely by the lady, mostly as a word processor. Steiner wrote his stuff on an old portable and she transcribed it on her machine, which used the small three-and-a-half-inch computer disks—I believe they are also called diskettes. Mrs. Steiner says that knowing that he was in danger, whenever he finished a certain number of chapters of his book, he would have her copy them onto an extra disk, encrypted a certain way—I gather many computer programs have provisions for such security measures. He would then put the disk into a protective mailer and send it to a friend in South America, a different friend each time. Apparently these friends were not given the access code or password that would let them read the disks; they were simply asked to keep them safe.'' Mac shook his head grimly. ''While Mrs. Steiner thinks she can remember the names of many of her husband's South American friends, she has no idea which of them he trusted enough to look after these precious fractions of his magnum opus. Incidentally, she says he sent the last one off last week; the book was finished, except for an appendix he was working on, and of course the final revision and polishing.''

I said, ''You'd think Mark would have kept a master list to remind him, if he should need them, which chapters he'd sent where.''

''He probably did,'' Mac said. ''It was probably hidden somewhere in the house; but you saw the house.''

I had certainly seen the house, although getting to it had taken some doing. The first contingent of cops that had descended on me had been bound they were going to arrest me for something, since there was nobody else for them to clap their cuffs on—nobody living, at least. And I was the man whose house had been blown up, whose lady friend had been killed, whose dog had been so hopelessly injured as to require euthanasia. Naturally, by police logic, I had to be guilty of something, if only of the heinous crime of self-defense, since there were a couple of extra stiffs lying around.

It had taken me a while to persuade them to take me, under escort, to 22 Butterwood Road on the south side of town.

When we got there, we found firemen pumping water onto the black, smoking, roofless shell of the house I remembered. The fire had been hot, quick, and obviously of incendiary origin. Later, I learned that it had not been merely a matter of tossing a couple of firebombs through the windows; a car had driven up and two men had managed the front door somehow—a passing jogger, thinking little of it, had noticed that one had carried a husky catalog case and the other had seemed to have trouble finding the right key—and had gone inside and spent some time there before coming out again; the fire had erupted a few minutes later. No electronic circuits or disks could have survived the heat that had obviously been generated, and I learned later that no fireproof safe had been found in the ruins. At the time I hadn't known that I was supposed to be interested in electronics.

"There were a couple of little girls," I'd said, looking at the hoses pumping water into the smoke.

My police guardians weren't interested in little girls, but a nearby cop glanced our way.

He called down the street: "Hey, Art, bring those kids over here."

Another uniformed man led them up to us. They were dressed in grubby jeans and T-shirts. The smaller girl had been crying, but the older one seemed to be very much in control of herself.

"You know these kids, mister?" their guardian asked me.

I said, "Hi, Andy. We talked on the phone."

She was skinny and had short blond hair and a pert face with wise blue eyes made wiser by a pair of large horn-rim glasses that made her look like a small edition of her mother. The younger one was slightly plump, with a pretty baby face and long brown hair down her back.

The older one said, "You're Mr. Helm. I saw you when Popsy brought you to the house that time."

I hunkered down on the sidewalk in front of her. From my own long-ago papa experience, I remembered that kids, like dogs, are best approached at their own level.

I said, "Andy, I've got some bad news for you. Your daddy's been hurt."

Her big eyes watched me gravely through the glasses. "He's not our real daddy, but we like him," she said, sounding like the chairman of a committee of two that had given the matter serious consideration. Then she asked calmly, "Is he dead?"

I nodded. "Yes, Andy, I'm afraid—"

At which point we were interrupted by a shrill female in a police uniform who accused me of being a sadistic brute, breaking the news of their bereavement to these helpless kids in such a crude and cruel manner. Considering that the helpless kids in question had fled one country ahead of its government's execution squads, had had their mother kidnapped in another country, and had just made good their escape from a home that had been torched, I hadn't felt they needed to be shielded from bad news, but perhaps I'd been wrong. Then Dennis Morton turned up and laid claim to them, saying he'd take them to the rest home where their mother was staying. The kids were marched away between him and the policewoman, who was making cooing, sympathetic noises at them. I saw Andrea Steiner look back, and I thought she winked at me, but I couldn't be sure.

"Useful assistance in doing what?" I repeated, when Mac didn't speak. I looked at him hard. I said, "So Ruth Steiner is going down to South America to retrieve some information about pernicious substances that's on computer disks her husband sent to various friends, a whole book of information; and you want me to go along and hold her hand."

"Yes, the lady has indicated that she will not cooperate with the organization that employs Dennis Morton, but she will with us. Rather than try to persuade her to change her mind, the powers that be have instructed us to protect her in her travels and give her any assistance she requires."

I studied him for a moment. I didn't need to ask why, when he'd always managed to keep us clear of antidrug operations in the past, saying that he had no intention of risking good soldiers in a lost war, he'd allowed us to be roped into

90

this shaky mission. There were two answers and I knew both of them. First and less important: Dennis Morton's superior had tried to give Mac hands-off orders, and he doesn't take kindly to being leaned on, so he'd wangled instructions from higher authority that let us take over the whole operation, and to hell with Morton and Co. But that was personal and of minor significance. More important was the fact that something needed to be done in South America, and as Ruth Steiner's bodyguard I'd be in a good position to do it.

I didn't need to ask, but to get things perfectly clear, I asked anyway: "We don't usually mess with the drug-interdiction business, sir. What's changed our policy, the threat of the nation being inundated by a flood of nickel marijuana and dollar cocaine?"

Mac said, "You're being willfully stupid, Eric. You know perfectly well that prohibited substances, or whatever the current jargon calls them, are not the real problem here."

I said, "Okay, I just wanted to get the priorities straight. What does my official brief include, if anything, beyond keeping the lady alive? I mean, are we interested in her damned diskettes?"

"Not particularly. Now that her husband is dead, they, and the book they represent, belong to the lady, as far as we're concerned. Of course, since we're required to protect her, we cannot allow her to be robbed by *anybody*, if you understand what I mean, Eric. We have jurisdiction. No one else has any right whatever to Mrs. Steiner's literary inheritance. You are entitled to use any means at your disposal to defend it." He stared at me hard for a moment to make sure I got the message: *If any other government agency tries to horn in, blast them.* Then he went on in softer tones: "If you should gain the lady's confidence to the extent that she'll entrust the disks to you, which doesn't seem likely at the moment, and she gives her permission, you can pass them along to us; but under no circumstances are you to antagonize her by trying to take her property against her will. I repeat, we are not particularly interested in obtaining Marcus Steiner's literary revelations."

I spent the afternoon in the basement with our armorer, having the theory and practice of Thuggee explained to me, since it seemed likely I hadn't seen the last of Vasquez's stranglers. The following morning I caught a flight west to Santa Fe—well, to Albuquerque; you have to drive the last sixty miles—so I could fly east to Miami two days later with Ruth Steiner.

It would have been simpler for me, already on the East Coast, to meet her in Miami, but although I didn't really expect action to be taken against her so soon, I didn't like the idea of letting her cross the country without me. Besides, we needed a little time together to develop a working relationship before we joined the tour group that was supposed to give us a bit of camouflage through South America.

As I now sipped my Scotch in the cocktail lounge of the MIA Hotel and nibbled at the Brie, which was satisfactorily ripe, I reflected that you had to hand it to the Thugs. Who would suspect you of being lethally armed just because you carried a slightly oversized silk handkerchief in one pocket and some change in another that could be knotted into one corner for weight—four or five quarters would do the job nicely, I'd determined. But airport security in Albuquerque hadn't given my most visible weapon a second look when I emptied my pockets at the magnetic gate; it had been just a fancy bandanna to them. They hadn't spotted the invisible ones, either; but then, they never do. Of course, arrangements had also been made for our local people to slip me a firearm in any country where I felt the need for one.

Ruth Steiner spoke after a little while. "I'm sorry if I seemed stuffy about your drinks."

I hadn't expected an apology. "Forget it."

She shook her head. "No, you'd better know that my first husband, the father of my girls, was an alcoholic." She drew a long breath. "He was in the wrong car when he was blown up. Nobody'd bother to booby-trap our old wreck, Richard's position wasn't that important—*he* wasn't that important, which was one of his problems—but he got so drunk at an official cocktail party that he staggered out and got into the wrong car by mistake, the one beside ours. It belonged to a visiting politico who'd earned a certain amount of hostility. The parking attendant had left the key in the lock—there was supposed to be perfect security on the premises, ha-ha!—and when Richard tried to start the car . . . *Boom*!" She shook her head. "They weren't very nice years, those last ones with Richard. Watching someone you once loved very much become somebody no one could love . . . Ever since, it gives me the creeps to see anybody drink, particularly someone I may have to rely on. Mark . . ." She stopped and cleared her throat. "Mark was very sweet about it after we were married. He liked an occasional whiskey, and particularly wine with dinner, but he knew how it made me feel, so he abstained." She smiled faintly. "Of course I knew he kept a cooler of beer in his truck and had one occasionally, but never when I was around. Not because he was afraid of me or what I'd say; simply because he didn't want to distress me. A very sweet guy."

Watching her, I remembered the first time I'd seen her, in the kitchen of their home, a slim, neat—well, except for the intentionally untidy hair—and rather plain girl in an inexpensive print dress, spreading peanut butter for two kids who didn't look much younger than she did. Today she was traveling in a striped blue knit shirt, a little faded-denim skirt, nylons, and low blue shoes. A blue cardigan, insurance against airline air-conditioning, hung over the back of her chair. She wore no eye makeup, and her eyes were big and blue behind the oversized glasses.

I sipped my Scotch deliberately. "I'm not a sweet guy," I said.

"I certainly hope not," she said.

"What does that mean?"

"Actually, I am not worrying about your alcoholic intake for my sake, and certainly not for yours, Mr. Helm. I just want to be certain you are not diminishing your effectiveness." She leaned forward, her elbows on the table. "You see, Mr. Helm, I want you in top condition; in good enough condition to kill Gregorio Vasquez for me. I have suffered quite enough at the hands of that man!''

The hatred in her voice, and in her small face, was quite impressive. That old man was certainly accumulating a lot of enemies.

I wasn't one of them. I mean, as far as I was concerned, Señor Vasquez was dead. He wasn't my enemy any more than he was my friend. He was simply a man who had ceased to exist at a certain moment, but who persisted in continuing to breathe. I merely had to see that he stopped.

Chapter 10

RIO de Janeiro was a big disappointment to me. I guess I'd heard too many wonderful things about this marvelous city on its fabulous beach washed by the gentle waters of the South Atlantic. There was no way it could live up to its advance billing, and as far as I was concerned, it didn't.

Oh, the scenery was moderately spectacular with the two famous peaks—Sugar Loaf and Corcovado (Hunchback) Mountain—rising from the great rocky ridge that splits the city in two, so that half of it has to be connected to the other half by a series of tunnels. (Corcovado's the one topped by the much-photographed statue of Christ the Redeemer.) However, I live seven thousand feet up in the foothills of the Rockies and I've seen a mountain, thanks. The legendary beach was impressive, to be sure, but I once spent some time in Waikiki, where you step out of your hotel right onto the gleaming sands instead of having to first fight your way across six lanes of traffic. (There's also a pretty fair stretch of sand, undisturbed by the noise and fumes of city traffic, at Varadero, Cuba; and don't ask me what I was doing in Varadero, Cuba.)

But my chief disillusionment in Rio concerned the people. Even in the fairly expensive hostelry to which we were taken, while they didn't look poverty-stricken, they didn't look especially smart or glamorous, either. Waiting, with the rest of the group, for our tour manager to take care of the red tape at the hotel desk, I watched a well-developed Brazilian girl in shorts and high heels heading for the elevators; moderately interesting, but hardly worth the trip, since my hometown is full of sexy Latin ladies in shorts and high heels. Still looking where the girl had vanished, I saw a sturdier figure appear, one I recognized.

"Oh, Jesus!" I said to Ruth. "Don't stare, but try to get a good look at the dame just coming from the elevators so you'll know her if you see her again."

We were waiting in an alcove off the lobby that was furnished with three overstuffed sofas in a loose C-formation and several big easy chairs, into which most members of our tour had settled; but I'd done enough sitting for a while and Ruth had felt the same way. We were giving our tired rumps a break by standing up, for a change, in the alcove opening, just out of the lobby traffic. The woman passed within ten feet of us.

It was the closest look I'd had of her—back in Santa Fe I'd been handicapped by having to pretend I wasn't aware of being under surveillance as she and her friends trailed me around. Like us, she was a bit rumpled this morning, in a beige linen pantsuit I'd seen before, that looked as if she'd spent the night in it, perhaps on a plane like us, perhaps even on our plane. I hadn't spotted her, but King Kong could lose himself on board one of those giant jets, particularly with a first-class ticket—I was still trying to recover from the strains and aches resulting from having to fold my six feet four, for most of a day and night, into the midget space provided in tourist class.

I noted that the woman had had her brown hair restyled from the stringy, straggling hippie mop I'd last seen. Short and smooth and glossy, it flattered her snub-nosed face and gave her a rather pleasant grown-up-tomboy look. She looked as if she used to play a mean game of golf or tennis before she took up homicide. As far as I could see, she showed no evidence of being on cocaine or anything else, but it's not my field of expertise and I don't really know what signs to look for. She walked by without glancing our way and went out the hotel's front door into the bright Brazilian sunshine.

"Yes, I'll know her," Ruth said. "Who is she?"

"One of the *Compañeros de la Hoja*, I think. *Compañeras?*"

Ruth looked surprised. "That freckled, bouncing phys-ed major? She looks too wholesome to . . . You do mean those people who were watching Mark and me?"

"And me, and Madeleine Rustin. They seem to have plenty of manpower. And womanpower. Although they lost one person of each gender in Santa Fe. Well, so did we. They're still a dog ahead of us, however." I cleared my throat. "Anyway, in case you're interested, that was Spooky Three who just went out."

Ruth frowned. "Spooky?"

"I call them all Spookies. That one's been following me around for the past several weeks, off and on. Chronologically, she's the third one I spotted of the four taking turns watching me back in Santa Fe. Spooky Three."

Ruth glanced at me. "Should they have found us down here so soon?"

I shrugged. "There was never any chance of their losing us for long, no matter how sneaky we tried to be, considering that you have to visit most of the obvious South American cities to look up Mark's friends and determine which of them received little three-and-a-half-by-three-and-a-half-inch presents in the mail. Maybe we could have slipped away briefly, but we have to figure that this continent belongs to Gregorio Vasquez. There's no practical way of getting from country to country except by plane. No matter what offbeat route we chose, his people would have spotted us at the first airport we hit, and passed the word. It was decided in Washington that we'd do better to play it straight and just follow along with this tour group, since it was hitting all the places you'd indicated plus a few more. We're supposed to act as if we're quite sure that the two of us can handle any problems that arise, although, as a matter of fact, we do have some backup if we need it. Maybe, thinking us cocky and careless and overconfident, Vasquez's people will get a little overconfident and careless themselves." I glanced over my shoulder. "What do you think of our fellow travelers?"

Ruth looked at our companions, slumped wearily and sleepily on the hotel furniture. There were seven couples. Ruth and I made eight; sixteen warm bodies. We'd all boarded the plane independently, so this was our first group get-together. Our tour manager, a Mrs. Tobler, whom we were supposed to call Annie, had made contact with each of us at the Varig counter in Miami, using our Weston Tours carry-on bags for identification. She'd helped us get our seat assignments and turned us loose with our boarding passes to make the flight on our own. Then she'd rounded us up at the Rio airport, directed us through immigration and customs, shoveled us and our luggage onto a waiting bus, and herded us into the hotel. She'd instructed us to introduce ourselves to each other while she picked up our room keys, and we had, but I doubted that many names had stuck in many minds; although I figured that Ruth's name and mine were probably imprinted boldly on one mind. The question was: which one?

Ruth moved her shoulders slightly. "It's a little early to form any opinions, isn't it? They look as tired as I feel. I seem to have been sitting in airplanes for a week; and how many hours did we lose, coming east? Two time zones from Albuquerque to Miami and two more from Miami to Rio? I never realized that South America was that far east of North America." She glanced at her watch. "That means it's barely six o'clock in the morning back home. Ugh! As soon as that woman produces a key, I'm going to disappear into my room, take a hot bath, and sleep the rest of the day and let the world catch up with me."

I said, "In that fistful of tour literature we were handed, there's a passenger list we'd both better memorize. There's also a schedule indicating that we have a get-together cocktail party and dinner tonight. It'll give us a chance to match the names to the faces. I understand that some of the people on the list canceled out after it was printed, and I believe two couples joined up too late to be listed—three if you include us. I'm particularly interested in the four people besides us who aren't on the list, but try not to let them know it. After

98

we've had a chance to get everybody sorted out, we'll compare notes. Okay?''

"What are we looking for?''

I said, "Even though we joined the tour at almost the last possible moment, it seems likely that one of those other unlisted characters joined even later, doesn't it? A *Compañero* who was assigned to keep an eye on us, once our travel plans were known, until his gang is ready to move in on us.''

Ruth shivered slightly. "It makes me feel, well, hunted, to think of all those eyes watching me.''

I said, "That's because you are hunted; we both are. If you have any arrangements to make here, be careful what phone you use. And if you have to leave the hotel for any reason, I'd better go with you. I'd hate to have you disappear on your first morning in Rio.''

She said, "No phone calls or excursions are needed, Mr. Helm. The contact procedures have already been established. I don't have to call anybody and tell them to meet me on the beach just to the right of the third wave, wearing a hibiscus in my navel.''

I laughed. "And you're not telling me what the established procedures are, right?''

She studied me for a moment and said quietly, "I know Dennis Morton would sacrifice me in an instant if it would buy him the information he wants. For all I know, you would, too. And I don't know about you, but Morton has absolutely no interest in seeing my husband's book published, certainly not before he gets the credit for catching Gregorio Vasquez and smashing the Evil Empire, as Mark so dramatically called it.''

"I'm not Dennis Morton,'' I said. "This is strictly a bodyguard job for me. What you do with the stuff you collect is your business. It doesn't figure in my instructions.''

Ruth Steiner said, "I hear you saying it, but how can I be sure? I want Mark's book published, and I want it published *before* Gregorio Vasquez is arrested or killed so that when he is finally brought to justice, one way or another, the news uproar will push *The King of Coke*, to use your rather tacky and inaccurate title—we'll have to think of a better one; Mark just called it Manuscript X2, since *Empire* had been X1—onto the best-seller list. I want it, not only for Mark's sake, but for my own and that of my girls. I have a little money of my own, and Mark left me some, but I'm strictly the housewife type; I have no marketable skills. These days it's very expensive to bring up a couple of kids and put them through college. I want to find all the pieces of Mark's book, I want to put them together, I want to see the book published, and I want it to sell a lot of copies and make a lot of money. I'm very mercenary about this, and I'm not going to have Dennis Morton's government gang, or yours, stealing Mark's thunder prematurely, so the book will be old hat when it comes out.''

I said, "Swell, but I thought I understood you to say something, earlier, about wanting Vasquez killed very dead, very soon.''

She colored slightly. "I was being emotional. I've had more time to think now—what else can you do on a plane?—and I've come to realize that building a secure future for Andrea and Beatrice is more important than avenging their stepfather.''

Then Annie Tobler was back, a hefty, businesslike female in a baggy pantsuit, with a red pugilist face surrounded by careful white curls. There was a dark little mustached man with her, who was formally dressed in a dark suit, white shirt, and silk tie. She introduced him as the local guide who'd be showing us around, but I didn't catch the name: it sounded as if she'd said Señor Avocado, which seemed unlikely. We got our passports back and were given our room keys.

"That little man's name wasn't *really* Avocado, was it?'' Ruth asked as we stopped in front of her door. She gave me her key when I held out my hand.

I said, "That's what I heard, too, but we could both be wrong.'' I used the key and preceded her into the room, discourteously and cautiously. It was a large and light and pleasant room, with a bird's-eye view of the beachfront boulevard and the beach itself—we were on the ninth floor. I checked the bathroom and the closet and turned to look at her. "I see they've already brought up your luggage, so there should be no immediate reason for you to open the hall door. Lock it after me. Call me if somebody knocks, and let me handle it. I'm going to unlock the connecting doors, if you don't mind."

She nodded. We stood there for a moment, a little awkwardly. Even if they have no reason to like each other much, two adult people, male and female, can't help but feel at least a hint of sexual tension, alone in a hotel room with a big, convenient bed—actually two beds—particularly a hotel room in a foreign country. I noticed that she didn't look too bad for a lady who'd just crossed two continents. Her feathery hairdo was as tidy as it ever got and her lipstick was straight, and not much can happen to a knitted shirt and denim skirt. If her eyes looked tired, whose didn't? I put her key into her hand and went to the hall door.

"Matt."

I turned. "Yes?"

"You're quite sure my girls are safe? Those people kidnapped me once to get information from Mark; they could try to take my children to get information from me."

I said, "I don't know if a certain government installation will ever be the same after those two little charmers get through with it, but your kids are as safe as if they were locked into Fort Knox."

While she was still under guard in the nursing home to which Dennis Morton had taken her I had, with her permission, flown her daughters to Arizona and escorted them to the Ranch, where they'd immediately been adopted by a couple of female agents recuperating from injuries incurred in the line of duty.

Ruth hesitated. "I don't believe I've thanked you properly."

"You're very welcome."

She licked her lips. "I don't mean just for finding a safe place for them. Before that . . . well, you were pretty heavy with that shotgun butt, and I let it prejudice me against you. But it has occurred to me that I owe you a debt that far outweighs a bump on the head. In a moment when you were surrounded by death and destruction—it must have been a dreadful experience, even if you've known a lot of violence— you still remembered two little girls alone in their home and made the telephone call that got them out of there before the arsonists arrived. Andy and Bea thank you. I thank you.''

I'm not very good with thanks, perhaps because I get so few of them. I said, ''I didn't talk much with your Bea, she was a little shy with me, but your Andy seems to be a smart and gutsy kid. We can't afford to lose any like that. . . . Well, call me if you see or hear anything that worries you.''

Chapter 11

THE following day we toured Rio in a large sight-seeing bus carefully designed to make it impossible to see the sights. Well, the passenger in a right-hand seat had something of a view out the window directly to starboard, and the passenger in a left-hand seat had some visibility straight out through the glass to port, but the poor souls on the aisle could see nothing but their fellow tourists on either side and the towering, head-high headrest of the seats in front of them. They could console themselves by thinking about how comfortable they could have been reclining in their lovely, supportive seats on the long cross-country ride they weren't going to take, and how safe they were, protected from whiplash under all conceivable circumstances. Ironically, the city buses we passed, of which there seemed to be hundreds, had nice low seat backs, giving a wonderful all-around view to the commuting local citizens, who didn't give a damn since they'd seen it before.

"Wouldn't you like to know just how many buses this big actually get hit in the rear hard enough to give the passengers whiplash?" Ruth asked.

She was craning her neck in a vain effort to see the passing points of interest being described by the little man up front with the mustache and the mike, whose name had turned out to be, not Avocado, but Alvarado. We were supposed to call him Roberto. I'd asked Ruth to take the inboard seat so I could use my camera, not that I'd get very good results, technically, shooting through the glass of the bus window, but at the moment I was just establishing my character as a

103

typical, shutter-happy, tourist type. Now I glanced at my seat companion uneasily; there's always something disturbing about finding somebody thinking your thoughts, particularly when it's somebody you don't particularly care for.

I said, "When the human race dies out, it will be because it was brainwashed to be so totally, completely, utterly safe that it no longer dared to keep on living, a risky business at best. The fact that we've managed to invent a tour bus that surrounds us with safety devices so completely that we can hardly catch a glimpse of the picturesque foreign scenes we've traveled several thousand miles to see, shows that we've got our priorities so badly screwed up that we're approaching extinction fast."

Ruth laughed and changed the subject. "That was quite a party we had last night," she said dryly. "A real bash."

Although they speak Portuguese instead of Spanish, the Brazilians seem to have pretty much the same customs as other Latins, which means that they don't dine until fairly late at night. Our American tour group had therefore had the hotel bar, and later the dining room, pretty much to itself until people started filtering in around nine, by which time we were getting ready to break up and go to bed. As Ruth had indicated ironically it could hardly have been called an orgy. Our traveling companions all seemed to be devotees of the modern cult of sobriety. With two Scotches before dinner and a couple of glasses of wine with the meal, I was the lush of the party—I had a feeling that the others, not necessarily excepting my traveling companion, had expected me to either pass out on the floor or break into happy song after such reckless indulgence in spirituous liquors. It had made me feel like an elderly gent yearning for the free and easy days of his youth, when nobody counted your drinks or, for that matter, expected you to apologize for your cigarettes. Gad, what wicked lives we lived back then!

"What did you learn from the male Ackerman?" I asked.

As I'd told Ruth, I'd wanted us to zero in on one of the couples who were not on the printed tour list, and she'd managed to corral a stocky older gent named Roger Ackerman, leaving to me his fairly young wife, Belinda, blond and plump and quite pretty. Roger had been wearing a sharply pressed cord suit that made me ashamed of my travel-creased seer-sucker, and Belinda had displayed her ample charms—as the old romances used to refer to them discreetly—in a confection of drifting blue-gray chiffon that undoubtedly made Ruth unhappy about her simple blue linen even though she'd got the hotel to press it so it looked smooth and crisp.

"Roger?" Ruth said. "Oh, Roger makes a lot of money doing something quite incomprehensible on Wall Street. Well, I guess it's only a reasonable amount of money; if he were a millionaire, he wouldn't be taking his enchanting new little wife—number three, I believe—on a cheap ten-thousand-dollar tour; he'd buy her a villa on the Riviera."

"Yes, I gathered they were married quite recently," I said.

Ruth said, "They live out on Long Island somewhere. I don't think he's our man. He seemed quite authentic as a money man; at least he had all the stuffy finance jargon at the tip of his tongue, right out of *The Wall Street Journal*. How did you get along with Belinda?" Ruth glanced at me slyly. "Why do I ask? You seemed to find a lot of interesting things to talk about. She's not unattractive in her overripe way, is she? If you like plump little phony blondes forty years old. And the dress she was wearing! Roger must have sold a lot of bonds, or whatever he sells, to pay for that little number."

Actually, I didn't think Belinda Ackerman was much over thirty; unfortunately she thought she looked even younger than that and acted accordingly.

I said, "Well, she seems to be a typical New York girl whose world is bounded by Connecticut to the east and New Jersey to the west—South America is just a confusing illusion to her, mildly interesting while it lasts. Unlike Manhattan, it doesn't *really* exist. Neither, of course, does New Mexico. Belinda was surprised to learn that we carried U.S. passports; she thought we came from a distant foreign land and it was clever of us to speak such good English. But then, she seemed to think that anything west of the Adirondacks was Indian territory.''

Ruth laughed. "I don't think you're being quite fair to the poor girl. . . . Did I hear the man say we're going to stop up ahead?''

I nodded. "Corcovado coming up. Hunchback Mountain to you. We get to ride a funicular railway to the top and take pictures of the Christ statue, lucky us.''

Ruth laughed again. "I get the impression you're not entirely sold on sight-seeing.''

"Hell, I don't mind sights; it's those damn cogwheel trains climbing up perpendicular precipices that get me. Just wait until we ride the cable car up to the top of Sugarloaf tomorrow, swinging gently and sickeningly in the breeze, and you'll see real panic. Ugh!''

Ruth studied me for a moment and smiled. "Well, a man who admits he's scared of heights can't be all bad. The ones I can't stand are the heroes who boast that they aren't afraid of anything. . . . Matt.''

Something in her voice made me glance at her sharply. "Yes, Ruth?''

She spoke without expression: "We seem to be stopping. When we get up there, find me a rest room, please. I feel a strange dizzy spell coming on; I'm going to have to wash my face in cold water to snap out of it. I'd rather you didn't get too far away.''

I looked at her for a moment. She was letting me know that action was imminent. I saw that she was not about to give me any additional information and that questions would not, repeat not, be welcome.

I said, "You picked one of the few places on earth outside my sphere of protection, but I'll keep myself as available as I can.''

"I didn't pick it. Messing about in johns is not my idea of glorious intrigue.'' She grimaced. "But there's one good thing about this stupid rendezvous: I'll have a toilet handy if I get so scared I'm in danger of disgracing my panty hose while I wait for this mysterious contact. Isn't that what you call it, a contact?''

It was interesting but a little unnerving, watching the rather reserved widow lady unbending to the point of making scatological jokes at her own expense.

I said, "Contact is the word. Good luck. Here we go."

It was a popular place, at the foot of the steep mountain and its funicular track. There were gaudy kiosks dispensing food, drinks, and souvenirs; and there was quite a line of people waiting at the train terminal. Our guides, big white-haired Annie and little black-haired Roberto, told us to have a look around while they checked the situation. As Ruth and I moved off I spotted a small, bright green building with a big sign: SANITARIO. I nudged my companion.

"I think that's the local word for the facilities, ma'am."

She said irritably, "I know, I lived in this country for several years, remember? But I have a feeling the rest room I'm supposed to visit is up above at the end of track. . . . Well, I'd better check this one out, just in case." She licked her lips. "Please don't go away."

I said, "One scream and I'll crash the door marked *damas* if it means my life."

I watched her disappear into the sacred, segregated premises. A slight figure almost thin, she looked more like a schoolgirl than a double widow with two half-grown kids. Waiting, I busied myself with my camera. Photographically, the zoom lens is the greatest invention since Kodachrome. The early ones weren't very sharp, but they've got them licked now, and just twisting the zoom collar of my 28-70 certainly beat switching back and forth between the two or three lenses I used to have to carry to cover the same focal range. I'd been instructed to stock up with a type of film I hadn't played with much, a fairly fast emulsion designed for the production of color prints. Back in my working photographic days I'd used slide film exclusively when I wanted color. However, for our present purposes, I was told, the color-print stuff, that I'd always considered suitable only for amateur snapshots, lent itself better to fast processing and checking.

107

I concentrated on some bright red flowers in a bed in the center of the patio, shooting from an angle that didn't give me the best light for the blossoms—don't ask me what they were—but allowed me to cover the door through which Ruth had disappeared, snapping everyone who entered that door. To be sure of getting a recognizable face, I took them coming out as well, not sighting through the viewfinder since they were looking my way, just letting the camera point casually in that direction while studying my flowery subjects and pressing the shutter release inconspicuously. The framing might be a bit cockeyed, but with the zoom lens at its wide-angle setting, I wasn't likely to miss completely, even hip-shooting like that; and the fancy auto-focus mechanism should give me sharp pictures that could be enlarged for careful examination by the backup crew.

"Hey, take our pitcher, mister."

It was my blond dinner companion of the night before, with a comfortably well-upholstered, gray-haired older woman whose name was . . . I dug around in my memory for a moment and came up with it: Grace Priestly, wife of Herman Priestly, a lean bald man with gold-rimmed glasses who had something to do with Texas oil. Like the Ackermans, they were not on the list, which made them possible candidates for a Spooky spot. Mrs. Priestly was wearing a print dress; Belinda Ackerman had on a crinkly brown jumpsuit with fashionably baggy pants that did nothing for her generous figure. My instructions were to supply photos of everyone on the tour as soon as possible, so I snapped them both, trying to get one in which the younger woman wasn't mugging for the camera in her cute, girlish fashion.

They vanished into the john and, presently, emerged and wandered over to one of the souvenir stands. At last Ruth came out, looking frustrated.

"No luck?" I asked.

She shook her head. "I couldn't stay in there forever. A woman told me there is another *sanitario* at the upper terminal, as I thought; I'll have to try that when we get there."

She giggled abruptly. "I'm glad it isn't a doctor's office and I don't have to give them another sample; I'm all peed out."

I looked at her for a moment, realizing that she was really a rather shy person whose faith in humanity hadn't been strengthened by her kidnap experience or, for that matter, by being thumped on the head by me. But she had apparently decided, after sharing a few airplanes with me and remembering that I'd saved her kids, that I wasn't so bad after all. In any case she was stuck with me, and she was damn well going to relax and be herself, and if I disapproved of her daring little rest-room jokes, to hell with me. Then Annie came to round us up: apparently there were so many people waiting for the funicular that we might have to stand in line for an hour, and it was almost lunchtime anyway. They'd decided to take us away and feed us; maybe the crowd would be smaller when we returned later. I heard Ruth groan softly beside me.

"Oh, dear, I wanted to get it over with so I could relax—well, until the next rendezvous."

"Where is that scheduled?"

She laughed. "Don't be nosy, Matt. I'll let you know when we get there."

I said, "I understand that our next stop after Rio is Iguassu Falls, Brazil's answer to Niagara. According to the poop sheet, it's just one hotel with a lot of jungle around it and a lot of water falling off some cliffs, a nice place to dispose of a body or two. Don't leave me working in the dark too long."

She hesitated. "All right. I have nothing scheduled for Iguassu; the next contact, after this one—if it ever comes off—is in Buenos Aires. Satisfied?"

Returning to the bus, we were delivered to a rustic-looking restaurant in town, where we all sat at one long table and our meat was brought to us in chunks on lethal-looking, fire-blackened swords. I made myself conspicuous by asking for Scotch and persisting even after Roberto warned me that it was terribly expensive here, senhor. A bottle of Teacher's was finally brought to the table and placed before me, with considerable ceremony; it had a strip of adhesive tape down the side marked in half centimeters. Apparently I could pour as much as I wanted; and at the end of the meal I'd simply be charged according to how many centimeters I'd lowered the liquor level. Drinking, I could see the guides, and my fellow travelers, deciding that they had a real bottle baby on their hands. Swell. Maybe the word would get around that the troublesome widow of Raoul Marcus Carrera Mascarena was being guarded only by an incompetent stumblebum who spent most of his time in an alcoholic daze.

I was reminded of a question I'd been wanting to ask and turned to Ruth: "What's all this stone business, anyway?"

"Stone?"

It was obvious that she was wondering if I wasn't already coming unfocused at the first sip.

I said, "Mark Steiner, Marcus Piedra. Operation Lapis. I suppose his next alias, if he'd lived, would have been Pebbles or Rockwell. But why the obsession with stones?"

She laughed. "It was a joke, a play on his real name, Matt. Don't you get it?"

I thought for a moment and shook my head. "I'm slow today. Bear with me."

"Maybe you'd be faster if you laid off that stuff."

I spoke deliberately: "I can see why your first husband blew himself up. It was quicker and less painful than being nagged to death."

She was silent for a little. "That was a nasty thing to say," she whispered at last.

"That's right. And so was your comment on my alcohol consumption. Which makes us even. Okay?"

She swallowed and, after a moment, looked around to see if our little interchange had been overheard; but everybody was prattling gaily around us.

"Marble," she said.

I frowned. "What about marble?"

"Don't be stupid. Where does the best marble come from?"

"Italy," I said. "Oh, I get it. But that's Carrara, not Carrera."

110

"He thought it was close enough. Carrera, Carrara, marble, stone, *piedra*. He thought it was amusing, and made it his literary signature, and later his alias when we had to go into hiding. He had a wry little sense of humor that would pop out when you'd least expect. . . . Oh, dear!"

She was groping in her purse, helplessly; I saw that her eyes were wet. I put my handkerchief, fortunately clean, into her hands, and she laid her glasses on the table and mopped at her face. She put the glasses back on and looked at me.

"I . . . I guess I kind of loved him," she said. "It still hits me occasionally. I'm sorry. Let me go make repairs, please."

Well, it was one reason for visiting a john; I wondered if she had another. I said, "Back in the corner, over there. Keep the hanky."

I watched her go. She had to make her way around a small corner table; and Spooky Three was sitting there. She hadn't been there earlier. I was annoyed with myself for getting so involved in conversation that I hadn't seen her come in. She was wearing jeans, a white T-shirt, and a man's blue shirt hanging loose and open like a jacket. There was a rather large, blond young man sitting with her, also in jeans and T-shirt. He wasn't one of the ones I'd seen in Santa Fe, so I cataloged him as Spooky Five. They were both careful not to look at Ruth as she walked past.

I became aware that Belinda Ackerman, on my left, had spoken. I said, "I'm sorry, what did you say?"

"I hope your . . . I hope Mrs. Steiner is all right."

I said, "Oh, Ruth's okay, she's just . . . Well, she lost her husband quite recently and I made a mistake and said something that brought back the wrong memories, or maybe you'd call them the right ones. She'll be all right as soon as she's washed her face."

Belinda asked casually, "You've known her a long time?"

I said, "Actually, I was more a friend of Mark, her husband; but after he died suddenly—it was kind of a traumatic business—well, she needed a shoulder to cry on and, well, one thing led to another. So we decided to park her two kids

111

and go away together for a bit and, well, really get acquainted and see just what we had, if anything. If you know what I mean.''

I'm not usually in favor of discussing my private relationships in public, but there was nothing to be gained by insisting on privacy here. They'd all be wondering about us, so give them the story, really not too far from the truth, of the brokenhearted young widow and mother clinging helplessly to her late husband's hard-drinking friend.

I'd kept my eye on the rest room as I talked, but it was Spooky Three's reaction that let me know Ruth was on her way back to our table. The freckled young woman gave a quick glance toward the rest rooms and then plunged into an animated discussion with her male friend, totally ignoring Ruth as she made her way past the table once more. It was really a pretty amateurish performance. I reflected that it didn't match the professionalism of the black-clad stranglers, one of whom had almost got me while his partner was making quite sure of Mark Steiner. Apparently, *El Viejo* used a lot of fairly low-grade manpower—and womanpower—for surveillance purposes but called on his elite units when killing time came. I found myself watching Ruth as she approached; I realized that, fairly amateurish herself, she was looking tremendously relieved and a little triumphant.

"Contact accomplished," she breathed as I helped her with her chair. "Now stay close to me until we get back to the hotel, Matt, please. I feel as if I were carrying a purse full of nitroglycerin."

Chapter 12

THAT evening she knocked on the connecting door
about an hour after we got back to the hotel, after spending
the afternoon bravely riding the cogwheel cars up Hunchback
Mountain and then climbing interminable flights of stairs to
the great white statue with arms outspread that looks benev-
olently down upon the city of Rio. Christ the Redeemer. He
has a fine view from up there, although I had a hunch the
panoramic shots I took, to maintain my role as an obsessive
tourist type snapshooter, would turn out a bit hazy. With sea
breezes to help out, Rio de Janeiro doesn't compare with the
Latin pollution champion, Ciudad el Smoggo, Mexico—
Mexico City to you—where the grunge is all confined in a
big bowl hemmed in by mountains. However, as L.A. has
learned to its sorrow, a handy ocean isn't a surefire smog
cure; and the Rio air isn't exactly crystalline.

I opened the door to see Ruth standing there a bit uncertainly, still in her sight-seeing clothes. She had something in
her hand: a small gray plastic square with some metal on it.
I estimated the dimensions to be about three and a half by
three and a half inches.

She licked her lips. "If . . . if I gave you this, what would
you do with it?" Then she laughed a bit sharply. "Oh, it's
not the original diskette that was slipped to me in that restaurant john; I'm not trusting you with *that*. I've just been
copying it so there'll be a spare."

Beyond her I could see, on the spindly writing desk set
against the far wall of her room, a small, flat, white computer
with a keyboard and a flip-up screen; clearly this was the

heavy object she'd been lugging through the airports in her carry-on bag.

I said, "Seems as if you computer aficionados are always copying everything, as if you're never quite sure it isn't going to fade away like skywriting. Don't you trust your magic machines?"

She said, "It's not the machine I don't trust, Matt."

"I see." I looked at her for a moment. "But you do trust me? I'm flattered."

She laughed shortly. "I've worked out a way of sending the disks to a safe place as I get them so they'll be waiting for me when I get home and start putting Mark's book back together. But even with you watching over me, something might happen before I can get rid of one. . . . I mean, there are the *Compañeros* or, as you call them, Spookies; and then there's Dennis Morton and his agency. Not to mention the fact that any South American city is a good place to get slightly mugged by independent operators. . . . I'm not thinking of just this diskette, but of the four others I'll be picking up as we go along with the tour. They're all scrambled, of course, so they're no use to anyone but me; but I just unscrambled this one enough to see that it covers Chapter Eleven to Chapter Nineteen of the book. It's obviously going to be like working a jigsaw puzzle. I have no way of knowing what disk Mark sent to whom; he said the less I knew about it the safer I was. I'll just have to take them as they come and put them into the right order when I get them all home. But I can't afford to lose a single one. Unlike Mark, I couldn't begin to replace any missing material from memory, even though I did help him a bit with the manuscript."

We were still standing in the doorway between our rooms. I said, "Come in and sit down. I'd offer you a real drink, but you'd think I was trying to sabotage your moral fiber. But there's Perrier and Coke, and a couple of fruity-looking local soft drinks. Name your poison."

She walked across to the window, presumably for a look at the ocean, and turned away, disappointed. However, although I didn't have the sea view she had, being around the corner on the side street, my room was as pleasant as hers in other respects, with some prints on the wall that were abstract and, as far as I was concerned, incomprehensible, but decorative and not too hard to live with. The place came well equipped; not only was there a small refrigerator with a bar on top, stocked with an assortment of miniatures, but there was also, in the closet, a little steel safe in which we were supposed to lock our passports and valuables, carrying only as much money as we thought we'd need for the day. Annie had given us the standing orders on the subject: men not to wear wallets in hip pockets, women not to carry purses dangling from shoulders, etc., etc. Apparently pickpocketing and purse snatching are honored professions throughout South America, so Ruth's fear of losing her property, either to the opposition or to local talent, was not unfounded.

When she didn't respond at once, I looked around from the bar. She'd seated herself in one of the two big chairs flanking the round table by the window, looking my way, but I couldn't read the expression on her small face.

"Well, what's it to be?" I asked.

Waiting, I twisted the cap off a tiny bottle of J&B for myself, and emptied the contents into a thick, low tumbler. Hooray for Argentina. No flimsy plastic U.S.-motel-type glasses here.

Ruth licked her lips. "Is there . . . is there bourbon?"

Startled, I studied her more carefully for a moment. "Look, you don't have to be wicked just because I am. If you don't like the stuff, for God's sake don't drink it just to keep me company."

She said, "You seem to have decided that I'm some kind of a prig. A self-righteous, teetotaler prig."

"The very worst kind," I agreed. "Sure. So you're a prig, so what? You don't have to unprig yourself just to get my help. For the moment, milady, I exist only to serve you, prig or no prig."

"Well, serve me that Jack Daniel's, then! No ice, just a splash of soda."

She had sharp eyes in spite of—or maybe because of—her

115

glasses; even from across the room she'd identified the black-labeled miniature on the bar. I shrugged, uncapped it, and dumped the contents into a glass.

"Now sit down," she said when I brought it to her. "It's time we had a little talk that isn't in an airport or on an airplane or a bus. Somehow I can't think very clearly with all those people around." She tasted her drink, licked the whiskey off her lips, and nodded. "Yes, I remember now that it did taste rather good in a nasty way. You won't believe this, but I really have no strong moral feelings about it, Matt. In fact, I used to enjoy having a pleasant drink or two with Richard until I realized that . . . that he couldn't control it any longer. So I quit drinking altogether. I suppose I was hoping it would at least slow him down a little, but it didn't. He just got very unpleasant about my precious sobriety, as he called it, but he kept right on. . . ." She stopped, and swallowed hard. "And then, afterward, when Mark came along, he assumed that abstinence was an important principle for me and, without being asked, sacrificed his own preferences. . . . Well, I told you. And when I got everything all straightened out in my head, it was too late, if you know what I mean. After Mark had gone to such lengths to please me, I could hardly tell him that he'd jumped to conclusions and I really wouldn't mind his having a whiskey now and then and might even like to join him occasionally. Maybe I'd have got around to it, probably I would, but . . . but time ran out on us. But after listening to myself nagging at you in that priggish way for two whole days . . . It got to be a compulsive Pavlov reaction, I guess, during those last awful years with Richard. Say 'alcohol' and little Ruthie automatically frothed at the mouth. It's time I stopped." She raised her glass. *"Salud!"*

I returned her salute and drank with her, wondering a bit about her motives. Well, she wanted a favor, obviously, and it's hard to ask favors of someone as long as you're treating him like a moral leper.

I said, "Where's that thing you were waving under my nose a minute ago?"

She fished it out of the pocket of her knitted blue-and-white shirt, hesitated, and laid it on the table between us, saying, "You still haven't answered my question."

I picked it up. Babes in their cradles seem to know all about computers these days, but it's not a standard part of the Ranch training, although I wouldn't be surprised if there was somebody there who could tell you what you needed to know about them if you needed to know it. I never had, and this was the first diskette I'd ever handled. It was approximately an eighth of an inch thick. Presumably it formed a protective envelope of sorts for a thin electronic or magnetic storage disk inside. There was a piece of shiny round metal in the center of the plastic, about the size of a quarter. There were two mysterious little holes in that, one centered and square, the other off center and oblong. I assumed they had something to do with the way the hidden disk was rotated by the computer, like a gramophone record, only, I suspected, much faster. A shiny, sliding metal gate at one side of the plastic square undoubtedly moved aside to expose the working surfaces when the machinery was in operation. Complicated.

I turned the diskette over and saw a label on which Ruth had printed with a felt-tipped pen: *MS-X2 (Ch. 11–19)*. I remembered her saying that Mark had called his current opus Manuscript X2. I decided not to flaunt my computer ignorance by commenting on the fact that the little object in my hand could hold nine whole chapters of a book—actually it could probably hold a lot more. Nowadays they can probably squeeze the whole Encyclopedia Britannica onto a single microdot. I laid the diskette back on the table.

I said, "In answer to your original question, let me quote my chief on the subject. His words were, roughly: 'If you should gain the lady's confidence to the extent that she'll entrust the disks to you, you can pass them along to us, but under no circumstances are you to antagonize her by trying to take her property against her will. We are not particularly interested in obtaining Marcus Steiner's literary revelations.' "

She licked her lips uncertainly. "And if I do trust you with it and let you send it to Washington, what will they do with it?"

"I can only guess," I said, "but I presume they'll put it into their computer and try to read it. When they find it's gobbledygook—coded as you say—they'll try to decode it. If they can't, they'll pass it to some mad government genius with a bigger computer who can."

Ruth smiled faintly. "You seem quite sure of that."

"Honey, they've got code busters in Washington who could decipher the secret of the Sphinx in sixty seconds flat, if the Sphinx had a secret and they wanted to be bothered with archaeology. And Mark was a good journalist, and a hell of a marksman, but I never heard that he was a computer whiz."

"No, he wasn't, but I am." Ruth laughed shortly. "Oh, I'm no genius hacker, but I do like to play with the things, and it doesn't take a genius to use the encryption feature that you find in a lot of programs. And I understand that if you lock up a document that way, it's really pretty secure against anyone who hasn't got the password." She hesitated. "Just a minute. I want to get something from my room."

She went out, leaving the diskette in front of me. It took her a couple of minutes. When she returned, the first thing she did was pick up the square of plastic from the table and slip it back into the shirt pocket from which it had come. Then she laid down, side by side, two more diskettes that seemed to be identical with the first, down to the careful hand-printing on the label.

"We wouldn't want to get them mixed up," she said. She tapped her pocket. "There's nothing on this one."

"Cute," I said.

She licked her lips. "It was . . . maybe we should call it a test disk. I wanted to see what you'd say."

I said, "So I said the right thing, goody." I looked at the disks on the table. "You're giving me these?"

"I want to be sure to keep Mark's book safe as I get it. One copy for you and one for Washington."

I looked at the disks a moment longer. I looked at her. "Strings?"

"What?"

"Are there any strings attached?"

She said, "There can't very well be, can there? I mean, either I take the risk of being the only custodian of the material, or I trust you and your people to help me. And once you have the disks, they're out of my control. But I would appreciate it if you don't let Morton and his associates have any of them until I'm ready for the story to break."

I said, "I'll pass your request along. It will probably be honored. Remember that my chief isn't very happy with the way Morton's chief tried to push him around. He's not going to go out of his way to volunteer assistance in that direction."

She looked at me and sighed. "Well, I hope I'm not being foolish, but there they are. All yours. Now you can take me for a walk along the beach so I can say I've at least walked along the beautiful beach in Rio, and then you can bring me back to the hotel and feed me."

Chapter 13

THEY tried for us as we sauntered along the wide, paved sidewalk between the boulevard and the beach. We had plenty of company there; apparently the evening ocean-front stroll was kind of a Rio ritual. There were three of them, suddenly appearing from behind a group of casual pedestrians. They were small and dark and shabby, and fairly young, one angling to block me off, away from Ruth, the other two heading to relieve her of her purse, even though she was holding it firmly with both hands, in front of her, in the approved South American female-pedestrian manner. (If you carry a backpack down there, you're advised not to wear it on your back, but to turn it around and hang it on your chest; otherwise they'll have the straps sliced off and the bag away before you know they're behind you.)

The combat computer spat out the answer almost instantly: grab the would-be blocker by the arm and use his momentum to sling him out into the roaring traffic to my right where the cars would mash him flat, step across far enough to kick the one just beyond her in the balls since he was more or less facing me, and at the same time, or as near as could be managed, whip the loaded end of the Thuggee scarf—I'd knotted some coins into a corner of it so it would be ready for action—around the neck of the nearer one facing away from me, cinching down on the silk with enough force to crack the vertebrae. I'd been practicing a bit on bedposts and other suitable targets, according to our armorer's instructions, and I was curious to see how well it would work. Then all I had to do, at my leisure, was kick the brains out of the one moaning and hugging himself on the ground and call for the disposers to haul away the garbage.

Except that while backup was available to a certain extent, it probably didn't have clout enough here to deal with several defunct youngsters who, whatever their character ratings might have been, had still qualified as Brazilian citizens. We were in a foreign land where, although they had the reputation of not being averse to a little occasional intramural homicide, they'd undoubtedly get upset if an agent of the lousy gringo CIA—all U.S. undercover agencies are considered to be CIA down there—infringed on their monopoly and indulged in killing games on their private playing field. Besides, I was supposed to be a fairly incompetent character.

No knives or guns were on display, so I had a little leeway in dealing with the situation. I tried clumsily to sidestep the punk coming at me, stumbled, and managed, kind of accidentally, to blunder right into him instead.

"Ooops, sorry, kid!" I said.

I reached out to steady him in a helpful fashion. As I pulled him to me I brought up my knee hard and he screamed, but the sound was muffled against my chest. I went down, kind of accidentally, taking him with me. I had him by his rather long hair now, over both ears, and I managed to bounce the back of his head off the pavement as we hit. His nearest associate—no knife there, either, I noted—was distracted by the scuffle, turning to look. I reached up helplessly, like a man having trouble getting to his feet.

"Gimme a hand, amigo. I'm not as young as I used to—"

When someone holds out a hand, the instinct is always to take it. He started to, and yanked back too late; I had his wrist. Off balance, he was easy to slam to the sidewalk. The same effort that had pulled him down helped to pull me up, and as I rose I managed to kick him hard in the side, kind of accidentally, driving the breath out of him. He tried to get up but couldn't, and wound up on all fours, gasping. I stepped around him, braced to tackle the third, with or without knife, but with his two friends on the ground, that one let go of the

121

purse he'd been trying to pull away from Ruth and took off with commendable speed. The one I'd kicked succeeded in rising; he fled, but more slowly, holding his side. The third one didn't know whether to nurse his head or his testicles, but he did manage to get up and scuttle away in a fragile and bowlegged fashion.

"Gee, this must be one of my clumsy days," I said. "I sure hope I didn't hurt those poor kids, bumping into them like that."

That was clowning, and Ruth, pulling herself together, gave me a pained look. I drew a long breath, standing there. It was a lovely, clear evening. Any time of day is lovely in any weather when you've survived another battle, whoever the enemy of the moment might have been, even one as young and ineffectual as today's. Here, I noted that beyond the shallows near the beach the ocean was very blue and that the offshore islands still held the sunshine that, blocked by the mountains to the west of us, no longer reached us on the shore. The beach wasn't crowded, but there were still a considerable number of bathers—at least they were wearing bathing suits. A few were actually trying the water; more were just lying around on the sand in sunbathing positions, even though there was no longer any sun. I was disappointed not to be able to spot any of the truly naughty bikinis, or monokinis, I'd been led to expect in glamorous Rio.

Quite a few people were still strolling along the promenade we were using. If any of them had noticed our little scuffle, they'd figured, just as they would have in any other city in the world, that it was our problem, thank God, not theirs. I spotted a couple of uniformed characters with submachine guns in the distance, also unconcerned. I'd seen them before, or their twins, as we waited for the traffic light to let us cross the boulevard. They were the modern Latin equivalent of the old beat cop, I suppose; but I had no impulse to rush over to them and report, breathlessly, the dastardly crime that had almost been perpetrated under their noses.

"Are you okay?" I asked.

Ruth had finished tucking in her shirt. She brushed at her denim skirt and straightened up, saying, "I will be as soon as you stop showing off and take me back to the hotel and get me something to eat. I think that's enough exercise for one evening, don't you?" She glanced down. "Incidentally, you seem to be losing a handkerchief."

I reached back and found that my Thuggee scarf, masquerading as a silk bandanna, was hanging out of my right hip pocket. I shrugged, pulled it free, folded it neatly, and tucked it back the way it had been, with one corner available for me to grab in case of need. I patted the left back pocket as a matter of routine; then I felt it again and began to laugh.

"What's so funny?"

"After all that, the little bastard got my wallet."

Ruth said, "But that's terrible. . . . Why are you laughing?"

"Well, you have to hand it to the kid. Obviously, when we collided, he grabbed the opportunity to reach around me and feel my pockets. He pulled out enough of the hanky to find out it was no use to him but the wallet was." I looked around on the ground. "He got it and it isn't here; which means that with his head cracked open, practically, and his balls screaming, he still hung onto it. A gutsy little punk."

Ruth started to speak, but stopped. Then she took my arm and we started walking back toward our hotel, a pale tower in the solid wall of tall buildings on the west side of the boulevard.

She spoke at last: "I suppose I'll get used to it eventually."

"Get used to what?"

"You. I don't know any other man who'd laugh at having his pocket picked, or admire the one who did it."

I said, "Hell, all he got was a four-ninety-five plastic job—a K Mart bargain special; I bought a couple of them so I have a spare—and ten bucks I just changed into local currency at the hotel. And what's wrong with admiring a young man who's good at his work?" I glanced at my companion. "In case you're worrying, he didn't get the disks, or my passport,

123

or my films, or my serious money, or my traveler's checks, or my credit cards. I don't have total faith in that little safe in the closet, so I'm carrying those here." I slapped a bulge under my left armpit. "A kind of shoulder-holster rig. Unfortunately it's under my shirt, so I have to practically undress to get at it. Wherefore I keep a little working capital in a cheap decoy wallet out where it's handy, and figure to lose it occasionally. I got into the habit after being cleaned out once, traveling in Mexico. Okay?"

Back at the hotel we passed up the formal downstairs dining room where we'd eaten the night before and took the elevator to the more casual restaurant on the roof.

"After all that excitement I'd better make a small detour," Ruth said as we emerged, indicating the two doors across the hall marked with stick figures, one skirted and the other trousered.

"I'll be right here," I said. "Incidentally, it's probably better if we don't talk about our little adventure."

She glanced at me. "Of course, if you think so, Matt."

Waiting, it occurred to me that if this went on, I was going to be uniquely qualified to do a scientific report on Latin American plumbing facilities, or at least the doors thereof. On the other hand, I'd better start exercising some water discipline, since in spite of picketing all these rest rooms, I seemed to have few opportunities to enter one and relieve myself without leaving the lady unguarded.

"Hey, we've got to stop meeting like this!"

It was Belinda Ackerman, in very short white shorts. Color-wise, the pale limbs she displayed would have been more attractive, at least to my taste, if they'd been a little browner, and to hell with cancer from the sky, but shape-wise, there was absolutely nothing wrong with the nicely rounded calves, and the ankles were surprisingly slim and pretty considering the plumpness elsewhere. She saw me looking and didn't mind: a girl would have to be fairly dumb to wear shorts that short if she objected to having her legs admired.

"Did you hear about Grace?" she asked.

124

"No, what about Grace?"

I still didn't have our whole tour group quite straight in my head, but I remembered that Grace Priestly was the gray-haired older woman I'd seen with Belinda and photographed, during one of my rest-room vigils. Husband: Herman. Bald. Glasses. Texas oil. Not on the official list. Belinda was eager to pass along the news.

"She and Herman went to look at that jewelry store around the corner, Stern's I guess it's called, and then took a walk around those funny little streets back there. I guess she was a little careless with her purse and all of a sudden it was empty. They'd slashed it open at the bottom so everything fell out. Of course, she'd left the important things in her room safe, the way we were told to, but she lost some money and a nice compact, she said, and they ruined a perfectly good leather bag, Mark Cross or something."

I said, "So Annie wasn't just whistling Dixie."

"You'd think with all the uniforms and machine guns around, folks would be safe on the street."

I couldn't help noticing that her purple silk shirt, loosely knotted in front, didn't conceal much more of her plump white breasts than the little pants did of her plump white legs. She bounced away through the appropriate door, and pretty soon Ruth came out to join me, looking neat and ladylike by comparison.

The rooftop restaurant had white garden-type furniture surrounding a small swimming pool—more a paddling and wading pool, I judged from the fact that a slim, dark young girl in a flowered one-piece bathing suit, with soaked black hair streaming down her back, wasn't even wet to the waist when she stood up in the middle. Of course, I could have gauged the water depth from her boyfriend, splashing play-fully beside her, but she made a more interesting measuring stick.

"Pretty," Ruth said, the first time she'd spoken since we'd sat down.

"Only pretty now, but she'll be a knockout senhorinha in a couple of years," I said.

125

Ruth said, "As a matter of fact, senhorinha is correct for the Portuguese in Portugal, but here in Brazil they give it a few twists of their own and their word is senhorita, very close to the Spanish."

I said, "I'll be happy when we get to Argentina and a language I'm familiar with, even though I don't claim to speak it much. Shall we order?" The waiter was hovering around us suggestively.

"That enormous fruit plate they're eating next door looks good," Ruth said.

"I'm a meat-and-potatoes man myself, but after the feed we had at lunch, I guess I'll go for the melons, too, or whatever they are. How about a drink, or are you back on the abstention kick?" She wasn't. Having settled all that to the waiter's satisfaction, I waited for him to leave and said deliberately: "Let's talk a little business. Five disks, you said earlier. Including the one you're carrying, right?"

She hesitated; then she said, "Wrong. I'm not carrying it any longer."

I looked at her for a moment, noting the small gleam of triumph in her eyes. She, too, like the kid pickpocket, had put one over on the cocky professional. I drew a long breath.

"You've had three chances to unload it since you left your room," I said. "You could have slipped it to the waiter just now while I was looking at the menu. You could have got rid of it in the rest room. Maybe somebody was waiting for you in there; or maybe Belinda Ackerman, who went in after you . . ."

"I wouldn't trust that roly-poly, blond, man-eater with a used Kleenex!"

I laughed and stopped laughing, watching her. "And then there's the possibility that the abortive robbery on the beach was a put-up job to let you make the transfer, in which case you are a damn fool, Mrs. Steiner. Pulling a stunt like that with a bodyguard in attendance could easily get somebody killed. At the very least it shows you don't mind making your escort look like an idiot."

She licked her lips. "I know and I'm sorry . I didn't realize. . . . I guess I've just seen too many movies with actors being excruciatingly clever, just like that, and nobody getting hurt.'' Ruth grimaced. ''Well, you don't have to worry about it happening again. Even if we thought we could get away, plausibly, with another phony mugging attempt, I have a feeling that volunteers are going to be very scarce after what happened to two of those boys, even if you made it look very clumsy and accidental. But in the confusion I did manage to slip my little package to the one who ran away unharmed.''

I said, ''So there are four pickups left to go. Presumably that means four cities, unless you've arranged to double up somewhere. Which four?''

She hesitated, drew a long breath, and said, ''I suppose, after the dumb trick I just pulled, I owe you. . . . All right. In chronological order: Buenos Aires, Argentina. Well, I already mentioned that. Santiago, Chile. Lima, Peru. Quito, Ecuador.''

I said, ''I can see why this tour was selected for you. It takes you exactly where you want to go.''

''And a few places I don't, like Iguassu Falls. Ugh.''

''Why ugh?''

''It's a hole in the jungle full of biting insects, and I've already seen it once. Richard took me when we were stationed here. I guess it's spectacular, all that water falling off all those cliffs, but once is enough.''

I said, ''My folks took me to Niagara as a kid, and just like you I figure, you've seen one waterfall, you've seen 'em all. And then, if I remember the schedule correctly, after Lima and before Quito, two cities where you have contacts waiting, there's Cuzco, Peru, from which we make a day trip by rail to the ruins at Machu Picchu and back.'' I shook my head ruefully. ''If you don't have business there, I'll be happy to pass up that excursion. Judging by the pictures I've seen, those damn Incas, or whoever they were, built their stone city on top of a mountain peak with thousand-foot cliffs all around; and you know how I am about high places.''

She laughed. ''Well, I'm not much for archaeology, myself. We can probably find something interesting to do in

Cuzco while the rest of them are riding little trains around the Andes and chasing dead Incas around the rocks.'' It would have been all right if she hadn't blushed.

I mean, she hadn't really said anything outrageous. There were undoubtedly, in Cuzco, interesting native markets and interesting souvenir stores galore, not to mention interesting Indians with interesting beasts of burden—Peru was the land of the llama, I recalled—and interesting museums and old churches. A fascinating place, according to the tour literature supplied us, Cuzco, Peru, eleven thousand feet in the air. There was absolutely no need for a girl to blush merely because she'd suggested that the city might have possibilities for a man and woman who'd deserted their tour group to spend a day together.

But her face did turn quite pink, betraying the thought that had come to her. I realized that the same thought hadn't been far from my mind. At least I'd become sensitized, let's say, to the point where I was looking hard for provocative bikinis, and very much aware of shapely legs and plump white breasts, and unnaturally intrigued by—if you want to call that unnatural—a juvenile senhorita in a snug, wet, one-piece swimsuit. What I mean to say is that traveling with a member of the opposite sex who's neither senile nor deformed, you can ignore the biological realities only so long before the pressure starts to build.

The waiter came to the rescue, placing our drinks before us. Ruth reached for hers as if it were the last life preserver on a sinking ocean liner and, for a recent nondrinker, did a good, fast job of inhaling about half of it.

"Did you hear about the Priestlys?" she asked without looking at me. "Belinda told me in the rest room that Grace had had her purse slashed. I didn't tell her about our little experience. . . ."

We discussed our tour companions extensively during dinner; they made a nice, safe subject. The melons, some of which I didn't recognize, were excellent, and the pineapple was a different fruit, sweet and tender, from the tart, stringy stuff served in all states of the U.S. except Hawaii. Then we were in the elevator and getting out at the ninth floor. I made a point of checking the rooms meticulously, both rooms, before I let Ruth come in. Then I beckoned her forward, into her room, and closed and locked the door behind her. We stood facing each other. She drew a long breath, looking up at me. Her lips were full and moist, and I wondered why it had taken me so long to realize that she was a very pretty girl.

"I . . . I'm a grieving widow," she said. "I really am, you know. I shouldn't even think of . . ."

"Mark wouldn't want you to grieve too long," I said.

She licked her lips childishly. "I don't know what . . . I thought I hated you. You hit me so hard with the butt of that big gun."

I reached out to touch the side of her head gently. "But it's all right now, isn't it?"

"Yes," she said, and suddenly she was in my arms, "it's all right now." But she held back for a moment. "You're supposed to take my glasses off before you kiss me, darling."

So I took the glasses off her, and moments later, some other things off her, and we determined in the most convincing way possible that everything really was all right now.

Chapter 14

THE scream brought me out of a sound sleep. Instinctively I grabbed the little knife I'd tucked under the pillow as I joined her in the bed. Kicking myself free of the bedclothes, I hit the carpet with a thump, rolled to get well clear, and on my stomach, spent a moment getting my diminutive weapon open two-handed, since it hadn't been designed for fast-draw work.

Actually it was a Swiss army knife about the size of the boy-scout knife I'd carried as a kid, but better equipped. This little red-handled implement had flat screwdrivers in two sizes, one also serving as a can opener while the other pried caps off bottles; in addition it had a Phillips screwdriver, a punch, a toothpick, and a pair of tweezers. It even had two blades, an inch-and-a-half job for fine whittling and a two-and-a-quarter-incher for heavy carving. Two and a quarter inches of steel isn't much, but it beats no steel at all, and the little slicer had the tremendous advantage that, with all its innocent-looking tools, it hadn't upset the airport inspectors a bit, either in Albuquerque or Miami. Well, they'd passed the Thuggee scarf also. Any sensible assassin who doesn't insist on packing a four-pound .44 Magnum with an eight-inch barrel through the gates won't find airport inspections much of a hindrance to his trade.

I'd taken my time with the knife because there had been another whimpering cry from the bed and I'd realized what was going on and felt a little ridiculous crawling around on the rug with a miniature stabber in my hand. But I finished opening the knife. You don't want to get into the habit of stopping halfway for any reason; the next time, that sharp little blade, open, might make the difference between life and death. Then I snapped it shut, rose, and dropped the knife on the chair toward which I'd tossed my clothes a few hours earlier, hitting with some, missing with others in my breathless haste, that contrasted strongly with the fine relaxation I now felt in spite of my sudden awakening. There was also, of course, a small sense of guilt, not involving the girl in the bed, but another woman with whom I'd shared a similar breathless moment not too long ago. I told myself that Madeleine would have laughed heartily at the thought that she'd expect me to be faithful beyond death. . . .

Ruth was thrashing around desperately in an effort to escape an invisible danger. "Oh, take them away, take them away!" she moaned.

I went around to that side of the bed and managed to knock something off the bedside table as I fumbled for the light switch. It turned out to be a fat paperback called *Trumpet in the Dust* by a best-selling novelist I'd heard of, named Johnson D'Arcy; the cover showed a terrified young lady fleeing a dark manor house that had light in one window. I guess I was still half-asleep; instinctively I picked up the book and replaced it tidily on the table before attending to the lady in distress, taking her gently by the shoulders.

"Easy now, take it easy," I said. Her eyes came open suddenly. "Dogs?" I asked.

She licked her lips and nodded. "They were just about to catch me again. Their teeth were all bloody. That poor man had tried to shoot them but it was dark and they were coming so fast and he missed and his friends were shooting from the edge of the field but they were too far away. . . ."

She shuddered. I sat down on the edge of the bed and held her. "Tell me."

"I don't want to talk about it!" After a little she drew a long, shuddering breath. "Well, all right. I suppose it's better to talk it out. Locked up in that room, I heard a sound in the middle of the night, and there he was, picking the padlock that held the bars shut, it was kind of a swinging grill.

131

He got me out through the window. We sneaked away, trying not to make any noise; then we ran. I never knew his name. I never really saw his face; it was night and he was in camouflage and all smeared with black. He said some friends were waiting for us with a car on the other side of the field. He hadn't expected dogs; he thought we had it made until we heard them barking. Then somebody turned them loose and we could hear them behind us, coming up fast. They weren't barking any longer, just rushing after us silently. When they got close, he told me to keep running and took out his gun and turned to deal with them, but it was too dark, like I said, and he missed, and his friends were shooting from the edge of the field, but they were too far away. The dogs charged him and knocked him down. Two of them. Well, I already said that, or didn't I?''

She was holding me tightly, her voice muffled against my chest. Neither of us had any clothes on. Of course, if I'd been a true gentleman comforting a troubled lady, I wouldn't have been aware of her nakedness, only of her distress.

She went on: ''I just stood there. I suppose I could have tried to find a club or something to beat them off; at least I could have taken the opportunity to run like he'd told me while they were still busy with . . . with him, but it was a big open field in which they were bound to catch me. So I just . . . just waited for them to come and kill me, too. And they came up to me and sniffed at me all around, later I found bloody smears on my jeans, ugh! I stood perfectly still. Then I heard the whistle—it was supposed to be supersonic, I think, but I have very good hearing—and the dogs started whining, and the whistle blew again, and they turned and trotted away.''

''Dobermans?''

She shook her head. ''Dobermans are the sleek, lean, dark ones, aren't they? I don't know much about dogs, but these were heavier. Big, stocky, yellow-brown brutes.'' She cleared her throat. ''I must have fainted. The next thing I knew I was in an ambulance. They caught some of the men who'd held me prisoner, but they never found the dogs or the old man who'd handled them.''

I glanced at her sharply. "How did you know he was an old man? Did he let you see his face?"

She shook her head and hesitated, thinking back. "Well, he was there with the dogs when they carried me into that house where they kept me. He *looked* old, a little bent and slow. Still fairly tall, but he looked as if he'd been taller, you know how they start kind of shrinking. Of course he was all in black and wearing a ski mask like all the others, so I never saw his face. He seemed to be quite fond of his dogs; you could tell by the way he touched them. He wore a big green stone on his left hand. He had spotty hands; that was another giveaway. He didn't say anything, of course, nobody said a word to me the whole time I was there, but I assumed he was showing me the dogs so I'd realize there was no point in trying to escape."

The information she'd given me made me forget, for a moment, that I was holding an attractive girl with no clothes on to whom I'd just made love. It seemed incredible that wealthy and influential and aging Gregorio Vasquez, originally of Colombia—wherever his current residence might be—would travel clear to New England to risk his neck supervising a minor abduction. On the other hand, it was equally incredible that a gang of kidnappers would burden itself with a shaky senior citizen unless he had a lot of authority. . . . Well, if the two-dog man was actually *El Viejo*, it was a hopeful sign. It meant that he didn't just hide in an inaccessible aerie handing out orders; he could occasionally be found taking part in the action, just like Mac, who sometimes gets antsy sitting in that office chair and joins us peons hoeing the fields.

Ruth said, "I'm sorry I woke you."

"Are you all right now?"

She hesitated, and her arms tightened around me. She laughed again, softly. "Well, there's only one sure way to find out, isn't there. . . ?"

In the morning, with shafts of sunlight lancing through the gaps between the heavy draperies at the windows, I left her asleep among the rumpled bedclothes, looking small and soft and young. The other bed in her room remained undisturbed, as did the two in my room. You might say we enjoyed a superfluity of beds. I suppose I could have mussed one of mine in the interest of respectability, but it seemed a waste of time and effort. Hotel employees aren't easy to fool about what guest sleeps where, and I saw no reason to try. We'd already resigned ourselves to the fact that our fellow tour members had had us living in sin even before we were.

I called down for breakfast for two and sat down to scribble a hasty report before shaving. I was dressed and tying my shoes when room service knocked on the door. The meal came on a rolling drop-leaf cart that the waiter unfolded to make a neat little formal table with a white tablecloth; he then uncovered and unwrapped and arranged things very carefully, including a vase with a single white flower, don't ask me the name. It was nice to see a man who took his profession seriously. There's another kind of room-service waiter, who shoves a loaded tray at you and runs. The man paused at the door and looked back.

"Can I bring the senhor anything else? Some ice, perhaps?"

Although I have, as I've already indicated, been known to take a drink upon occasion, I don't need ice at 7:30 in the morning even in countries where I trust the water, soft or hard. However, "ice" was the word that had been chosen, perhaps because somebody figured that down here south of the equator, but pretty far north of Antarctica, ice wouldn't figure in normal conversations often enough to cause confusion. I could see some objections to the choice, but I hadn't been asked. The bureaucratic geniuses who set up these operations never ask.

"Ice, what's that in Portuguese?" I asked. We were supposed to go through some linguistic nonsense to confirm identification.

"*Gelo*, senhor. It is very close to the Spanish *hielo*."

"I've been expecting you," I said. "As a matter of fact, the stuff you're to pick up is in the ice bucket in the bathroom.

134

It seemed like a suitable place for it, under the circumstances. What do I call you?''

"Armando will do.''

He was a slim, moderately tall, middle-aged gent in black pants, a white long-sleeved shirt, and a black bow tie. The formal tie, the thick, smooth black hair, a small black mustache, and a dark poker face gave him the look of a rather snooty headwaiter condescending to do a little work below his station.

I said, "Sure, Armando. Are you local or will I be seeing more of you on this tour?''

"I have your schedule; you will see me again. We will continue to make certain that your hotel rooms are clean of electronic surveillance and explosive surprises, as well as possible. It will have to be a hasty check each time, since the hotel desk seldom knows very far in advance which members of a tour will be assigned to which rooms. I suggest, therefore, that after being given your keys, you delay a few minutes in each new hotel before using them. You almost caught our security specialist yesterday.''

"Sorry about that," I said. "I'll take us to the bar for a drink next time.''

"Of course, the limited time available is not altogether a handicap. It reduces the enemy's opportunities as well," Armando said. After a moment he went on: "Elsewhere, under normal circumstances, we will continue to assume that you are capable of protecting yourself and the lady without assistance, as you did last night; however, if we see anything very elaborate being prepared for you, we will let you know. Incidentally, the three young hoodlums you encountered are known to operate around these hotels; it seems unlikely that their attempt to rob you was anything but a coincidence.''

I saw no reason to tell him that Ruth had indicated otherwise. I said, "You'll find a computer diskette with the films. Mrs. Steiner tells me it's a copy of one she was given yesterday. She says she's scrambled it in some computerized way so we can't read it without her password. She's just giving it to us for safekeeping—one copy for me, one for Washington—in case her original goes astray. Even if Washington should manage to read it, she hopes that it, and the ones to come, will not be released for action until she's ready to take advantage of the publicity that will result. Well, it's all in my covering report, if anybody can read my hasty scribbles."

"I will transmit your suggestions orally as well."

"I'll want a gun at Iguassu Falls."

"Any particular kind of gun? We don't have a great selection. They are quite strict about guns here."

"Any old clunker will do," I said.

"Ammunition?"

"One cylinder or magazine will be enough."

"Very well." He stepped into the bathroom and came out holding a white plastic bucket by the swinging gold handle— well, it looked like gold. He opened the hall door and looked back, speaking rather loudly: "Just one moment, senhor. I will return with the ice you requested. . . ."

When I entered Ruth's room, the bed we'd shared was empty, and the window draperies had been pulled aside to let the daylight in. I could hear her in the bathroom. I tried to tell her that food awaited her, but with water running she didn't hear me through the closed door, so I crossed the room and knocked.

"Breakfast, ma'am," I called.

She opened the door, holding a comb and wearing a short beach coat, striped blue and white, with a belt that she hadn't got around to fastening around her. As I'd already discovered, her body, while constructed on economical lines, wasn't really skinny anywhere. She covered herself without any haste or embarrassment, reminding me that although she sometimes looked like a kid, she'd buried two husbands, so she was used to having a man around in the morning. We faced each other for a moment, assessing our new relationship, but we were both experienced enough to know that it wasn't something to be talked about.

"Breakfast is getting cold," I said.

"Yes, darling, I'll be with you in a minute," she said.

136

Chapter 15

SUGARLOAF was a bitch. Getting to the top of the tall, rounded peak, I discovered, didn't involve just one cable car, but two, with an uneasy transfer stop on an intermediate knob of rock. Both cars were crammed with sightseers. Trying to stay protectively between Ruth and the other passengers wasn't easy, but my bodyguard duties helped to distract me from the fact that we were hanging by a fragile thread—well, wire cable—over a bottomless abyss. Well, almost bottomless. In my next incarnation I suppose I'll compensate by becoming an intrepid airman or mountain climber, or maybe even a steeplejack. It'll be a welcome change.

The view of Rio from the top of Sugarloaf was spectacular, but I'd already seen one spectacular view of Rio from the top of Corcovado. I didn't need another, thanks. The only view that really interested me, aside from the sight of ground that was reasonably horizontal, was that of Spooky Three lurking near the lower terminal when we finally made it back down there. She was wearing the beige pantsuit I'd seen more than once already; but although it was neatly pressed today and made her look quite respectable in her healthy tomboy way, it was hardly an invisibility costume. The tall boy with whom she'd lunched the day before in the restaurant with the smoky swords, Spooky Five, was acting as backup and, in jeans and T-shirt and windbreaker, was only a little harder to spot.

Next day we were expertly packaged, labeled, and shipped by air to Iguassu Falls, flying over a mat of dense green jungle through which silvery rivers gleamed. It was raining a little when we set down on the Iguassu airstrip, a change from the bright Rio sunshine. We were met by a bus with a driver and a smiling girl guide, not quite pretty but close enough, an improvement over dour little Arturo. They took us to the Itaipu Hydroelectric Plant on the Paraná River and drove us across the dam, which was new, high, and impressive, with a lot of water roaring down the spillway and throwing up clouds of mist. We spent about thirty seconds in Paraguay across the river, turning the bus around, then we returned to Brazil and, in the administration building, were shown a film of the dam's construction.

The rest rooms, that came in handy after the bouncing bus ride and the dull half-hour sit, were marked MASCULINO and FEMININO. Photographing the toilet traffic as usual while waiting for Ruth to emerge, I had a little chat with Belinda Ackerman, in white jeans that were under considerable tension and a purple silk shirt that, by way of contrast, didn't provide much restraint. She thought it was wonderful the way I seemed to find photogenic subjects everywhere.

Then onward to the Brazilian national park at Iguassu Falls and a picturesque old pink hotel with white trimmings. I didn't think much of our accommodations as far as security was concerned—I get nervous in ground-floor rooms with big windows and lush vegetation outside providing convenient cover for any approaching malefactor—but they were carefully done in old-fashioned style. There were tall, black, lathe-turned bedposts and old engravings on the walls. At least they looked enough like old engravings to pass muster if you didn't look too hard. The bathrooms were frankly modern, however, neatly tiled and offering all toilet conveniences including bidets.

I spent some time in my room organizing the rudimentary location notes I'd made to go with the day's take of pictures. Finally, I removed the half-used roll still in the camera, added it to the collection, put everything into the ice bucket provided with the room, and loaded up with fresh film. Shortly afterward I heard a light code knock on the hall door. I opened to admit Armando. Good timing.

"Are the accommodations to your satisfaction, senhor? Can I bring you anything, some ice perhaps?"

He was in just about the same black-and-white waiter get-up I'd seen him wearing last. I wondered how he'd managed the transition to this hotel, but money is very effective down there, as elsewhere; and his position wasn't necessarily official. No guests and very few employees are likely to challenge a man who marches through a sizable hostelry dressed pretty much like the rest of the staff and acts as if he knows where he's going and what he's going to do when he gets there.

"Ice, that's *gelo* in Portuguese, isn't it?" They like us to maintain the ID nonsense even after it's become unnecessary and ridiculous. "Yes, we could use some ice, thanks. The bucket's in the bathroom."

He glanced at the connecting door and lowered his voice: "I have been instructed to inform you that a preliminary check has been run on the credentials of all members of your tour; they seem to be what they claim. The computer diskette you sent could not be read by our people; it has been passed along to the proper technical section for analysis."

So my fellow travelers were all genuine, at least as far as a preliminary check was concerned, which didn't necessarily mean they were harmless. And Ruth's computer had apparently managed to cook up a reasonably impenetrable code.

"What about the pix?" I asked Armando.

"Excuse me?"

Apparently his English wasn't quite up to my photo slang. I said, "Pix. Pictures. Photographs. The color negatives I sent in. Have they got around to developing and printing them yet?"

He said, "Pix. I will have to remember that. Yes, the pix have been processed; and the results seem to be quite interesting."

"Don't keep me in suspense."

"There were one hundred and forty negatives on the four rolls submitted. Among those images, I am informed, two faces reoccur with statistically significant frequency, one male, one female. That is, of course, excluding the members of your group.''

I studied the prints he gave me and said, ''Yes, those two have been doing a pretty conspicuous job of surveillance. I saw the big blond guy for the first time having lunch with the girl yesterday, and I saw him again up on Sugarloaf today. The dame has been following me around for over a month. She had three helpers back in Santa Fe, but I haven't seen any of them since we left the States. Maybe she left them behind and, when she got down here, picked up Blondie as a substitute.''

Armando said, ''We have no information on the man as yet. We do have an identification of the woman.''

''Great, who is she?''

''Apparently she has no record as a criminal or as an international agent of any kind; no matching photograph was found in any files we would normally access. I am informed that her identity probably would have remained a mystery if one of our female colleagues hadn't come into a certain office on another errand, and noticed the prints on the desk, and asked what in the world we were doing with photographs of Pat Weatherford. Apparently our lady agent was a tennis aficionado, the kind that can tell you precisely who won Wimbledon in what year, against whom, and with what score. Patricia Weatherford seems to be a typical wealthy young Yankee woman, riding horses, sailing boats, and flying airplanes. However, her *afición* is tennis. She is a player of professional caliber. She made a brilliant debut as a young girl, and great things were expected of her, but apparently she never quite lived up to her early promise. Our agent who identified her expressed the opinion that Miss Weatherford could have become a truly top-ranking player if she had been a little hungrier and worked a little harder; but prize money, of course, meant nothing to her, not with the Weatherford fortune behind her.''

I said, ''My God! *Those* Weatherfords?''

What I knew about the Weatherfords was what everybody knew: their wealth was old railroad money multiplied a good many times by modern manipulation. A while back I spent a little time in Newport, Rhode Island. One of the local landmarks was the magnificent old Weatherford summer mansion, still in family hands. I wondered what the hell a Weatherford scion—well, scioness—was up to, following me around two continents.

"Anything else?" I asked.

"It may or may not be significant, but another reason Miss Weatherford never quite made it to the top in tennis seems to be that instead of dedicating herself wholly to her sport she spends much of her time, as well as her money, crusading for various causes. Ban the bomb. Equalize the women. Preserve the jungle. Protect the animals. Purify the water. Save the ozone." Armando shrugged. "She seems to be a member of a great many organizations, none particularly dangerous as far as can be determined. Some are feminist groups like NOW, of course, but she also belongs to ASPCA, MPS, Greenpeace . . . the list covers most of a typewritten page, and I did not memorize it all. Here's a dossier on the girl, complete with her worthy affiliations. No unworthy ones seem to be recorded."

"No mention of Vasquez, eh?" I glanced at the paper he'd given me. "What's MPS? It sounds like a disease. Massive Paranoia Syndrome?"

"Along with several others, it has not yet been identified; they are working on it." He raised his voice. "I will bring your ice, senhor."

After he'd left for good, I opened the ice bucket he'd taken away and then returned to me, and found the gun I'd asked for. It was a smallish automatic pistol, a fairly beat-up Browning equivalent of the .380 Llama I'd once taken from Ruth. Well, I'd said any clunker would do. While I was keeping my target firmly in mind, I wasn't expecting to find him within pistol range very soon. I either had to learn where he was and go there, or get him to come to me, somehow. In the meantime I just wanted to demonstrate that I took my bodyguarding seriously. The gun's magazine held thirteen cartridges. As I finished checking out the weapon Ruth knocked on the connecting door and came in. She paused briefly, seeing the pistol; then she came to stand in front of me.

"Are we expecting trouble?"

"If we weren't, you'd be taking this tour alone, wouldn't you?"

I eased the magazine into the butt, slapped it home, and tucked the weapon away inside my shirt. Ruth was still standing before me. Something in her attitude caught my attention at last. One of her hands was held behind her; and she looked like a little girl bringing Daddy a secret present she wasn't quite sure he'd like.

"Matt," she said, bringing the hand into sight. It held another pair of cute little three-and-a-half-inch computer diskettes. "For your collection. And Washington's."

I maintained a poker face as I examined the two disks. It seemed inadvisable to show annoyance merely because the perverse lady who'd been put into my charge liked to play tricks on her stupid bodyguard. I read the hand-printing on the visible label: *MS-X2 (Ch. 27–34)*. Eight more chapters accounted for.

I spoke carefully: "I thought you said your next contact would be made in Buenos Aires. . . . Oh, hell, don't look so guilty. Sit down. Be comfortable. Have a drink." After supplying our liquid needs and seating myself, I raised my glass to her. "Sneaky, aren't you?"

"Matt, I—"

"Let me guess," I said. "I kind of twisted your arm and got you to tell me that the next rendezvous was to be in Buenos Aires. You got scared that I'd watch you too closely when we got there and learn more than you wanted me to, or call in some help and set a trap of some kind, so you got in touch with the gal in B.A. and told her to hop a plane and rendezvous with you where I wouldn't be expecting a meeting."

She glanced at me sharply. "How do you know it was a woman?"

I said, "Nothing was delivered to you here in the hotel.

142

Our rooms were checked by friendlies right after the keys were issued; that's why you and I stalled around sampling that lousy local sugarcane tipple they were handing out free in the lobby. So nobody could have left anything for you here, they'd have spotted it, and you've had no visitors. The rest room at the Itaipu power plant is the only other place I haven't been as close to you as a Band-Aid since we left Rio. And you didn't go into the *masculino*. Ergo, your contact was feminine. Logic.'' I looked at her for a moment. ''You've got three more contacts ahead, Ruth. They'll come a lot more easily, and safely, if you take a deep breath and decide to trust me.''

I always feel silly and naive talking about trust these cynical days, but you've got to at least give it a chance occasionally, or you'll never find it when you need it.

Ruth drew a long breath. ''There are . . . things you don't know, Matt. I wish . . .'' She stopped. After a little, she said, changing the subject deliberately, ''I saw that woman in the lobby. The one with freckles you call Spooky Three. I wonder what her real name is.''

I asked, ''Do you ever watch tennis on TV?''

She frowned, puzzled by the apparently irrelevant question. ''Tennis? I'm not much for watching TV sports unless I'm very bored or sick in bed. What about tennis?''

''I've just been informed that the gal's name is Patricia Weatherford. She's a fairly well known tennis pro; she's also a very wealthy girl.''

Ruth looked startled. ''Oh, *those* Weatherfords.''

''Right. She also seems to be mixed up with a lot of do-good organizations, some Lib-type, but mostly of an ecological bent. I can't see the significance of that at the moment, but there may be some. Here.'' I passed her the paper Armando had left me. ''Do these outfits mean anything to you? NOW and Greenpeace, all right, everybody's heard of those, but what's a group called EGG?''

Ruth laughed. ''I just happen to know that one, it's the Earth Government Group. FOR is Friends of the Redwoods. SOSO is Save Our Sea Otters. But what's MPS?''

"If you find out, let me know."

"Well, you've got to give Miss Weatherford credit," Ruth said. "At least, unlike a lot of wealthy people, she's not throwing her money away on yachts and fast cars and expensive clothes. Apparently she's trying to save the world or some small part of it."

I grimaced. "That's exactly what I'm afraid of. I'd rather tackle a dozen wicked criminals bent on destroying the world than one self-righteous crusader determined to save it. And I wonder how this super-idealistic, world-saving dame can justify her association with a world destroyer like Gregorio Vasquez?"

Ruth hesitated. "Maybe it's blackmail. Maybe he's got something on her, like cocaine. Do they test those tennis pros for drugs the way they do football or baseball players?"

I shook my head. "I don't know much about the sport, but I don't think so. However, the Weatherford doesn't look like a druggie, for what it's worth. And I do know that her associate, the grenade-happy gal I killed in my backyard, was quite clean. There was an autopsy. Which, come to think of it, if Weatherford is clean also, would seem to indicate that I was wrong about her and her friends belonging to the *Compañeros de la Hoja*, who apparently consider coke the food of the gods and use it in their sacred ceremonies." I frowned. "It begins to look as if the *Compañeros* are one outfit, call them *El Viejo*'s professional soldiers, and the Spookies are just auxiliary troops, amateurs, that the old man uses for routine jobs like surveillance."

"But what are Miss Weatherford and her Spooky friends after if they're not involved with drugs?"

"We know what Frederica Tolson was after at the end," I said. "But I doubt that her motives are typical."

"Tolson?"

"The gal in my backyard. She may have had some fine public reasons for being there with her bag of bombs, although it's hard to see what they could be—as far as I'm aware, neither Madeleine Rustin, nor Happy, nor I, had been wrecking any ecology lately—but there seems to be no doubt

144

that privately the girl was simply avenging herself on Madeleine for spoiling her face. That's presumably why she accompanied the *Compañeros* on their commando raid against my mini-estate, instead of sticking to peaceful surveillance like her friends.''

Ruth frowned. ''Who was the girl, anyway?''

''Her father is a prominent Milwaukee surgeon. He couldn't believe she'd really tried to kill me, I just had to be lying. He was going to have my scalp, until it was pointed out to him that regardless of my veracity, there was no doubt that his darling Freddie had been packing a shopping bag full of illegal army-surplus whiz-bangs, one of which she'd already used to commit a murder when I nailed her to the fence—two murders as far as I'm concerned, but the legislature and the legal profession don't seem to feel about dogs the way I do.'' I drew a long breath and went on: ''Anyway, rather than have his little girl remembered as a bomb-throwing nut, Dr. Tolson dropped his Helm vendetta. But apparently, while he's not in the Weatherford class, he isn't hurting for money and wasn't stingy with his Freddie girl. So what are these well-heeled dames and their male friends up to, teaming up with Gregorio Vasquez's crude, coke-sniffing stranglers?'' After a moment I shrugged. ''Well, I suppose it will all become clear eventually, if we live that long. Who was the B.A. girl?''

''What?''

''Your contact from Buenos Aires, whom you actually met in Itaipu?''

Ruth hesitated and said reluctantly, ''Her name is Leonora Otero, known as Lenny. Argentinian. She's a journalist with whom Mark worked several times. I met her once; quite a handsome lady. It's been a few years and I don't know how well she's aged; mostly what I saw of her today was a pair of high-heeled black pumps in the adjoining booth; but the ankles were still nice. Black nylons, in case you're interested. Her relationship with Mark was basically professional—if he needed political information from Argentina she'd help him out—but in years past he may very well have slept with her on occasion. He never said and I never asked. His sex life before we met was none of my business. But I lucked out there in Buenos Aires. I had to work much harder in some other cities and sit on the phone for hours checking various possibilities; but in B.A., Lenny was the first person I called and she *had* received a little package from Mark not too long ago. She was glad to be rid of it.''

"She must have been, to fly several hundred miles just to go to the can. . . .''

I stopped, as somebody knocked on the hall door. It wasn't just polite knuckle rapping, it was hefty, imperative fist pounding. I got up hastily and gestured toward the connecting door.

"Get into your room, quickly.'' I took the disks from the table and held them out. "Here, take them and hide them. Listen if you can and use your judgment about joining the party.''

She took the disks. "Matt, be careful.''

"You too. Now get out of here.''

The pounding came again. An accented male voice said: "Open please the door!''

I hurried Ruth through the connecting doors and waited until she'd closed and locked the one on her side; then I went to the hall door, that was rattling under a new assault.

"Be so good as to open immediate!''

"Coming! Don't break it down,'' I said.

I turned the latch and stepped back. The door was slammed open violently. The man who stood there was a big surprise. The accent I'd heard and the demanding, arrogant hammering had had me thinking in terms of hotel security or local cops, but he was neither uniformed nor Latin: a stocky older man with rather thick silver-gray hair that had obviously been combed back earlier, straight and smooth, but was disordered now, hanging in untidy wings on either side of his flushed and angry face. He was wearing handsome yellow slacks and a blue short-sleeved sports shirt open at the neck, very colorful, but one shirttail was escaping from the expensive pleated pants. I had a little trouble dredging up his first name. I hadn't really spoken to him except to say hello since the tour's inaugural dinner, and Ruth had had more dealings with him that night than I had. However, I had no trouble remembering his last name: Ackerman. Mr. Roger Ackerman, of Wall Street and Long Island, apparently more than a little drunk.

"Where'sh Belinda, you bashtard?" he demanded, slurring his words badly. He glared around the room. Finding it empty except for me, he marched up to me, letting the hall door close behind him. "Did you really shink I wouldn't notish the way you and my wife have been looking at eash other, the way you've been meeting and laughing in dark cornersh—laughing at her shtuffy, impotent old hushband no doubt! Where'sh she hiding, you bashtard, in the bashroom?"

He moved that way unsteadily. I started to get angry; then I shrugged and went past him to fling open the door and let him have his look. Who wants to argue with a jealous drunk?

"See for yourself," I said. "No Belinda."

Then the back of my head seemed to explode, sending a strange, electric, tingling sensation down my arms and legs. As the fireworks died away the tiled bathroom floor came up to meet me.

Chapter 16

WHEN I began recording environmental data with some accuracy once more, lying on the floor, I became aware that my drunken attacker, instead of kicking me to a pulp as might have been expected, was kneeling beside me to frisk me expertly. He'd got the beat-up prop gun from my waistband, so it had already served its purpose, and he was slipping the cheap decoy wallet from my hip pocket: the spare I'd put into service after being robbed in Rio. I reflected hazily that I seemed to be having a hard time hanging on to K Mart's bargain plastic. But this was hardly the behavior of an older husband, mad with booze and jealousy, punishing the man he thought to be his young wife's lover.

I suppose I should have felt good about it, although it's hard to feel good about anything involving a battered skull. But I'd firmly resisted the temptation to grab either or both of the two Spookies whom *El Viejo*, or whoever was running this operation for him, had persisted in waving under my nose. By the looks of them, my shadowers were by no means tough professionals hardened to interrogation; it should have been easy enough to open up wealthy Miss Weatherford or her handsome sidekick, or both. I could probably have made them eager to tell me everything they knew, and after the way I'd been haunted by their persistent outfit for weeks, not to mention their involvement in what had happened to Madeleine and Mark and Happy, it would have been a pleasure to work them over. The trouble was that they probably didn't have any information worth extracting. They wouldn't have been paraded so openly and vulnerably before me if they knew anything that would lead me to Gregorio Vasquez.

I'd figured that if I was patient, somebody more important in the hierarchy, and better informed, would reveal himself. Now he had. All I had to do was simply turn the tables on him and beat the information out of him. Simply.

Finding nothing of importance in the wallet, Ackerman patted me in an exploratory way and located the concealed shoulder-holster rig in which I carried my documents and serious money. He unfastened my shirt and, rather than go to the trouble of undressing me extensively to remove the underarm purse, just pulled it around to where he could get at it, unzipped the various compartments, found what he wanted, and making a little breathy sound of satisfaction, removed it. Then I heard him close the zippers neatly again. I felt him put the money holster back under my armpit and pull my shirt more or less into place. He even tucked the wallet back into my hip pocket before rising. A tidy man.

"You can open your eyes now, Mr. Helm," he said, without any alcoholic speech impediments. "Sit up if you wish. I hope your head isn't giving you too much pain."

I sat up with a great dramatic effort, groaning pitifully. I saw that Ackerman was rising and tucking a blackjack into his hip pocket; he'd known I wasn't altogether out and he'd been ready for me to try something. I was glad I hadn't. Another crack on the cranium I didn't need.

I touched the back of my head gingerly. "Ouch! Oh, Jesus, that hurts!"

Stoicism seldom buys you anything; let the opposition know what a softy you are and how terribly you're suffering. They love it. The man standing over me produced a silenced .22 Colt Woodsman pistol, an obsolete weapon, but in its day the preferred assassination tool of many undercover organizations. Although at least as old as my Browning relic, which he'd tucked inside his waistband, this was a well-cared-for piece; and it's hard to wear out a quality firearm that's kept in good condition.

"I apologize for the violence," Ackerman said. "However, it was a necessary precaution."

I licked my lips and said ruefully, "Pretty tricky, Mr. Ackerman. First you play cop outside the door, with a corny Latin accent, to get me to open up all unsuspecting, and then you put on a betrayed-husband act so that, knowing myself to be pure and innocent, I won't take your wild accusations, or you, very seriously. . . . And where my brains were hiding while all this was going on is a question I prefer not to answer."

Ackerman said, "You have a certain reputation, Mr. Helm. It seemed necessary to take you completely by surprise to avoid, at the very least, an unnecessary and undignified struggle in which someone could have been hurt."

His speech bothered me; he didn't talk like, or look like, a typical employee of a South American drug baron. Even the gun was wrong; I was under the impression that they generally like the big, noisy, macho blasters, .357 minimum. I reminded myself that I really had very little experience with the breed. They undoubtedly came in all shapes and sizes; hell, *El Viejo* presumably had bank presidents, not to mention other presidents, working for him. Anyway I still, with a king-size headache, probably wasn't very sharp on nuances.

I touched my bruised scalp again, winced, and said, "Well, I surely am happy that nobody got hurt. And I won't ask why you couldn't just knock on the door normally and state your business without all this horsing around. I'm sure it will all become clear eventually."

"I'm sure it will. . . . Please sit over there." When I'd made a production of pulling myself up painfully, tottering a few feet, and lowering myself into the indicated chair, Ackerman spoke over his shoulder: "Bring her in, Belinda."

The connecting door opened and Ruth came in followed by plump Mrs. Ackerman, still in her tight white pants and loose purple shirt. High-heeled white sandals. Stainless-steel Smith & Wesson revolver, five-shot, caliber .38 Special, the new ladies' model with the rosewood grips. Ruth was also

150

dressed as last seen, in her standard tour costume of denim skirt and open-necked knitted shirt. She didn't seem to have taken any damage, but her eyes were furious, as was her voice, rushing into indignant protest as soon as she saw me.

"Matt, she barged right through the connecting door and waved her silly gun at me, and opened the hall door for that man, you know the one, who immediately started tearing my things apart; he's still in there making a mess of . . . Matt, you're hurt!" She hurried across the room to me. "What in the world do these crazy people think they're doing? She pawed all over me, searching me, damn her! What do they want? Are you all right?"

My dull mind wanted to ask about the still-unseen man I was supposed to know, but Ackerman's impatient expression told me I'd better let my curiosity wait.

"Just a small dent in my skull," I said to Ruth. "And a large one in my pride. Sit down, sweetheart, and I'm sure the nice man will explain everything."

"Yes, do sit down, Mrs. Steiner, please. Keep an eye on both of them, Belinda." Ackerman laid his pistol down once more and spoke to me: "Mrs. Ackerman is a competent marksman—excuse me, Belinda, markswoman—so I hope, Mr. Helm, that you have no grandiose plans in mind for altering the balance of power here."

I said, "There's nothing grandiose in my mind at the moment." I looked at Belinda Ackerman. "I'm deeply hurt. Here I thought you always smiled at me so pretty because you found me attractive!"

The blond girl laughed. "Oh, I do, darling, I do! It's always nice when a girl can combine business with pleasure."

But her big blue eyes, emphasized by the long, dark, curling lashes and the elaborate baby-doll makeup she always wore, were cold and wary, and the revolver resting on her plump knee was quite steady as she perched on the nearby cocktail table. Then Ackerman looked around impatiently and walked to the connecting door and told somebody to hurry up, returning to his former post near us. Moments later a familiar figure appeared in the doorway between the rooms—well, I'd only met the guy once but I hadn't forgotten him: Dennis Morton, the young hero who'd backed down from a confrontation in Santa Fe.

Some pieces of the puzzle fell into place, and I started to get mad. I mean, I'd thought I'd accomplished something, getting Ackerman to reveal himself, and it didn't please me to learn that I'd called the wrong coyotes out of the brush at the expense of a damaged head.

Ackerman looked around. "Finished, Dennis?"

Dennis Morton said, "I've done all I can with her laptop; it's not a very powerful machine, sir."

He was as neatly shorn and shaved as he'd been in Santa Fe, wearing a crisp seersucker suit and a flowered sport shirt open at the throat. He was also wearing his gun, in the same place as last seen, high on the right hip well back under the suit coat. He'd been a little reluctant with that, once; but apparently he was an eager man with a computer. The look he sent in my direction indicated that he hadn't forgotten me, or our last meeting, either.

Well, at least I'd been right about something: the fact that the Ackermans had not been on the tour list had been significant, although not in the way I'd expected. And they hadn't been spotted in our hasty preliminary check because, as a government man with, presumably, a reasonable amount of clout, he could undoubtedly—just as we could—make his official records, and the records of associates like Belinda, conform to whatever identities he chose to employ. His cover would be proof against a casual search, although our research boys and girls in Washington would undoubtedly penetrate it eventually and feel very proud of themselves as they made their report next week or next month. Being a kindly soul, I wouldn't ever dream of asking where all this great information had been when I needed it.

Ackerman asked Morton, "What did you find in there?"

The younger man said, "She's got a little portable computer with a hard disk—that's the built-in job that has a very large storage capacity and will handle some reasonably elaborate programs. The program she's working with has a fairly secure encryption feature; the people in Washington can undoubtedly break it but I can't. There's a separate drive that lets her copy stuff from the hard disk onto a three-and-half-inch diskette or, for that matter, from diskette to diskette. She has a couple of boxes of blank disks. And hidden in her toilet kit, I found two diskettes that, according to the labels, are identical copies of a missing original and hold Chapters Twenty-seven to Thirty-four of Mr. Steiner's book, which he apparently called Manuscript X2, or MSX2 for computer purposes. Those are the ones I was trying to read just now but the machine wanted a password and I couldn't supply it.''

Ackerman frowned. ''You say the original is missing? You searched the room thoroughly?''

''Yes, sir, and Belinda searched Mrs. Steiner; she does not have it on her person.''

Ackerman frowned. ''Well, here is another disk I took from Mr. Helm just now. Chapters Nine to Eighteen, according to the label. It's probably also coded or encrypted or whatever you call it, but you'd better put it into the computer and make sure.''

''Yes, sir.''

After Morton had disappeared into Ruth's room, Ackerman looked at me and said, ''Well, Mr. Helm? I see by your face that you're beginning to get a grasp on the situation at last. Do you know who I am?''

I said, ''You must be the boss, lucky man, of that handsome character who just left us, the one I met in Santa Fe who bluffs so easily.''

''Morton wasn't sent to Santa Fe to secure any loose cannon that rolled his way; he had other work to do.''

''Then he should learn to concentrate on his work instead of trying to make a sideline of collecting firearms that don't belong to him. And his commanding officer should learn that it's unwise to tangle with experienced old Washington politicos who have more influence than he does.''

I was trying for a reaction and I got it: the gray-haired man stepped forward and slapped my face hard. He stepped back to glare at me.

"That power-hungry old goat!" he said harshly. "The assignment was *mine*. Vasquez is *mine*! I have lived with this case for years; he had no right to—"

He broke off, breathing hard, apparently unaware in his anger that he'd just changed the situation drastically. A moment before, we'd still been colleagues after a fashion, working toward the same goal, Gregorio Vasquez, for the same employer, Uncle Sam. The fact that Ackerman had tricked me and struck me down to gain an advantageous position wasn't a serious matter between us. A judicious tap with a sap, no harder than necessary, is quite forgivable in our racket; I had no right to resent the one he'd given me. It was strictly business. However, a gratuitous slap in anger was a different matter entirely. That was not permitted. The Ackerman season was now open, he'd just opened it himself, and if a good shot offered itself, I'd have no qualms about taking it; but there's never anything to be gained by talking big and mean and blustery about it. Why warn them?

So I just sat there without raising my hand to my stinging face and said, "I don't suppose that Ackerman is your real name, or that Belinda, here, is really Mrs. Ackerman."

The gray-haired man said, "Call it a working partnership, like yours and Mrs. Steiner's. And for purposes of reference, Ackerman is as good a name as any." He sounded, for a moment, quite reasonable; then his calm and his voice broke: "That aging gray spider sitting in his dingy little office sending his young men out to kill, like the Old Man of the Mountain!"

I said, "We're all aging, every day of the year; and if you're referring to me as one of Mac's young men, I thank you for the compliment. But unlike the Old Man of the Mountain, he doesn't pass out hash with our orders, damn it."

"I will not tolerate humor involving drugs!" Having put me into my place, Ackerman drew a long breath and went on: "It was simply an exercise in influence to him! He cares nothing for the evil done by men like Gregorio Vasquez; he cares nothing for the terrible disaster that faces us now, if the man is permitted to saturate our country with his vicious product at bargain prices.''

I said, ''He cares. He cares about cancer, too, and AIDS, and nukes, and the national debt; but he doesn't feel that we're qualified to solve those problems, either. And power and influence may have had something to do with his taking over this mission against his usual policy—after all, you did throw him a direct challenge—but as it happened, we were involved already. I suspect he was happy when you gave him an excuse to take over; he thought that his way I wouldn't create a nasty hassle by tangling with you and your mission on my way to the target, since it is my mission now. Clearly he was wrong.''

''*Your* mission!'' Ackerman's face had lost its healthy pinkness, replaced by an angry flush. ''*I* was the one who realized the possibilities of Mark Steiner's research—well, he was calling himself Raoul Marcus Carrera Mascarena then, and writing as Marcus Piedra. *I* was the one who offered protection to him and his family if he'd come to the U.S. *I* was the one who managed to save his wife when she was kidnapped. We lost a good man in the process. *I* was the one who, when his first American identity was compromised, arranged to give him and his family a new home and identity out west. And then this ungrateful woman whose life we saved turns around and—''

Ruth, who'd been listening to all this in silence, now stirred and spoke harshly: ''Ungrateful? What's to be grateful for, that after all the promises of perfect security you made my husband before we came to this country, your people actually watched over us so carelessly that almost right away a man slipped into the backseat of my car with a bottle of chloroform? So your clowns managed to repair that damage after I'd gone through almost a week of hell, big deal! I'm supposed to be oozing gratitude all over for that? And why should I be grateful, anyway, to a man who never let me see him?'' She drew a long breath. ''There's nothing to make a girl feel grateful like being treated as a blabbermouthed nitwit who can't be trusted when important schemes are afoot that concern her and her children. Mark told me he wanted me to sit in on his discussions with you, but you kept screaming security. So as far as I'm concerned, all your big talk about the wonderful things *you* did for us is a lot of . . . a lot of bull. The great, marvelous things that were done for us, like letting me be kidnapped and my husband be killed, were all done by Mr. Morton and his merry men. All right, if you're the one who gave the orders and want to take the responsibility, what have you done about the fact that in spite of your fine promises, Mark is dead?''

"My dear lady . . ."

"Never mind that dear-lady nonsense!" Ruth said sharply. "I'll tell you what you *haven't* done. You haven't come out of your beautiful, secure anonymity to comfort the grieving widow and apologize for the fact that you and your underlings failed dismally to keep your promise of safety, the promise with which you lured us to the U.S. I haven't heard a single word of regret or remorse from anybody in your idiotic undercover circus that let Mark be murdered as easily as I was kidnapped. I haven't even heard anybody—not Mr. Morton and certainly not you—promise to make up for your total incompetence, at least a little, by making certain Mark's murderers are brought to justice.''

"Mrs. Steiner . . ."

Ruth went on, unheeding: "All you people cared about when he died was getting hold of his book, because you thought it might give you the answer to some of your drug problems. Well, I didn't give a damn about your stupid problems; I wanted Mark's assassins found and punished. So I turned to an organization in which people had the odd notion that murder is a slightly more heinous crime than substance abuse, to use the silly name you people have for it.'' She glared at Ackerman. "I was a new widow, my husband was *dead*, and all your boy Dennis could think about and talk about and hound me about was that lousy manuscript! I presume he was acting under your instructions. Well, there'll

be six-foot snowdrifts in the jungle outside that window before either of you ever lays hands on that book, Mr. Roger
Ackerman!''

Ackerman stepped forward and slapped her hard.

Chapter 17

I always wonder about these sluggers: how do they manage to live so long with both hands still attached? The normal human reaction to being slapped—at least it's my normal human reaction—is to perform at least an amputation, if not a total extermination; so how do they continue to survive intact?

"Watch her, Belinda!" Ackerman snapped, stepping back.

But Ruth made no effort to lunge at him; she just set the spectacles straight on her nose, touched her mouth with her fingertips, saw the blood, and dug a crumpled Kleenex out of a skirt pocket to hold against her split lip.

"This disk is also coded, sir." That was the boy wonder returning from Ruth's room.

"And you say you can't break it?" Ackerman asked.

"I'm afraid not, sir. Not with the facilities I have here."

"Very well. We'll try it another way. You'd better get behind Helm and hold your pistol to his head. Correction, make that my pistol. It's silenced, so it shouldn't disturb anybody if you have to use it. Here, take it and lend me yours. Belinda, I believe you carry cigarettes."

"Yes."

Ackerman said, "It's a dirty habit and an unhealthy one, but it has advantages. Light one, please. You can put away your weapon; I'll watch the woman." He moved to stand before Ruth, holding Morton's revolver. "Now, Mrs. Steiner, I want two things. I want the password or computer code or whatever it takes to unscramble the text on these disks. And I want the names and addresses of the people here in South

158

America to whom your husband sent the remaining disks on which he recorded his book. We still lack Chapters One to Ten, Chapters Twenty to Twenty-six, and however many chapters he wrote beyond Thirty-four. You can start by telling me how many there were altogether."

Ruth glared at him over the wad of Kleenex. "What will you do if I don't tell you? Hit me again?"

"No, but Mrs. Ackerman will apply the lighted end of her cigarette to Mr. Helm's chest. And Mr. Morton will blow his brains out if he tries to object—well, let's be generous and allow him to squirm just a little, shall we? And small moans will be permitted, but no loud screams that could disturb the occupants of neighboring rooms. . . ."

"I don't believe this!" Ruth protested. "You work for the U.S. government! And you know that I'm a respectable American citizen; I was married to a member of the Foreign Service and later to a well-known author. Mr. Helm works for the U.S. government just as you do. What gives you the right to march in here with . . . with your slaps and your torture; what makes you think you can get away with it?" She appealed to me: "Matt, has he gone absolutely crazy?"

I shrugged. It wasn't the time or place to go into the question of Ackerman's sanity. As far as I'm concerned, they're all nuts, but then I've spent my life in a fairly hard-boiled profession and I never can understand the soft-boiled folks who make careers of saving people from their own bad habits. Go ahead and smoke up a storm for all I care. It's your emphysema.

I said, "Maybe yes, maybe no, but for the moment he has the guns. Moral and legal rights are all very well, sweetheart, but in the crunch it's the guns that count, always."

Ruth licked her lips. "But how can he expect to get away with—"

Ackerman didn't want us to get into that. He snapped, "All right, Belinda!"

The blond girl, with the cigarette dangling between her lips, pulled open my already unbuttoned shirt with both hands. When she leaned over me, I got an intimate view of

159

her chest in return: the rather spectacular white breasts were, I noted, quite unconfined inside the purple blouse. At the moment I didn't find them unbearably stimulating, but I'll admit to a small reaction, of which she was aware. She smiled at me affectionately, puffed hard on the cigarette, blew the smoke into my face, and pressed the glowing coal against my breastbone.

There was the well-remembered, instant blaze of pain, of course, and the familiar smell of burned chest hairs and scorched skin mingled with the odor of tobacco. I mean, I'd played this scene before too many times, with all conceivable variations. I'd long since learned that suffering doesn't become any easier with practice, but this time, at least, I didn't have to pretend it didn't hurt, as is sometimes required. I believe I performed the expected squirm-and-moan act quite convincingly; and how much of it was truly an act is none of your damned business.

"You sadistic bitch!" I gasped. Corny verbiage was also expected.

Belinda grinned. "I'd just love to hurt you a different way, lover, and have you hurt me right back, but since this is all the fun we can share today, just relax and enjoy it. Your lady friend doesn't seem to be talking, so . . ." She leaned forward again.

"Forty-three!"

That was Ruth's voice, sounding a bit dim through the pain haze, as Belinda set another small part of me afire.

Ackerman's voice said, "What did you say, Mrs. Steiner?"

The girl above me withdrew temporarily, leaving my chest throbbing. I saw that Ruth's face was set and shiny. She'd taken the Kleenex from her mouth. The bleeding had already stopped. There was some swelling of her lower lip where Ackerman's blow had caught her. Maybe a double amputation was in order. You wouldn't want to go to all the trouble of chopping off one just to have him learn how to slap even harder and oftener with the other.

Ruth snapped, "You wanted to know the number of chapters, damn you! There are forty-three of them. The total number of manuscript pages completed is five hundred and thirty-four. There was to have been an appendix—Mark thought it would come to some fifteen pages, for a total manuscript of about five hundred and fifty double-spaced pages—but he never got enough of the final section written out, and revised to his satisfaction, to put it on a disk and send it away.''

"Very well. Now the names."

"What will you do to them if I tell you who they are?"

It was time for me to be brave. I whispered hoarsely, "Ruth, you don't have to. . . . Hell, in this business a little toasting session is all in the day's work. These dumbos always reach for the cigarette or the soldering iron or the blow-torch and think they've invented a lovely new form of interrogation, as if the Spanish Inquisition hadn't beat them to it by centuries! I've had it done to me so many times I'm practically fireproof. Don't tell the bastard a damn thing you don't want. . . . Ahhh!''

"Don't be a hero, hero," the plump girl said, taking the cigarette away and puffing it back to good, bright ignition.

"Well, Mrs. Steiner?" Ackerman asked.

Ruth hesitated.

"Ahh-ahh!" I said as Belinda did her stuff once more. I decided that the antitobacco crusaders had missed one good argument against the filthy weed: Mrs. Roger Ackerman.

"That doesn't seem to be one of your fireproof spots, lover," she said solicitously. "But let's check it out again. . . .''

"Ahhhhh!"

"Stop it, stop it!" Ruth cried. "Please, what is it you want to know, Mr. Ackerman?"

"Where are your other contacts to take place?"

She licked her lips. "Lima, Santiago, Quito. There was supposed to be one in Buenos Aires, but I switched it to Itaipu at the last minute."

"The two disks Mr. Morton found in your room, are they copies of the one you just received at Itaipu?"

"Yes."

161

"Where is the original?"

"It was . . . picked up a few minutes ago. A man came to the window and I handed it out to him." She shook her head quickly. "You don't need to know who he was. As a matter of fact, I don't know who he was, myself. Over the phone, I'd asked Lenny Otero to arrange it, just giving me time to fire up the computer and run off a couple of copies of the disk before I passed it on."

Ackerman pounced on the name. "Otero? Is that the name of your Buenos Aires contact, or somebody here in the hotel?"

Ruth looked annoyed with herself, then she shrugged. "What difference does it make? She doesn't have what you want any longer. Lenny's the one in Buenos Aires."

"You made two copies?" Ackerman said thoughtfully. "One for you and one for Mr. Helm?"

"No, one for him to keep for me and one to send to his people in Washington. The same as I did with the disk I got in Rio. One copy of that must already be on its way to Washington, since you found only one on him."

"To Washington!" Ackerman turned on me sharply and started to speak, but changed his mind. He swung back to Ruth: "But no copy for you? That seems odd."

She said sharply, "Nothing odd about it! The way I had it planned, we'd have one copy of each diskette with us, the one Matt was holding, in case I needed immediate access to it. There was no sense in my carrying still another, and I didn't want too many floating around. Three seemed enough to ensure . . . Well, if one of the originals didn't make it by the route I'd arranged, there would be Matt's copy right at hand, and if something should happen to that, there would still be a backup in Washington."

Ackerman was silent for a little. At last he asked, "These friends your husband trusted to safeguard his work, were they all female friends? You said your contact in Buenos Aires was a girl. And the one in Rio? We think your rendezvous there was also a *sanitario*—in that restaurant where we

162

had lunch on Monday, am I right?—which would make her a woman, too."

Ruth drew a long breath. "I'm afraid my husband was kind of a ladies' man in his younger days, Mr. Ackerman. Of course he also had a good many male friends and acquaintances down here, but yes, the people he asked to keep his disks safe for him were all women." She grimaced. "Fortunately for this project, as it turned out, he hadn't been exactly reticent about his . . . his premarital relationships. Or you could say he'd just been painfully honest when he came courting me, to use the old-fashioned term, telling me what kind of a man I'd be getting and swearing that it would never happen after we were married, even though keeping a mistress was an old Spanish custom. He kept his word. He . . . he loved me. But I did get to know a considerable amount about the women in his past. Strangely, he seemed to have remained friends with practically all of them. Well, he was a very nice guy. I even kept meeting them socially when I accompanied him on his journalistic travels around South America. A bit embarrassing at the time, knowing what I knew, but useful later when I was trying to track down the ones who'd received the disks."

"Yes, I can see that. Now the names, if you please."

She licked her lips. "I can't. . . . What will you do to them?"

"They will come to no harm if they turn over the disks."

"I'm afraid I don't trust you. If . . . if one of them gets a bit stubborn, you'll hurt her, too, just as you're hurting . . . No, I don't think I care to betray them to you!"

"Belinda!"

When there was no immediate groan from me, Ackerman looked our way. Belinda Ackerman—whatever her real name might be—was taking a final long drag at the stub of her cigarette. She crushed it out deliberately in one of the hotel ashtrays.

Ackerman said irritably, "Belinda, you are not on stage; a dramatic production is not required. Just light another and . . ."

The blond girl shook her head. "No."

Ackerman looked startled. "*What* did you say?" he demanded.

Belinda spoke calmly: "That's enough sadism for little Linda, the Krafft-Ebing girl. I've had my kicks for today, thanks, Mr. Ackerman; now let the boy wonder take a crack at it. Hell, this guy owes him one, from what I hear, or vice versa. I'll just hold the gun and watch the fun for a change."

I should have noticed. I suppose, if I hadn't been distracted by my own discomfort, I would have seen that the girl was in trouble. Her voice had been steady enough throughout, but now her face was quite pale, even a little greenish, and there were drops of perspiration on her forehead. She'd sweated through her sexy silk blouse under the armpits.

I didn't like it. I prefer to deal with psychopathic creeps. The girl had suddenly become human, just a hardworking junior agent who'd been plugging away to the best of her ability at the new job assigned to her. She'd been professional enough not to let herself be distracted by the right and wrong of a spot of interrogation—ethics don't play a very large part in our training—but in the end what she'd been ordered to do had turned out to be just a bit too much for her. Maybe she was just a nice girl at heart. Too bad. It's easier to pull the trigger on the opposition when the time comes, or push the blade all the way home, if you can tell yourself you're dealing with a bunch of conscienceless freaks from outer space, not real, vulnerable human beings.

Ackerman asked, "Are you refusing . . . ?"

"The poor girl's got a weak stomach." This was the handsome character holding the silenced automatic. He laughed scornfully. "I haven't. Certainly not where this quickdraw cowboy is concerned. Let me take over as she suggests, Mr. Ackerman."

"Well, all right." The older man threw a baleful look at Belinda. "But I'll speak with you later, young lady."

After that it was just more and worse of the same, complicated by the fact that Mr. Dennis Morton clearly wasn't accustomed to defiling his lungs with tobacco. This led to a considerable amount of coughing as he sucked inexpertly to keep the cigarette fired up and choked on the resulting smoke. A real comedy routine; but the fact that he was aware of making a fool of himself with the unfamiliar fags after volunteering so bravely for torture duty only made him all the more eager to take it out on me: he was faster to start a burn than Belinda had been and slower to stop. Ruth stalled a little, but gradually she let it all come out. The woman in Santiago was Conchita Perez. Address. The woman in Lima was Rafaela Hoffman. Address. The woman in Quito was Evelyn Herrera Gonzales. Address.

Then there was a little silence. At last Ruth looked up at Ackerman and asked sharply, "Well, are you satisfied?"

"One more name," he said.

"There aren't any more!"

"Oh, yes there are. There is. The name of the man or woman, I presume back in the States, to whom you're sending the original disks after you get them copied. . . . Dennis!"

"Oh, stop it!" Ruth said wearily. She sighed. "Why don't you use your brains for a change? Who in the world would I send them to except Mark's publisher?"

After taking a moment to consider her answer and decide that it made sense, Ackerman asked, "The name of the firm?"

"For heaven's sake! You can read it off any copy of his first book; if you knew your business, you already would have. Horizon Press. New York. I don't have the street address in my head. . . . Oh, all right, all right, don't start *that* again, let me think! 243 Mackey Street. Zip 10022, if I remember right. Actually, our dealings were with one of their senior editors."

"Name?"

"Paul Rentner. But I'm not sending them to him directly. We were sneaky, we didn't think it would be smart to address the packages so obviously to a publishing house, so Paul

165

arranged to have a young associate editor receive them at home and bring them to him at the office. Elizabeth Johns.''

"Address?"

Ruth gave it, and Ackerman copied it into the little notebook in which, rather clumsily since he also had to juggle Morton's revolver, he'd been recording the information as it was extracted. He flipped to a new page.

"And now," he said, "now we'll have the code or whatever you computer people call it, please, Mrs. Steiner, and the unpleasantness will all be behind us.''

"No.''

"Dennis!"

"You're getting tiresome," Ruth said wearily. "I'm not going to give it to you. You can fry him to a crisp—I'm sorry, Matt—and you can toast me like a marshmallow on a stick, but you won't get that out of me. I know there are drugs that could make me talk, but if you had access to those you'd have used them already instead of going in for these . . . primitive methods.'' She drew a deep breath. "Forget about Matt, Mr. Ackerman. He doesn't have the information you want, and nothing you do to him will make me give it to you. He's a nice enough person, but he doesn't mean that much to me. Tell your junior-grade inquisitor to come over here and work on me. I assure you, he'll die a long, lingering death from lung cancer before I talk, if he doesn't rupture something vital first, the way he keeps coughing. . . .''

The slap knocked her glasses off. I decided that a hatchet would be too quick; when the time came I'd do a slow job with a dull hacksaw. No-Hands Ackerman.

"You've been stalling, you bitch!"

She made no move to touch her bruised cheek; she just straightened up in the chair, adjusted her glasses once more, and laughed at him.

"That's right, I've been stalling," she said. "I've been making you work for a lot of names and addresses that mean nothing at all, because even if you get the disks, what good will they do you if you can't read them? Oh, I'll be sorry to lose them; they represent Mark's last work and I hate to see it wasted; besides, I had greedy hopes. . . . But never mind that. Obviously there's a drug-related evil no one talks about, that's worse than the drugs themselves: the lovely power the so-called drug wars give to certain ambitious, ruthless people, the power to push and slap people around with impunity. The majority of your colleagues are probably honest and sincere and maybe even reasonably considerate law enforcement people, Mr. Ackerman, but you and men like you make the whole noble crusade stink. As far as I'm concerned, you're a much greater danger than Gregorio Vasquez; at least everybody knows what he is. He's not a hidden menace like you, a secret threat to everything our country stands for. As I said before, you'll never get your hands on my husband's book. You'll never use it to further your dirty career. Never!''

Chapter 18

ACKERMAN took a quick step forward. He was pale with fury and he might very well have smashed Ruth's face with the revolver he was holding if Belinda hadn't stepped forward quickly and caught his arm.

"Please, Mr. Ackerman! Somebody's coming!"

Footsteps approached the door and stopped. There was a polite little knock, very different from Ackerman's recent assault on the panels.

"Matt?"

It was a woman's voice, that of our tour manager, Annie. Ackerman reached out and grabbed Ruth's chin left-handed to hold her head steady. He placed the muzzle of his gun— well, Morton's gun—between her eyes. I decided that the way he kept losing his temper, he might be a bit screwy after all, as Ruth had suggested; or perhaps the fact that he was on very shaky legal ground here, actually no legal ground at all, was affecting his nerves adversely—not that any of us spend too much time brooding about legality.

Ackerman glared at me over Ruth's head and whispered, "Answer, Helm! Very, very carefully!"

I raised my voice and said, "Yes, Annie?"

She spoke through the closed door: "The tour to the falls is about to start. You and Ruth said you were planning to come with us."

It was no time to be clever; the room was infested with too many nervous people with guns. I said, "I'm sorry, I think we'll have to pass after all. Ruth's a bit tired."

The woman outside the door said, "Oh, that's too bad!

Well, we'll go ahead without you. When she's had a little rest, maybe you can just take her across the road in front of the hotel and over to the river, it's only a couple of hundred yards. You can get a nice view of the cataracts from there, and you can follow the cliffs upstream toward them as far as she feels like walking, there's a good path along the edge. It's quite a spectacle. You really shouldn't miss it.''

"We won't. Thanks, Annie.''

We heard her walk away. When her footsteps were no longer audible, Ackerman released Ruth and backed away from her. Relieved of the strain of staring cross-eyed at the threatening gun barrel, Ruth blinked a couple of times and drew a shaky breath. Dennis Morton, still holding the silenced pistol to my head, sighed deeply.

"Mr. Ackerman,'' he said after a moment. "If I may suggest . . .''

"Yes, Dennis?''

"I'll do whatever you say, of course, sir, but . . . well, we've already spent a lot of time in this room and we don't really need Mrs. Steiner's information, do we?''

"Explain.''

"We know where the disks are now. Once we have them all, Washington can take it from there. Those boys are real pros and I'm sure they've long since figured out how to deal with the kind of encryption provided by an off-the-shelf computer program available to civilians. Even back during the coldest cold-war days, the Russians with all their facilities couldn't keep their secret communications secret from us very long; do you think a housewife with a battery-powered portable is going to?'' He cleared his throat. "As I said, it's only a suggestion, sir.''

It sounded reasonable, but I sensed a hidden uncertainty. Mr. Dennis Morton didn't have quite as much faith in the Washington computer geniuses as he pretended. He was simply, like Belinda but in a slightly different way, losing his nerve. He was beginning to realize that his fanatic superior had put them all into a very unhealthy situation in a foreign land, and he wanted to persuade Ackerman, diplomatically, to get them the hell out of there before the Brazilian police, or somebody, broke in the door and found them abusing a couple of helpless victims, with illegal weapons in their hands.

Ackerman was not a man sensitive to hidden uncertainties; he was nodding thoughtfully. "You make a good point," he said. "And we have, as you say, spent too much time here. Very well, but I think we had better keep Mrs. Steiner in reserve, so to speak, just in case she's cleverer than you think—or our cryptographers are stupider, which is not inconceivable. If so, well, we have access to interrogators who have better techniques than we have, and they'll be able to obtain the information from her, I'm sure."

Ruth licked her lips. "I don't understand. How are you going to keep me in reserve, as you call it? Lock me up somewhere?"

"Oh, no, dear lady," Ackerman said. "You and I are going to put on a great performance for the other members of the troupe as, although deserted and humiliated by our respective partners, we stubbornly accompany them through Argentina and Chile and all the other beautiful South American countries we've paid to see. I presume you've alerted your husband's female friends in Santiago, Lima, and Quito to expect you with this group, so we'd better not confuse them by traveling independently. In the meantime, for the benefit of our companions, we'll play the betrayed husband and the deserted mistress, seeking consolation with each other."

Ruth stared at him. "Just exactly how are you planning for me to console you? If you think for one little moment—"

He laughed shortly. "You flatter yourself, Mrs. Steiner. Your body attracts me not at all; I'm merely interested in the contents of your brain. And particularly your late husband's brain. We'll merely associate in a friendly fashion as we travel, you and I, drawn together by shared adversity. We'll explain to Annie what has happened and give her a note from the missing lovebirds addressed to her, telling how they were

170

compelled to run off together by a passion greater than . . .
Well, you can fill in the clichés for yourself, I'm sure. Signed,
with apologies, Belinda and Matthew. It will be a scandal in
a teapot, it will make us—the two pitiful rejects—objects of
great curiosity, and the whole tour group will be so pleasantly
titillated by this romantic escapade that nobody will ask any
awkward questions about Mr. Helm's disappearance, or Belinda's. Or Dennis's, for that matter; but since I've been careful to keep him out of sight, they aren't likely to miss him.
As for Annie, I'm sure a lady of her experience is hardened
to having strange things, including mate swapping, happen
on her tours. All she really cares about is having all warm
bodies accounted for.''

Ruth frowned. ''And just what's going to make me cooperate with this wild scenario?'' She laughed sharply. ''Oh,
I see! Instead of keeping me imprisoned, you're going to take
Matt off somewhere and hold him so you can use him as a
hostage while I help you get the rest of the computer disks.
I suppose you'll threaten to do dreadful things to him if I get
stubborn, maybe even kill him.''

Ackerman said, ''It's pleasant to deal with an intelligent
woman.''

''You're forgetting one thing,'' Ruth said. ''You're forgetting that this intelligent woman has already told you to go
right ahead and set fire to Mr. Helm if you like. Or do anything else you care to. He doesn't mean all that much to her.''

I said, ''Gee, thanks loads, sweetheart!''

She ignored my interruption and went on: ''I'm a reasonably humanitarian person, Mr. Ackerman, and I won't let
somebody suffer if I can help it; but one has to draw the line
somewhere. What I'm trying to say is that this man is really
just a bodyguard type to me. I'll admit I slept with him once,
just once; he's reasonably presentable, and when you've been
married, you do get lonely for . . . But that doesn't mean I'll
jump through hoops for you just because you threaten him.
I owe him nothing; actually less than nothing, since the fact
that you're here, and in control of the situation, proves that
he's failed at his job of protecting me just as you did.'' She

laughed shortly. "I don't seem to have much luck with my government protectors, do I? Well, he took his chances and lost and we're sorry about that, but I've got two daughters to look after and my own life to live and I'm not going to worry too much about a government gunman who doesn't seem to be very proficient at his work." She looked at me directly. "Sorry, Matt, but that's the way it is."

She was really quite good. She was putting on the best performance possible under the circumstances. There's nothing more tiresome than the old TV hand-wringing routine in which the heroine, when the pressure comes on, immediately starts to moan and weep with desperate concern for her threatened hero and instantly agrees to all demands no matter how outlandish. I mean, we all know the script and the outcome, but we do like to see the girl display a little backbone before the final curtain.

Ackerman also knew his lines; he said, "Very well. Since you say the man can be of no use to us . . . Dennis, you know what to do. Take him to the place we selected. Belinda had better back you up. Mr. Helm is supposed to be tough, although I've seen no evidence of it."

Morton spoke bravely: "I don't need a backup, sir. I can handle him."

Ackerman was impatient with this posturing. He snapped, "You will take Belinda anyway; it's time for her to disappear and she might as well be giving you a hand. But she'd better first write her farewell note, hers and Helm's. . . . Belinda, there should be some hotel stationery in the top drawer of that bureau. Here's a pen if you don't find one there."

Then they did some pistol juggling. The silenced .22 went back to Ackerman while Morton reclaimed his own .38. Belinda, freed from guard duty, sat down at the desk and started writing. It didn't take her long. She showed the result to Ackerman, who gave her a sharp, offended look and started to speak, but checked himself.

"Very well, I suppose that will have to do." He looked my way. "Now, Mr. Helm, you will sign your name below

Belinda's. Underneath you will write 'Las Cataratas Hotel' and the date, please.''

He found a slick cardboard folder, actually the one containing the hotel's room-service menu, put it on my knees for something to write on, placed the letter on top of it, and handed me the pen. I took a moment to read what I was signing:

Dear Annie:

It's awful and it's wonderful and sometimes I think I can't bear it. We're going away together, so just cross us off your passenger list, no refunds expected. I hope our leaving like this won't make any trouble for you. Tell that tired old man I was married to that I'm sorry to have to hurt him; but Matt and I knew the moment we met that it just had to be.

Belinda Nunn

It was quite an impressive piece of creative writing to have been dashed off in minutes, on demand. I scribbled my name below Belinda's and added place and date as instructed. Ackerman retrieved the letter and passed it to Belinda, who folded it, put it in a hotel envelope with airmail trimmings, sealed it, and, given back the pen, scribbled a name, presumably Annie's, on the front.

Ackerman looked at me for a moment and said to Belinda, "Button his shirt." When this had been done, he said to Morton, "You can take him away now."

"Yes, sir. Come on, you!"

Ackerman spoke again: "If you can put him over the cliff without any shooting, so much the better, but take no chances with him. Use your gun if you have to. Down there, nobody'll hear the report and by the time the body goes through the rocks of those rapids and washes ashore downriver, if it does, it's unlikely that anybody'll notice a little bullet hole. . . . All right, on your way. After it's done, stay out of sight again and keep in touch with me as arranged."

"Yes, sir. All right, you!"

We were almost at the door, Belinda going ahead to open it, when Ruth spoke behind us: "What . . . what are you going to do to him?"

That was all right. It was a dumb-dumb question, the answer had just been given, but it was stupid-time now as we put the final touches on the gripping drama we'd just played.

Ackerman said, "Really, Mrs. Steiner! He means nothing to you, you just said, so why should you be concerned. . . ?"

"Oh, my God, you're going to *kill* him!" Heedless of Ackerman's long-barreled .22—well, long if you count the silencer as barrel—she jumped out of her chair, ran to me, and threw her arms around my neck. "Oh, my darling, I'm sorry, I'm sorry, I thought if I put on a cold-blooded act, maybe . . . Oh, my dear, I didn't really mean. . . !" She whirled on Ackerman. "All right, all right, you win! I'll act out this ridiculous charade with you. Just promise me he'll be safe and I'll get the remaining disks for you."

It was still a little obvious, a little corny, but much better than if she'd yielded without any preliminary struggles. Men like Roger Ackerman, whatever his real name might be, like to admire their own cleverness and ruthlessness. He'd want to believe that he'd really broken her will with his threats; now he hurried to capitalize on his victory.

"You'll get them *and* tell me how to read them?"

She hesitated and let her shoulders sag in a defeated way. "If you promise not to hurt him anymore."

"Tell me now!"

That brought a show of resistance: "Oh, no! We'll do it in Quito, the last stop before the whole tour flies back to Miami. You bring Matt to me there, alive and well; and when we're ready to board the plane, with all the others around so you don't dare touch us, I'll give you the password."

Ackerman frowned suspiciously. "How do I know, once you have your man safe, you won't just laugh at me and get on the plane together and fly away?"

"You have my word, for whatever that means," Ruth said. "And what can you lose? By that time you'll already have all the disks. As your man says, even if I should go back on my promise, which I have no intention of doing, your experts can undoubtedly decode them for you eventually. But considering the way you got the material, do you really *want* to have to ask another government department to help you read it if you don't have to, Mr. Ackerman? Somebody might get curious, particularly since one disk is already with Matt's people in Washington, who may very well—you'd know more about this than I do—use the same government decoding experts as you do. If you take the gamble of trusting me, and win, you'll be able to print out Mark's book at your leisure without taking anybody else into your confidence.''

Ackerman hesitated, shrugged, and spoke to Morton: ''You heard the lady. All right, she has a deal. Take Helm to the hideout we discussed as an alternative solution and hold him there until I let you know where to bring him. . . .''

The orders were accompanied by a wink, unseen by Ruth, that effectively canceled them. Well, there had never been a chance that after recklessly reclaiming ''his'' mission by force from the government agency to which it had been assigned—our agency—Ackerman would leave the government agent involved, me, alive to complain to Washington.

Chapter 19

IT was a pleasure to get out of that room at last, even with a gun in my back and a river in my future. For the moment there was nobody in the corridor outside. I wondered if Armando was keeping an eye on my door, or Ruth's. He might well be, but the instructions I'd left with him concerned keeping her safe, not me. There'd be no officer-needs-assistance signals; I was strictly on my own. Well, it had happened before. Belinda, ahead of me, stopped so abruptly I almost ran into her. She turned to speak to Morton.

"I'd better be the one to take him through the lobby and down the walk, until we're past the biggest mobs of tourists," she said. "I can snuggle up to him so nobody sees my gun; if you walk that close to him, they'll think you're both queer."

Morton didn't like it. "Mr. Ackerman said I was to . . . The arrogant bastard is *mine*, damn it!"

"My God, you're welcome to him; I wouldn't dream of depriving you. I just want to get us all down there without attracting attention; then you can have him back with pink ribbons. Now be sensible and just follow a couple of steps behind us and pretend you don't know us."

She linked arms with me and drew me close, with her other hand inside the shoulderstrap bag that she pushed against me as we walked side by side. I was aware of her perfume. Perversely, far from attracting me, a heavily scented lady always makes me wonder if she's trying to cover up the fact that she hasn't had a bath lately. Still, I reminded myself, the girl had—well, eventually—balked at performing Ackerman's painful brand of interrogation; a point in her favor.

I was aware that Morton was following at a discreet distance, from which he'd have a clear shot if I tried anything. We made our way through the lobby, which was moderately crowded. There were people clustered around the hotel desk, checking in or out; this late in the afternoon, probably in. Outside the front door we were greeted by a gray mist of rain. There were quite a few tourists out here as well. Some foresighted characters displayed colorful raincoats or umbrellas. The others were either strolling along ignoring the thin drizzle courageously or hurrying through it uncomfortably, the latter hunched over and, in the case of the women, shielding their hairdos with inadequate purses, newspapers, or guidebooks.

The picturesque old hotel, with jungle behind it, was set at the head of lush green lawns that sloped gently down toward the road by which we'd arrived; beyond that, the paved walk we were now following led across more lawns to the Paraná River, invisible at first at the bottom of its chasm—but here, in the open air, the rumble of the falls upstream was a constant reminder of its presence. I realized what Ackerman had meant when he told Morton not to worry about a shot or two: down by the water the noise would undoubtedly cover the sound of a pitched battle.

A pair of young men came strolling up the path together; they were briefly intrigued by the well-developed blond girl tap-tapping through the drizzle beside me on her high heels, but they obviously thought a ripe young lady like that was wasting her time snuggling up to a well-worn character like me.

"Keep moving!" Morton snapped from behind me when I paused. "Well, all right, take a look at your last scenic wonder, Wonder Boy."

I've known better times for sight-seeing, but you're supposed to grab eagerly at any reprieve you can get, no matter how short. It was really an impressive spectacle: several miles

177

of high, jagged cliffs with all the water in the world pouring off them and shattering into clouds of roiling white mist.

As we stood there another loud noise was added to the continuing roar. I saw a neatly carved and varnished wooden park sign ahead reading HELICOPTERO, with an arrow directing customers to the sight-seeing flights, before the whirlybird itself came into sight over the river. It seemed like an ugly intrusion: one should be allowed to listen to the hypnotic thunder of the falls undisturbed by the clatter of internal combustion engines. Well, I understand that the ancient peace of the Grand Canyon is also broken by the racket of airborne rubberneck traffic.

Morton, still behind me, spoke again: "Damn, I hoped the rain had grounded it! Well, we'll just have to time it right so nobody reports any falling bodies, won't we?"

It was time for me to act naively shocked and distressed, as if I'd just realized I was to be killed, after all. I spoke plaintively: "But Mr. Ackerman promised Ruth. . . !"

Behind us, Morton laughed scornfully. "What the Steiner bitch doesn't know won't hurt her. By the time she learns you're dead, if she lives that long, she'll have served Mr. Ackerman's purpose. Hell, all we really need are the disks; as I told Mr. Ackerman, deciphering them should be a piece of cake with the right equipment. And where the hell would we keep you safe around here, a clever-ass like you? Oh, I don't underestimate you, Helm, even if you did look better making brave noises in your own front yard than moaning and groaning down here in Brazil. But did you really believe that crap about an alternate hideout? The only hideout we've got for you is right down there in all that nice, churning water. . . . All right, if you've seen enough, move it!"

We turned onto the cliff path. It was wide and paved, and followed the edge, more or less, sometimes allowing us to look straight down into the rushing river below, as well as across the broken water to the falls themselves. The wooden railings didn't look remarkably sturdy or well maintained; but then, where precipices are concerned, any protective barrier short of solid, reinforced concrete looks inadequate to me. We passed another neat park sign directing tourists of various nationalities to the LANCHONETE-ECHAPORA-SNACKBAR. Off to our right, the helicopter came and went noisily, but its racket seemed to diminish as the sound of the falls grew louder with our approach.

Occasionally the path would wander into the tangled woods for a bit, cutting across a point or promontory. Once Belinda shied abruptly, like a startled mare, as a rodent the size of a Pomeranian lumbered across the wet path ahead. She gave a sharp, nervous, little laugh.

"My God, if that's what the local rats look like, I don't want to see the cats! Keep moving, Buster!"

On the next inland excursion we stopped in the shelter of a big tree at the side of the pavement. The rain was coming down more densely now. I could feel water trickling down my neck, but it wasn't one of my major worries. I'd been wet before and survived it. I noted that we'd stopped where a side path toward the river left the main trail. It was blocked by a wooden fence and a gate to which was nailed a faded sign: INTERDITADO POR MOTIVO DE SEGURANCA. There was a funny little squiggle under the C. Although my Portuguese is nonexistent, my rudimentary Spanish, a very similar language, let me figure out that the path was forbidden for motives of safety.

These motives did not seem to impress my guards. After a quick look up and down the main path, at the moment empty in the rain, Morton went forward and untwisted the rusty baling wire that had been used to reinforce the decrepit gate latch. He opened the gate, waved us through, secured the latch once more, and followed us into the trees just as a small child in jeans, sex indeterminate, came running down the main path, splashing happily through the puddles; we could hear the mother, still out of sight, shouting at him/her in Portuguese or Spanish, I couldn't tell which.

Reaching the end of the path, I found the situation just as bad as I'd expected. I mean, down there they don't have our obsession with safety, and they don't close off paths and nail up warning signs for just any minor peril. This was a booby trap dangerous enough to catch even their reluctant attention. The trail emerged abruptly from the trees onto what had once been a small, paved, fenced area on a shelf of rock overhanging the rapids. It had obviously been a special little observation point with a magnificent view of the falls, now close enough that the ground was wet with drifting mist as well as rain.

The only trouble was that the river below the promontory had undercut the rock. Most of the paved area, with its railing, had fallen into the torrent—I couldn't help wondering if they'd lost any tourists in the collapse. The pavement ended raggedly over nothing, as did the broken safety fence on either side. Ugly cracks in the remaining asphalt indicated that more large chunks of the cliff underneath were settling, getting ready to fall. It wasn't really, I reflected grimly, a very good place for a gent afflicted with acrophobia.

"Hold it!" Morton snapped. "Back up!"

Glad to do so, I moved back obediently, with Belinda. Morton waved us to the side of the path where we were shielded by jungle brush and trees. We could hear the helicopter coming; then it appeared, clattering loudly. It made a circle near the falls and headed back downstream.

"All right, Belinda. He's mine now!"

"You're welcome to him," the girl said.

She was pretty wet by now, her fluffy blond hair damply matted, her thin purple blouse dark across the shoulders. She regarded me for a moment and seemed about to say something, perhaps good-bye; then she shrugged and moved aside without speaking. Morton gestured with his gun. He'd held it in his pocket during our walk, but it was in the open now. The pleasure of getting to deal with me seemed to have dispelled the uncertainty I'd sensed earlier. He didn't even seem to notice the penetrating rain that had made him as wet as the rest of us. Well, one of us was going to get even wetter; the question was which one.

I'd made my preparations as well as I could. Having watched me squirming and squealing pitifully under interrogation, making no attempt at resistance, clearly afraid even to utter an angry protest, signing my name to anything that was put in front of me, and marching obediently where I was told, Morton would be thinking by now, I hoped, that this loudmouthed Helm clown was really just a big false alarm, nothing to worry about. That was one of my facedown cards; the other was that he'd once suffered a serious humiliation at my hands. He wouldn't kill me immediately. He'd want to get his revenge first.

"Get out there, hotshot!" he snapped, with a wave of the gun. "Go on, move! Unless you want to die right here."

I looked at the short-barreled revolver and backed away onto the precarious shelf of cracked asphalt. He followed, stalking me. I glanced fearfully over my shoulder and acted shocked at where I found myself, ten feet from the brink—it didn't really take much acting. Well, if my real fear made my phony panic more convincing, at least I was putting the damned disability to some practical use at last. I took a terrified step to the side so I could grab at the wooden railing for security.

"Keep going!" Morton ordered.

Clinging there, I threw another frightened look backward and shook my head desperately. I gasped, "I can't, I can't! You're going to have to shoot me right here, damn you! I . . . I c-can't go any closer. My G-God, it's hundreds of f-feet s-s-straight d-down!"

Actually I didn't think the cliff was over fifty feet high at that point, but it was no time for niggling accuracy.

Belinda's voice said, "The poor man is frightened of high places. I saw him on the cable car in Rio, riding up to Sugarloaf, he almost wet his pants he was so scared."

"My God, a secret agent with vertigo. Shades of Alfred Hitchcock!"

Morton's laughter was a shout of joy; he had his vengeance in spades. I sank to my knees, clinging to a fence upright. Huddled there, a trembling bundle of panic, I saw his feet approach across the wet asphalt. I knew that being the man he was, he was bound to kick me at least once. He did. I took it in the ribs and grabbed his ankle and lunged forward;

he might be braced for a pull but he wouldn't be expecting a shove. I hoped. I also hoped that the gun would now be waving high as he tried to keep his balance. I heard it go off but nothing hit me. I got his other ankle and, still on my knees, shoved my head between his legs and reared upward with him riding my neck ridiculously, like a horseman facing the tail of his mount. With a major effort, throwing his legs free, I bucked him off violently, hurling him toward the end of the world—well, at least the end of his world.

Afterward, I stood there for a moment gasping, incapable of movement, wondering how many muscles and ligaments I'd strained, how many vertebrae I'd cracked, with that Herculean heave. I turned slowly and saw nothing there, no man, no gun, not even a smear on the wet black pavement, although he must have hit and rolled a bit before he went over the edge. I couldn't possibly have thrown him all the way clear, or could I? A scream hung in the air, barely audible over the roar of Iguassu Falls.

It was still not a nice place for a man who got dizzy on a high curb, if you'll excuse a bit of exaggeration. I stumbled away from the lousy precipice into the reassuring shelter of the trees. Only then did I remember Belinda, but she was nowhere to be seen. The noise of the falls seemed to be everywhere. Still breathing heavily, weak with reaction, I started back toward the main trail, but stopped at the sight of a high-heeled white pump—no little fairy-tale Cinderella slipper, but a good-sized female shoe—lying in the middle of the path in the rain. There was no girl in the pump. I bent over to pick it up. Then I heard a soft footstep behind me and realized belatedly that I was being stupid for the second time that day. I tried to duck, but the scarf went around my neck, tightening instantly.

I kicked backward and hit nothing; that was the expected response and my attacker was ready for it. I groped for my pocket knife, but realized that I'd never get it open in time to cut myself free. Thrashing around wildly was a waste of effort. There was really nothing for me to do but wait for the wrench that would crack my neck, but it didn't come. I simply drifted off into gray, airless unconsciousness.

Chapter 20

My first thought upon awakening was that I seemed to have managed it again, and survived it again, with a large assist from luck. Using my clumsy, alcoholic, acrophobic self as a decoy, I'd lured another predator out of the jungle; and this one hadn't eaten me, either, at least not yet. I hoped I'd attracted the right tiger this time.

It's not considered proper professional behavior, after being rendered unconscious, to pop up wide-eyed and ask: *Oh, my goodness, what happened, where am I?* I knew what had happened, and I could still hear the roar of Iguassu Falls, so I couldn't have been transported very far from where I'd been captured. Without opening my eyes or moving my body conspicuously, I took inventory. Moving would have been difficult in any case, since I seemed to be roped in a sitting position, to a tree, perhaps. There was a sore place on my head. Well, I had an explanation for that, I remembered getting sapped in my hotel room; but I couldn't recall the origin of the funny little itching sting in my upper left arm.

The familiar lump of the Swiss army knife seemed to be missing from my pants pocket; in its place was a larger bulge I couldn't identify. I added to my store of exotic knowledge the fact that being strangled with a soft scarf beat being throttled by hard fingers, as had happened to me once or twice in the past. Fingers tend to bruise; but the scarf had left no hurting memories behind. My cigarette-scorched chest, however, was still quite painful. . . .

"Helm, wake up, damn you!"

It was a throaty, sexy, female voice and I'd heard it before.

Things were coming back to me. It was the voice of the girl I'd known as Belinda Ackerman who'd last signed her name as Belinda Nunn, and I remembered clearly that any woman less nunlike would be hard to find.

Her voice went on insistently: "Who the hell grabbed me like that, just as you were heaving pretty boy into the drink? I was so busy watching, and that damn waterfall was making such a racket, I didn't notice the guy sneaking up behind me with a noose or something. . . . I thought he was going to wring my neck! How'd he get you, the same way? Where the fuck are they taking us?" After a moment her voice went on: "Oh, stop playing possum, there's nobody back here but us trussed-up turkeys. I *know* you're not dead, you can't be! They just stuck you with something when you started coming around like they did me. Didn't they?"

That explained the bee sting in my arm. There was a panicky note in Belinda's voice; apparently she didn't want me to be dead now, leaving her alone in her captivity, although she'd been raising blisters on my hide only a little while . . . It occurred to me that I didn't really know how much time had passed since we'd left my hotel room, and Ruth Steiner, and the man who'd given the torture orders, Roger Ackerman. I pulled out all the names—Dennis Morton's also, although he no longer counted—to make sure the mental machinery was working properly.

However, while my memory seemed to be intact, I was becoming aware that my initial, hasty, hazy appraisal of my present circumstances had been badly flawed. What I was leaning against was too soft to be a tree, the noise I was hearing wasn't that of a waterfall, the air I breathed didn't smell like jungle air, and there was a certain amount of vibration that had been unaccounted for in my preliminary status report to myself.

I opened my eyes to see above me, shockingly, instead of vines and trees and leaves and blue sky, the low ceiling of an airplane cabin. The lights were on, and my first thought was that I'd been unconscious so long that the sun had set; then I realized that there was daylight up forward where the cockpit was shared by pilot and copilot—or perhaps the second man was just riding shotgun up there. Aft in the cabin, however, the window blinds had been drawn, presumably so we'd have no idea of where we were being taken, not that there was much chance of my recognizing the South American landscape below, but I could at least have got some idea of our direction from the sun.

The plane seemed to vibrate more than a jet. On the other hand, although I had a view straight ahead between the heads of the two men up there, I could see no fan up forward. Okay, give it two propeller-driving motors, one in each wing. Although small by airlines standards, it would probably have seated a dozen people, give or take a few, if there had been seats for them all. However, up forward there were only the two cockpit seats. Then there was a large vacant space with slots in the floor to which seats had once been secured. Finally there were the seats we were occupying, back against the rear bulkhead.

Having been wrong about everything else, I wasn't surprised to find that I'd been wrong about the method that had been used to secure us. We weren't tied, we were taped. Well, that figured. Rope isn't necessarily a part of an airplane's equipment, but no flying machine takes off these days without a roll of silver duct tape on board; they use it for sticking the bird back together whenever it starts falling apart. I was fastened to my seat by two or three wraps of tape around my arms and upper body and several more around my thighs. I saw that Belinda was similarly secured. At the moment she was looking at the floor and sniffing like a hound on a hot trail.

"Grass!" she said.

It was her line of business and Ackerman's, not mine and Mac's. By most modern standards, although not those of my super-pure tour companions, I'm really an innocent. I stick to Scotch and martinis—booze does seem pretty innocent these narcotic days—and an occasional glass of wine with my more festive meals. Champagne for a real celebration. I know very little more about the other kinds of happy stuff than the average drug-free citizen.

The plane had not been swept out recently and there were scattered stalks and crushed dry leaves on the floor; but it could have been feed for starving Peruvian llamas for all I knew. Or cared. Except that the fact that we were being transported somewhere in what, if Belinda was correct, was a drug-smuggling plane, seemed to indicate, like the strangling scarves that had been used on us, that we'd wound up in the right hands at last, traveling toward the right destination, and maybe even the right man: the high priest of the *Compañeros de la Hoja*, the old man who'd died some time ago but who didn't know it yet. I hoped I'd get to break the news to him soon.

"How long have you been awake?" I asked the girl beside me.

"Just a few minutes. We must have been out quite a while; I'm practically dry. The last thing I remember was that damn rain running down inside my clothes as they kind of walked me between them to a van they had standing by; I never knew we'd been transferred to a plane until I woke up strapped to this seat. Christ, I bet I look like something fished out of the river." She was silent for a moment, clearly thinking of something—well, somebody—who probably hadn't been fished out of the river yet. "You're a sneaky bastard, aren't you?"

"I don't know what you mean."

"The hell you don't, Helm. My God, the way you were whining and moaning while I . . . Sorry about that, incidentally."

"All in the day's work," I said. "No hard feelings."

"And then on your knees clinging to that fence post like a scared little boy freezing in panic on a high diving board . . . . And waiting until he moved in close to kick you—you knew he'd do that, didn't you?—and flipping him off the cliff so neatly, gun and all! Well, it couldn't have happened to a nicer creep. But you don't mind making yourself look bad, do you?"

I said, "The world is full of folks trying to impress other folks with how brave they are; but the ones who survive are usually the ones who don't mind looking cowardly when required."

"I figured you were putting on an act," she said. "That's what gave me the idea."

"Idea?"

"Do I look like a girl with a weak stomach?" Belinda glanced down at her rather substantial figure and laughed. "Don't answer that question! But you were making such a fuss about a few little burns—considering the kind of tough guy you were supposed to be—that I figured you just had to be acting a part and had some kind of a plan. I was looking for an escape hatch, anyway. That guy was beginning to scare me."

"Ackerman?"

She nodded. "I mean, he was way out of his tree, you know what I mean? Moving in on another government department like that, with guns yet! Even if it *was* our assignment in the first place, shit, it was only a job. But when it happened, he ranted around like a hellfire preacher I heard as a kid, like he had the Word from Above, and anyone who interfered with his sacred mission of salvation was obviously in league with the Forces of Evil, since he was the only one who could save us all from sin and Satan. Only with Mr. Ackerman it was coke and *El Viejo*."

"He didn't trust us—me—to do a proper job?"

"He said you weren't *concerned*; you didn't *believe*. You didn't really *care*; you were merely engaged in a puny private vendetta. You were after Vasquez, not because he was wicked, not because he'd brought pain and death to millions of people, not because he'd even made a religion of that vicious addiction, but merely because he was responsible for your girlfriend being killed. A gal named Rustin, he said. Madeleine Rustin?" It was a question.

"That was her name," I said. I found that I had to clear my throat for some reason. "A very nice girl. They got my Labrador retriever, too. A very nice dog. But why does Ackerman care who reaches the old guy first? I mean, what he yearns for is a drug-free world, right? And one big step in that direction is the elimination of Gregorio Vasquez, right? Whether he does the job for beautiful idealistic reasons or I do it because the bastard's assassins killed my big yellow dog, what's the difference?''

Belinda laughed scornfully. ''You can't be that naive, Helm. What Mr. Ackerman wants is a beautiful drug-free world, sure, but a beautiful drug-free world presented to humanity in a moving public ceremony by Mr. Roger Ackerman—applause, applause—not privately by a jerk named Helm. Wake up and smell the incense, Buster. Shy and self-effacing saints we don't got nohow; they're all into PR these days.''

I nodded, accepting this, and said, ''So you got scared.''

''That's right. A girl's got to look out for herself. Suddenly here was this high-grade bureaucratic creep I was working for going totally ape, and giving me his big save-the-world pep talk—well, save America from being buried in nickel-and-dime drugs—and telling me to kidnap the widow of a best-selling author and torture an agent of the U.S government, my God! I went along for a little—it's always easier just to do what the boss tells you, I guess—but like I said, I was getting scared. He'd have me killing people next!''

I spoke deliberately: ''You're delicate or something? You've got some weirdo objection to killing people?''

She looked at me sharply, startled; then she laughed abruptly. ''All right, I admit I didn't quit giving you the cigarette treatment because I'm such a softhearted slob; I did it because I decided it was time to bail out before I let the man order me into trouble he couldn't get me out of.''

''Just bail out, or actually change sides?''

She licked her lips. ''Well, hanging from a parachute with *everybody* shooting at you is kind of lonely. I figured, even though you were in a bad spot at the moment, you were a lot tougher than you were acting and would probably wind up on top in the end. Maybe, if I gave you a hand, you'd give me a break later. . . .''

"I didn't notice you giving me any hands."

"Why do you think I talked Dennis into letting me be the one to escort you down to the river? I hoped you'd understand that the softhearted little girl who couldn't really bear to burn you wasn't going to shoot you, either, if you made a run for it. But you didn't."

I said, "Even if I'd got the message, and believed it, Dennis stayed in too good a position behind us, and was just too damn eager to shoot me for old time's sake."

Belinda said, "I really wasn't going to let him kill you, I swear it! I had my gun ready when we got down there, but you took care of him yourself before I could make up my mind to. . . ." She drew a long breath. "Maybe I hesitated too long, but damn it, Helm, I'd never shot at a man, just those big paper targets that are supposed to look like men! But before that I did help you out by giving him a big phony story about how scared you'd been on that cable car in Rio, since you obviously wanted him to think you were practically helpless with vertigo. Remember?"

I remembered, and her story had been closer to the truth than she seemed to know, but if she was really hoping to gain my trust, she was plowing a barren field; I don't even trust the certified colleagues Mac sometimes assigns to work with me. However, the girl and I were in this predicament together and there was no reason not to accept her assurances on a tentative basis, hoping we could work together to get ourselves out of it. Which didn't mean I'd turn my back on her carelessly.

"Well, I'm not holding any grudges, if that helps," I said. "As I said, getting slightly scorched is all in the day's work. And at the moment, at least, we'd better cooperate if we're both going to get out of this alive. . . . Oh, Jesus!"

"What is it, Matt?"

I didn't answer; I was watching the man in the copilot's seat. He'd looked aft to check on us; now, satisfied that we were still safely secured, he turned away from us, and I was remembering a tallish, black-clad man throwing just such a look behind him before he went over my six-foot backyard fence like a great cat. . . .

"Palomino," Mac had said as he shoved a manila folder across the desk to me.

I'd said, "Nobody's named Palomino. A palomino is a horse."

That had been in Washington, after I'd spent a dull morning looking at photographs of varying degrees of technical excellence—mostly they hadn't been excellent at all—representing black-haired killers, known hit men, about five ten, about one-seventy, who might have some connection with the South American drug trade. I'd finally narrowed it down to half a dozen who might have been the man I'd seen crouching over Mark Steiner's body. Mac had selected the most likely candidate, a man who'd been seen in the company of Gregorio Vasquez on several occasions. I'd read the condensed dossier he'd shoved across the desk:

Palomino Escobar, Hector. (For cover names employed refer original file.) Five eleven and a half, one-eighty, hair black with widow's peak, sometimes modified by razor. Eyes brown. Skin olive. Face narrow, nose long, broken once, lips thin, teeth large, chin pointed. Mustache often worn, dimensions various. Identifying marks: aside from nose break, none known. (For fingerprints refer master file.) Not known to drink excessively. Occasional use cocaine, frequent marijuana. No known homosexual tendencies. Heterosexual relationships numerous, tending toward violence. Adequate pistol, poor rifle, excellent edged weapons, adequate unarmed combat. Preferred MO: strangulation (wire). Associated Medellín to '86, current affiliation unknown. Responsible for following deaths (confirmed): DEA Agent James Pollard, Miami, May '86. Also Felix Bustamente, San Juan, Jan '82; Roman Soldana Parral, Key West, Sep '83; George Larragoite, New Orleans, May '84. . . .

Okay, so I'd missed the height by half an inch and the weight by ten pounds. The hit list went on, showing one or two kills a year. There was also an impressive catalog of unconfirmed deaths attributed to Palomino by sources of varying degrees of reliability.

I reflected that the record keepers could now add for this year: *Raoul Marcus Carrera Mascarena (alias Mark Steiner), Santa Fe*. They could note that Palomino's current employer was no longer unknown. They could also bring the modus operandi up to date: our boy was no longer enamored of the wire noose, he'd found an ancient weapon he, or his employer, liked better. . . . The fact that he'd killed a DEA agent was not a matter of great concern to me; it wasn't as if he'd got one of ours. Even then, well, we're not exactly a little band of brothers. We can't be responsible for every dumb government employee who puts his neck into a noose, or a Thuggee scarf, at least not until we're asked to be.

But the man had killed Mark, who'd been a good journalist and a friend of sorts as well as a guest in my house, and Palomino had also been accomplice to a couple of other killings of which I disapproved. On the other hand, I'd disposed of his two associates on that mission with an outsized bowie knife. He might consider that sufficient reason for disliking me; and we were in his hands.

I'd been looking for a tiger and apparently I'd found one.

Chapter 21

THE landing must have looked spectacular. I would have preferred to be standing safely on the ground watching it. In the curtained cabin, I just heard the warning thumps of the wheels being lowered; then the plane tilted sharply as it turned, presumably to line up with the unseen runway. After straightening up for a moment, it dropped suddenly and sickeningly, elevator fashion, and slammed onto the ground hard enough to drive me down into my seat and strain the tape that served me as a safety harness. I was still listening for the crack of a breaking axle or the bang of a blowing tire when I saw, dead ahead through the windshield, big, junglylooking, vine-laced trees rushing at us. We came to a stop with a little, very little, to spare.

I drew a long breath. "Goddamn all macho Latin stunt pilots!"

Belinda said, "Where the hell are we?"

Up forward, Palomino had again turned in his seat to keep an eye on us. I managed to get a glimpse of my watch at last and saw that it was now well past four in the afternoon; we'd left my room in Las Cataratas Hotel a little before eleven. Belinda's question seemed to hang in the air between us. I tried to work out a reasonable answer, but it wasn't easy. I didn't know what course we'd flown, I'd been unconscious for part of the time so I didn't know how long we'd been airborne, and I didn't know how fast a plane like this would fly. However, a conservative estimate of four hours in the air at a hundred and fifty miles per hour would put us six hundred miles from Iguassu Falls, in any direction, which gave us a large choice of countries. Paraguay was definitely a possibility, we'd actually touched that in the tour bus; and Uruguay, Argentina, and Bolivia were all within reach, if I remembered my hasty preflight atlas research correctly. Peru probably wasn't, way up there in the Andes overlooking the Pacific Ocean. . . .

A voice asked sharply, *"Who in the world is that woman?"*

Palomino had opened the cabin door when we stopped taxiing. Now I could see a silhouette in the bright opening. Female silhouettes, unless viewed with the chest area in profile, are almost indistinguishable from male silhouettes these trousered and long-haired days—in fact, the boys and girls seem to make a point of it—but the voice was unmistakably feminine, speaking English touched by one of those slightly affected eastern-girls'-school accents.

Palomino sounded surprised at the question. "On your recommendation to Señor Vasquez, I was ordered to bring here the tall hombre I see once before up in the *Estados Unidos*, the one who make such business with the big knife, and the muchacha who travel with him. This I have done."

"This you have not done!" The woman's voice was harsh. "You managed to get the proper hombre, all right, but goddamn it, the muchacha isn't Ruth Steiner!" When Palomino didn't speak at once, she went on: "Damn it, Hector, how could you make such a mistake? This isn't the woman I asked you to bring. This isn't the woman Mr. Vasquez wants!"

I reflected that *El Viejo* must really be an impressive old character, for this upper-class Yankee dame—judging by her accent—to call him Mister.

Palomino said stiffly, "Señorita, I bring the lady you say, the *rubia*, the blond one who is with the man."

Throughout all this, the pilot was writing in a notebook, perhaps the ship's log, paying no attention to the proceedings. He was just the guy who ran the streetcar; the problems of the passengers meant nothing to him.

"For heaven's sake, I described her as a skinny blonde!" The woman ducked to enter the cabin, studying us as she approached. She went on: "This one may be blond, at least

194

as long as she keeps the bleach bottle handy, but you can hardly call her skinny!''

"She is not fat," Palomino protested, and of course by the standards of his country—of most Latin countries—where anorexia is not fashionable, Belinda's well-rounded figure was practically perfect, maybe even a bit on the economical side. He said: "They come out of his room together. If she is not the Señora Steiner, who is she?"

The woman with the classy accent was standing over me now. The cabin lights were still burning, although the motors had stopped and I could see her clearly; and of course I knew her. Well, it was about time we met formally; we'd been covering the same ground for weeks. Spooky Three, otherwise known as Patricia Weatherford. Today she was looking very sporty in tailored chino shorts and a short-sleeved shirt of the same material, with epaulets. Her tennis-player arms were brown and muscular, as were her legs, terminating in white ankle socks and jogging shoes, or maybe they were tennis shoes.

She was frowning at Belinda. She spoke to Palomino without turning her head: "Actually, I know this woman. At least she's one of the tour group we've been keeping under surveillance for you. However, I have no idea what she was doing in Mr. Helm's room; I thought his affections were otherwise engaged. Her name is Ackerman, Mrs. Roger Ackerman. Her husband is considerably older. I've seen her talking with Helm, but it never occurred to me there was enough attraction there to cause a mix-up. . . ."

Palomino said stiffly, "There would have been no meex-up if the right woman had been pointed out to me, as I asked, so I would know her on sight."

"And I reminded you, and Mr. Vasquez, that Helm had seen you once at fairly close range. You'd given him good reason to remember you, up there in New Mexico. We had to keep you out of sight; we couldn't take the risk of his recognizing you and being warned. . . . Tell me what happened."

Palomino clearly wanted to carry the argument further,

but he checked himself and said, "I follow the plan we have agreed; I wait until your man in the hotel lobby signals that they have gone to their rooms. Many people are in the corridors, I wait until I can approach without being seen, but a woman comes, a big woman with a red face and white hair. I wait around the corner as she knocks on the man's door. In answer to her question I hear him call her Annie and say that Ruth feels not well and they will not take the tour to the falls. Good, I think, they will be in the rooms with all their companions elsewhere, as I want them. More people pass; then I start for the door, but step back quickly. These two are coming out, and there is a younger man with them. What younger man? This I have not been told. The signal was to be made when they were in their rooms alone."

"It's impossible to watch a hotel room constantly without attracting attention, you know that. I suppose somebody could have slipped in. . . . Well, obviously, somebody did. More than one somebody. Go on. What happened then?"

Palomino said, "I step back quickly and wait to let them pass me. He walks behind, a very serious young man who holds a gun in his pocket. You tell me the two who are wanted have a relationship. These two walk arm in arm, so close, so loving; I never doubt that she is the one with whom he travels, the one with whom he sleeps, you say. They proceed to the river. What happens at the river I cannot see until I make my way through the forest quietly, then I see a struggle on the cliff. The man fights, the woman has a gun now, also, and waits for the moment that will let her shoot without hitting the man. A true woman, I think, prepared to kill to help her man. But the man requires no help, he is strong, he throws the enemy into the river far below. While he is so engaged I take the woman and drag her into the bushes; then I take the man as he comes up the path still breathing hard from the fight and not alert, foolish enough to pick up the pretty white shoe I leave for him to see. And now you say she is not his woman, not the one we want? How many women does he have?"

Before Patricia Weatherford could answer, the pilot

slapped his notebook closed, glanced at his watch, and said something to Palomino in Spanish or Portugese—at any distance, the two languages sound too much alike for me to distinguish between them. Palomino nodded.

He spoke to Patricia Weatherford: "Ricardo says the plane must leave quickly; it is not good to leave the runway uncovered too long, even though not many aircraft fly this way. . . . You are quite certain this is not the woman *El Viejo* wants?"

"Unlike some people, I'm not likely to mistake a plump sexpot for a scrawny intellectual, even if both are blond!"

"Very well. It is a bad mistake. I will fly with Ricardo and consult *El Viejo* and determine his wishes. You and your friends will remain and watch over these two until I return."

"Damn it, you can't leave us in this hole in the jungle, that wasn't the plan at all! You're supposed to stay and help us!"

"*Sí*, I was ordered to stay and assist you with the interrogation, and then arrange an aircraft for your immediate return; but we cannot learn the addresses and the password *El Viejo* desires from a woman who is not here. So you must wait. I suggest that while I am away you find out who was the man who was thrown into the river, who is this woman, and how comes she to be with this man in his room. If he cannot learn about her from his own sources—you say she is the Señora Roger Ackerman?—*El Viejo* may request further information from you by radio, although he prefers to keep such traffic at a minimum."

Patricia Weatherford asked uneasily, "How long will you be gone?"

The man shrugged. "*Quien sabe?* I may be instructed to capture the right woman and bring her here; it could take time. Or it may be that I will never return."

"Hector, damn it . . . !"

The dark man said calmly, "It may be that having made this mistake with your kind assistance, Señorita, I will be shot, and another will take my place. Mistakes are seldom forgiven in *Los Compañeros de la Hoja*. However, at the moment there is only one mistake for *El Viejo* to forgive, if

197

he is feeling merciful; I do not wish to seal my fate by taking hasty action and making another. Or by broadcasting such a matter over the air, asking for instructions. You have food and accommodations. There are four guards for the laboratory. The captain of security who commands them will help you get settled, but he and his men have their own duties. You, and the three associates who flew in with you, have responsibility for the prisoners. Do you wish a *pistola*?''

The girl spoke angrily: ''No, I don't wish a *pistola*! I hate *pistolas*! The deal was that you people would handle the rough stuff.''

Palomino said dryly, ''The deal was that you and your people would supply the accurate information before we *Compañeros* handled the rough stuff. You had better change your mind. . . . On second thought you had better have enough weapons to arm your friends as well. I have already seen this man kill twice, not to mention an associate of mine he chopped to death just out of my sight; he is not one to be controlled by unarmed guards. . . . Señor Helm.''

I cleared my throat and said, ''Yes, Señor Palomino.''

''So you know my name.''

I said, ''We have access to pretty good records. Not that your record qualifies as good in the moral sense of the word.''

He smiled thinly. ''Neither does yours, amigo. I have read it. Very well, we know each other, we have seen each other in action. Let me give you warning, as one specialist to another. What is out there''—he waved an arm at the plane's open doorway—''what is out there is not the kind of Yankee wilderness in which you know how to operate—your dossier describes you as an experienced outdoorsman. But this is Brazilian jungle, in which no white man can operate, and very few Indians. Even if you managed to escape from this facility and elude pursuit, you would simply die out there. Please take my word for this. . . . Yes, Ricardo, we go, we go, *un momentito*.''

I might or might not heed his warning, but at least I'd learned one thing from his speech: after all the hours of flying, we were still in Brazil, or he wanted us to think we were. Well, it was a big country, occupying the whole upper right-hand corner of the South American continent, if I remembered the atlas correctly. Palomino made his way past the forward seats and came aft, carrying a large roll of silver tape. He made us bring our wrists together, with some difficulty because of the way our arms were secured, and taped them that way. Then, tossing the roll of tape to Patricia Weatherford, who'd stepped aside, he produced a moderately large, single-bladed pocket knife and cut the tape that held us to the seats; but when we started to rise, a commanding gesture restrained us.

"One more thing," he said. "You must understand that I am having you preserved because *El Viejo* himself may wish the pleasure of deciding your fate. However, I have left instructions with the captain of security that if either of you should disturb the functioning of our installation here in any way, he is to have you shot without waiting for further orders. Remember that you have little value for us. The woman who was accompanying you earlier, señor, the one I was supposed to bring, is said to have information that would have justified our tolerating some annoyance to keep her alive; I doubt that you or this lady have any." He paused briefly, perhaps to give me a chance to proclaim that my head was stuffed with priceless knowledge. When I didn't—he wouldn't have believed me, anyway—he went on: "The captain, Hernando O'Connor Rojas, is a man who knows violence. He is proud of his position here as guardian of one of *El Viejo*'s important facilities. He is not happy at being asked to function as a *carcelero*, a jailer, and he will welcome an excuse to dispose of you permanently. I suggest that you refrain from giving him one." He turned away to address Patricia Weatherford: "Now, señorita, let us find arms for you and your friends. . . ."

Five minutes later we were on the ground watching the plane taxi to the end of the runway. I noted that my guesses had been correct: it was propeller-driven, with a motor in each wing. Ricardo jumped it into the air with everything

199

roaring, and cleared the trees with something to spare, leaving us alone in the trackless jungle.

Well, not quite trackless, there was a village of sorts, and not quite alone, since Palomino had turned us over to a stocky gent with a heavy automatic pistol on his belt, whom I disregarded for the moment. I might not have another chance to look around outdoors. First things first.

Standing there with my hands taped in front of me, I made a quick survey of my surroundings. The jungle greenery all around us looked tangled and impenetrable, giving weight to Palomino's warning. The airstrip was paved, pretty fancy for a boondocks runway. It was very short, explaining Ricardo's slam-bang tactics. There was some bulky material piled along the far side that I couldn't identify without a closer look. Under the trees at the end, which had been scorched by fire, was some wreckage draped with camouflage netting. I guessed it to be what was left of the plane of a less competent pilot who hadn't quite got his flying machine stopped, or airborne, in time. The strip was at the rear of the village, which was small enough that I could see right through it to a sizable river in front that flowed eastward, judging by the sun. The current wasn't fierce, but it was strong enough to break the surface of the brown water with occasional boils and swirls. The green, green jungle overhanging the far bank looked just as inhospitable as that on this side. Snake and jaguar and orchid country.

The village itself consisted of a couple of dozen primitive-looking huts of varying sizes loosely grouped around an open area that didn't perform any obvious function. Although you'd think the arrival of a plane would be considered an event in an isolated jungle community like this, I'd seen no curious little brown aborigines rubbernecking at the noisy bird from the sky.

The pistol-packing gent beside me, the captain of security, with the unlikely name of Hernando O'Connor, was wearing rumpled khakis and a uniform cap without insignia. Although the holster prevented me from seeing it clearly, the weapon on his belt looked very much like the old .45 Colt auto, Model 1911. A small dark man stood beside him, also in khakis and cap; this one carried an AK-47 assault rifle or reasonable facsimile thereof, aimed in our general direction. Almost as many imitations of the Kalashnikov-designed blaster have been manufactured as of the Browning-designed hand cannon; I wouldn't have been surprised to learn that both of these weapons had been made right here in Brazil. Just in case I should manage to get my hands on one, I reviewed in my mind the controls of the AK-47. The old .45 was no problem. I could strip and reassemble that blindfolded. In fact, in order to pass our firearms qualification at the Ranch, we have to do just that.

It was a hot day. In that humid climate, just standing in the sun at the side of the runway—the asphalt looked ready to melt and run away—made the perspiration start all over my body, reminding me nostalgically of arid New Mexico, where you have to make a major effort to work up a sweat. Belinda was tidying herself as well as she could with her wrists taped, but there wasn't a great deal she could do about her bedraggled appearance, that was emphasized by the fact that she was missing one high-heel shoe.

My own slacks and shirt had also deteriorated significantly, but I satisfied my undemanding sartorial standards by peeling off the strips of tape that still clung to me here and there, the ones I could reach. I pulled some off Belinda's back, and she did the same for me. Then she gave a little sound of recognition and pleasure, and tugged something else free, and dropped it on the ground: her missing white pump. Apparently Palomino—very considerate for a professional strangler—had tucked it into my pants pocket for safekeeping. She maneuvered it upright with a grubby bare foot and stepped into it.

Patricia Weatherford, standing near us, spoke impatiently to the captain of security: "Can't we get into the shade?"

He shook his head minutely. "A moment, please, senhorita."

Then he checked the sky carefully and determined that it was empty except for a large, soaring bird of some kind, probably the local brand of buzzard. He fished a whistle out of his shirt pocket and blew it three times. Men came running out of the shacks. They were mostly dark-faced and black-haired, but instead of displaying the scanty loincloths or total nudity that might have been expected in those jungle surroundings, they were wearing assorted pants and shirts; most needed shaves and a couple had mustaches. Hardly the beardless children of nature native to the area, if I remembered my *National Geographic* correctly.

O'Connor waved toward the runway, and with three armed men in khakis directing them, they spread out to attack the stuff I'd noticed piled on the other side of the paved strip, and started hauling it across to our side. It turned out to be an instant cornfield. Well, maize, milo, you name it; farming is out of my line. After the heavy strips of painted canvas were all in place, the men scurried around planting bushes and weeds, and even a few saplings, on and around the camouflaged runway: an Indian village wouldn't be expected to cultivate its communal garden too meticulously.

Eight unarmed workers, I thought, and five armed *Compañeros* including Captain O'Connor. And Patricia Weatherford and the three unseen associates who'd been mentioned, also with weapons—the girl was standing nearby with the plastic grocery bag she'd been given by Palomino, heavy with four revolvers and a couple of boxes of ammunition. She held it away from her, warily, as if it held live rattlesnakes that might bite her poisonously through the plastic. There's nothing I love, in a tight spot, more than a gun-hating, gun-fearing opponent. It was a big potential advantage for our side, particularly if her associates shared the same prejudice. On the other hand, the odds were at least seventeen to two and might be worse; there could be more men still in the huts. . . .

O'Connor had stepped forward to inspect the phony grainfield; now he returned. "So. Now you can go, senhorita. March, you!"

I was aware of Belinda walking close enough to brush against me occasionally; apparently the girl required physical contact in times of stress. The gent with the AK-47 followed behind us; O'Connor and Patricia Weatherford walked ahead. The tennis girl had a neat, muscular rump that moved nicely inside the tailored chino shorts. That was, of course, strictly irrelevant, but I noted also that the huts were mostly phony: modern prefabs covered with enough poles and sticks and grass to give them a primitive look that might deceive an aerial observer who didn't fly too close. A few, however, looked as if they might be genuine, part of a real native village that had once occupied this spot, but I didn't get near enough to be certain of that. I could hear a generator thumping somewhere. The odors that reached me were not the ones of excrement and cooking and garbage that one would expect to encounter in a primitive jungle community. I could smell diesel exhaust; there was also a chemical fragrance that was vaguely familiar.

Belinda wrinkled her nose. "Coke!"

I said, "Who needs drug-sniffing dogs with you along? I didn't know the stuff smelled like that, kind of sweetish."

"Actually the leaves are pretty odorless; what we're smelling is the solvents they use in processing the stuff. I can give you the chemical names, but they wouldn't mean anything to you."

I said, "Don't be superior, sweetie. I happen to have managed a minor scientific degree at one time. Although it's kind of rusty, I might just possibly cope with those painfully complicated chemical terms if I really put my mind to it. Complicated terms like methyl alcohol . . ."

A gun barrel nudged me in the back. "No talk!"

Fine. The opposition included one timid specimen of the guns-are-ghastly persuasion and one character who, on the other hand, took firearms so lightly that he used them for poking and prying. With enough such opponents I might even be able to handle nine of them, leaving only eight for Belinda to deal with.

Then we were at the hut that, apparently, was to be our home away from home. Patricia Weatherford knocked on the door and a man opened cautiously. She gave him the plastic grocery bag.

"Around this place they pass out firearms like lollipops," she told him. "You'd better load one, if you know how. It seems that we're drafted for jailer duty."

"But that wasn't in the bargain!"

Patricia Weatherford said grimly, "There's been a stupid foul-up; Palomino kidnapped the wrong female and blames us. Now let us in, Charles. We can discuss the bargain later. And do load that gun! This man is supposed to be dangerous."

Charles was the blond boy I'd seen her having lunch with once. He wanted to ask questions, but restrained himself and backed into the room to let us enter. O'Connor, pistol drawn, escorted Belinda and me inside and waited, covering us, while Charles passed weapons to the other two in the room and opened a box of ammunition and put it on the table. It was a useful demonstration of competence and otherwise. Charles, and a tall, thin, black girl with dramatic features and a big Afro, at least knew what buttons to push in order to open the weapons for loading, but a roly-poly little middle-aged gent, with thinning dark hair plastered to his scalp in a fore-and-aft direction, had to be shown. Miss Weatherford waved away the piece that was offered her, with a grimace of distaste.

"Very well, senhoritas, senhores," O'Connor said. "As you say in your country, they are all yours. Take good care of them. Do not permit them to cause me any difficulties if you wish to preserve them alive."

He went out, closing the door behind him. Patricia Weatherford was looking at the revolver that remained on the table. After a moment she shrugged and picked it up, released the cylinder the way she'd seen it done, and stuffed cartridges awkwardly into the six chambers. I could read the printing on the box: *.38 Special, 158 grain Lead RN*, meaning round nose. Standard police ammo.

"All right," she said, closing the weapon and tucking it into the waistband of her shorts. "I suppose I'm obliged to join you in this primitive firearms ritual. Now let's put them in the other room and make sure they're secure. Jerry, bring that roll of tape, please."

"Miss Weatherford," I said.

She turned to look at me coldly. "Oh, you know my name, too. You seem to know everybody's names."

"Not everybody, but we try," I said. "Do you mind telling me what this is all about? Who are you people? I gathered from what Palomino said that you're not part of his—well, Gregorio Vasquez's—semireligious gang of stranglers."

The girl showed me a small smile. "No, we do not worship at the shrine of the leaf; we're not *Compañeros de la Hoja*, thank you very much."

"Then who the hell are you?" I asked. "And what did you all have against Mark Steiner that made you hound him and his family across two continents?"

Patricia Weatherford looked startled. "Oh, you're wrong, we had nothing to do with whatever happened to him in Peru! None of us had ever even heard of him until he escaped to the U.S., and published his book, and Mr. Vasquez made a certain pronouncement. . . . My dear man, we had nothing against poor Mr. Steiner. He was simply worth a million dollars to us."

Chapter 22

THE shack was divided into three parts. We'd already made the acquaintance of the all-purpose front room, a kind of dormitory boasting four rickety cots, a battered table with four beat-up chairs, and back in one corner, some rudimentary kitchen facilities. A partition cut off the rear of the building to make—we learned when we were herded back there—a small bedroom, or maybe cell would be a better word, containing two more cots and not much else. It was a dark little hole because boards had been nailed across the single window to take the place of bars. Another partition, with a door, cut off one side of that space. The door was open, giving us a tantalizing glimpse of some white plumbing. It had been a long plane ride.

"If that's a bathroom, you'd better let me at it, unless you want me to pee-pee all over your floor," Belinda said.

The handsome ebony female who'd elected to guard her asked, "Why should we care if you piss your pants, white girl?"

"Well, you'd have to live with the stink, black girl," Belinda answered.

Patricia Weatherford said, "Fight your racial battles on your own time, Lenore. Take her in there. Be careful, Palomino said she had a gun when he grabbed her, so it's likely she knows how to use one."

"Blondie's not going to get to use *my* gun, don't worry your pointy little head about that!" Lenore said. She nudged Belinda with the barrel of the weapon in question. "You heard the lady, go unload it before you lose it."

They disappeared into the bathroom. Another gun-barrel poker, I reflected; the world was still full of them, in spite of the fact that I've had to deal with several and those aren't poking any longer. Presently Belinda emerged from the john with her blouse hanging outside her pants; she'd apparently managed to zip and unzip, but tucking in had been beyond her, bound as she was. She was clowning relief; for an inexperienced operative she was holding up well. She could be forgiven for overdoing the funny business a bit trying to show how unscared she was. She was prodded over to one of the cots in the little room while I was allowed to take my turn at the facilities under the supervision of Charles, who at least knew enough to keep a discreet distance between me and the end of his gun barrel.

At first I'd assumed that the hut had been built as housing for the workers in this happiness factory, but on second thought I decided that it had probably been intended as quarters for the management, since in this part of the world it was unlikely that mere laborers were afforded such fancy plumbing. What I entered was an honest-to-Pete little prefab bathroom with running water—I wasn't given time to determine if the hot-water faucet actually ran hot—a molded shower with a mildewed curtain, and a flushing john. I did note that the window was too small for escape purposes. The place wasn't surgically clean, but it wasn't outrageously filthy, either.

Emerging, I was ordered to sit on the cot beside Belinda, whose legs were already taped together. Patricia Weatherford strapped my ankles with the silvery stuff while Charles kept me covered in a reasonably intelligent fashion, although I was fairly sure that he'd never before pointed a gun at another human being. I noted that Lenore was waving her piece around in a careless manner that would have got her thrown off any respectable shooting range. On the other hand, the plump little man whom I called Baldy in my mind, since his name had not been revealed to us, was concentrating hard on not shooting anybody, or himself, with the terrifying implement that had been wished off on him. Amateur night in the jungle. After rechecking our bonds, Patricia Weatherford signaled to her troops and they withdrew to the other room, closing the door behind them.

Belinda drew a long breath. "All right, now tell me what in the world is going on here!" she said. "What's all this about a million dollars?"

I'd had time to think it over and to realize, rather abashed, that we'd all managed to disregard one of the most significant factors in Mark Steiner's recent history.

I said, "Baby, you have a short memory. You forget—we all seem to have forgotten—that some time ago the late Ayatollah Khomeini offered five million dollars for the author of *The Satanic Verses*. I gather that his successor hasn't withdrawn the offer, quite the contrary. Then Gregorio Vasquez, the copycat, offered one million for the author of *The Evil Empire*. I don't think anybody's cashed in on Salman Rushdie yet, but it seems as if *El Viejo* may just possibly have paid off for Mark Steiner, although why this Spooky gang didn't simply take their million and run remains to be determined."

Belinda licked her lips. "But that's crazy! I mean, the Weatherford has lots of money of her own, and I get the impression her friends aren't exactly starving, judging by the one that got killed in Santa Fe. So why would they need—"

I said, "Us po' folks do try to get along with what we have, ma'am; it's the *ricos* who're forever trying to pick up an extra million or two. . . . But we're wasting time; they'll be back to question us any minute. We'd better settle the ground rules for possible engagement while we have the chance." I drew a long breath. "First of all, don't jump the gun. In the movies they're forever making monkeys of themselves trying to escape prematurely and getting themselves clobbered, just to keep the action moving on the screen. Forget it. We don't give a damn about moving any action; if we have to sit here for a month waiting for the right moment, we sit. Or it may look good to me five minutes from now. I think I've been through this a few more times than you have, so let me call it. Wait for my signal. If you go without it, you're on your own; and if you get yourself crippled up doing it, I won't carry you when the time comes; I'll just leave you. Understood?"

Belinda made a face at me. "Ain't you the tough one? All right, I understand. What else?"

I said, "When we do make a break, if we make one here, remember that this is not a drill. I repeat, this is not a drill."

"And just what do you mean by that?"

It was time for the Speech, the one I find myself giving, in self-defense, to all the rookies and amateurs I seem to wind up with, before battle is joined. I always have to remind them that they're in the real world now, not the bloodless TV dreamland they grew up in.

I said, "I mean that this is not a fun-fun game with paint-firing guns and rubber knives. This is for real, baby, and I don't want to be shot in the back by somebody you forgot to finish off. I want to know for sure that once you leave some-body on the ground, he isn't coming after us, ever. Or she. Take an extra moment if you have to, to do the job right, but *do* it. Okay?"

I heard her swallow beside me. "Okay," she said after a moment. "I read you, Chief."

I said, "There's just one exception. The Weatherford girl. I've got a use for her."

"What . . . Oh, never mind. I won't ask. Obviously it's love at first sight. . . . Oh, God, here they come again."

They were marching back in, in a purposeful way, having presumably held a council of war in the other room to decide how to deal with us if we proved recalcitrant. Leading the parade was the tall black girl, Lenore. She walked past me briskly and stopped in front of Belinda, looking down at her in a speculative way, like a cat lazily appraising a cornered mouse. Patricia Weatherford, less eager, came up to me and hesitated a moment before she spoke.

"You heard what Mr. Palomino said before he left. We have to know who this woman is and what she was doing in your room with another man—"

"Two other men," I said.

209

The freckled girl frowned. "Two? Nobody has said anything about—"

I said, "If whoever you had watching me had done a reasonably professional job of surveillance, instead of just loafing in the hotel lobby ogling the pretty Brazilian girls, he'd have seen them bust in on me; and he wouldn't have been quite so quick to give Palomino the go-ahead signal for the kidnapping."

Charles, standing behind the girl, asked sharply, "What was I supposed to do, lounge conspicuously for hours in the corridor outside your door?"

The girl said, "Never mind, Charles, he's just trying to provoke us. Who was the second man, Mr. Helm?"

"Who the hell would he be?" I asked. "Belinda's crazy husband, that's who!"

"That would be Mr. Roger Ackerman?"

"No one but," I said grimly. "Apparently Mr. Ackerman has a few sexual problems due to aging that make him very sensitive about the fact that his young wife is attractive to men. . . . Hell, I'd never laid hands on the girl! But he'd seen her smile at me, I guess, she smiles at everybody, it's no crime, but it gave him jealous ideas, and when his Number One Boy, who seemed to take surveillance a little more seriously than some people, saw her slipping into my room, he tipped off the boss and . . . Jesus, when I answered the door the old bastard came through it like gangbusters, foaming at the mouth and waving a gun. The guy was nuts. He was going to have his gofer kill us both and dump our bodies in the river, for Christ's sake!"

Patricia Weatherford took a moment to digest this; then she asked, "If your relationship was really so innocent, Mr. Helm, what was Mrs. Ackerman doing in your hotel room?"

I was making it up as I went along, using the same phony straying-wife theme that Ackerman had employed as a distraction, for just about the same purpose. If they bought it, okay; if not, they'd believe the truth more readily for having been made to work for it. But I was a little slow in thinking up the next answer: just what *had* brought Belinda innocently

210

to my room, in this version of the script? That's the trouble with improvising; you can talk yourself into a corner before you know it. Before I could speak, Belinda intervened.

She laughed sharply. "Don't ask him what I was doing there; he never got a chance to find out. Ask me!"

The Weatherford girl said, "Very well. What *were* you doing in Mr. Helm's room, Mrs. Ackerman."

Belinda said, "To hell with innocent relationships; I'd had too damn much innocence at home! I was trying to get fucked."

Chapter 23

A little silence followed Belinda's pronouncement. I had to restrain a grin. Obviously the girl understood what I was doing, just putting out smoke, and she was playing along to the best of her ability, aware of the basic principle that a statement that makes you look bad is always believed a lot sooner than a statement that makes you look good.

Patricia Weatherford seemed to be startled by the frank response. "But you'd spoken to the man less than half a dozen times! We were watching and we'd never seen anything to indicate . . . Are you trying to say that you deliberately visited the room of a man who was practically a stranger, just a casual tour acquaintance, in order to . . . ?" She hesitated, too fastidious, perhaps, to repeat the vulgar term.

Belinda said, "Seduce is the genteel word you're looking for, baby. . . . What the hell could I do? I had to get it somewhere, damn it; that old fart I was married to couldn't get it up anymore. We'd just tried again. He didn't even want to anymore, and he'd never thought much of morning sex anyway, but I made him try. Nothing! My God, I was ready to climb the walls, so I picked the only guy on the tour who wasn't senile, and didn't have a battle-ax wife sitting in the same hotel room, and looked like a reasonable character who might be willing to do the little girl a great big favor—"

"They're both kidding you!" This was the black girl, speaking to Patricia Weatherford. "They're just cooking up a dirty story between them to keep you happy."

Patricia glanced at her irritably, seeming reluctant to dis-

212

miss Belinda's interesting nympho fantasy. "What makes you think—"

"Just *look* at them!" After a moment Lenore went on quickly, "*Think* about it! I'm not saying that Mrs. Sexy here wouldn't climb into any bed that was handy, but if her husband is a respectable businessman—and we checked him out with the rest of the tour, remember—can you see him casually ordering his private secretary or whatever to throw his wife and her lover off a cliff? No, they're just trying to sell us a hot passion triangle to keep us away from what they really . . . What's the matter with your chest, Mr. Helm? I've noticed that you act as if it's hurting you." A moment later she had my shirt open and was pointing to the cigarette burns. "It looks as if somebody's been interrogating this man rather drastically, Pat. Don't you wonder why?" She looked down at me. "And please don't try to tell me it was just dear old Mr. Ackerman trying to make you confess to being his wife's lover. According to you, he was already taking that for granted when he broke into your room, wasn't he?"

She was a smart girl, and we'd played around long enough. I started to speak and let my words trail away. After a moment I gave an elaborate shrug of resignation.

"All right, damn it, what do you want to know?"

"First, why don't you tell us who burned you like that?"

I jerked my head toward Belinda. "Hell, she did." That silenced them again and, after a little, I went on: "Well, she started it. When she started feeling a little icky about it, the boy scout took over."

"The boy scout?"

"Dennis Morton. The jerkoff I tossed into the Paraná River. It was a real pleasure."

Lenore said triumphantly to Patricia Weatherford, "I damn well knew just by looking at them that they weren't even close to being lovers!" She spoke to me: "What did they want you to tell them?"

I said, "It wasn't me they were working on, really, it was

213

Ruth. They figured her for the softhearted type who couldn't bear to see a man suffer.''

"Ruth Steiner? Well, what did they want from her?''

I made the black girl work for it, but she wrung the whole gripping story out of me gradually. It was augmented by an occasional contribution from Belinda.

At last I said, "Well, that's about it. Ruth agreed to get the disks to save me, but having me alive made Ackerman nervous, and he figured, the way things stood, if he got rid of me, Ruth wouldn't know until after she'd kept her part of the agreement, and there'd be nothing she could do about it then. He'd already have what he wanted. So he tipped the wink to pretty boy, who was willing but unable. I flipped him into the river, like I said. When I looked around, Belinda was missing. I went looking for her, and your boy Palomino got me with his lousy scarf, making two guys I'd let sneak up behind me inside a few hours. Not the brightest day of my life.''

Patricia Weatherford, who'd been listening in silence, letting Lenore carry the ball, drew a long breath and asked:

"Why?''

"Why what?''

"Why would you bother to go looking for a female monster like you make Mrs. Ackerman out to be? First, you say, she burned you with her cigarette, and then she came along to help this Dennis Morton murder you. Why would her disappearance concern you in the least, Mr. Helm? I'd think you'd thank your lucky stars the sadistic bitch was missing and simply run away from that spot as fast as you . . . Lenore, I think this time you're the one who's being kidded!''

"I disagree. . . .''

Patricia waved aside the black girl's interruption irritably and went on: "I have a much easier time believing in a homicidal love triangle than in this implausible tale of a career bureaucrat in government service ordering the torture and assassination of a fellow government employee just because the second man had usurped a mission originally assigned to him! I don't doubt that there are people in the government

214

who take their drug enforcement work very seriously. Maybe they even make something of a religion of it, and who can blame them—it's something nobody can help feeling strongly about—but this is simply too ridiculous!" She stepped up to me and studied me for a moment. Then she slapped me lightly across the face. "I think you're still playing games with us, Mr. Helm! I think it's time you stopped trying to make fools of us with tales of panting nymphomaniacs and wild-eyed fanatics. At least give us a story that makes sense!"

It was too bad. I entered her name carefully, just below Roger Ackerman's, in the People-Who-Can't-Keep-Their-Hands-to-Themselves file.

After a moment I said, "Okay, okay, I'll give you a sensible story, if you insist. It's about a good-looking dame, born in the chips, if you know what I mean, family really loaded. And it's not as if she were a poor little rich girl condemned to a life of dull party-going and coupon clipping; the kid's got talent, she's athletic, she's shown she can be right up there with the good ones in a certain sport." I shook my head as she started to interrupt, and went on, watching her: "No, let me finish, Miss Weatherford. So what does our heroine do? Well, this attractive and talented babe who's got all the money in the world decides she needs another lousy little million. She gets a bunch of her greedy friends together to help her track down a man she's never met and keep him located until they can sell him for blood money to one of the worst drug peddlers in the world. . . ." I held up my hand when she stirred angrily under my regard. "Oh, that's quite all right, Miss Weatherford. I know it's too wild a yarn; I don't really expect you to believe me."

The girl was quite pale; the freckles showed clearly on her square, rather boyish face. "You don't understand," she breathed. "You just don't understand!"

"That's right," I said. "I surely don't understand. It seems like such a waste. I mean, you go to all this trouble to arrange it, tracing Mark Steiner to where he's hiding under a new name and identity out west, trailing him around, checking on his friends and his friends' friends, following them for weeks to learn their habits and make sure they won't interfere at the last moment, very thorough, and then you let yourself miss out on the very best part of it.''

She licked her lips. "The best . . . What do you mean?''

I said, "I mean, baby, after sending for the stranglers, why weren't you there when they moved in? You did send for them, didn't you? Vasquez wouldn't trust an amateur outfit like yours to carry out the actual execution; he had his own trained assassins for that. But he wasn't about to expose those valuable men unnecessarily in a foreign land where they couldn't operate inconspicuously—many of them probably can't even speak English—when a bunch of nice American boys and girls, who'd blend right into the scenery, were willing to do the pick-and-shovel work for a mere million. Your job was to case the situation and let the *Compañeros* know when it was time to do their stuff, wasn't it? But how could you bear to stay away and miss the show? Jeez, it was really something, Miss Weatherford! I mean, the way Mark Steiner's face turned blue when your pal Palomino pulled the scarf tight, and the way his neck cracked like a tree breaking in a high wind, really a beautiful sound—well, if you're into people dying violently a million bucks' worth!''

I guess the tennis people would have called it a big forehand, a powerful, open-handed swing to the side of my face that really rocked me. I mean, the girl had muscle. Roger Ackerman's feeble slaps had been love taps by comparison.

"You simply don't understand!''

Then she was burying her hands in her face and running out of the room, sobbing. The blond boy, Charles, stepped forward angrily.

"Don't talk to Pat . . . Miss Weatherford like that!''

I looked at the black girl, who was apparently the most sensible, if also probably the meanest, of the lot.

"Please enlighten me, ma'am,'' I said. "Just what is this thing I don't understand?''

But it was Baldy who answered. He came forward, still holding the loaded revolver he'd been issued as if afraid it would bite him, which is actually a pretty good way to handle a loaded gun. He stopped before me and spoke pedantically.

"There are plenty of people in the world, Mr. Helm," he said. "There are too many of them, actually. We had to make the decision. One man's life, the life of a member of a species that is in no danger whatever of extinction, against the survival of a whole species that is about to disappear from the face of the earth. It was unfortunate about Mr. Steiner, or whatever his name was back in his native land—"

"Raoul Marcus Carrera Mascarena," I said. "If you're going to kill them, you should at least have the decency to remember their names right."

"We kill nobody!" Baldy said sharply. "I made that clear to Señor Vasquez: we are an organization for peace and preservation. However, with our affiliated organizations, we have members all over the United States, and with the help of this membership network, I told him, we might be able to get him the information he required, for a price, the price he had already offered. What he did with that information was no concern of ours." The plump man shrugged. "Apparently, his reward had found no takers up to that time. He was willing to settle for our terms. As you probably know, we twice found him the man he wanted, once in the east, where his men apparently fumbled the job, and again in the southwest, where they were more successful." He shook his head sadly. "It was really too bad about Mr. Steiner. It would have been easier on the consciences of some members of this group, at least, if the man selected had been a wicked person whose death would have benefited society. However, Señor Vasquez had not offered his first reward for a criminal type, he'd offered it for the author of *The Evil Empire*."

"His first reward?" I said. "I hadn't heard of any others."

The bald little man smiled thinly. "Well, you wouldn't, would you?"

"Why wouldn't I?"

"One is for you."

I felt Belinda give a startled little jump beside me, but I

had no trouble controlling my reaction. It wasn't such a big deal. People have wanted me dead before and been willing to pay for it.

I asked, "Satisfy my curiosity. How much am I worth today?"

The bald man shrugged. "Only five hundred thousand dollars, I'm afraid, and in your case there were no conscience pangs. On the record—*your* record, which we finally managed to obtain—you are obviously the kind of man society can well do without. I tried to drive up the price on the grounds of risk, you are supposed to be somewhat dangerous, but half a million was as high as Señor Vasquez would go for you. And another half million for Mrs. Steiner. Here again the sentimentalists in the group made some difficulties since she is a woman, as if that made a difference, but I managed to convince them that if we turned down this money, we'd never reach our financial goal—three million was the project estimate, and we've received some eight hundred thousand in contributions, which, with the sum already received from Mr. Vasquez, leaves us short a million, two. The two hundred thousand we can probably raise somehow; but there are no angels waiting in the wings with million-dollar checks, none but Mr. Vasquez."

I said, "With angels like Gregorio Vasquez, who needs devils?"

Patricia Weatherford was returning, looking somewhat red-eyed and pink-nosed.

She sniffed and said, "I'm sorry, Dr. Weems."

Baldy, or to give him his real name, Weems, merely nodded, and went on addressing me: "The money means nothing to Vasquez, of course. His unpleasant business makes him that much in the time he takes to blow his nose; and as I pointed out to him, it was well worth another million to him—actually I asked for two million, one for each of you, but the old man drives a hard bargain—to be rid of the widow who might actually be able to assemble the scattered chapters of her late husband's manuscript, and of the government killer

218

assigned to protect her while she does it. Particularly since said government killer has a personal grudge to settle with *El Viejo*.''

I said, ''I love this government-killer routine. If I got up and started to hop toward that door, what would you do, Dr. Weems?''

He shook his head ruefully. ''I suppose I would have to try to shoot you. I would probably miss, but Charles wouldn't; he is quite a good shot, aren't you, Charles?''

''I get along with a gun,'' the blond boy said modestly.

Which meant that he, like the late Mark Steiner, was probably a pretty good marksman, on targets. The question was: how straight could he shoot with somebody coming at him?

I said, ''So it turns out that we're all killers together, but you two simply haven't been smart enough to get a government to finance your homicidal impulses.''

The bald man shrugged. ''However you want to put it. If a cause is important enough to die for—a Greenpeace member died, you'll remember—it is important enough to kill for.''

I said, ''I knew we'd get to a noble cause sooner or later. Just what is this great cause Mark Steiner and Mrs. Steiner and I, and maybe Mrs. Ackerman as well, are being sacrificed for? And why? I mean, the freckled lady over there has money to burn, I'm told; she should be able to produce a couple of mil without breathing hard. Why doesn't she, instead of becoming accessory to the murder of an investigative journalist who was doing good work in his field, and of his wife, the mother of two children. I won't mention myself, since you feel I'm not an asset to society, but those two people qualify, don't they? Are you certain that the good you'll do with the blood money you got for Mark will be greater than the good he would have done if he'd been allowed to keep on writing?''

The freckled girl said breathlessly, ''Oh, God, I wanted to give the money, but I'd long since gone through everything

219

I'd won at tennis, and the trustees wouldn't let me touch my principal. They said they had to draw the line somewhere; they said I'd wasted enough on crackpot causes. Crackpot? The survival of the world is a crackpot cause?''

The little man said, ''As far as Mark Steiner was concerned, what contribution was he really making? All he ever wrote about was drugs, that nonsense. A totally artificial situation. Pretty soon they will pass the same stupid laws against chocolate candy, very bad for you, and we will hear a great many fine speeches about the war against obesity and the terrible Hershey cartel. And people will shoot each other in the street for Nestlé's bars worth a thousand dollars an ounce.'' He shook his head. ''The crime with which we deal is not artificial; it is the very real crime of extermination, in this case the extinction of yet another marvelous species that can never be replaced, that the world cannot afford to lose. Our wonderful aquatic friends in the southeastern United States are dying daily for want of protected refuges. With all due respect to the labors of the Nature Conservancy, and the rather ineffectual club that's working in the same direction, the Crystal River is not enough. The MPS has an option on a suitable area on the other side of the state where the need is desperate—''

I interrupted: ''What's an MPS?''

The black girl, Lenore, said, ''Dr. Weems is a professor of marine biology and probably the world's greatest expert on the manatee, which he has studied all his life. Knowing that she'd supported a number of similar movements, both privately and as a director of the Earth Government Group, he went to Patricia for help. Between them they organized a branch of EGG called the Manatee Preservation Society—''

I'm afraid I was very rude. I couldn't help it. I don't hold with ridiculing people's religions or beliefs, but it just burst out of me: I interrupted her with a hoot of vulgar laughter.

I shouted, "My God, Belinda, did you hear that? We're going to die so they can finance a home for a bunch of lousy sea cows!"

Chapter 24

THE cot was pretty crowded with two of us on it. The fact that we had our wrists taped in front of us made things awkward, preventing me from assuming any of the positions I normally would have when sharing a bed with a girl, even with the purest intentions. So we wound up lying on our backs, squeezed together precariously side by side, staring at the ceiling. At least it was precarious on my side; Belinda had the wall to hold her in place. After a little she giggled softly.

I said. "Share it. Don't keep it to yourself."

"It would be interesting to see if we could, all tied up like this, wouldn't it?"

"Oh, my God!" I said. "Here we are, bound hand and foot with death staring us in the face, and the dame can't think of anything but sex!" After a little I said, "Don't wiggle, damn it. You'll shove me off on the floor. . . . What the hell are you doing?"

"I've got pretty strong nails; I thought maybe I could peel some of that tape off your wrists. . . ."

"That wasn't a wrist you were groping, baby. And I told you, just relax and let me call the shots, please."

"Well, excuse me all to pieces!"

I didn't want her angry, so I explained: "As Palomino pointed out, there's an awful lot of mean jungle out there. Just because we can get loose from this tape, maybe, doesn't mean it's a good idea right now. Let's stick it out for a while and see how the situation develops. Stick it, tape, that's a pun, get it?"

"Ha-ha. Just so it doesn't develop a bullet in the head,"

she said tartly. She lay beside me in silence for a little; at last she asked, "Just what the hell *is* a manatee?"

"Well, it's smaller than a whale and mostly it's bigger than a seal, although I guess some sea lions and walruses will go that large. A thousand pounds or so, full-grown. It's a placid, blimplike beastie, with a couple of flippers and a tail, that kind of paddles around in coastal waters—I think the range runs from Florida to Texas—and eats grass. A very peaceful animal, I understand. I've heard of attacks by walruses and whales, but never by sea cows. No aggression and not much sense of self-preservation. In particular, it has no sense at all about motorboats. Manatees are forever getting themselves killed by propellers along the Intracoastal Waterway and other channels; in fact I've been told that you rarely see a manatee without a prop scar or two. It seems to be just about the biggest cause of manatee mortality; which I suppose is why these folks are plugging for manatee preserves that are off limits to powerboats, at least, if not to all boats and people. They have a point. I'd hate to see the big ugly gentle things die off, myself. The catch is, I'd hate worse to see me die off. And Ruth Steiner. And you."

"I was waiting," she said. "I thought you'd get around to me sooner or later, but I wasn't quite sure." Belinda was silent for a little; when she spoke again, it was on a different subject: "These people, the ones in the other room, they're kind of crazy, aren't they?"

"Who isn't?" I said. "Your boss is killing people, or trying to have them killed, for a little white powder; these people are killing people, or having them killed, for a big black mammal. Well, folks get pretty hysterical about saving the whales and the elephants, why not the sea cows? It's the old crusader syndrome. It used to be just souls that had to be saved for Christ with a sharp sword or a hot auto-da-fé, but nowadays everybody's saving everybody and every-thing—human, animal, vegetable, or mineral. It's a fine ide-alistic impulse, no doubt, but apparently some of these world saviors are getting fanatic enough to sacrifice human lives for their pet salvation projects, which seems like overdoing it. But that's enough amateur philosophy. Let's shut up and get some sleep.''

In the business, you learn how to do it, or you don't last long; an insomniac agent can turn into a dead agent very fast. I was tired enough that I had no trouble drifting off, and if I had any dreams, they're none of your damned business; but suddenly I was teetering on the edge of a precipice and somebody was trying to push me off into the bottomless void. . . .

''Take it easy! Don't tear it, damn you!''

Clawing for a handhold, I'd managed to grasp a flimsy bush growing on top of the cliff, that turned out to be Belinda's blouse.

She said irritably, ''God, you were *really* asleep! I didn't think you lethal guys ever slept.''

''How many lethal guys have you known?'' I asked, releasing her and trying for a little more of the cot. She wasn't leaving me much. I noted that the light in our room was fading. Somebody'd opened the connecting door, presumably to look in on us, and left it ajar. Artificial light from the other room spilled through the crack, along with a murmur of conversation and some other sounds that I identified, tentatively, as the clatter of eating implements against plastic dishes. The slanting beam of light only made our room seem darker, too dark to read my fancy digital watch since I couldn't reach the pushbutton that illuminated the numbers. When Belinda didn't answer my question, I asked, ''What made you decide to kick me out of bed?''

She said, ''I just nudged you a little to wake you up. Maybe we're going to get fed. At least I think somebody brought in some food, but they don't seem to think much of it. Listen.''

I heard the black girl's voice: ''Damn it, I know a goat when I eat one! Don't tell me mutton, no sheep was ever this tough.''

Dr. Weems spoke judiciously: ''The flavor is . . . very interesting.''

''Somebody'd better take some to the prisoners.'' That was Patricia Weatherford. ''We can't let them starve.''

"Why the hell not?" Lenore asked callously. "I'll bet pretty soon Vasquez will send word to have them shot, anyway. Like Palomino said, they're no use to him."

"Well, let them die with full tummies," said the voice of the blond boy, Charles. "And I don't see why we have to keep talking about it. I know the project is terribly important and we have no other way of financing it, but this is still a dirty business and we don't have to talk about it."

There was a brief silence; then the Weatherford's voice asked, "Where are you going, Lenore?"

"Somebody said to feed the animals."

The door swung wide, spilling more light into our rapidly darkening room. The black girl entered cautiously, a lean, faceless silhouette with a gun; then she saw us on the cot, revealed by the light from behind her, and relaxed a little. She found a bare bulb hanging from the ceiling and pulled the chain.

"My, don't you two look cozy on that little cot. You can sit up now." She laughed, watching us as we helped each other struggle upright, and said, "What's the matter, Blondie, scared? Don't worry, we're not going to shoot you . . . yet. Right now, all we're going to do is feed you, not that you need it. With that figure, you could live on your own lard for a month. No wonder your old man couldn't get it up, it must have been like fucking a rubber balloon. . . ."

Patricia Weatherford, coming in behind her, said, "That's enough, Lenore. Just cover me while I cut them loose enough so they can eat."

I'd managed to dig my fingers into Belinda's thigh, to keep her from responding angrily to the insults. The freckled girl did the job with a small, pearl-handled penknife, freeing both our wrists and our ankles. Dr. Weems came in with a steaming bowl in each hand. The blond boy, revolver ready, was playing backup at the door, but it was still an amateurish performance and I didn't think we were going to have much trouble when the time came. The big problem would be recognizing it when it did come. As for the stew, well, it was food and I'd tasted worse, but not very often. Afterward,

225

they let us use the bathroom; then they taped us up again and left us with the light on and the door open. After a little Belinda drew a long, angry breath.

"She's mine! When we go out of here, the black bitch is mine!" When I didn't respond to this, she said, "Tell me, just why don't you want the Weatherford dame killed, aside from those cute freckles?"

I didn't like talking about it, even though it seemed unlikely that this pseudo–jungle hut was wired for sound. I don't really believe in psychic emanations, but somehow things you talk about seem to occur to other people more often than things you don't. However, I'd leaned on the girl pretty hard and I had to give her something in return.

I said, "I got a quickie version of her background. Miss Weatherford can fly. She's got an amateur pilot's license of some kind."

Belinda said, "License or no license, I don't think I want to be aboard when a Sunday bird girl tries to get a plane off that sawed-off airstrip. It looks bad enough with a real pilot at the controls; I thought Ricardo was going to wind up in the trees, both coming in and going out of here."

I said, "Say we get loose and overpower the manatee boys and girls. The way they handle firearms, it shouldn't be too difficult. We make sure that no matter what we do to the others, including Lady Lenore, the Weatherford survives. We tie her up, take the guns we've liberated, and dispose of Captain O'Connor and his security force. If we did the first part of the job quietly enough so that we have the advantage of surprise, we may even manage that. Let's just hope the workmen don't have arms enough, or interest enough, to interfere. We try to time the whole thing for when we know a plane is coming in; then we let it land and get control of it somehow."

Belinda swallowed. "Wow, you rattle it all off as if you thought it would be easy!"

"Not easy, but possible," I said. "People have these oddball notions about other people. They may be totally ruthless, themselves, but they never quite believe that anybody

226

else is. They expect a little hesitation, a little menacing chit-chat, at least, before the hammers fall and the guns go off. Particularly from a pretty woman. If you walk out there, even with a cocked Smith and Wesson in each hand, Hernando O'Connor and his four male Latin chauvinists will be quite sure they can sweet-talk you into letting them get close enough to disarm you. You should be able to get a couple of them, at least, while they're telling you how you should put down your guns, beautiful lady, because you are obviously made for loving, not shooting, and you couldn't possibly mean to hurt such handsome and virile gentlemen. . . . Meanwhile, of course, I'll be sneaking up behind them to deal with the ones you leave alive. That's one way we might work it; there are others. We'll have to see how it breaks. But the plane will be the hard part.''

She grimaced. "Harder than dealing with the four MPS loonies and the five security guards: nine armed people?''

I said, "Forcing a pilot to fly you somewhere is very tricky, in fact practically impossible. Once in the air, he has your life in his hands. No matter how menacingly you wave your gun at him, he knows you can't afford to shoot him, not unless you're capable of handling a plane yourself, which I'm not—or unless you have another pilot in reserve, which is where Miss Weatherford comes in. Like you say, getting off that strip is probably beyond her aeronautical capabilities, although, athletic as she is, she may be better than we think; but once we're airborne, her presence will help me keep Ricardo, or whoever, in line. He'll know that if he gets too tricky, I can shoot him and figure on her bringing us down somehow, if only as a matter of self-preservation. . . . Well, let's wait and see how it goes.''

Belinda said wryly, "I hope we don't have to wait too long. Being wrapped up in duct tape and eating goat isn't my idea of a tropical vacation.''

Actually, we were there a full week. It rained off and on and the roof leaked; otherwise nothing much happened of interest, except that I was moved to the other cot to keep us from working on each other's bonds or whispering in each

227

other's ears. On the evening of the sixth day Lenore came marching in to us with her gun at mealtime, as usual; but there was malicious triumph in her attitude today.

"Better make the most of dinner, Blondie," she said. "Our lady führer just got the word from Captain O'Connor. It came over the radio. Seems like that old fart, Vasquez, has finally made up his mind, and we go out of here in the morning as soon as it's light enough for the plane to land. *We* go. The captain has other orders about you; and I don't think you'll be eating breakfast, honey, so like I said, you better savor every mouthful of this meal. Lousy though it is, it's probably your last."

We went through the usual routine of eating and peeing and were taped up again—the silver stuff was getting pretty low on the roll, I noted, but if the black girl was correct, it didn't have to last much longer. It had been nice of her to let me know it was time to go to work. After they'd left us, I lay considering what I had to work with: a trick belt buckle and a little knife in each shoe and a silk handkerchief. Strangely, Palomino had taken my Swiss army knife but left me the gaudy bandanna; apparently it hadn't occurred to him that this could serve the same purpose as his lethal black scarf. The fact that he'd missed the other hardware wasn't surprising. It was designed to be missed, and he was presumably trained for strangling, not searching. One knife would have been enough; however, our armorer had explained that it had seemed advisable to have the shoes show up in the X-ray machines with identical-looking steel shanks. Actually, I don't think he expected anybody to compare my shoes so carefully; he just likes to have things tidy and symmetrical.

I made my plans and waited for things to settle down. They had a kind of watch system; one would stay awake for two hours and then arouse his, or her, relief. Each one was supposed to take a good look at us upon assuming the duty. Tonight the first shift belonged to Patricia Weatherford. She took a step into our cell, saw that we were where we were supposed to be, and started to turn away; then she changed her mind and came over to my cot and stood looking down at me for some time.

At last she drew a long breath and said, "I'm sorry about this, Mr. Helm. I wish you'd try to understand. . . ."

When I didn't give her any help, she left the sentence incomplete and turned and walked away, slowly. She was obviously stalling, hoping I'd call her back and say something to her, either something nasty that would prove I deserved to die, or something noble that would tell her that I really appreciated what a wonderful thing she was doing, preserving a unique and precious species from extinction, and that I forgave her for sacrificing me, among others, to do it. I don't know. I have no trouble understanding the world destroyers like Gregorio Vasquez, but the world saviors like Patricia Weatherford mystify me, which undoubtedly says something unpleasant about me.

I decided that my move should be made about 11:30. I didn't want to have to deal with a freshly awakened guard but I wanted to give this one time enough to get sleepy. Later in the night, or morning, they might get even sleepier; but I didn't care to cut things too fine. This way, if things didn't look right on this watch, I'd have time to abort and try again later. I set my mental alarm and closed my eyes. . . .

A scuffling noise aroused me. It took me a moment to realize what it was; then I turned my head and saw Belinda halfway between our two cots. Kind of like a jackrabbit in slow motion, on hands and knees, the idiot girl was making awkward progress toward me, right out in the open room under the grimy light bulb, where anyone just glancing through the door couldn't help but see her.

"Get back!" I hissed, waving her away as well as my bonds permitted. "Get back to your cot, damn it!"

But she kept coming, and I didn't dare speak again. Reaching me, she grabbed me by the arm with both tethered hands and shook me violently.

"Damn you!" she whispered. "Damn you, they're going to kill us in the morning and you just lie there snoring!"

I said, "I told you to wait for my signal, Belinda."

She looked at me for a moment, her anger fading. "Oh, shit, did I goof? I was so scared—"

"Never mind," I said. "Just get back where you belong before. . . . Oh, Christ, she's heard you, here she comes! What the hell are you doing?"

What she was doing was kissing me passionately, kneeling beside my cot. Well, it wasn't exactly an original idea, and if we'd been dealing with pros, it would have been a waste of time; I couldn't believe even amateurs would fall for it. But it wasn't a bad way to waste time, and I cooperated to the best of my ability. We got as close as our bound hands allowed and let ourselves work at it breathlessly, oblivious— well, almost oblivious—of the approaching footsteps. Then Belinda lifted her head irritably.

"Go away!" she snapped at the freckled young woman standing over us. "If you're going to sell us to the butchers tomorrow, you can at least . . . Go away!"

She put her mouth to mine again, without waiting for a response. After a while we heard footsteps moving away.

"Okay, now my belt buckle," I whispered after a certain amount of time had passed. Being somewhat distracted, I wasn't quite sure how much. I kissed the lady's ear. "You said you had strong fingernails. It's covered with foil that's supposed to peel off. It's sharp underneath, so be careful, don't cut yourself. . . . Hold it, something's happening out there!"

Somebody had come into the hut, several somebodies. I heard a chair fall over; apparently Patricia Weatherford had spilled it, getting to her feet hastily. I heard her voice.

"What . . . ? Oh, you want me to move over that way? All right, but why does it matter where . . . *Oh, no! Oh, don't, please don't, no you can't!*"

Then the automatic weapons opened up.

I rolled off the cot on top of Belinda, and got us both underneath it, and flipped it over onto its side between us and the doorway end of the room. Hard as that mattress was, it ought to be good for something, like stopping a bullet, or at least slowing down a ricochet. The racket of several assault rifles set to full auto firing at once beyond the open door was unbelievable. Belinda had burrowed against my back as closely as her bound hands allowed; I felt her cringe at each new burst in there. The Latins have a love affair with the rat-tat-tat guns, they purely love to hear them sing their murderous, staccato songs. The shooting continued longer than there was any sense in; there weren't all that many people around to be killed. Actually, when it has to be done, I prefer to use just one bullet per target. Economical.

At last there was silence in the other room. I heard a command being given and figured it was our turn, but there was nothing to be done about it. Nobody came through the door.

"Who are they?" Belinda breathed at last.

"Oh, I think it's Senhor O'Connor and his crew. Those Kalashnikovs have a pretty distinctive sound; I've heard them before."

I heard her swallow hard in the darkness. "You're very calm about it. They're going to kill us next, I suppose."

"Actually," I said, "I think they're gone."

"Oh, Jesus!"

"Are you okay?"

After a moment she whispered, "I . . . I guess so. I just . . . just never died before."

I struggled to my feet, and set the cot upright, and helped her up, and guided her to it. She moved like a sleepwalker, and sat down heavily, and rested her face against her bound hands.

"Are you okay?" I asked again.

She looked up irritably. "Don't keep asking that. Sure I'm okay. I didn't even wet myself. I'm great. What do we do now? Isn't it about time to put the Great Escape back on the tracks, Mr. Houdini? Move around so I can reach that buckle."

I said, "Never mind the buckle."

She stared at me. "But we've got to get out of here before they come back and—"

I said, "Don't be stupid. If they'd wanted to kill us, we'd be dead."

"But—"

I said a little impatiently, "Sweetheart, how many shots were fired in the other room?"

"I don't know. Hundreds, by the sound."

"And how many bullets came our way?"

"Well, none . . . I don't understand what you're driving at!"

I said, "Four or five men emptied four or five assault rifles in there, maybe even reloading a time or two, and not one bullet passed through this room; even though the walls aren't thick enough to stop a marble from a kid's slingshot. Doesn't that say something to you? Doesn't it tell you that they were very careful not to direct their fire this way? I assure you, baby, there's just no way it could be accidental. Hell, they even made the Weatherford girl move before they opened up, I'll bet so she'd be standing against one of the other walls, not the partition between the rooms." I grimaced. "They obviously had their orders: shoot as much as you want, boys, have lots and lots of fun, make lots and lots of noise, but if you send one stray slug into that other room, *El Viejo* will eat your *cojones* on toast in the morning. Or whatever 'balls' translates to in Portuguese."

"But if they want us alive, why haven't they come for us?"

"Because they're in no hurry. The plane won't land until dawn. Meanwhile they're waiting to see if we'll come to them."

"You mean, they're lying in wait outside . . . ? How do you know?"

"Because if they've got any brains, they've got to be. Look, we ought to be pretty panicky in here, wouldn't you say, after hearing all that shooting next door? We'll be expecting the same firing squad to come for us any minute, won't we? As you did. So if we have any getaway secrets we've been saving, that Palomino didn't spot when he searched us, now's the time we'll trot them out, right? And slip out of here triumphantly—right into the arms of the waiting security guards, with all our hidden tricks and weapons on display, ready to be confiscated."

Belinda sighed. "I suppose you know more about it than I. . . . So what do we do?"

I said, "It's obviously no use trying to make a break tonight, with everybody on the alert, so we just catch up on our sleep some more. And this time, if you want to share a cot with me, I get the inside."

They came for us well after daylight.

Chapter 25

RICARDO made it again, although I thought I heard the topmost leaves of one jungle giant slap into the underside of the plane lightly, just a farewell pat, as our hero pilot jumped us off the runway and shot us skyward like a jet, with the wheels slamming home and the straining engines shaking the plane to pieces—at least there was enough rattling and clattering and buzzing that I expected some important parts, like the wings, to fall off before we were clear. But we made it, apparently without losing anything essential, and Ricardo put us into a tight left turn that laid the aircraft over and would have let me—I had the seat on that side—look down at the asphalt strip we'd just left if the cabin curtains hadn't been drawn, as before. Presumably the workers were already hurrying to turn it back into an innocent cornfield.

I became aware that Belinda was squirming beside me. She seemed to be trying to accomplish something with her feet, hampered by the tape that bound her legs together. Palomino, still riding shotgun, hadn't strapped us in as thoroughly as on our last plane trip. Perhaps because he was running short of the stuff—he seemed to have retrieved the diminishing roll he'd left with the late Patricia Weatherford—he'd simply let us retain the tape that had been put on our wrists in the hut, earlier, and secured our legs. I suppose it improved our chances of escape, but at the moment, at least, there was no place to escape to, and I was beginning to wonder if escaping was such a great idea, anyway.

"What the hell are you doing?" I asked Belinda.

"My shoes!" she said, with a grimace of disgust. "Ugh, I can't bear to . . . ! Oh, God, I'm going to be sick again!"

I said unsympathetically, "Well, if you have to, aim it the other way, please; I'd rather not have it in my lap. And you'd better leave your shoes on even if they are a bit messy. If things happen in a hurry, we'll have problems enough without you limping around barefoot."

Actually, there wasn't much blood on her beat-up pumps, but there had been no way either of us could have avoided stepping in it a little. With four people shot to pieces in the front room of the hut, the floor had been pretty well flooded. They still hadn't been removed when we were taken through. The ones who'd been asleep had apparently managed to make it off their cots before the bullets cut them down; and they all lay where they'd fallen, sprawling gracelessly in the congealing lake of gore: the tall, blond boy who hadn't wanted to talk about it, the handsome black girl with the big racist chip on her shoulder, the balding little professor who loved sea cows, and the sturdy, freckled, young woman who should have been playing in the French Open or Wimbledon or whatever prestigious tennis events they run in the spring, instead of conducting wild-eyed money-raising projects in the Brazilian jungle. But they do get blinded by their great shining causes; and I suppose it could be argued that being totally concerned, even if it leads to occasional excesses, is at least a slight improvement over being totally unconcerned.

I saw Belinda stare for a moment at the bodies; then she stumbled outside and I could hear her vomiting helplessly. Urged on by Captain O'Connor, I followed more slowly. I'd seen dead people before, both fresh and stale, and they don't affect my digestion much, but as I picked my way out of that butcher shop I knew I was going to miss Spooky Three even if she had slapped me pretty hard. I'd become kind of used to looking over my shoulder and seeing her there. I glanced at the captain of security, whose heavy face didn't look like that of a humorist, but he'd had his little joke nevertheless, leading them to think, happily, that they were leaving this place on the morning plane. . . .

Belinda had stopped trying to poke off her shoes. She also seemed to have conquered her recurring nausea, but her eyes were still wide and shocked.

"Why?" she asked. "Why would they kill them?"

The antecedents of that were a little scrambled, but the meaning was clear. "A mistake was made," I said. "In that business, when a mistake is made, you kill somebody, it's standard operating procedure. It keeps the boys and girls on their toes. Palomino half expected to die, remember. He knew somebody had to. The choice was between him, the MPS gang, and us. Aren't you glad *El Viejo* didn't choose us?" When she didn't answer, I went on, "Besides, they'd served their purpose; what more could they do for Vasquez? This way he even saves a little blood money, not having to pay them off a second time, although I doubt that figured largely in his calculations; he's got the stuff to burn."

Belinda started to speak again, but changed her mind and settled back in her seat. It was a long flight, and I was starting to wonder about the fuel situation, even though a lot of gas had been pumped aboard at the cocaine-factory when Ricardo and Palomino picked us up; but at last our pilot dove suddenly and made one of his crash-bang landings on a rutted dirt airstrip that fought right back. We were allowed to relieve ourselves in the nearby bushes, one at a time, while Ricardo dragged the camouflage netting from a stack of fuel drums at the side of the strip and filled the plane's tanks laboriously by means of a hand pump. Then we were leg-taped again and airborne again after the usual noisy acrobatics.

"Oh, my God!"

Startled out of a semidoze, I looked at Belinda. She was staring forward, past Palomino's head, and by straining sideways a bit I could get almost the same view through the windshield. It was a jagged wall of rock that reared up spectacularly against the sky ahead, capped with white even now, at the end of the South American summer. Or maybe, up there, it was the beginning of winter.

There are times in eastern U.S., and elsewhere, when I

236

get a little impatient with folks who talk about mountains when the rocky stuff to which they're referring only goes up a mere mile or so into the air. Hell, in Santa Fe I live at seven thousand feet, and at one time, in the winters, my wife and I used to drive fifteen miles up behind town several times a week to go skiing at ten thousand. That was back when I indulged in innocent pastimes like matrimony and skiing. But the South American mountains are high enough to earn anybody's respect, even that of an old cliff dweller like me. In fact, there are twenty-thousand-foot-plus Andean peaks that, I believe, are as tall as anything the Rockies have to offer, or maybe even a little taller.

Belinda drew a long breath. "My God, are we going through *that*?"

"If we can't go through it," I said, "we're in deep shit, baby, because I doubt very much that this puddle jumper has the guts to climb over it."

But it turned out to be Ricardo heaven. He found a crack in the wall of rock and snow and hurled us into it and took us through it exuberantly like a kayaker happily shooting the rapids of the Rio Grande. A few dead people hadn't bothered my stomach at all, but even though the curtains prevented me from seeing the wing tips flirting with the walls of the winding passes we were penetrating, the plane's gyrations soon had me wishing there was a seasick bag handy, just in case.

To the best of my knowledge there were no mountain ranges of significance in South America except the Andes, which ran down the western side of the continent. Since we seemed to be crossing them, we pretty well had to be heading for one of the countries on the Pacific coast: Chile, Peru, Equador, or Colombia. I remembered that Colombia was Vasquez's original stamping ground. On the other hand, Mark Steiner had been hounded out of Peru, so obviously *El Viejo* had strong connections there, also—the Peruvian Andes were, after all, the ancient home of the coca leaf—and Peru was closer. I decided that if I were a gambling man, I'd put my money on Peru.

"Oh, Jesus, I think we're really out of those damned rocks at last!" Belinda spoke in an exhausted voice, as if she'd personally carried the plane the whole way through the mountains; and of course she had, with my help. Now Ricardo was flying reasonably straight for a change, but it didn't last. Belinda sighed. "Oh, God, what's he doing now?"

We'd made a right turn and seemed to be following the western flanks of the Andes northward. This lasted for quite a while. I'd expected us to lose altitude once we were through the high passes; but if anything, the plane seemed to be trying for even greater elevations. At last there was some more twisting and turning and Ricardo reached for his microphone, spoke into it, listened, and made some adjustments to our course, descending. He set us down on a paved runway without a jar, as if to show us he could do it that way, too. The guy really could fly. Then Palomino was cutting us free once more, legs and arms both, and instructing us to clean the tag ends of tape off each other.

"This is a different jungle, señora, señor," he said, "but please to understand it is our jungle. The police are ours and the taxi drivers are ours and the hotel people are ours. No one will help you escape us. It is known that anyone who assists our enemies, particularly U.S. government enemies like you, will soon die. And it is also known that anyone who assists us will be well paid for his efforts. So it is much better for you if you cooperate, okay?"

Belinda said, "Sounds like that place in Colombia, Medellín, where the drug lords blow up all the judges and politicians who don't play ball."

I said, "I don't think we've come quite that far." I glanced at Palomino. "Cuzco, Peru?"

Palomino frowned. "What makes you say Cuzco, señor?"

I should have kept my mouth shut; it's never smart to be clever. But it had been said, so I breathed deeply and patted my chest. "I can feel it here. I'm pretty used to altitude; if I can feel it, it's got to be at least ten thousand feet. Over three

238

thousand meters. How many cities with real airports do you have at that elevation? Cuzco is the only one I've read about."

Palomino said, a bit stiffly, "Cuzco is at the approximate elevation three thousand seven hundred meters or eleven thousand feet, so I suggest you refrain from any violent activity until you become accustomed."

I said, "Well, that's one way of keeping prisoners in line, take away their oxygen."

We found the sun low in the west, hot and red, when we descended to the pavement and could look around. It was a small airport, but a sizable jet was parked near the terminal and we could see people at the gates waiting for the word to board, too many people for Belinda's peace of mind.

"Oh, God, I can't go through that crowded building looking like this, I haven't been out of my clothes for a week, I'm a disaster area!" she protested.

But a car had come onto the field and was approaching our little plane, a block-long black Cadillac limousine, polished until it shone like a diamond, transportation deluxe. However, the windows were dark, at least from the outside, and when we'd been ushered into the capacious rear, the uniformed chauffeur pushed a button and both doors clicked softly. I didn't even bother to confirm that we were locked in.

But if it was a jail cell on wheels, it was certainly a luxurious one. Unfortunately, my first reaction to the plushy interior was to remember that I needed a shave and a bath, and a clean shirt wouldn't hurt a bit. Maybe Belinda's dainty concern for her appearance was rubbing off on me. Palomino had got into the front seat. A glass partition prevented me from hearing what he said to the driver, but the car began to move. No officials had come near us; apparently no representatives of *El Viejo* had to worry about foolish formalities like customs and immigration.

Cuzco turned out to be a city of very narrow streets full of shabby pedestrians moving in all directions and yielding the right of way only reluctantly to the vehicles, which were not very numerous. The long Cadillac had to proceed slowly because it was a close fit in many places and could only barely make it around the corners, like a semi maneuvering in a New York alley. I wondered how many kidnap victims had had the privilege of riding in the most conspicuous car in town. I hadn't taken Palomino's pronouncement that Cuzco was a wholly owned subsidiary of *El Viejo*'s operation too seriously. Naturally, since it would make us easier to manage, he'd do his best to trade on the image of all-powerful South American drug lords presented in the U.S. press and make us believe we were completely surrounded by enemies. However, the spectacular Cadillac indicated, at least, that he felt no need to keep a low profile here, even though he was transporting a couple of unwilling guests.

Reaching the center of the city, we passed a couple of churches or cathedrals that would have rated a second look if we'd been in the mood for religious architecture. The chauffeur squeezed us through some particularly narrow lanes; at last he started to turn into an alley leading to the rear of a massive old building that looked like a hotel, but stopped when he found it completely blocked by a tour bus that was just discharging passengers.

"Hey, there's Grace; that's our tour!" Belinda said quickly.

Palomino was already speaking to the driver, who was backing us out of there; but I saw white-haired Annie and dowdy Mrs. Gloria Priestly and lean husband Herman. I also saw, sharply dressed in yellow slacks and a white sport shirt, Roger Ackerman, who'd ordered me killed (join the club, Roge, old boy), and beside Ackerman I saw a slim young woman with ragged light hair who glanced casually at the retreating Cadillac but could not, of course, see us behind the dark window glass; it was like one of those dreams where you can see everybody but you're not really there, so nobody can see you. Ruth wore her short blue denim skirt and one of her short-sleeved knitted shirts, this one striped red and white. As the movement of the Cadillac cut off my view of the narrow alley she was allowing Ackerman to escort her toward the door of the hotel.

Palomino had picked up a microphone, and his voice

reached us from hidden speakers: "An unfortunate delay,"
he said. "We must wait. I suggest that you serve yourselves
with drinks; the bar is in front of you. But do not drink too
much. Don Gregorio Vasquez Stussman is expecting you for
dinner, and you will find much refreshment there."

Chapter 26

"I don't believe this!" Belinda said.

"I don't believe it, either," I said. "I didn't know there was a civilized woman alive who could leave a bathroom in such a mess."

She laughed. "Whatever gave you the idea I was civilized, darling? Oh, God, look at my hair! Well, at least it's clean for a change."

She'd spent the best part of an hour scrubbing and shampooing herself and just soaking in the big bathtub. Now, wrapped in a long, white terry-cloth robe provided by the hotel management, she was tackling the coiffure problem in front of the dresser mirror, yielding me the bathroom at last only because we'd been given a deadline and time was running out on us.

"What don't you believe?"

I asked my question through the open bathroom door as I leaned forward to operate my safety razor more accurately. Aside from sporting a heavier crop of whiskers, the face that confronted me in the mirror didn't seem to have changed significantly since I'd last shaved it, certainly not for the better.

"All this," Belinda said. "First the old fart has Palomino pump us full of sleepyjuice and fly us off into the lousy jungle and dump us on a bunch of nutty ecofreaks he's paying to beat or squeeze or burn some information out of me, except that Palomino grabbed the wrong girl and I don't have any. So this doddering character—*El Viejo*, the Old One, for God's sake!—lets us sit there a month or two all wrapped in duct tape and eating boiled goat while he's making up his senile mind; and then, bingo, he has the freaks massacred and us hauled out of there and given the VIP treatment: a limousine, a hotel suite with our own best clothes from our own suitcases laid out on the beds all pressed and pretty, and a formal invitation to dinner, if you please! Bring that hair dryer over here, will you, darling, and plug it in for me; I don't seem to have got it all dry in back." When I'd done as she'd asked, she looked up at me. "You look kind of dumb, half-lathered or whatever that goop is. I thought all men used electric mowers these days."

I said, "This way I don't have to worry about what kind of oddball juice they have when I'm traveling in oddball places. Mr. Gillette does a pretty good job of making his blades available just about everywhere."

She licked her lips, not yet lipsticked, but full and rosy nevertheless. "Do you want to make love to me?" she asked. "Just a quickie, to make up for all the times we couldn't on those damn little cots?"

I grinned. "There you go again. Nothing but sex, sex, sex. You know you don't really want to; you're just making seductive noises because you think you ought to."

"No, because I'm scared," she admitted readily enough. "And do you know what really scares me, stupid me? Not being tortured or raped or killed, but getting all dolled up in chiffon and nylons and then getting all messed up again; it was humiliating enough in jeans. What do you think the old creep is up to with this crazy dress-up charade? Why is he going to all the trouble of cleaning us up and giving us our own clothes back?"

"Our own clothes is easy," I said, returning to my razor and speaking between gingerly strokes of the blade. "If Vasquez just wanted us decently dressed for the occasion, whatever it may be, he could have bought me a new suit and you the latest evening gown from Paris, but all that would have proved was that he had plenty of money, which we already knew. He's showing his power. He's showing us that wherever Roger Ackerman, your revered leader—"

243

"Ex-leader."

"Vasquez is demonstrating that wherever your former leader, a U.S. government operative of some standing, stashed those suitcases in or around that hotel in Iguassu Falls after he'd sent you and Morton off to give me a nice swim in the Paraná River, *El Viejo*'s people were right there watching, ready to produce the hidden luggage for *their* leader anytime it was wanted. As for what else he has in mind, beyond confusing us thoroughly, I have no idea."

That wasn't quite true. I felt reasonably sure that surrounding us with luxury, after subjecting us to a week of hardship, was intended as an apology of sorts from Vasquez; and when men with unlimited power start apologizing to you and being very nice to you, you know damned well they want something from you and will squash you flat if they don't get it. In any case, I didn't believe for a minute that it was just by coincidence that we'd been held prisoner precisely long enough for a certain tour to reach Cuzco.

Clearly Vasquez had been waiting for Mark Steiner's young widow to get here before having us flown here. Why he wanted us all together, I couldn't guess, but whatever he intended, it seemed to be something he couldn't do—or at least couldn't do so easily—in Buenos Aires, Argentina, or Santiago, Chile, or even Lima, Peru, the preceding stops on the tour's sight-seeing schedule. Apparently, it could only be done, or at least it could best be done, here in Cuzco, at eleven thousand feet, a fairly high elevation for an aging gent who, if I remembered correctly, was just about to celebrate his seventieth birthday.

I recalled that Mark Steiner had hoped to attend the celebration—not too closely, say at three or four hundred yards—with a rifle in his hands and me assisting him as a sort of big-game guide. Well, it has been called the biggest, or at least the most dangerous, game on earth; and if it was, Gregorio Vasquez was certainly a trophy specimen. I closed the bathroom door—after a week of togetherness I felt I was entitled to privacy for my bath—and started the water running in the tub.

"Just put it right over there," I heard Belinda say when I opened the door at last.

I hadn't heard the knock. Belinda was admitting a waiter with a tray holding two hollow-stemmed glasses and an ice bucket from which protruded the neck of an aristocratic-looking bottle. He set the tray on the cocktail table by the window and turned. For a moment, seeing the ice bucket and the familiar costume of white shirt and black pants, I'd thought it was Armando, but it was another dark-faced man I didn't recognize. Well, I was a big boy now. I could solve my problems all by myself without outside help. I hoped.

"With Don Gregorio's compliments," the man said to Belinda. "Do you wish me to open it, señora?"

"Sure, pop the cork," Belinda said.

After doing the honors skillfully, the man withdrew. I lifted the glass he had given me.

"To happy landings."

"Ugh, don't remind me of that damn little plane and those crazy mountains." She glanced at the clock radio on the bedside table. "Better drink up and get dressed, darling, it's almost seven o'clock. *El Viejo* must be running on Yankee time. I thought they never had dinner before ten P.M. in this part of the world."

Now she was dressed the way I'd seen her at our tour's get-together party in Rio de Janeiro, in gray-blue chiffon with pale nylons and silver sandals; and she'd managed to fix her blond hair very attractively, even though it hadn't had any professional attention recently. She was really quite a pretty woman, and I guess a world filled with nothing but skinny dames would really be kind of dull. Dressing myself, I found that my old blue-and-white seersucker suit had been expertly pressed, and my white wash-and-wear shirt had been ironed for the first time in its life. The dress shoes I'd brought along for such formal emergencies had been polished to a blinding shine. They had the same hidden features as my everyday shoes, and I checked and found that the armorer's handiwork had not been disturbed, which worried me a little, since it was sloppy security for a bunch of pros. On the other hand, maybe they knew all about the hidden knives and figured they'd just let me think I was putting something over on them: how much damage could I do with a couple of little blades I couldn't even reach without removing, and half dismantling, my shoes? I was tying my necktie when somebody knocked on the door.

"Coming," I said. Belinda was making some nervous adjustments to her chiffon draperies. I waited while she fussed with herself; but at last I said, "Let's not keep the don waiting."

She gave the dress a final smoothing and threw me a bleak look. "I've got this weird feeling. . . . I guess I'm just hoping, after getting all dressed up like this, I don't wind up getting blood all over it," she said, and I knew she was remembering the sprawling, sodden bodies in the hut. Suddenly she stepped close and hugged me tightly, her body soft and warm under the filmy dress. "No, damn you, don't kiss me, you'll smear me. Anyway, I offered you a chance at something better than a kiss and you blew it. Now let's get the hell out there and sing for our suppers."

Palomino was waiting in the corridor. He indicated the direction and walked behind us. I knew he had a gun, he'd displayed one on the plane, but it occurred to me that I didn't particularly want to escape. I'd done all right so far, just paddling along with the current. Indications were that I was getting closer to *El Viejo* all the time, and I found that I was really curious about what he had in store for us after these elaborate preliminaries.

"No, señora, proceed to the front door, if you please." Palomino's voice checked Belinda, making her way through the lobby ahead of me, as she started to turn toward the sign indicating the dining room. Palomino continued smoothly, "When the streets are crowded, vehicles must come to the rear of the hotel, but it is not so crowded now. Please to step outside and enter the car that awaits us."

The big, ornate hotel doors opened right onto a narrow street; you could see why tour buses and limousines were sent around to the rear during rush hour, whatever that might mean in Cuzco. The long black Cadillac was parked in front with two wheels on the sidewalk to leave some room for traffic to pass. It was still broad daylight, and I didn't notice that the town was noticeably less packed with pedestrian humanity than before, but perhaps there were somewhat fewer vehicles.

I helped Belinda into the backseat of the car and followed her inside, noting that there wasn't as much legroom as before because the jump seats had been set up; apparently more passengers were expected. Palomino didn't get in; he left our door open and waited beside the car. Presently, four people emerged from the hotel. I knew two of them. Ackerman was behind, being led by a dark-faced gent in black. In front, with another black-clad escort, was Ruth Steiner in a blue linen dress I recognized; she'd worn it the night Belinda had first displayed her chiffon. The man beside Ruth tried to help her into the Cadillac, but she shrugged off his hand and started to get in unassisted—and stopped abruptly, seeing me.

"Matt!"

"Please to get in, lady." That was her escort, getting impatient after a second or two and reaching for her arm again.

"Hi, Ruth," I said. "Join the party."

I held out my hand to help her, moving over to give her room beside me—to hell with the jump seat—aware of Belinda, on the other side of me, watching us knowingly. I guessed that she had some theories about me; and something had certainly made me fairly uninterested in the sexy lady with whom I'd just spent a week in fairly confined circumstances. I realized now that something had been started between Ruth Steiner and me one night in Buenos Aires—or maybe earlier, perhaps even back when I slugged her with a shotgun—and that I was enough of a one-woman man not to be very susceptible to other female stimuli until it was finished, one way or another. I felt Ruth squeeze my fingers tightly before releasing them, settling herself beside me.

On the sidewalk, Roger Ackerman was doing the standard Hollywood-hero bit. They always feel they have to prove something by resisting the irresistible. Palomino had moved in to help the other two men in black, but even though they were three against one, Mr. Ackerman was not, by God, going to let any goddamn greasers push him around—but of course they did, shoving him into the Cadillac and slamming the door on him. I heard the locks click. The two I didn't know went back into the hotel. Palomino got into the front seat of the limousine and spoke to the driver. The big car started to move in its smooth and silent way.

Ackerman pulled himself off our feet and onto one of the jump seats. He started to straighten his tie and smooth his disheveled hair—and stopped, becoming aware at last of who sat facing him.

"You!" he said, staring. "But you're dead!"

Chapter 27

A paved highway took us out of town, but we soon turned off onto a winding gravel road and started climbing. At the top of the grade Palomino ordered the car brought to a halt; his voice reached us through the intercom.

"Perhaps the ladies would like to see the animals."

The rear windows slid down silently. A group of Indians with broad brown faces, wearing bulky colorful costumes, moved toward us accompanied by over a dozen llamas. They were handsome beasts. The big ones were about the size of small cow ponies but more slenderly built; they had a proud, alert, independent look, posing with their heads held high on rather long necks. The little ones, leggy and very fuzzy, were being carried around like puppies by the Indian kids.

"Oh, God, aren't they *cute*!" Belinda exclaimed, reaching out to pat one that was held up to her. "Can I give the little girl something?"

"It is expected," Palomino's electrified voice said.

"For Christ's sake, did you kidnap us just to show us a roadside zoo?" Ackerman asked irritably.

Clearly being in the hands of a polite and considerate kidnapper bothered him. Maybe he was afraid that we were remembering that this wasn't the way he ran his abductions; and feeling my chest still very sore, and seeing a small scab on Ruth's lip, I did find the thought coming to mind. Belinda slipped some local currency to the kid at her window and gave the baby llama a final pat on the nose. The window glass slid back up and the car started to move once more, but we did not resume the recrimination session that had been interrupted, perhaps because everything had been said.

Ruth had, of course, expressed conventional dismay at Ackerman's perfidy. She'd pointed out that he'd sworn I'd be safe if she cooperated with him, but judging by his surprise at seeing me alive, he'd ignored that promise. Ackerman had acted very shocked at the accusation; he'd protested that she'd misunderstood his reaction completely. He'd merely heard from official sources the disturbing news that a male Caucasian body, naked and battered beyond recognition, had been taken out of the Paraná River far downstream from the Iguassu Falls; it had not yet been identified. He, Ackerman, had assumed that the body was mine and that I'd panicked and tried to get away from Dennis and Belinda and had fallen into the river accidentally. Or perhaps Dennis, with a personal grievance, had exceeded his instructions, but there had certainly been no termination order from him, Ackerman. . . . At this point Belinda had called him a liar, describing what had actually happened at the river and why; this had led to an acrimonious exchange, which she'd brought to a conventional close by telling him he couldn't fire her since she'd already quit. Then Ackerman had turned his attention to me. When we stopped for the llamas, he'd been telling me, in effect, that I was certainly going to be made to pay for my brutal assassination of a fine young agent with a promising career ahead of him who'd merely tried to murder me. . . .

Considering that we were all helpless captives in a locked vehicle, being transported against our wills toward an unknown fate at an unknown destination, this bickering was a big waste of time and verbiage. Clearly, instead of fighting with each other, we should have been figuring out how to cooperate against our captors. Still, the arguments had kind of cleared the air and brought everybody up to date on everybody else's activities.

"How did they get you?" I asked Ruth, beside me.

"I was waiting in my room for Roger to take me down to dinner. When somebody knocked on the door, I opened expecting to see him; well, he was there, all right, but obviously a prisoner. I couldn't react fast enough; one of those men grabbed me and had me out in the hall before I could slam the door shut.''

"Are you all right?" I asked.

"Oh, I'm fine.'' She glanced at the man facing us. "Roger's been a perfect little gentleman all week, even if his word of honor doesn't seem to be worth doodlesquat.''

Belinda spoke up from the other side of me: "I'm sure you'll be glad to know, Ruth, that Matt's been a perfect little gentleman all week, too, damn it. . . . God, look at those fields! You wouldn't think a horse—or even a llama—could keep its footing up there, let alone pull a plow.''

It was a magnificently rugged landscape in the low red light of evening, but the truly remarkable thing was that practically all the mountainsides that weren't solid rock, no matter how high or steep, were cultivated. I wouldn't have wanted to climb some of those fields, even on hands and knees; if you ever started sliding and rolling, there'd be no stopping you. You'd wind up with a heroic splash in the river a couple of thousand feet below.

Gradually, as we drove, the light faded and the peaks ahead lost the last light of the sun. The chauffeur turned on the headlights, and soon there was nothing to see but the twisty mountain road ahead and sometimes not even that as the beams swept out over a black abyss. Occasionally we'd pass a village with a few lights showing, but we met no traffic, which was just as well; there wasn't room for much besides the big Cadillac. Often there didn't seem to be room enough for that. Trying to keep track of the altitude—as far as direction was concerned, the fading glow in the sky more or less behind us told me we were moving roughly eastward—I sensed that the downgrades were generally somewhat longer than the upgrades, and I no longer had that tight, eleven-thousand-foot feeling in my chest. We seemed to have come down a bit, even though we were heading deeper into the Andes.

I remembered that the Machu Picchu ruins, which should

251

lie in this general direction, were actually at a lower elevation than the city of Cuzco, according to the tour material that had been given us. But it didn't seem likely that Don Gregorio was bringing us all together, all dressed up, for a visit to the lost city of the Incas that had been discovered, if I remembered correctly, by a gent named Hiram Bingham. Of course the local Indians had known where it was all along.

Then the chauffeur made a sharp turn off the main road, such as it was, and put the limousine to a steep climb up a track that would have challenged the borrowed little four-wheel-drive Subaru I'd left in New Mexico. The headlights gave us a glimpse of a couple of heavy stone gateposts going by; shortly thereafter we saw a large stone house ahead, with illumination of its own. There was a wide, lighted terrace in front of the house, and on it a wheelchair awaited us occupied by a white-haired man in evening clothes. A black-clad attendant stood behind the chair. A dog sat beside it.

"Please to disembark now," Palomino said to us through the intercom. "Don Gregorio wishes to greet you. . . . But first a word of warning. Some in your party, perhaps all, have been seeking *El Viejo* with violent intentions. I will not threaten you; I will merely suggest that you wait to hear what your host has to say to you before you commit suicide by attempting to abuse his hospitality."

The locks clicked and Palomino opened the door on Ruth's side. We clambered out and approached the wheelchair in a straggling group. The seated man was, of course, considerably older than the photographs I'd been shown; they never manage to keep those file pix up to date. The hair had not been totally white in the last snaps I'd seen. However, the aquiline features were unmistakable, particularly the bold blade of a nose. The body was thinner than I'd visualized it, and the right leg was in a hip cast that was supported by the raised footrest of the chair. Vasquez waited for us to stop before him.

Then he said, "You are guests at Casa Coca. I joke. The name is Hacienda San Gregorio. Strangely, it was not named by me, or for me, but I heard the name and found that it

252

filled my need for a pied-à-terre in this area. I am Gregorio Vasquez Stussman. This is Bravo.'' He patted the dog's head. ''Whatever plans you may be entertaining against me, please do not feel it necessary to harm Bravo. He is a very friendly dog.''

I heard Ruth make a choked sound beside me. Her hand grasped my arm tightly, and I remembered that this was probably one of the dogs that had chased her, and killed her rescuer, when she was escaping from her first kidnapping. I could see that Bravo was a very large young Chesapeake, but little more than a pup. He'd go seventy-five or eighty pounds already; he'd wind up close to a hundred when he got his full growth. He had a fine massive head and a tightly curling, yellow-brown coat. They are not attack dogs; they were bred to retrieve waterfowl under extremely rugged conditions; but unlike Labradors and goldens they are not blessed with unending tolerance. A Chessie may give you the first bite, but unlike his gentler retrieving cousins—my lost Happy, for instance—he'll sure as hell bite back.

Vasquez looked at Ruth and spoke deliberately: ''You are Mrs. Steiner, whose husband wrote one book containing much nonsense and some truth about my business and was killed while writing another. . . . And you are Mr. Helm, assigned to protect her as she searches for her husband's electronic manuscript, but with certain personal motives for seeking me out, am I correct?'' When I nodded, he turned to Belinda and Ackerman. ''And you two feel a sacred obligation to save mankind from one of its innumerable bad habits; it might have been better if you'd directed your earnest salvation efforts toward tobacco or masturbation. . . . No, no, we will talk later. Right now I am sure you would all like an opportunity to 'freshen up,' as I believe it's called. Señor Palomino will show you the facilities. I do not believe in the barbaric Yankee custom of cocktails, so we will meet again at the dinner table.''

El Viejo's mountain hideout—one of many hidden sanctuaries, no doubt—was not a treasure house of fine old paintings and priceless period furniture, but it was not a vacation cottage in the Berkshires furnished out of the Monkey Ward catalog, either. The house was roomy and massively built, and everything in it was sound and solid. The bathroom to which Ackerman and I were directed had been remodeled quite recently with new U.S. plumbing. Roger had nothing to say to me, which was fine, since I had nothing to say to him. Finished in there, we waited out in the long hall, under Palomino's supervision, for the ladies to join us.

"This way, please," Palomino said.

The dining room to which he directed us was big enough for a table that could have seated eight people, or maybe even ten if they were skinny, but was set for five. The tablecloth was linen or as close as made no difference; the china was thin and gray, marked with a colorful crest; the glasses seemed to be crystal or a good imitation; the flatware was silver and also sported a crest. Having associated, upon occasion, with aristocratic Scandinavian relatives who also went in for shields and crowns and lions and unicorns, I'm not particularly impressed by heraldic symbols, but I noted that Belinda, as soon as she was seated, picked up a fork to study the markings with unabashed curiosity. With Ackerman beside her, she'd been put to the left of the place setting at the head of the table that had no chair; Ruth was on the right, with me to talk to if Vasquez proved boring. I doubted that we'd be holding any lengthy conversations.

Then Don Gregorio, as he seemed to be called locally, was wheeled to his place by his silent attendant. Bravo trotted alongside the chair and sat down at a hand signal.

He said, "I hope no one objects to a dog in the dining room, but I must ask you not to feed him. We would not want to give him any bad habits, like begging at the table, would we? Were you very strict with your dog, Señor Helm?"

I shook my head. "I'm afraid Happy was a terrible beggar, Señor Vasquez."

"I wish to state that I regret your loss very much. It was certainly not intended—"

Ackerman made an angry sound. "Did you drag us all this way to talk about *dogs*, for Christ's sake?"

Vasquez said calmly, "As you Yankees say, first things first. Now we talk about important things like dogs; later, perhaps, we discuss unimportant things like people. I'm certain that Señor Helm will agree with those priorities."

I said, "All the way."

"But first we eat," Vasquez said. He didn't smile, but there was, let's say, a certain twinkle as he went on: "I was intending to serve *cabrillo*, but consulting Señor Palomino, I learned that there is a certain prejudice. Do you know what *cabrillo* is, Mr. Ackerman?"

"No, I don't talk Spanish."

Ruth said, "As a good New Mexican of about two years' standing, I know that a *cabrillo* is a young goat."

Belinda said, "Goat, ugh! Don't they have any cows or chickens south of the equator?"

Vasquez laughed shortly. "Apparently Palomino was correct; there is a prejudice. So I am happy to announce that you will be served good Argentine beef. Now let us commence, and let us not spoil our meal with business talk; that will come later. Do you know about the nearby Machu Picchu ruins and how they were so heroically discovered by a gentleman named Bingham . . . ?"

It was quite an elaborate, European-style meal, with one course following another and a different wine for each. Our host gave us the history of Machu Picchu and the Incas in considerable detail; then he told us about the cultivation of the coca leaf and its many uses, recreational, medicinal, and religious.

"In your country you encounter only the evil side of this versatile substance," he said, looking at Ackerman. "But today, here in Peru, you have seen the kind of fields cultivated by the natives. Do you think over the centuries they could have sustained such effort at such an altitude without the support of coca, Señor Ackerman? As for the religious aspects, I believe your country permits the use of peyote in certain religious ceremonies. . . ."

Ackerman spoke sharply: "It's ridiculous to compare a fairly harmless hallucinogen like peyote with a poison like cocaine! Anyway, I think the most recent court cases involving peyote have been decided the other way.''

''Ah, so your vaunted freedom of religion is just another Yankee sham,'' Vasquez said. ''Well, after we have finished our discussion, Señor Palomino and his associates will demonstrate one of the less secret religious ceremonies performed by the *Compañeros de la Hoja*; I think you will find it very entertaining.''

''Discussion?'' Ruth said. ''What do we have to discuss, Mr. Vasquez?''

''Peace,'' Vasquez said.

Chapter 28

THERE was an interruption while coffee and after-dinner drinks were offered around. I settled for some brandy that was a little hard to track down as it rolled around in the bottom of a snifter the size of a kid's balloon. Coffee for Ruth, a gooey-looking liqueur for Belinda, a Scotch for Roger. Vasquez, taking nothing, apologized for keeping us at the dining table, but the other rooms were small, he said, and he thought we'd be more comfortable here. I thought it more likely that Palomino, stationed at the door to the kitchen supervising the black-clad attendants who hovered around catering to our every whim, had suggested that it would be easier to control us if we remained grouped neatly at a table than if we were allowed to sprawl around untidily on sofas and easy chairs.

Finally, with everyone taken care of, Vasquez leaned forward to address us: "Now to business. I am an old man, and as you can see my bones are becoming brittle—the doctors do not seem to be certain whether my hip broke because I fell, or I fell because my hip broke. In any case I no longer thrive on conflict. That is why I have brought you here gently and fed you well. I think in most instances we can resolve our disagreements without violence. So, ladies and gentlemen, this is a peace conference. Let us hope it will be more successful at generating useful compromises than most such conferences." As he sat back, folding his hands, I noted belatedly the ring with the green stone that Ruth had mentioned.

Across the table from me, Ackerman stirred indignantly.

257

"If you think . . . This is a big waste of time! I don't compromise with drug dealers. If that means you'll have me shot, go ahead and shoot!"

"Shooting is what we are trying to avoid, Mr. Ackerman. There has been sufficient shooting. . . . I will be honest with you," Vasquez said, addressing all of us. "The killings at *Estación Seis*—Station Six—in Brazil, where two of you were held for a while, can easily be explained as the result of some young Americans—well, three young Americans and an evil old professor leading them astray—looking for drugs and getting too close to a major operation. Unfortunately, it means sacrificing a productive laboratory to the police and the press, but so be it. However, while this incident was required, it rather limits my options, as your businessmen might say. We cannot have too many wandering *Americanos* dying violently down here; it gives this continent a bad name."

I reflected that the son of a bitch had a nice, dry sense of humor, which didn't make him any less a son of a bitch. But it was nice to see the smoothie approach so nicely done. He and Palomino. The toughies know you hate them and will clobber them instantly at the first opportunity; the smoothies think they can get you to like them or at least respect them, and thereby slow you down a bit when the time comes. Well, it's been known to work under favorable conditions, with susceptible subjects. There even seems to be a syndrome of sorts leading captives to love their captors. So far I've managed to stay immune.

Vasquez was still talking: "There is also the fact that some of you are working for your government, which makes things slightly awkward, since your country takes these matters with ridiculous seriousness. For instance, a certain U.S. agent was killed in Mexico; you have probably heard of the case. It happened a considerable time ago, but your country is still making more trouble about it than one would think a single man would be worth to a country of endless millions. Well, it is a form of trouble I can survive if I must; but I would prefer not to. Therefore I will not shoot you unless you force me to, Mr. Ackerman, even though you are not employed by

258

quite such a well-advertised U.S. agency. Mr. Helm's organization, I understand, avoids publicity, and is less likely to call for government action when it loses an operative; but it is reputed to have a very long memory, and I prefer not to spend what life I have left to me looking over my shoulder. As for Mrs. Steiner, she is the widow of a fairly prominent literary figure, and her death or disappearance would also cause some inconvenient notices in the press. This is why I have brought us together here.''

Ruth started to speak and checked herself. It was Belinda who spoke: ''What about me?''

Vasquez regarded her for a moment and said, ''I gather that you have quite recently severed your connections with the U.S. government, so you can hardly claim protection there, Miss Nunn—I believe that is your correct name. We will discuss your problem later. Right now, let us commence with your former associate. Mr. Ackerman, what would satisfy you?''

''To see you extradited and standing in a U.S. courtroom answering for your crimes!''

Vasquez smiled thinly. ''If you could guarantee that I would be standing, it might be worth it, since the doctors do not promise that I will ever stand, or walk, again,'' he said. ''But consider, what kind of a triumph would that be, trying and convicting and sending to prison a doddering old fart like me?'' Vasquez glanced at Belinda without expression; a little color came to her face as she realized that her hotel-room remarks had been recorded—as had, obviously, the conversation in the Cadillac where she'd thrown her government job into Ackerman's face. Vasquez went on: ''You can see that I am a helpless cripple, and the fact that I have brought you here for such a ridiculous reason—in such a violent business, how can I ever expect to find peace?—should indicate to you that I am mentally, as well as physically, incompetent, totally incapable of controlling the far-flung empire of crime I will be accused of manipulating for your country's destruction.''

Ackerman said quickly, "Then you admit that you intend to flood the U.S. with cheap drugs?"

Vasquez shrugged. "This room is flooded with delicious odors and there is a roast on the sideboard with considerable meat remaining. Yet Bravo sits beside me, resisting this terrible temptation. Should I concern myself with the fate of men who have less self-control than a dog? Should you? And even if you do, do you really wish to put a senile cripple on trial when you could prove to your employers, and your press, that the infamous Old One is really only a figurehead; the real power behind the South American drug trade with connections all over the world, both financial and religious, is the much younger man you will produce as your prisoner—"

"What the hell are you driving at?" Ackerman demanded.

"Hector, please come forward."

Palomino left his post to stand beside Vasquez on the side that was not occupied by Bravo.

Vasquez said, "Ladies and gentlemen, I give you Señor Hector Palomino Escobar. Or, rather, let us say that he gives himself to you, Mr. Ackerman. Hector made a mistake; and mistakes are not tolerated here, as he well knows. The others involved have already been punished. Hector was given a choice of punishments; he sensibly chose this one. An American prison will be a country club compared to what he would normally have had to endure to atone for his error. And having given his word, and being a man of honor, he will give your officials much incriminating evidence about the international drug transactions he will freely admit to having controlled in my name; he will also, with my permission, proudly claim to hold my position as the high priest of the *Compañeros de la Hoja*, the Companions of the Leaf, the new religion of cocaine that is taking the world by storm. And, finally, he will confess to the ritual execution of the sacrilegious journalist Steiner who had managed to penetrate the mysteries of the *Compañeros* and was about to reveal them in print." Vasquez leaned forward. "It will be a spectacular trial, I assure you. And you, Mr. Ackerman, *you* will be the agent who receives the credit for bringing to justice this mastermind of crime! Consider it, Mr. Ackerman, consider it carefully. As you might say in your country, it sure beats a bullet in the brain.''

Ackerman drew a long breath, but said nothing. Vasquez made a signal and Palomino returned to his station by the door. One of the waiters, if that's what they were, poured another dollop of brandy into my big globular glass. Vasquez looked at me as I tried to corner it.

"And you, Mr. Helm," he said. "While Mr. Ackerman is thinking things over let us hear what would satisfy you."

"I'm satisfied," I said, lowering the snifter, my least favorite type of booze container; why make liquor so hard to catch? But the brandy was excellent. I went on, with a glance toward the lady on my left: "As long as Mrs. Steiner is unharmed and allowed to go about her business without interference, I'm satisfied. That's my job. Granting that I haven't been in a position to work at it for a while, and am even kind of handicapped at the moment, it's still my job. As long as she's simply attending a pleasant dinner here with friends I have no reason to object; but if the situation should change, I'll carry out my orders to the best of my ability. It may not be a very good best, under the circumstances, but good or bad, you'd better count on it."

Vasquez nodded approvingly. "A clear statement. Do you feel the same sense of responsibility for anyone else at this table, Miss Nunn for instance? You two recently spent several days together."

I looked across the table and spoke deliberately: "Belinda's a nice kid, but she's no responsibility of mine, no."

Vasquez looked at me hard. "You realize what you are saying?"

I said, "I've been here before, sir." It always helps to throw in a respectful "sir" or two; even the smartest ones go for it. I continued: "I'm just one man, sir; I can't be responsible for the whole world. My instructions do not involve the protection of anyone but Mrs. Steiner. As far as I'm concerned, all others are on their own."

Belinda's face was pale, but her voice was steady enough: "Well, now I know how it feels to be thrown to the buzzards! Thanks loads, you bastard!" She looked at the man beside her. "I don't suppose I'll get any support from you, either!"

"You quit rather loudly, remember?" Ackerman said, with some satisfaction. "If you want support, buy a girdle."

Belinda started to make an angry retort, but gave it up. I saw that her eyes were frightened. She signaled the nearest attendant for a refill of the sticky stuff in her little glass.

Vasquez said, "Mr. Helm, do you wish me to believe that you are here entirely because you were ordered to protect Mrs. Steiner, that you have no personal—"

"Personal means nothing in my business, sir."

Vasquez cleared his throat. "Then we are in different kinds of business. Personal means much to me, Mr. Helm. My son was killed, as you undoubtedly know. I mean to exact payment by doing everything in my power to damage the arrogant country responsible. But you claim that you are not motivated at all by the death of your lady friend, Madeleine Rustin? Not to mention that of your dog, Happy? You have no desire for vengeance? If you'll excuse my saying so, you do not look like a forgiving man. And I do not think you are a very good liar, Mr. Helm."

I said, "Everybody tells me that, but I keep trying."

Vasquez said, "To be frank, I feel no real responsibility for the woman's death. She chose to disfigure another woman, who retaliated violently; we merely employed the girl's anger for our purposes. In this case, the fact that the implement used, a grenade, was supplied by people employed by me, is not significant; without it, the scarred young woman would simply have accomplished her purpose with another weapon. Do you agree?"

After a moment I nodded reluctantly. "Okay, Madeleine asked for it in a way, I suppose, although she had plenty of provocation. But Happy—"

"Where the dog is concerned, the nature of the weapon is certainly significant," Vasquez said. "If no explosives had been provided—if the girl had been forced to use a knife, say, or a gun—the dog would most likely not have been harmed. To this extent I owe you, as I believe you say in your country. There is no way I can make complete restitution, but—"

He turned his head to speak to the silent attendant behind the wheelchair, a large, heavy man with rather long black hair, and a piratical black mustache in a round, almost Oriental, face. The man pulled something from his pocket, a dog leash, snapped it onto Bravo's collar, and gave a little jerk, signaling the dog to rise.

"Un momentito."

Vasquez's voice sounded oddly hoarse. His hand reached out to touch the massive head of the Chesapeake pup, who looked around and gave it a couple of licks before it was taken away.

"Very well, Bo." Vasquez watched the dog being led around the table and spoke to me. "Take the leash, Señor Helm. The dog is yours."

Well, they do it down there. *Mi casa, su casa* and all that stuff. I said, "No, I—"

"Please do not tell me that no dog can replace another dog in a man's affections; I am well aware of that. But this is the best I can do. You will want another hunting dog eventually, and Bravo is a good one with a fine pedigree. . . . But you confuse him; he thinks you reject him. You are a dog man, you know what he wants. Do it."

I didn't give a damn about hurting Vasquez's feelings by rejecting any presents he might choose to give me, but as he said, I was a dog man, and you don't leave a young dog standing around bewildered. I started to offer the back of my hand in the customary way so Bravo could check my scent.

"Oh, no! Be careful!"

That was Ruth, beside me. She'd cringed as the dog was led past her chair; I remembered again her reasons for being afraid of them, and particularly of this one.

Vasquez said impatiently, "Go ahead, Mr. Helm, make his acquaintance. Bravo does not bite."

263

Ruth spoke sharply. "How can you say that? I was there, I saw—"

Vasquez shook his head. "It was dark and you were frightened; you did not see what you thought you saw," he said. "Mr. Ackerman, you oversaw the rescue of Mrs. Steiner, in which one of your agents lost his life. Now give us the truth. Was there a single tooth mark on the dead man's body?"

Ackerman licked his lips. "My report . . ."

Vasquez made a sharp gesture. "Of course your report would state that the poor fellow was ripped apart by vicious hounds. You would hardly admit officially—at least not if there was an alternative—that your people are so incompetent that they fire their guns at random in the dark and shoot their own colleague. You covered up by putting the blame on my dogs and somehow persuaded a medical man to make the proper findings. Mrs. Steiner's hysterical testimony was all the additional confirmation you required. But we are not official here, so please be so kind as to let us have the truth."

Ackerman shrugged. "All right. With two big dogs charging around in the dark, and an agent and the subject in apparent danger, somebody got trigger happy and let a shot go when he couldn't really see his sights. Melvin's spine was smashed by a thirty-eight-caliber bullet. There were no bites."

Ruth licked her lips. "But I *saw*—"

Vasquez said, "It was a totally incompetent performance from everyone except the dogs, Mrs. Steiner. The dogs did what they were supposed to; they alerted us to a stranger on the premises. But they were not supposed to be released. Why release them? If there had been a duck or a goose to be retrieved, very well; but they were not man-hunting dogs. But an idiot boy, hearing that the prisoner was escaping, opened the kennel door. So there the dogs were, released after being penned most of the night, and I presume they did what dogs do under such circumstances. Having done it, and finding themselves still free, they looked around for entertainment and saw some people running and, of course, ran to join them. One gun began to fire, and then more guns, making them even more eager; gunfire, to them, meant re-trieving business, their main purpose in life. One of the run-ning figures fell down; they investigated that and went on to the standing figure beyond, trying to find the reason for all the interesting shooting: there simply had to be some dead birds, somewhere. At that point they heard my whistle and came in, disappointed at not being able to bring me a single feather.''

I saw that Ruth was remembering her misinterpretation of Happy's behavior when she'd slipped into my yard with a gun; then she recalled something else and said stiffly, ''That's a good story, Mr. Vasquez, but they were bloody; there were smears on my clothes where they'd sniffed me.''

Vasquez cleared his throat. ''You have to understand about Chesapeake retrievers; they are bred to operate under very severe conditions. Tell her, Mr. Helm.''

I said, ''A golden retriever will cry pitifully if you tap him lightly with a folded newspaper; a Labrador may wince if you slug him with a baseball bat; but you can run over a Chesapeake with a truck, or shoot him, and he won't con-descend to admit he's hurt. They're really tough. . . . I sup-pose your two dogs had blood on them because they were wounded, Mr. Vasquez?'' I made it a question.

Vasquez nodded. ''Mr. Ackerman's man, the one who performed the rescue, seems to have been a different breed of marksman from the ones who were firing so wildly from the edge of the field. Before he was shot by his friends, he put a small groove into Bravo's skull—you can see the healing scar—and he put two bullets into Bravo's dam, Bella. She died with her head in my lap as we drove away. But of course, being stoical Chesapeakes, neither she nor Bravo gave any indication of being wounded.'' Vasquez drew a long breath. ''So, after all the dogs I have had, Bravo is my last and I give him to you, Mr. Helm. He needs training, he needs hunting, he needs to be taken for long walks in the mountains. He does not need an old man in a wheelchair. Take him, *por favor*, as payment for the debt I owe you.''

It was a sentimental moment that would have played well

on the TV screen. Anything involving mean old men humanized by lovable dogs plays well on the TV screen. I had to remind myself that this was a fallacy, and that a good man with dogs could still be a very bad man with people. But I took the leash and scratched the dog's ears briefly. He really was a good-looking pup in his husky Chesapeake way. Big Bo returned to his station behind Vasquez. Ruth stirred beside me.

"And what about the debt you owe me, Mr. Vasquez?" she demanded harshly. "My husband is dead. Are you going to offer me another husband to replace the one you had killed?"

Vasquez regarded her for a moment and asked, "Why are you here, Mrs. Steiner?"

She frowned at the question. "You know perfectly well why I'm here! I'm here because your men grabbed me at the hotel and brought me here. If you mean, why am I in South America, you know that I'm here to retrieve the computer copies of my husband's book, the manuscript of which was burned when your arsonists destroyed our house. Fortunately, as you're well aware, Mark had sent copies of everything to friends in various cities of South America. Fortunately for me. Not so fortunately for you. It's all on the diskettes, everything Mark found out about you; and he found out plenty!"

"Diskettes like these?"

With a small flourish, like a magician producing a live white rabbit, Vasquez held up a thin stack of computer disks; I couldn't tell how many until he spread them on the tablecloth like a short hand of cards. Three. Disregarding duplicates, there had been only two the last time I'd been involved with them; well, according to what she'd told me, Ruth had been supposed to pick up another in Santiago, Chile—but I was willing to bet that wherever it had appeared on the tour, it was not Santiago.

"Where did you get those?" The sharp question didn't come from Ruth, but from Ackerman.

Vasquez spoke without expression: "Your communications with Washington do not seem to be entirely secure, Mr. Ackerman.''

"You snoopy son of a bitch!"

Vasquez said calmly, "Let us say merely that I am a man who keeps an eye on his own interests. I hold here Chapters One to Ten, Chapters Eleven to Nineteen, and Chapters Twenty-seven to Thirty-four of Mr. Steiner's work. Would anybody care to inform me how many chapters the manuscript contained."

I said, "Forty-three."

Ruth looked at me, sharply and accusingly. Vasquez merely nodded. "So there are still two disks missing, if Mr. Steiner sent off, for safekeeping, book sections of approximately equal length. Where were the last two contacts to be made?"

I said, "Lima, Peru, and Quito, Equador."

Ruth was glaring at me angrily. "Matt, what in the world do you think you're doing?"

I said, "Shut up, sweetie. I know that masochism is habit-forming, and I suppose if I let you, you'd stay stubborn and get beat up some more and love every minute of it, but my job is to keep you intact as far as possible and you look prettier without another fat lip. So answer the man's questions or I will."

"Matt, damn you—"

I said, "For Christ's sake, Ruth, what's the point of holding out now? You got where you wanted to be, didn't you? You're right here, and there's your man, so why go through a lot of tight-lip nonsense now?"

She glared at me, but before she could speak again, Vasquez said, "These disks are encrypted, Mr. Helm. Do you have the password that will enable us to read them?"

I shook my head. "No, but she'll tell you—"

"I will *not* tell him!"

I looked from her stubborn face to the man at the head of the table and said, "Mr. Vasquez, let's stop playing games. Don't harass the girl just for fun; you know you don't need her cotton-picking password. You know there's nothing on those damned disks of any interest to you. I don't know how you know, but you do. If you didn't, you'd have waited until you had all five diskettes before you brought us in like this.''

There was a little silence. Ruth was staring at me. "Matt, how long—''

"How long have I known?'' I shook my head. "Don't play tricks on a pro, Ruth. How long was I supposed to believe in these ladies' john contacts that always took place somewhere where they hadn't been scheduled? The restaurant instead of the funicular. Itaipu instead of Buenos Aires. And the pickups, my God! A gang of street kids trying to mug us, a mystery man sneaking up to your hotel window— an invisible mystery man, because I was kind of nervous about those ground-floor windows and kept my eye on the approaches to yours as well as I could. Obviously, you were just making it up as you went along—''

Ackerman said, "You mean the bitch never met anybody at all?''

I said, "The lady simply announced a successful contact whenever she felt like it, always picking a place where nobody had been watching her too closely. Then, back in her hotel room, she cooked up a new disk on her handy-dandy little computer and presented it proudly as what had been given her in the potty place.'' I hesitated. "She had a contact scheduled for Santiago, Chile. Did she make that?''

Ackerman said, "No, and she acted very upset about it, but then we took a bus tour to Valparaiso and she came back from a public john all smiles.'' Ackerman glared at Ruth. "But there had to be something on those damn diskettes; Dennis said it came out gibberish because he didn't have the code or password, but *something* was there!''

Vasquez said, "D'Arcy.''

We'd almost forgotten where we were, and who'd brought us here. Now we all looked toward the head of the table.

After a moment Ruth said, "So you figured it out.''

"One of my clever young computer men did,'' Vasquez said. "This business, like any other, is very dependent on the computer experts nowadays; and we employ some of the best in the world. I am told that the password is Anemone, which seems to be the name of a minor female character in a best-selling romantic novel called *Trumpet in the Dust*, written by a certain Johnson D'Arcy, who, strangely enough, seems to be a woman. You slipped a little, Mrs. Steiner, having the book in your possession, even though it was one of half a dozen you carried.''

She said, "I know, but we left so hurriedly that I hadn't finished my preparations; I had to keep it around so I could copy it into my computer at odd moments, all encrypted like a real secret. I thought, if I brought a whole bunch of books to read on the tour—well, I always do—nobody'd spot that particular one. But I can see how a smart and persistent computer expert with a big machine and a lot of fast typists to feed it could set up a program that would check out every word in every book I had along. So he finally came to Anemone—she really appears only twice, well into the story—and hit the jackpot.''

Vasquez nodded. "I did not understand all the technical verbiage, but I gather that was approximately the way it was done.'' He regarded her for a moment. "And now, Mrs. Steiner, let me repeat my original question. Why are you here?''

Ruth licked her lips. "Mark's manuscript was gone, burned to ashes. My home computer was destroyed with the disks that held my copies, including the backup copies. We were always talking about putting those in a safe place, but we never got around to it. But it occurred to me that you couldn't *know* there weren't any backup disks floating around, Mr. Vasquez, so I invented some and spotted them all around South America to make it easy for you. I was going to do it all by myself, but then I got hold of Matt's organization, since I realized that I was out of my depth and I'd never reach you alive without protection. At least I thought I wouldn't, although, as Matt points out, I do seem to be here, don't I?''

"I see,'' Vasquez said. "So these imaginary disks—well, this carefully encrypted romance—were just a scam, if I have the right word, a scam to bring me out of hiding. And when your scam finally brought us face-to-face, what did you intend to do?''

Ruth's face was pale. She licked her lips once more. ''Why,'' she whispered, ''why, I was going to kill you!''

Vasquez nodded slowly. He made a signal to the big man behind the wheelchair, and Bo drew him back from his place at the table far enough to clear the immobilized leg, swung him around, and wheeled him around to Ruth.

''Please to stand up, Mrs. Steiner,'' Vasquez said. When she'd done so and turned to face him, he looked up at her from the chair and said, raising his hand, ''Bo.''

The big man took out a sizable automatic pistol—another .45 Colt or one of the many imitations—and placed it in his employer's hand. Without looking down, Vasquez jacked back the slide to cock the hammer and feed a cartridge into the chamber. He reversed the weapon and held it out to Ruth, who hesitated but took it.

Vasquez said, ''I am here, señora. Do what you came to do. . . . Oh, just one moment. I am sure you are willing to die to achieve your vengeance, but you may hesitate on account of your friends. Hector.''

''*Sí*, Don Gregorio.''

''When I am dead, you will take no revenge on this woman or on the two American agents. You will transport them back to their hotel in the city and release them.''

''*Sí*, Don Gregorio.''

''The other woman is yours, of course, as you were promised in return for your word on the other matter.''

I saw Palomino glance toward Belinda, his poker face not quite concealing the fact that he was a man regarding a woman he found desirable, which was a surprise to me; I hadn't considered him that impressionable. Belinda looked toward me; but how many women can a man protect at once, anyway? So far I hadn't even done much for the one I was assigned to.

"*Sí*, Don Gregorio."

Ruth was still holding the weapon in an awkward manner. I said helpfully, "The trigger is the dingus sticking out the bottom."

She didn't deign to look at me. Her face was very pale. She drew a long, shaky breath and aimed the gun at Vasquez.

"Very good, Mrs. Steiner." His voice was quite calm. "As Mr. Helm said, the trigger is the dingus sticking out of the bottom. You have come a long way, and played many clever games, to pull it. I suggest you do so now."

You had to hand it to the guy, unflinchingly facing a loaded and cocked weapon in the unsteady hand of a white-faced woman whose family he'd hounded from continent to continent, a woman whose husband he'd had killed. . . . Of course there was always the possibility that the gun was gimmicked, but I didn't think so. He was an old man and he was well aware that death would come for him soon; if now, so be it. . . .

"Oh, my God, I can't do it!"

I saw a faint smile of triumph touch Vasquez's face. Well, he'd earned it, gambling on his assessment of Ruth Steiner's character. Then the triumph was replaced by shock as Ruth buried her face in her hands. Well, nobody minded her little display of emotion, but in the process she dropped the gun— simply let go of it, as if she'd forgotten its existence, and let it fall.

Mark should have taught her better, of course, but he shouldn't have had to. You'd think, safety-minded as they are, they'd give high-school firearms-ed courses right along with drivers-ed so everybody would have sense enough not to bounce cocked automatics off tile floors. Clearly the gun was not gimmicked; Vasquez knew what was coming and so did Bo, instinctively swinging the wheelchair away as if he could beat a bullet. All I could do, still sitting at the table, was lift my feet hopefully.

Then the automatic fired with a deafening crash, and I felt something tug at my pants leg; and all hell broke loose in the fancy dining room as if the ringing, reverberating report had been a signal for everybody to go crazy.

Chapter 29

THEY came bounding into the room like a troupe of acrobats, from both doors, the one that led to the living quarters where we'd been allowed to use the johns, and the one that presumably led to the kitchen, since that was where the food had been coming from. They were dressed in black like the attendants who'd served us—black seemed to be the uniform of the day—but the newcomers didn't seem to like the five men already there, who quickly formed a defensive phalanx around the wheelchair while Bo steered it toward the kitchen door. Apparently, in addition to waiting on the table, these were Vasquez's personal bodyguards.

I got a startling freeze-frame image of Palomino, still at the door toward which they were moving, raising the gun he'd showed before and aiming it directly at Vasquez. But okay, it made sense: clearly *El Viejo* had overestimated his subordinate's loyalty. Rather than be surrendered to the authorities for extradition to the U.S. in his chief's place, only pretending to be Mr. Big, the younger man had summoned the *Compañeros* with whom he'd been working, men who'd become accustomed to taking his orders, even though Vasquez was the true high priest of the order. He was taking over for real. It wouldn't be the first time in criminal, or political, history that a number two had moved himself up to the one spot by means of the dagger or the bullet—but the two men faced each other for an extended instant and again, as when Ruth had held the gun, the easy, point-blank shot was not fired. . . .

Not that I was standing there just watching the show. I

only caught that one vignette out of the melee as I made my own move. I didn't bother with the gun on the floor, everybody knew about that and I figured it would be the most popular piece of hardware in the place. I avoided the pistol rush, therefore, and dove for the sideboard and got my hand on the husky, wedge-shaped knife with which Palomino had carved the roast to Vasquez's directions. I was just in time— I could feel one of the *Compañeros* closing in on me from behind, and I heard the soft, familiar swoosh of a swinging scarf. I got the blade up, edge out, in the position that had worked before. The scarf whipped around both my neck and the knife; I waited for the man to give me enough pressure to cut against; then I sliced down, hoping that Palomino kept his tools sharp.

He did. The keen blade parted the cloth easily, and I used the backhand swing I'd employed before, but the carving knife, while substantial, didn't have the length or heft of the outsized bowie I'd used in Santa Fe, and maybe this man ducked a little faster than the one I'd had to deal with there. I just chopped him across his ear, but it was enough to shock him into momentary immobility. I finished the turn, and drove the blade into him and wrenched it free and stepped aside as he went to his knees. Now I became aware that the handsome dining room had suddenly become an untidy battlefield with chairs overturned and the tablecloth pulled halfway off the table and broken glass and china all over the floor. I couldn't see Palomino any longer. The wheelchair contingent was holding at the kitchen door; but to hell with Vasquez, he'd keep. Or maybe he wouldn't, and that was okay, too.

At the moment I wanted two things: a girl and a gun, but there was no telling who'd retrieved the fallen weapon, so I was probably going to have to settle for the girl, if I could even manage that. Ruth's blue dress showed up well among the black costumes that filled the room. She was still where I'd left her at the table, but now she was trying to free her throat from a tightening scarf. Apparently the *Compañero* behind it hadn't made a good swing in the confusion and

274

she'd managed to get her hands under it, but although she was straining desperately, she wasn't strong enough to loosen it. . . . A man came at me with a knife using the old ice-pick attack; I sidestepped the clumsy downstroke, went in over it, and slashed him across the forehead. Unable to see through the sudden curtain of blood, not quite sure he hadn't been blinded permanently, he stumbled away. I drove the knife into the side of the man who was trying to strangle Ruth and pulled it free, ready to hit him again if necessary, but he released the cloth, falling. Ruth clawed the scarf off her neck and started to throw it aside, but I grabbed it and pocketed it. I never can understand these people who're forever discarding perfectly good weapons that may come in handy later.

Thinking this, leading her away from the table, I felt my foot turn on something, and there was the automatic. Apparently I'd given the locals too much credit, if credit is the proper word. Well, they're not as firearms-oriented down there, but I'm still baffled by folks who can't be bothered to keep track of the neighborhood artillery or pick up any stray pieces lying around. Still, there it was, and I scooped it up left-handed and got the knife up in time to counter another scarf attack from behind. This time I really leaned into that backhand stroke—Miss Weatherford would have been proud of me—and felt the knife chop through the neck meat and reach the spine. Still no decapitation, but it was a satisfactory job of putting the guy out of commission for so light a blade, and no finish blow was required. I set the safety on the heavy pistol and tucked it into my pants and looked around.

Bo was still battling for an opportunity to retreat through the kitchen door with his crippled leader. He was using a dining chair to beat off the attackers. He was a big man and the furniture wasn't up to the job; it was disintegrating in his hands. Only two of the bodyguards remained beside him, the others had been pried away from the phalanx and were either down or fighting for their lives elsewhere in the room. As I looked a concerted effort by the Palomino forces swept away Bo's last allies, leaving him struggling alone. Then the old man in the chair, who'd sat watching the battle without expression, gave a short command. Bo hesitated, and stepped aside, lowering the shattered chair.

Vasquez faced the black-clad *Compañeros* without speaking. I expected them to rip him out of the chair and stomp him into the floor, and they surged forward to do just that; then they stopped without touching him. I don't suppose I'll ever know what stopped them; maybe they won't, either. Well, he was, after all, the high priest of their perverted religion. Maybe it was the habit of respect, or maybe it was just the admiration for courage that still persists in some societies although ours seems to have dismissed it as mere macho posturing. Whatever the reason, he remained untouched, until Bo spat contemptuously and swung the wheelchair around and pushed it through the doorway and out of sight. . . .

Elsewhere, the battle still raged. I said, "Let's blow this dinner party, ma'am, it's getting to be a drag."

"Stop showing off and get us out of here!" Ruth's voice indicated that after being choked like that, she was still a little behind in her breathing.

I saw that on the far side of the table Ackerman was still on his feet, with blood running down the side of his face; he was going through some unarmed-combat routines and seemed to be pretty good at the *Ha-Ha* stuff. I caught a glimpse of Belinda's blond hair and light gray dress; she was trying to wrench herself away from two men who were dragging her by the arms toward the door leading to the living quarters, presumably as a prize for Palomino. I hadn't thought the guy was that human.

Some of Vasquez's bodyguards were still on their feet, struggling to survive. A machete waved over the fray by the windows and I guided Ruth that way, first checking to make sure I really wanted to go that way; but although in that part of the world all the better homes have broken glass on the walls and bars on the windows, there were no bars here. Of course. No burglar would have the temerity to break into the home of *El Viejo*. The gent with the machete was laying about him lustily when I slipped up behind him. It seemed a pity to grab his uplifted arm from behind and wrench away the weapon and let him face his enemies unarmed, but I wanted that blade; and whether he'd been on Palomino's side or Vasquez's—probably the latter since he'd been fighting alone—he certainly hadn't been on mine.

"Grab a chair and knock out that window," I said to Ruth. "Do a good job so we don't slice ourselves too badly climbing out. I'll try to hold them off; let me know when you're ready."

It was the old Custer's Last Stand routine, except that poor old Yellowhair had had no escape window behind him, and no lovely lady, either. Suddenly I realized that I was feeling good, very good, a strange feeling for a gent who was probably about to be killed, either in this shattered dining room or out on a rocky hillside I hadn't even seen by daylight, in a totally foreign land, the natives of which were distinctly hostile. But I'd been cautious and conservative long enough—long enough to get me here at last, close to the target. Now I could forget about being clever, which wasn't really my forte, and concentrate on surviving, which was. I heard glass breaking behind me. With the heavy machete in my right hand and the sharp carver in my left I established, shall we say, a defensive perimeter, and made them pay bloodily for encroaching upon it. . . .

"All right, it's ready. The ground is only some four feet down." Ruth's voice was still hoarse from the scarf.

"Go on out, I'll be right after you."

I heard her scrambling out and swearing in an unladylike manner as cloth ripped somewhere. "All right, I'm out, most of me. . . . Come on, Errol Flynn, stop playing Robin Hood or whatever! Let's get *out* of here!"

I passed the carver back. "Hold this for me."

It was pistol time now; and I shot one of them left-handed and the rest backed off. I handed the machete out to Ruth. The sights and sounds of combat were diminishing. Belinda was gone from the room and Ackerman was either gone or down where I couldn't see him. Somebody, presumably a

277

Vasquez guard, was still putting up a tough resistance in a corner, but he was the last. The place was a wreck, but at least we'd got a good meal out of it.

I spoke to the *Compañeros* facing me: "The first one who comes out this window after us is dead. *Muerte*, get it?"

I spoke in English, but they seemed to get the general idea. Covering them, right-handed now, I backed myself out through the opening, groped for footing, and found it only a little way down. I stood up incautiously, tearing hell out of my seersucker jacket, that had hung up on a nail or something. I yanked it free.

"Ah, you found it, too," Ruth said, a dim figure in the darkness beside me, but not so dim that I couldn't see that something drastic and unfortunate had happened to the skirt of her linen dress. "Can we go now?"

"I'll take the machete. You keep the knife."

We seemed to be at the rear of the house with a steep hillside above us. I took us about thirty yards up the slope and glanced back. Nobody showed at the lighted window from which we'd come, but that wouldn't last.

"I want you to keep going," I said to Ruth. I looked around for a landmark. "Head for that big white rock way up there. Find a hole nearby and crawl into it and stay there. Don't move, don't breathe, as they say in the X-ray room. Just stay there. If somebody tries to crawl in with you, use the knife. Well, unless it's me."

"What . . . ? Oh, why do I bother to ask? You're going hunting."

"We call it creating a diversion."

She touched my shoulder lightly. "Just don't let them divert you, darling."

Then she was gone. There were silhouettes at the window now. I laid aside the machete and took out the gun again, and found a steady two-handed rest on a rock, and fired once. Somebody screamed down there. I set the safety and put the gun away, picked up the machete, and climbed on after Ruth. It was easier going now that my eyes had had time to become adapted to the night and I could see the dim shapes of the

278

rocks and brush. Somebody else was on the hillside, hurrying after Ruth, who, less accustomed to moving in the dark, was making more noise than I was. Crouching behind a bush, laying aside the machete once more, I let him go past, intent on his female quarry. I rose up and whipped the liberated scarf, the one that Ruth had been about to discard, around his neck, from behind—and the damned thing didn't work. Well, sure, it cut off his wind all right. Any garrote will do that, but I couldn't seem to apply the right wrenching strain to the cloth to crack the vertebrae. I'd seen Palomino do it and had the armorer demonstrate it to me, but it simply didn't work for me; I had to pin the guy down and choke him to death. Clearly, Thuggee was not my religion. I started to hide the body, which was stupid; instead I hauled him over to a big light rock and draped him across it.

I picked up the machete again. Ruth was a pale shape above me, working her way up the hillside—mountainside, rather. With my vision still improving, I could see the distant top now, high against the night sky. The stars were very bright at this altitude, whatever it might be; they reminded me of home, where we also got some pretty fair celestial displays at night.

Below me, the hunt was getting under way. I've never quite understood the standard movie chase scenes where the pursuit goes on endlessly and nothing happens to anybody except perhaps a few harmless bullets bouncing off the landscape. Why doesn't the jackass hero ever ambush his pursuers and discourage them by taking out a few of them, instead of forever running ahead of them witlessly like a rabbit, dragging the breathless heroine with him?

My light seersucker suit, although damaged and no longer immaculate, wasn't the best uniform for night fighting, and taking off the jacket would only make things worse since my shirt was white; well, I'd just have to be careful and pick good cover. I watched them for a little and spotted one who was either more eager than the rest or had found easier going; he was well in the lead. I set a course to intercept, moving cautiously from rock to rock until I was in the right position.

Waiting for him to come to me, I heard a shout as somebody found the body I'd laid out for them. My man was looking that way, over his shoulder, trying to learn what was going on down there, when he came past me. Crouching low, I saw a leg appear and chopped with the machete. He gave a wild howl and dropped to one knee, reaching down for the place that hurt.

"Ah, Dios, Dios!"

He was in a perfect position, and I rose and swung the heavy blade with all my strength, two-handed, and almost made it at last. Well, those old boys with their big axes often had a bit of trouble doing a clean and total job, even with the neck resting on a block; that's why the guillotine was invented. There was a lot of blood, of course, all of it in fact, as I cut the object free and set it on a high rock nearby. Crude and nasty, I admit, but you can't afford to be fastidious with a whole religion chasing you.

They were coming my way now, drawn by the screams; but I'd heard a voice I'd recognized, taking charge down there behind me, and I had the answer now. It was an obvious answer, the first thought of every outnumbered clown in trouble, but that didn't obscure the fact that it often worked and I didn't have a great deal of choice. Instead of fleeing the oncoming hordes, I crawled toward them and found myself a good spot a little aside from the direct line between them and the object so clearly silhouetted on its rock. Soon the first ones were stumbling past me blind and gathering to stare up at the exhibit, jabbering angrily in Spanish. I gathered that the name had been Miguel, and that whatever he'd been alive, he was an irreplaceable treasure dead. But nobody seemed eager to pick up his head and return it respectfully to his body.

One of them spotted movement above, perhaps Ruth, perhaps just a leaf in the breeze, and they charged off in pursuit. More of them came past, paid their respects to the head, and chased after the rest. At last the lean, black-clad figure of Palomino moved past me, but a little too far away, with too many men close to him. I could have tried it, but I knew he'd stop at the head, and he did. He gave a command, and it was taken down and carried away with the body. He gave additional commands that organized a skirmish line across the mountainside. He moved aside to study the situation above, stopping only ten feet away from me. A moment later I had the pistol in his back.

It's not the recommended way of dealing with a man trained as we are—you don't want to get that close—but these were the folks who left guns all over the floor, so I thought I was safe in assuming that he didn't know the firearms tricks any more than I knew how to work his lousy scarf.

"Helm?" His voice was soft.

"Who else?"

"If you shoot me, they will kill you."

"If I don't shoot you, they'll kill me. Unless you tell them not to."

"What reason have I to do that?" he asked calmly.

"I could say your life, but let's assume that we're both brave men who don't fear death. But I think, if you keep me alive, you'll find me very useful. . . . Quick now, send them off before they figure out what's going on!"

Three or four men, coming up, had realized that something was wrong although they couldn't tell exactly what in the dark. They were moving toward us uncertainly.

"*Jefe?*" one said questioningly.

"Go with the others." Palomino gestured up the slope. "Join the line. You should be no more than three meters from the next man." At least I thought that was the appropriate translation.

"*Sí, jefe.*"

The group went on. I said, "Well, they're still taking your orders, but for how long with the Old One still alive and kicking and nobody willing to lay a hand on him? Seems to me your takeover is in serious trouble, amigo."

He drew a long breath. "I was certain that the foolish gringo woman would shoot. The shot was to be the signal, as you saw, and the gun did discharge, even if accidentally. But a proper Spanish widow, avenging her husband, would

281

have emptied the whole magazine into the body and spat on the body."

"And if Ruth didn't shoot, or missed, you were ready to do the job and blame it on her. Only, when the time came, you couldn't do it. The old loyalty was too strong."

"Loyalty!" He spat out the word. "What kind of loyalty is it that will sacrifice a man whose whole adult life has been spent in faithful service—sacrifice him for a small mistake, easily corrected." He drew another long, ragged breath. "No. You saw. I could not shoot, either, any more than that sentimental woman. And these men, my *Compañeros*, they take my orders here, at least for the moment, but I cannot order that because they would not obey, could not obey. He has been our leader too long. He is the true high priest who has presided at all our ceremonies and interpreted all our mysteries. I thought I could do it, but I was incapable, as you saw. There is no man here who can kill *El Viejo*."

"You're wrong, there is one man, if you're willing to deal," I said.

Chapter 30

THE rooms behind the kitchen had, I suppose, originally functioned as servants' quarters; but Vasquez had apparently chosen to make them his private suite. I couldn't quite understand the reason for his choice at first, not until I realized that the house was level here, allowing the wheelchair a clear shot into the dining room and even to the front door, whereas the bedroom wing of the house kind of straggled down the mountainside with a step here and a couple of steps there. I once had to serve behind a wheelchair in the line of duty, not to mention having occupied one occasionally after getting myself damaged, and I remembered how all the casual little stairsteps that architects love to stick into totally unnecessary places had suddenly grown into major obstacles.

There was a man stationed at the door. Palomino waved him away and spoke to me.

"Be careful of Bo, he is very strong and dangerous."

"Thanks, I've seen him in action, remember?"

"I will wait outside." He smiled thinly. "It is all right, I will keep my word. This time. But you drive a hard bargain. I was really looking forward to enjoying the blond muchacha—the other blond muchacha." He made a little bow of apology toward Ruth, standing beside me. "And I fail to understand why you must have the man who once ordered you killed. He is a little battered, but he would have served very well at one of our forthcoming ceremonies in which a young man who is being initiated will prove his skill with *la bufonda*."

"That's the scarf?" I asked. "It's *phansi* in Hindustani, I believe, and the Indian sect employing it was first known as the Phansigars, meaning stranglers. Then of course there were the Dacoits and the Thuggees. I read up on it a little." I was just talking casually to keep him from realizing that my bargaining position was really pretty weak. It occurred to me that the rites in which the novices of the *Compañeros de la Hoja* proved their neck-breaking abilities might teach me what was wrong with my own scarf technique, but it didn't seem advisable to ask for a guest card. I said, "It's better for you this way. No more wandering *Americanos* disappearing in the wildernesses of South America; no dead Yankee agents to upset our government, very bad for business. Señor Vasquez had the right idea."

Palomino gave me his limited smile again. "Yes, I am certain that you have my welfare much at heart. But you speak sensibly. Blood was spilled, and my people, primed for violent action, went out of control, but it is just as well they did not succeed in destroying the hated gringos as they wished. I will abide by our deal." He glanced again toward Ruth. "Do you come with me, señora?"

"She stays here," I said. "I need her to hold the dog."

"Very well. I go so my people can see that, whatever happens, the blood is not on my hands."

He strode off, and the door closed at the end of the corridor. Ruth was glaring at me.

"Hold the dog? Have you lost your mind?"

I said, "It's just a very nice Chesapeake pup, and it never killed anybody. It's not the Hound of the Baskervilles, and it's time you stopped having nightmares about it."

She said angrily, "I'm scratched and bruised and dirty, and my only good dress is in rags; and you want me to undergo amateur therapy!"

I'd had to climb up the mountain to find her—she wouldn't have revealed her location to anybody else—and help her out of the little cave in which she'd gone to cover, hiding herself quite well, with her knife ready. But she'd broken down a bit when she realized that it was over and had clung to me tightly.

However, I no longer seemed to be one of her favorite people.

She spoke abruptly, after a brief silence: "Oh, never mind the dog, I'll hold the damn dog. But do you realize what you're doing? All you're doing is turning Vasquez's whole gigantic enterprise, that Mark died fighting against, over to another, younger man, the man who . . . who really killed him!"

I said, "Hell, if you want a crack at Palomino, I'll lend you the gun again. Be my guest."

She licked her lips. "That's not fair! You know it's something I just can't do to anybody. You saw. . . . Well, maybe if somebody's actually trying to kill me, or hurt my children, but not . . . not in cold blood. I thought I could, but I can't."

I said, "Well, it's your grudge; it's not my grudge. And I'm not here to solve Ackerman's problems, either. Drugs are his concern, not mine. Maybe he'll be happy to learn that Palomino has no intention whatever of burying America in a flood of cheap cocaine; he plans to keep right on charging whatever the traffic will bear. Whether that's good or bad is up to the drug experts, but actually it's Palomino's real motive: he couldn't bear to think of all those millions going down the drain just so Vasquez could take revenge on a whole nation for his boy's death. The other business was just the trigger that finally set Palomino off."

Ruth was studying me closely. "Matt, what is your concern if it isn't revenge and it isn't drugs? What are you really here for?"

"To keep a certain lady alive," I said. "Those were my official instructions. Of course, in our outfit, a lot of instructions aren't even given unofficially. It's simply taken for granted that we understand what's expected of us."

"And what is expected of you, and how do you expect to accomplish it standing out here in the hall talking to me? Talking rather loudly, I notice."

I said, "Hell, I'm just waiting for an invitation. . . . Ah, I think it's about to be delivered."

Somebody rapped on the inside of the door. "Señor Helm. Are you . . . are you lonely?"

I had heard the voice before, bellowing in angry Spanish during the battle in the dining room. I saw no reason to educate Bo to the difference between "alone" and "lonely."

I said, "There is a lady with me."

There was a brief consultation on the other side of the door; then Bo said, "It is permitted that you enter with the lady."

The door opened. I let Ruth walk in ahead of me, followed her in, and turned and shot Bo twice in the head as he was locking the door behind us. The noise, as always indoors, was tremendous, leaving my ears ringing. The big man fell facedown and didn't move. A trickle of blood ran across the floor that here, as in the dining room, was covered with rather crude tiles, probably of local manufacture, the kind that artsy gringos will travel miles to find and pay fancy prices for. Covering Vasquez, I moved to the door and checked to make sure it was securely locked.

"Bravo, no!"

The curly-coated brown dog had shifted uneasily beside the wheelchair, but Vasquez's command checked him before he could move. Ruth, white-faced, was staring at the dead man.

I said, "The leash is in his right-hand hip pocket. Get it, and go get the dog. Walk up to him slowly, speak to him— *good Bravo, good dog Bravo*—let him sniff your hand, and snap on the leash, and lead him away from the wheelchair. Okay?"

"Matt, I . . . What in the world do you think you're—"

I said, "For Christ's sake, Ruth, go get the fucking dog before he gets all worked up and I have to shoot him!"

Then everything waited while she approached the body gingerly, pulled out the leash, and started toward the wheelchair.

"Not that way!" I snapped. "Don't get between us. Come around behind me."

Vasquez and I watched her approach Bravo cautiously and hold out a nervous hand. "Good Bravo, good doggie."

I said, "Stroke his head a little. Okay, now the leash. You're doing fine. Now give a little jerk to the leash and come this way. Great. Stop right there. I want you to hear what this is all about, although I can't understand why it's such a mystery to everybody. Mr. Vasquez, do you have some questions?"

It was a monastic white room with heavy dark furniture rather like the supposedly ethnic stuff that had come with the little house I'd bought in Santa Fe. There were none of the religious objects you usually see down there, Christs and crucifixes and gold-framed pictures of the Virgin Mary. Vasquez had his own religion, and it wasn't Catholicism. He had watched the whole performance without expression; I'd have hated to play poker with the old guy. Now he glanced toward the body by the door.

"I suppose that was necessary."

"Yes," I said. "If I didn't take care of him before, I'd have to deal with him afterward."

"Afterward. I see." Vasquez sighed. "I thought we had agreed that none of you had reason to—"

"No. Where I was concerned, we didn't agree to that at all. We just agreed that I had no personal reason."

"I see." After a moment he went on scornfully: "So you are working for the drug enforcement people just like your friend Mr. Ackerman. Anticipating that he would prove unable to touch me legally, they sent a government assassin to deal with me when he failed. You."

I said irritably, "This is the damnedest case: nobody who's involved seems capable of keeping his, or her, eyes on the ball!"

"The ball? I fail to understand—"

I said, "As far as I'm concerned, as far as my organization is concerned, Mr. Vasquez, you can peddle your shit until hell freezes over. We disapprove, we think you're a terrible man, but your business is not our business. As Roger Ackerman would be the first to point out, he's paid to worry

287

about drugs and so is a whole army of dedicated government employees; but that's not what we're paid for."

Ruth spoke, beside me: "What are you paid for, Matt? I asked you in the hall just now, but you just talked around it."

I said, "We're the counterassassins, baby. When somebody's so big and tough and deadly that nobody else can handle them legally, the nice law-abiding little government boys and girls call on us to handle them illegally. Like when somebody who considers himself untouchable starts putting million-dollar prices on authors' heads. That's when the word goes down and the wolves go out. Just call me Lobo for short."

Vasquez said, "This is why you have come? Because the money was offered?"

I said, "Yes, Mr. Vasquez. This is not considered acceptable behavior. I have been sent to discourage it. As a former journalist of sorts, I am happy to do so." Nobody spoke for a moment; then I went on: "Salman Rushdie went to the British for help. I don't know what kind of preventive measures are being taken on his behalf. I would like to think that the old ayatollah didn't die a natural death, and that the new one is soon to go, and they'll continue to fall until the bounty is withdrawn, but the British are gentlemen and I'm undoubtedly only dreaming. But we're not gentlemen. Raoul Marcus Carrera Mascarena, alias Mark Steiner, came to the U.S. for help and we failed him; the least we can do is make certain you don't ever threaten another writer or journalist or TV reporter or whatever with your drug millions, and that anybody else who considers silencing his critics with the same threat will think again." I glanced at Ruth. "Please take the dog out into the hall. I'll be with you in a minute."

Spring in New Mexico had a great deal in common with fall in Peru. There was the same mountain chill in the air even on a bright day. At the rifle range I shot sixty rounds, the quota I set myself. The bullets went pretty much where I wanted them to, with only a few fliers. I was getting back into shape, mentally as well as physically; Mac had commented on the fact that my after-mission checkup had shown considerable improvement over my previous evaluation.

"Operating at eleven thousand feet seems to have done you good," he'd said.

The window behind him showed a green Washington; it's a lousy city, as far as I'm concerned, but if you've got to go there, spring is the time. Maybe I'd take in the cherry blossoms on this visit; I'd never seen them.

"Did Armando make out okay?" I asked.

"Yes, he apologizes for not being able to help you at the end, but he couldn't penetrate the security."

"He did all right; he's a good man," I said. Curiosity made me go on: "I had him pass along a computer diskette. Did our backroom boys manage to unscramble it?"

"They said that those standard encryption programs are really very good; but the password was Anemone and the text was some chapters from a novel by a lady named D'Arcy. A rather sexy novel, they said."

I said, "I'll have to read it sometime. Have you heard anything from Roger Ackerman?"

"Having tried to have one of my people killed, Mr. Ackerman is hardly likely to get in touch with me," Mac said stiffly. "I gather he took quite a beating, but unfortunately he seems to be recovering well. Do you wish any action taken there?"

I said, "Hell, no. If we start going after every fanatic we meet, we'll never get any work done; the world is full of them. Besides, when he's on his feet again, he'll probably go after Palomino, and that's not half a bad idea. There just wasn't anything I could do about the guy, the way things worked out." I shrugged. "One thing, I doubt that we have to worry about Señor Hector Palomino Escobar putting prices on writers' heads, no matter what they scribble about him. I believe he got the message."

"I have been thinking about the Rushdie problem," Mac said thoughtfully. "It is really a matter of world concern,

Eric. Since the British seem reluctant to deal with the current ayatollah, whatever his name is, maybe . . .''

I said hastily, ''Don't look at me, sir! I don't speak Arabic worth a damn.''

It turned out that cherry-blossom time was over, which was just as well, since I wouldn't have taken time to see them anyway, getting out of Washington as fast as I could. I didn't think he was serious, but you never know. Now I packed my gear back into the Subaru and called the dog. I had to admit that he was better about answering the whistle than Happy had been, but I had a hard time keeping him in the rear seat of the car. I suppose he was used to limousines where he rode up front with the chauffeur.

I said, ''No, goddamn it, get in *back*! Kennel up, you pigheaded mutt! What does it take to get it through your thick skull—''

I broke off, because a very familiar van had just rolled into the parking area; for a moment I expected Mark Steiner to step out and start pulling his shooting equipment out of the rear. But it wasn't Mark, of course. I went over there.

''Hi, Ruth.''

''Hello, Matt. The girls wanted to say good-bye to you.''

''Only the girls?''

She said, ''Is Bravo giving you trouble?''

''It takes a while, but he's a good pup.''

She said, ''That was the last thing he asked, in that room, wasn't it? That you'd really take his dog and look after him.''

I said, ''The trouble with this business is that the bad guys often have redeeming traits and the good guys are often real bastards. . . . What's that?''

She was holding out to me a small plastic box, a square, about half an inch thick and four inches to the side. I glanced at her, took the box, opened it, and looked at the computer disk inside.

She said, ''No, this is not Mark's book; that's really gone, just as I said. But I told you once that there was an appendix he hadn't finished. For every name in the text there was a footnote referring the reader to a fairly complete dossier on the person mentioned, at the rear of the book. Mark kept a backup copy of the appendix in his tackle box or whatever you call it, right here in the van. Actually, it holds more really incriminating stuff than the main body of the text." She pushed it into my hand. "It's yours. Do what you want with it. After all, you saved my life."

I looked at the disk for a moment; then I grinned. "If it's all right with you, I think I'll send it to Ackerman, from the two of us."

She looked startled. "To Roger? But—"

"Coals of fire," I said. "If it helps him get Palomino, think how he'll hate us, wondering every minute if we're going to pop up and claim the credit." I stopped grinning. "Besides, he'll probably make better use of the information than somebody who goes by the rules, and I don't really think the drug business should be encouraged, even though it's not my problem, officially speaking."

After a moment Ruth said, "You're really kind of a nice guy, in a way."

I said, "I don't hold grudges very long, just long enough to keep me in adrenaline when I need it."

"Of course, you're also kind of an awful guy, in a way," she said.

We stood for a moment in silence, in the cool high-country sunshine. The Jemez Mountains on the horizon were not as spectacular as the Andes. The two little girls were picking up spent cartridge cases as if they were pretty seashells on the beach. It occurred to me that I wouldn't really mind having them as my little girls.

"It wouldn't work, Matt." Ruth's voice was soft.

"I know."

"I don't think you do. You think I'm a super-sensitive little idiot who can't bear to pull a trigger and can't stand thinking about that old man you executed so deliberately, not to mention the others. . . . Oh, I saw what you did with that machete. Ugh. But it's not that, really. It's just that the dangerous work you do . . . well, I've had two husbands who died violently. I don't need a third. The girls don't need another dead daddy, damn it. And what if . . . what if somebody shooting at you were to hit one of them?''

Then the little girls came running, and I told them that the short, fat ones were .45s, the medium ones were either .38 or 9mm, and the little bitty ones were .22s.

"I got to shoot a twenty-two in the secret place where we were," Andrea said proudly.

"Mommy's going to get us a puppy," the little one said. "She promised."

I glanced quickly at Ruth. She smiled. "That's another one I owe you. I think I can stand a puppy now, if it's a small puppy."

There was a little pause; then I said, "It's okay, Ruth. Everything is okay. Take care."

I watched the van drive away. I'd left the car door open and Bravo had gone off again, but he came racing in to the whistle as before and jumped in where he was supposed to, making the little station wagon rock on its springs. He was a very substantial pup and I looked forward to seeing him with a duck in his mouth. Or make that a goose; he had the size for it. When I reached home, there was a car parked in front of my gate. It wasn't one of the workmen who were doing the final repairs in back. One of them might be driving a small red sports car shaped like a watermelon seed; but this was Sunday. I remembered another Sunday when I'd seen a UPS van that wasn't.

Then Belinda Nunn stepped out of the little car and came back to me. She was wearing some kind of a baggy jumper outfit, I guess current fashions aren't supposed to be flattering, but I remembered a rather brave and uncomplaining young woman in grimy jeans and a pretty lady in chiffon, and it didn't matter anyway. After a while, knowing what they are, remembering the times you've shared with them, you start to disregard how they look at any given moment.

"This is a hard place to find," she said.

"Next time let me know and I'll send out the Saint Bernards with the brandy."

She glanced at Bravo. "Well, you've got a dog that's big

enough." She glanced toward the house. "Do you have anybody in there, Matt? Or are you planning to move anybody in?"

I said, "Ruth just stopped by with her girls, to say goodbye, if that's what you're asking."

"I guess it is," Belinda said. "Well, you are kind of a target, and I didn't think she was the kind to want to live in the line of fire."

"She has her daughters to think of."

"Sure. Well, in that case . . ." After a momentary pause Belinda went on: "There was some unfinished business. It's the only time in my life I ever spent a week with a man and finished as pure as I started. I thought that if you had nobody else on your mind, maybe we could . . . Well, aren't you curious, too?"

I was.

About the Author

Donald Hamilton has been writing Matt Helm novels for over twenty-five years. He is also an experienced yachtsman and marksman, and has written books and articles on sailing and shooting. He is currently living on board his 38-foot motorsailer in Westbrook, Connecticut.